In Bed With

In Bed With

EDITED BY

Jessica Adams, Maggie Alderson,
Imogen Edwards-Jones
and Kathy Lette

VIKING
an imprint of
PENGUIN BOOKS

VIKING

Published by the Penguin Group
Penguin Group (Australia)
250 Camberwell Road, Camberwell, Victoria 3124, Australia
(a division of Pearson Australia Group Pty Ltd)
Penguin Group (USA) Inc.
375 Hudson Street, New York, New York 10014, USA
Penguin Group (Canada)
90 Eglinton Avenue East, Suite 700, Toronto ON M4P 2Y3, Canada
(a division of Pearson Penguin Canada Inc.)
Penguin Books Ltd
80 Strand, London WC2R 0RL, England
Penguin Ireland
25 St Stephen's Green, Dublin 2, Ireland
(a division of Penguin Books Ltd)
Penguin Books India Pvt Ltd
11 Community Centre, Panchsheel Park, New Delhi – 110 017, India
Penguin Group (NZ)
67 Apollo Drive, Rosedale, North Shore 0632, New Zealand
(a division of Pearson New Zealand Ltd)
Penguin Books (South Africa) (Pty) Ltd
24 Sturdee Avenue, Rosebank, Johannesburg 2196, South Africa

Penguin Books Ltd, Registered Offices: 80 Strand, London, WC2R 0RL, England

First published in Australia by Penguin Group (Australia), 2008

1 3 5 7 9 10 8 6 4 2

Cover and text design by Allison Colpoys © Penguin Group (Australia)
Cover photograph © M. Deutsch/zefa/Corbis
Typeset in 12.5/18 pt Fairfield Light by Post Pre-press Group, Brisbane, Queensland
Printed and bound in Australia by McPherson's Printing Group, Maryborough, Victoria

National Library of Australia
Cataloguing-in-Publication data:

In Bed With – / edited by Jessica Adams . . . [et al.].
9780670070398 (pbk)
Short stories, Australian.
Short stories, English.
Adams, Jessica.

823.0108

penguin.com.au

Contents

Kicking while Singing

ANNEY SHENTON

It's six weeks since I gave up sex and I'm feeling fine. I have survived another work week without being fired and I'm heading home, smiling with the knowledge there will be no overdue bills in my mailbox, no messages from debt collectors shoved under my door.

It doesn't occur to me to worry about finding a half-naked man sprawled in my doorway. But there he is, lying where the welcome mat would be if I had one. He's in the place I imagine the dog I plan to buy will lie in wait for me each day. Although his face is pressed into the porch, and it is almost dark, I'm fairly certain I don't know him. A back like that, arms like that, I would remember.

'Excuse me,' I say, nudging his ribs with the tip of my shoe, but he doesn't stir. I kneel and put my hand to his back, which rises and falls rhythmically. I'm sure now that he is a stranger. I know I have never touched this back before. My touch-memory is the most reliable thing about me.

His hair is dirty blond and greasy and would be over his collar if he was wearing a shirt, which he is not. I lean in closer and smell sweat but not booze. I touch his back again, prodding, saying, *hey, excuse me*, but saying it softly, prodding gently, because I'm not sure I want him to wake up right away.

In my head I hear the voice of my therapist. Her name is Cookie and she has changed my life. For the first time in years my rent is not overdue. I have a kitchen full of groceries. I have kept a job for over a month. I am thinking of buying a car.

And now there is a man with nice arms and a lovely back asleep on my porch and I am pretending to wake him whilst actually just enjoying the feel and the look of him and I hear Cookie saying, *when you sexually objectify a person you deny their humanity.*

I rock back on my heels and think it through. I *have* been objectifying this person on my porch but that has nothing to do with sex. That's one thing Cookie doesn't understand, actually – she thinks my promiscuity is the result of seeing other people as sexual objects, when, in fact, the opposite is true. I like to look at and sometimes touch objects, but I only ever want to fuck people. As long as I look at this man as an attractive object my desire is theoretical. But once I start wondering who he is, why he is here, where is his shirt . . . once I start wanting to know the things about him that are not his

2

back and arms and hair and – yes, I noticed, his denim-clad arse and long, thick thighs, then, *then* I am in big trouble.

'Hey!' I shake him with both hands. 'Wake up! Hey!' I shake him again, my fingers digging hard into his shoulders. It suddenly seems very important that I get him away from my front door.

He stirs and mumbles into the floor. I stand while he drags himself to a sitting position.

'Hello,' he says, smiling as though I am exactly who he expected to see when he opened his eyes. He is, I guess, in his early forties. His beard is a few days old. 'How you doing?' he says, sleepy voiced and glassy eyed.

'I can't get into my house,' I say and he looks around, his face wrinkling up. It's as though he's only just noticed that he is on a porch with a stranger and not in his own bed with a lover. He looks down at his chest, which, is, yes, as lovely as his back. Lovelier maybe, with its sparse grey-blond hairs and girlish pink nipples. He smiles again as though he too enjoys looking at it.

He stands and I notice his feet are bare. No shirt, no shoes. *Underwear?* I can't tell. Me, I always wear underwear now. Cookie explained that it was just like when smokers quit they have to throw out their lighters and ashtrays and give up all the things they associate with smoking, like coffee or red wine. We had a whole session where we made a list of all the things I had to get rid of: condoms, lube (purse-size and bedside), vibrators, dildos, handcuffs, butt-plugs. She said I had to get rid of my porn collection and was surprised

I didn't have one. I think she thought I was lying because most sex addicts have home emporiums of porn, but not me. I like flesh in the flesh. I never got off on images.

Anyway, when we were finished going through the stuff I had to chuck out we made a list of things I had to buy. Number one was underpants. Years ago I realised I was spending a fortune on undies because I kept leaving them behind at parties or in parks or toilet cubicles. So I stopped replacing the pairs I lost and before long I didn't have any and that had worked out just fine. But six weeks ago I went out and bought a drawer full of sensible cotton knickers. I wear them every day. I even wear them to bed.

I suspect the man on my porch does not wear underwear to bed, if he wears it at all. He is looking directly at me, his hands in his pockets pushing his low-slung jeans lower, revealing a delicate, teasing trail of fine dark hair. Six weeks ago I would have assumed the eye contact and stance meant he wanted to fuck me and I would have acted on that assumption and within two minutes I'd have his jeans off and his (potential) underwear between my teeth.

'I'm going inside now,' I say, putting my key in the door. 'There's a phone booth in the pub across the road.'

'Right, ah, I don't have any money.'

The door is open. I know he is behind me, watching me. I cannot invite him in. He could be dangerous. I know I am.

'I can give you some change for the phone,' I say, but damn it, even as I say it I am walking through the door and he is following and I am in my body in a way I haven't been since the Easter Show.

That was where it happened, where that final straw was laid upon that poor old camel. I had a job selling tickets to Sideshow Alley. I worked in a tiny booth at the top end of the alley and whenever people approached I'd say 'how many' and then whatever number they said I'd tear off that many orange tickets and hand them over and take their money and put it in the little zip bag I wore around my waist.

A couple of days into the job, I was sitting in the break room, which was really just a one-man tent behind one of the bigger display tents halfway along the alley. I'd just eaten an entire bag of fairy floss and was wondering how to get the stickiness off my hands, when the World's Strongest Man came in and sat beside me. When I say beside me I mean *beside me*, like I was on a milk crate and he picked up another milk crate and put it right up against mine so that the plastic was touching and so was our skin.

You know those summer nights when your inside smells like rum and your outside smells like coconut oil and the heat and booze makes you confused about which is inside and which is out? That's what having the World's Strongest Man pressed against me in that tiny tent felt like.

New people – strong or not, leopard-skin-loincloth or not – always create in me a rush of questions. I wanted to know how the milk crate could hold his weight and whether I would be crushed if he lay on top of me and how he felt about having people stare at him all day and whether he might like it if I kissed him and if he knew I wanted badly to know how it would feel to have the World's Strongest Man inside my body.

And it turns out that the milk crate wasn't holding his weight, it was just steadying him while he held his own weight in his glutes. It turns out, also, that he didn't mind being stared at all day but hated it when people talked about him like he wasn't there and, also, he did like it when I kissed him and he was happy I wanted to know what having the World's Strongest Man inside my body felt like. It felt, by the way, the same as having any other man inside me except that the outside of my body was hidden and protected by an enormous tent of muscle and fat. I was not crushed, only cocooned.

But there really wasn't much room in there and he really was very large and so it was perhaps inevitable that the tent of muscle and fat covering me would soon himself be covered by the half-collapsed tent of the Sideshow Alley break room. But even that felt okay, like the world was getting smaller, closing in as we closed in on each other, like the sky was falling in as our bodies collapsed into each other. So even with the canvas slapping against us and even with the sound of people saying, *oh my God, they're still going!*, even though I could see over his shoulder the shadow people plucking at the collapsed tent, trying to get us out, we kept fucking and when the World's Strongest Man said, *I will always remember you*, I came hard and kicked the last standing tent pole.

I ended up in hospital, which is where so many of my

stories end. Either there or at the police station. This time it was a bit of both, actually, because there was a cop by my bedside taking a statement. The World's Strongest Man had been charged with public indecency and I would be too. I had been charged with this before, locked up overnight even, but this time, the cop told me, I could go away for a while. There are only so many times a person can be warned.

So the cop asked what had happened and I told him. I told him about the smell and the skin and the feeling of being enclosed. I told him how it's hard for me to remember to not do these things because I find people so interesting and I want badly to connect. I tried to explain that I feel life is too short and precious to let people pass through without taking a moment to experience them fully, to feel what they're made of, to know who they are rather than how they appear.

The cop asked if I felt like that with him and I told him, *yes*, that I'd been wondering the whole time what it must be like to go from tackling bag snatchers to pulling dead teenagers out of car wrecks to watching over thirty-year-old women who forget they're not supposed to fuck in public, and I'd been wondering if he ever went home and took off his uniform and looked in the mirror and realised he wasn't a cop at all but just a kid like the one he'd arrested outside the pub earlier that night.

And although the door was closed, it was a hospital after all, and of course there was no lock, and of course a doctor came in while my cop was mid-thrust and then another cop came and there were whispered meetings in the hallway and eventually the new cop (who stood far away in the open door-way and did not look at me as he spoke) said that I would not be charged this time but that I had better get myself sorted out because next time . . . And he left.

Then the doctor who was observing me for concussion referred me to Cookie, and I told her that the World's Strongest Man/cop incident was the last of a long line of incidents that ended tragicomically. She said I was a classic addict, that I was using sex to disguise other problems in my life and that I had to abstain until those other problems were under control.

I didn't want to go to jail or get another concussion so I took her advice. I went cold turkey and quickly discovered that she was both right and wrong. She was right that I needed to stop so I could regain control of my life, but she was wrong that the sex had been a way of covering up my real problems. As soon as I stopped fucking, life became easy. Sex hadn't been a way of concealing my problems – it had been the straight-out cause of them.

And so here I am, abstinent, employed, sober, in control. In my hallway is a half-naked man looking at me as though this is the end of a long date during which we both drank too much wine and laughed at things that tomorrow would not seem funny.

'Do you want to use the phone then?' I ask him, point-ing toward the kitchen. I am conscious that not long ago I wouldn't have offered this because the phone would have been disconnected.

He nods and moves toward the kitchen. His back fills my view. I crash into it when he stops suddenly. We stand like that: my face against his back, my startled hands on his hips. I stare at the freckles on his shoulderblades. I can smell his hair, which needs to be washed and combed.

'I don't have anyone to call,' he says. My hands landed on his hips by accident, but I am sliding them around to his front on purpose. My face is against his back because he stopped short, but my lips are opening because I want them to.

'I don't have anyone to call, anyplace to go, anything to do,' he says and I can taste the truth of what he says. He is salted by the days of having nowhere to be. I lick the salt and his hips twitch beneath my hands. I know this is trouble, but I have been this man, standing someplace strange, not having anyone to call, anywhere to go. I have been him and I have been kissed and made to feel that standing in a strange place, being strange, was a fine and human thing to do.

I move my hands up over his chest. I pull on his soft girl's nipples until they feel hard like mine. I kiss his back, his neck, his shoulders. Every new place I move my hands or mouth I am afraid he will decide, *that's it*. I'm scared he will say, *stop*, he will call me a freak, he will say, *what kind of woman are you?*, he will run.

'Is this okay?' I ask, kissing up the side of his neck, pressing my breasts into his back.

'Sure,' he says. 'I mean, it's quite surprising.'

I stop everything. My face is hot against the back of his neck. My hands hang limp at my sides. 'I'm sorry.'

'No, it's good. Nothing ever surprises me any more.'

For a second we stand still, both facing the kitchen, not touching. Then he reaches back and takes my hands. He presses them against the front of his jeans. I am as thrilled as I was the very first time I felt a boy's swollen crotch and realised what it meant.

I remember Cookie again. *An erection is a reflex*, she told me. *It's a response to stimuli, not a sign of love, not even a sign of connection.* I realise I am doing it again, confusing compulsion with connection, taking a body part personally.

'Obviously,' he says, his cock pulsing through his jeans into my hands, 'I enjoy being surprised.'

I try not to take that personally but my cunt has begun pulsing, *sympatico* with his cock. I pull away, spin around too fast and hurtle, head swimming, into the living room. I sit on the sofa that I bought with a credit card given to me on the strength of my four weeks continuous employment at the bank. My last sofa was stolen along with all my other furniture and electrical goods. I know who took them: the junkie boyfriend of a moon-faced girl who gave amazing head. While she was going down on me, or maybe afterwards while I was passed out from exhaustion and pleasure, he cleared the place out.

The man is crouched in front of me. He looks like his heart has been broken. 'Do you want me to leave?' he says, but before I can answer he starts unbuttoning my navy polyester bank-clerk blouse.

I kick off my shoes and close my eyes. I think about the time that I lived in a squat and a reporter came to the door and asked to talk to the residents. He had black hair cut like Julius Caesar's and his eyes were watery blue behind thick glasses. We had this chair at the squat, a lovely old brocade thing, and when the reporter sat on it he looked so right, so beautiful, like a boy-king on his throne.

I believe in embracing beauty wherever it appears, I told him and he laughed as though I was mad and so I stripped him and made him believe in the beauty of himself on an old chair in an inner-city squat. Later, after his article was published and we were all evicted, the others said the reporter had used me, but I don't think that's right. I would have answered all his questions whether he'd fucked me or not. It wasn't his fault I couldn't resist unexpected loveliness.

I've been evicted before and since. I never felt like it was such a big deal until Cookie put it all together for me. She pointed out that each of my bouts of homelessness was preceded by inappropriate sex. The reporter; the son of a landlady; the wife of a landlord; the incident with the smashed windows; the thing in the communal swimming pool. And that's not counting the times I've lost my job and therefore my ability to pay rent. That goes something like: boss, boss, co-worker, customer, customer, boss, delivery guy, co-worker, boss's son, delivery guy, World's Strongest Man.

There is a mouth on my left nipple, a hand on my right breast, another hand on my thigh. I open my eyes and notice that I have left the front door open. If anyone strolls past they will see me here on my sofa, ending my abstinence, inviting in chaos.

'The door,' I say, thinking of the neighbours, the police, charges, trouble.

The man looks over his shoulder and begins to move away from me. As he turns I notice the head of his cock poking up above his waistband. I am right behind him as he slams the door. I push him back into the living room and tackle him to the carpet in the process of removing his jeans. They are too large for him and slide off easily.

'No underwear,' I say, wrapping one hand around his cock, using the other to weigh his balls.

'I lost them,' he says, his hands tugging at the waistband of my work skirt. I am still a trainee and this skirt belongs to the company but when the man yanks the zipper so hard that the surrounding fabric is ripped apart I don't care. It's just a job; there are plenty more. There is only this one chance in life to have this man rip my skirt while I knead his silky balls.

'How?' I ask, half-standing, kicking free my ripped skirt.

'Forgot them on someone's floor, I think.' He pulls me down so I am sitting on his crotch. I grind against him while he claws at my regulation beige pantyhose, ripping holes large enough for his hands.

'I thought I was the only one that happened to,' I say, but my words come out like gurgles and I'm not sure he under-stands. I can feel my wetness seeping through the cotton and nylon as I rub myself against him. I want to be naked but I can't seem to stop moving against him.

He rolls me off him, pushes me onto my back, rips away

the remaining shreds of my pantyhose. He bends his head to my crotch. He hovers there a second then plucks up the waistband of my underpants between his teeth. He looks up at me, a mangy dog, proud of its find, reluctant to let it drop.

'Take them off,' I plead, desperate to have his mouth on my cunt. He shakes his head and his beard scratches my swollen clit through the cotton. Then he places his hands on either side of his mouth and begins to drag my pants down. He moves slowly, his chin, beard, mouth and nose, teasing me as he moves down. He leaves the underpants stretched between my knees and leans over me, his hands stroking the insides of my thighs.

'Tell me about this tattoo,' he says, pointing to the word *Forever* on my right hip.

'Later,' I say, reaching for him with my whole body.

He stays between my thighs and slides a finger into my cunt, then another and another. I force my legs wider, feeling my knickers stretching beyond repair. He smiles at me, that same smile he gave me when he first woke up on my porch, and I am sure I will never regret abandoning abstinence now that I have felt that smile through the hand moving inside me.

Then his hand is out of me and on his cock. His slippery fist works up and down while his other hand presses into my belly, holding me down. I struggle against him and kick my restrained legs. 'Tell me about the tattoo or I'll come,' he says. He's not kidding around: his hand is pumping, his balls are shiny and tight, his breathing fast.

'I used to love a girl whose body was covered in tattoos,'

I say, and he slows his pace but keeps his hand moving, nodding for me to go on. 'Most of them were ugly, and some of them were just weird, but I loved her because she believed each one meant something important. She was always starting arguments, then right when things were getting heated she'd rip off her shirt or pull down her jeans. "It's like this," she'd say, pointing to a goldfish or lily or some ugly gnome. "You know?" And I never did, but it didn't matter.

'She was really insecure, always asking me if I loved her, if I wouldn't prefer to be with a man. So I went and got this tattoo so that next time she asked if I loved her I could flash it at her and say, "It's like this, baby". I thought it would make her happy.'

He takes his hand off his cock. 'Did it?'

'No.' I lift my hips to meet his hand. He works his fingers in one by one and when I say, *come on, please, more*, he thrusts his whole hand in and slams his body down on mine.

'What happened with the tattooed girl?' he asks but I don't want to talk about anything sad or anything at all. I lift my head and kiss his lips and to my relief he kisses back.

I scrape my nails down his spine and then grab his beautiful arse, teasing the crack with my fingertips, stroking his arsehole, then pressing it, then slipping the tip of one finger inside. He moans and grinds the head of his cock hard against my clit. My cunt is gripping and squeezing his hand so hard I am worried his bones will be crushed. I tell him I have never wanted to fuck someone so much in my life and he says, *I know*, and then asks if I have any condoms.

I start to cry, because I am as close to mad with desire as I've ever been and I do not have any goddamn condoms. I keep crying because I remember why I do not, and I am confused that I gave up sex because I was always taking stupid risks, and here I was again about to take a stupid risk because I didn't have a condom because I had sworn off doing this thing that would not be so risky if only I hadn't thrown out all the condoms, and I meant what I said to him – I really, really have never wanted anything so much as I want to fuck this man right now.

He gets off me, grabs his jeans, runs from the room. I am crying and horrified and agonisingly aroused and before I can untangle my ruined underpants from my ankles and follow him I hear the front door open and slam shut. I stagger naked into the hall and see my handbag on the floor. I don't need to pick it up to know that my wallet is gone.

I stand in the hall, staring at my bag. I can't seem to make myself move. The thing is that although this has proven beyond doubt that I lose all sense when I am aroused, although I am cold and hurting and most likely penniless until next pay day, I am not sorry. I felt real just now, fully alive, and that has not been true for six long weeks. It doesn't matter that it ended badly, only that while it lasted I was connected to another fragment of humanity. For a while I was not so very separate.

The door opens. He is there, red-faced, chest hair plastered to his skin with sweat, my wallet in one hand, a vending-machine packet of condoms in the other. I start to cry again and he takes my hand and leads me to the sofa, removes his jeans, lies on top of me and kisses me until we're grinding and grunting again.

And at last his cock is inside me and it is the oddest feeling. It's like I've been running for weeks and now I have stopped. My heart is racing and my hands are clawing at his back and my hips are moving fast, fast, faster, but inside I am utterly peaceful. When I come, I black out for just a second, and when I recover I feel as though I've woken from a very deep sleep.

I open my eyes and am looking right into his. His face seems to break apart and his body stiffens and I am shaking from the inside with the force of his orgasm. He collapses onto me and I lock my legs around his thighs not wanting him to move, not yet.

'What are you doing here?' I ask and he sighs and presses his scratchy face into my neck.

After a minute or so he begins to talk, his words rushing in to my ear as though they've been trapped inside for too long.

'I had a girlfriend once who liked to read to me while I went down on her. I don't remember much of what she read but this one thing has stuck with me, from Bukowski: "Sexual intercourse is kicking death in the ass while singing." And that always seemed right to me. I've tried to not do things like this. I've tried to live like a respectable human being, tried to connect with people without sticking my dick in them. I went a couple of years once, never touching another body. And life was easy. I had money in my pocket and food in my belly and a roof over my head. But the whole time I could see Death straight on ahead, just his back, as he sauntered along at a reasonable distance. I'm just following along behind death, I thought. It might take fifty years, but some time I'm going to catch up with him and he'll turn and look at me and I'll be so tired of just walking along looking at his back that I won't fight. I won't kick him in the arse, I'll fall gratefully at his feet.

'So, I started up again. Kicking death in the arse while singing, that's the only thing that makes me want to keep living. I've been told it's an addiction, an unhealthy compulsion, and that's probably true, but so what? So sometimes I end up running naked, pants in hand away from a pissed-off boyfriend I didn't know existed, leaving behind everything I own in the world and collapsing exhausted on a random porch too tired to care whether the owner calls the police on me. And sometimes . . . Sometimes the police do not get called and there is no pissed-off boyfriend and instead of yelling and running and losing everything there is this. And this is good. The only good.'

'Yes,' I say, 'I know exactly what you mean.'

'Yes,' he says, kissing my throat and eyelids and lips. 'Yes.'

Twenty-seven Mattresses
(a fairytale, reinvented)

CAT DEVONSHIRE

Of course I wasn't a virgin. *That* was the first lie I told – that, and the one about my father being king. They should have seen it coming, really. Beauty *and* brains both at once – I mean, most *real* princesses are kinda dumb, and the lack of genetic diversity has managed to breed in many of them a kind of horsey, gormless look, which, though not actually *ugly*, is hardly the stuff of fairytale.

And that's what I'm selling. Fairytale. The one thing everybody wants, from the dumbest of plain-vanilla princes to the most exotic of wicked witches. And though, personally, if given the choice, I'd take an adequate gene pool over royal blood any time, it was no good in a scam like this, where the guy wasn't a freak (so many are) and his parents were both fabulously wealthy *and* borderline psychopathic about good breeding.

I've scammed some people in my time. We scammed them together, Wolfie and I – Wolfie, my bedmate and partner in crime. He ran the one with the fake glass slipper, though the one with the golden goose was mine. But the best of all our scams was the last, the one with the princess and the pea.

Dammit. I missed Wolfie. I missed his hands, which were larger than most but could play you like an accordion without ever missing a single one of those little buttons; and those eyes that could leave scorch marks on the bedroom wallpaper; and his smile, which was mostly big-bad-wolf with just a trace of little-boy-lost . . . Not to mention the rest of him, which was little short of spectacular. But given that the last time we'd exchanged words I'd just scammed him out of the proceeds of a rat evacuation in Hamelin and left him doing time while I made off with the earnings, I wasn't expecting a happy reunion any time soon.

He'd promised me from his prison cell that if we ever met again he'd take his riding crop to my arse. But talk's cheap, I figured (besides, he knew I'd enjoy it too much). Meanwhile, there was money to be made – most particularly among the sons of rich parents who had made their fortune in commerce and badly needed a princess bride . . .

The deal was this: spend the weekend at their place, and let the family check me out. If his folks were satisfied that I was the real deal and not one of the many fake 'princesses' doing the rounds, then the final decision would go to the son.

False modesty aside, I wasn't expecting any resistance

there. An hour alone with the guy would do it; it was the parents who would need convincing. Still, I was pretty confident. I was posing as foreign royalty from a conveniently distant land, with a lively retinue to support my act – footmen, a maid, a trumpeter; not to mention the voice coach, the dresser and the dancing-master; plus fans, shoes, gowns and jewellery for all occasions. You can guess it cost me a fair bit. But it was worth the investment.

The mark was an only son, recently returned from the wars: good-looking, clever by all accounts, and loaded with the good stuff. My plan was simple. I'd done it before. The first step is to seduce the guy, then to win his parents' approval. After that, it's in the bag; I get him to sign a pre-nup in my favour then, as soon as the wedding's over, I'm off into the sunset with my share of the dough before you can say *'happily ever after'*.

Like I said, I'd done it before. I wasn't expecting difficulties. So you can imagine how surprised I was to arrive at my destination to find out that Wolfie had got there before me, running the Prodigal Son scam, no less – long-lost heir returns – and was sitting there between his proud old parents, dressed to the nines, watching me with those blowtorch eyes and fingering his riding crop. The whole bottom half of me melted like ice cream right there and then.

'So pleased to meet you, Your Highness,' he says.

Well, I should have backed out, of course. Packed up my things and just got out. But I was curious, wasn't I? It looked like Wolfie had a new scam going, and I wanted in on it. And

I was cocky enough to think that I could make him come round; he'd always been a sucker for me, and from that hungry look on his face I could almost believe he still was.

So I played along. Who wouldn't have done? I'd spent my last cent on setting this up, and I badly needed a return on my investment. So, when Wolfie didn't throw me out, I thought: Hello, let's see what gives, and exerted every inch of my charm to make sure that both he and the would-be parents-in-law were gobsmacked, bedazzled and captivated.

It wasn't difficult. Like I said, bountiful nature has been more than generous. A small waist, a decent rack and a more-than-adequate derrière can take a girl a long way and, properly showcased with a dazzling smile and vivacious manner (helped by an occasional glimpse of silk stocking from beneath an embroidered petticoat), will usually obtain a result.

Oh, he was good – Wolfie, now playing the attentive son, respectful and affectionate. We played them both like violins and, boy, it was good to work with him again. We had that rapport. We always had.

Better still, he needed me. He'd managed to pass himself off as their son, but the parents weren't completely stupid, his fortune was tied up in a trust, and he couldn't touch a cent of it until he was safely married. Which was where I came in, of course. He needed me – I needed him.

I tell you. It was beautiful.

I found out the next part later that night, when they showed me into the bedroom. A bedroom the size of a ballroom, with a marble floor and silver drapes and a claw-footed bath the size of a ship – all a bit *nouveau riche*, of course, but pretty impressive nevertheless, with mirrors on the ceiling and angels on the floor and chandeliers all dripping with crystal and a whole gallery of family portraits staring down with palpable disapproval onto the canopy of the largest four-poster bed you could ever imagine.

Oh, boy. That bed. I'd never seen anything like it before. Draped with muslin and silken brocade; sheets of the finest, whitest linen; all garlands and gilding and burnished wood and scented with hyacinth and patchouli.

And the mattresses. Twenty-seven mattresses, reaching halfway up to the ceiling – goose-down and silk and dandelion fluff, all piled up on that fabulous bed . . .

'I trust you'll be comfortable, Your Highness.' That was Wolfie, the look in his eyes warning me not to comment.

As if I would. I knew the score. I knew he was planning to visit me later – that bed was irresistible and I'd been thinking how nice it would be if Wolfie and I got together to celebrate our reunion in style.

'I'm sure I'll sleep like an angel,' I said, looking straight into his eyes. I ordered an ice bucket of champagne, then dismissed the maid (making sure he heard), kissed the dear old parents, gave Wolfie one of my sweetest smiles and said goodnight to one and all.

They left me to bathe and disrobe. Then I climbed into bed (using the stepladder thoughtfully provided), slipped naked between the scented sheets and waited for my partner in crime.

He turned up half an hour later, still dressed for riding.

I greeted him from my downy perch, sheets drawn demurely up to my chin.

'So what's with the twenty-seven mattresses?'

'To check you're a real princess,' He grinned as he said it and my heart did a little double flip (I never could resist that grin). 'Turns out you all have such sensitive skin that even a dried pea under the mattress can bring you out all black and blue.'

I stared at him. '*That* old wives' tale!'

He shrugged. 'My folks are traditionalists.'

Well, that made it almost too easy, I thought. A couple of comments at breakfast time – a sigh, a complaint at the lumpy bed – and it was happy ever after for both of us. And it felt so good to be with him again that for a moment I almost forgot the promise he'd made me last time we met.

'Of course I may give it a little *help*.'

And he started to climb up the stepladder, coat, boots and spurs and all. Under the sheet, I shivered a little and my heart did that double flip again, and something between my legs tugged and responded, and I realised then that we were alone, that the maids had all gone home for the night and if he were minded to settle old scores, no one would be there to hear the sound of a riding crop being vigorously applied to a lady's behind, or the sound of that lady squealing for mercy.

'Is that a riding crop in your hand . . .?'

'Oh, but I've missed you, sweetheart,' he said, pulling away the coverlet. I was beginning to think I'd made a mistake – that carnivorous look was in his eyes and wolves have *very* long memories – but it was far too late to back out now. I put my arms around his neck and kissed him softly on the mouth. I know it isn't usual for a wolf to taste of wild strawberries, but this one did, and it made me tingle all the way down to my toes.

Then his hands were on me, and for a minute I gave myself up, rubbing against him like a cat, feeling the roughness of his clothes against my belly and my breasts, feeling shivery and hot at the same time, his teeth – not rough, but not quite gentle – tweaking insistently at my nipples, one hand moving between my legs, the other finding the sweet spot at the base of my spine, crowned with a double dimple.

I'd forgotten how well we fit, he and I. We fit like two pieces of a broken heart; his hands a perfect D-cup, my body and his a perfect match. I snaked towards his groin at last, reaching for the buttons on his fly.

'Not so fast, my love,' he growled, and then he moved with lethal speed, turning me over onto his knee, lifting my buttocks invitingly into the air. 'You and I have unfinished business.'

Now Wolfie is definitely a bottom man. Mine is plump and sensitive and he gives it plenty of attention in bed. But this time I was getting slightly concerned that the attention might take a less welcome form and I wriggled and ventured to suggest that maybe he would be more comfortable if he put aside the riding crop.

'You know, I think I'll hang onto it.'

He and I have played these games before. But I never thought he quite *got* them, somehow, and although he understands that it's easy to turn me on with a couple of brisk smacks to the derrière, he doesn't really know about punishment.

Or so I thought, for about half a second, until the crop came down resoundingly across my unprotected backside.

This isn't a turn-on at all, I thought.

'Ow!' I screamed, and grabbed my behind. Next time the crop came down on my hands.

I uttered an expletive and struggled to escape.

'Now, now. That's hardly ladylike,' said Wolfie and, though I couldn't see his face, I thought I could hear the smile in his voice. 'A delicately bred young thing like you.'

And now he began in earnest. I squealed and swore to no avail – I'd sent the maid away myself. The crop felt nothing like his hands, which, though strong, would at least have diffused the pain evenly across my spread buttocks. This instrument, however, with its flexible shaft, seemed to focus all its energy into a searing line. He used it most efficiently, making sure the blows were spread out so that maximum coverage was ensured. My anguish was exquisitely keen; I felt as if my arse were being branded with hot irons, and the thinness and manoeuvrability of the crop meant that the tenderest parts of my intimate anatomy were by no means neglected. I wailed and pleaded and threatened in vain.

At last I began to see how the pea-under-the-mattress trick would work. He must have planned it that way from the start; a good scam and a neat little vengeance to boot. After tonight my backside would surely display dramatic enough results to convince even the most cynical of my royally sensitive complexion.

Finally, he released me, grinning, and I scooted up the bed out of reach, settling – with the utmost delicacy – onto one of the giant pillows. 'I *always* keep my promises,' he said, with an appraising glance at my flushed face and dishevelled ringlets. 'Besides, you deserved it, didn't you?'

My hands crept sullenly to the afflicted areas. It's amazing how quickly the initial pain fades; my bottom was still sore, of course, but the blistering heat was dying away and there was a new feeling between my legs – an urgent, stinging, *nipping* sensation that was not at all unpleasant.

I tried not to give that too much thought. Revenge, not sex, was first on my list.

Discreetly, I reached under the pillow for the object I'd concealed there earlier, too far away to use until now. I slid my hand around its comforting bulge. The life of an adventuress being filled with perils and uncertainties, I've always found it useful to carry a loaded pistol at all times and, if I hadn't been so foolishly preoccupied with memories of happier days, my double-dealing vulpine associate would have got it in the balls the minute he reached the top of that ladder.

Well, better late than never, I thought, unholstering my phallic friend.

Three minutes later, the balance was redressed and Wolfie had been relieved of his shirt and breeches and was spread-eagled, face-down on the bed, hands and feet tied to the posts with the green silk ribbons from my discarded corset.

I took a minute to appreciate the view while I stood over him, crop in hand, contemplating where to begin.

Of course, it was easy. A few well-placed strokes along the crack of his arse soon got him howling for release, but silk ribbon is astonishingly strong and, try as he might, he couldn't get free, only pull it cruelly tighter, chafing his wrists and ankles raw.

I took my time – I deserved it – kneeling beside him to touch the nape of his neck with my lips, moving around him on all fours to investigate every part of his captive body, pausing, sometimes to lavish attention on his hands, his feet, his shoulders, his balls, the backs of his knees, at others using the crop on him, making him flinch and yelp like a pup.

He had feigned indifference as best he could. But now there was no mistaking his arousal. I poured myself a glass of champagne, then I took a cube of ice from the bucket and ran it down the curve of his spine, rubbing it across the bud of his anus, making him shiver and cry out.

'*Please*,' he said.

'Swear you won't cause trouble.' In fact I was almost as ready as he, and the tingling between my legs had intensified to a waspish buzz.

'Okay.' He nodded. 'I promise.'

So I freed him from his silken restraints and lifted both his hands to my mouth, kissing and tonguing the marks on his wrists, mouth awry with the sour taste of his sweat and of his broken skin. I allowed myself a moment to note that his cock was just as spectacular as I'd remembered it, and then I was on him, straddling him, pushing him down, knees locked around his waist, hands clasped around the nape of his neck.

'At last, a part of you that doesn't lie,' I said, guiding him swiftly between my legs, allowing him to thrust into me with a low growl of pleasure. He pulled me closer, moaning as he did, his hands reaching urgently for my breasts.

I could feel him trying to speed up, but kept him beneath me all the time, controlling his movements, easing back as his hips jerked convulsively towards me so that he all but whimpered with frustration.

'I swear on my life,' he gasped between clenched teeth. 'When I get hold of you again, you're going to wish you'd never been born.'

I laughed. 'Admit it, Wolfie,' I said. 'You liked it.'

He closed his eyes and moaned gently, arching his back against the mattress. I tightened my knees around his ribs. 'Please,' he said in a hoarse voice.

'I'm sorry. I didn't quite catch that,' I said.

But who can resist a man who can beg?

Both of us came almost at once – at least, we did for the first time, as something like a rocket went off between us and, for a moment, we were a single point of exquisite sensation, all senses numbed in the face of the orgasm that racked us both, leaving us shaken and breathless and trembling and raw.

After which, still keeping him at pistol point, I forced him down the ladder again, flinging his clothes and his riding crop after him from the topmost mattress.

It wasn't just that I mistrusted him; he'd sworn an oath – on his life, no less – and I wasn't going to be caught napping again.

'No hard feelings, sweetheart,' I said, 'but I think I'd feel safer sleeping alone.'

He gave me a hurt look that had all the authenticity of a lead sovereign (I should know, I've peddled a few), and spread his hands in a *Who? Me?* shrug.

'Don't give me that,' I warned him. 'Now get some sleep. We both have a long day ahead of us. Oh, and next time, Wolfie, if you don't mind . . .'

'What?'

'Take your fucking boots off.'

Angel Gabriel

SAMANTHA SUTTON-PLACE

It began with a storm, the closure of several airports on the eastern seaboard and the plane's subsequent redirection to Dulles, Washington. Once on the ground, there had been the usual hours of waiting, queues of stranded passengers and harassed airline officials. A temper tantrum had secured her boss the last seat on a flight to New York, leaving her to spend a sleepless night in the bland surroundings of an airport motel.

In an ideal world, she would have flown home the next morning, at worst the afternoon, with a trip to the Smithsonian Museum squeezed in to ease the pain of an enforced stopover. In an ideal world, she would not be on a dirt track hundreds of miles south of Washington, negotiating a rented car round the switchbacks of oppressively dense mountains, jet lag inducing her to squint at directions to some lone cabin in the woods. What was this? *Deliverance*? Certainly she would not be wearing a crumpled suit to meet her company's lead author, especially not one with a visible grease stain from a blob of mustard that had slithered off the skin of a Bratwurst straight on to her lapel. Good God, had she been at the Frankfurt Book Fair only yesterday? No, lunch with her boss had been the day before and it had been while she was dabbing at the mustard with a napkin that he'd accused her of being jaded with her work and given her the sort of pep talk that any fool could see was a prelude to being sacked. She was not jaded, that much she knew. Hers was a different problem, a problem so insidious that she had always known it would catch up with her in this job, just as it had caught up with her in every job before now.

But where had it begun, this, this . . . *deficiency* of hers. For the millionth time she tried to track it backwards. Her childhood had been normal, her emotional history free from trauma or abuse. There had been no creepy uncle reading bedtime stories while his hand explored her under the darkness of her blankets. Her parents talked about sex openly, appropriately. They undressed in front of her and slept naked when the summer's heat overpowered them. She might have been an only child but she rode her bike and scraped her knees along with every other kid in the neighbourhood. At school she formed crushes on a variety of doltish jocks but, when the time came, not one of them left her weeping and abandoned on prom night.

She discovered sex at six years old. On her stomach, on

the floor, legs bent up like a frog, she rubbed against the carpet, feeling the friction through the thin cotton of her panties. By nine, she'd discarded the panties, preferring to allow the rough fibres of the carpet to sting the pale-pink slit of her couchie until she felt shivers course through her body and her throat turn dry. One day, her mother gently informed her that the 'couchiewaggle' as she had dubbed it, was a pastime best practised in private – but this was her first and only indication that pleasure and secrets and guilt all lived together in one mutually dependent, if neurotic, group.

At fifteen she began to wonder how it would feel to be penetrated by something other than her own finger. One evening, she spread herself open in front of the long mirror of the bathroom cupboard and watched, fascinated, as the opaque, white length of a dining-room candle slid in and out of her body. At seventeen she read Jerzy Kosinski's *The Painted Bird*. Thoroughly aroused by the sexual degradations of the Kalmuks and of poor, stupid Ludmila's couplings with goats and horses, she realised that the time had come to step out from behind the curtain of self-love and have sex for real.

He was older than her by two years. She liked the smell of his neck and the feel of his lips against hers, but as soon as he sprung an erect penis from his pants and fumbled it between her legs, the minute he clawed her breast and gnawed at her nipple, she experienced not pleasure, but dismay. She had not bargained on being made to touch the softly ridged skin of his scrotum, or share the drool hanging off the edge of his mouth. Moreover, she was surprised by the speed of it all – who knew that boys were bicycles with twenty-seven gears and no brakes? Suddenly the absolute control she had always enjoyed over the act drained away, and down the tubes alongside it went desire.

This and subsequent teenage forays she initially dismissed as a minor programming fault in her sexual DNA, a malfunction she assumed would be corrected with patience and experience; but soon she began counting the years by the number of failed and miserable sexual acts which peppered them.

She relieved her frustrations at night. Masturbation remained her comfort, her constant companion. She loved the way it made her breath shorten, then stop altogether; she loved the paralysing rush through her body, the drugged sleep that always followed. She kept a bottle of mildly scented oil by her bedside table. She experimented with toys of different shapes and textures. Once, on a whim, she cut the tip off a red chilli pepper and rubbed it between her legs. As the tingle turned to a burn and the heat grew stronger, she pushed the chilli into herself, drew it over the delicate bridge of her perineum, then slipped it into her rear hole, creating a trail of fire that burned through her body the entire night.

She worked in publishing. An old-fashioned imprint based in New York, which published works at the forefront of the American literary scene. As marketing director, she was careful not to date within the boundaries of the office, but she experimented on the periphery of the business. The literary editor of a newspaper, the red-headed manager of a print factory, a first-time author she'd accompanied on a national book tour. Every time she prayed it would be different. Every time she was floored by the realisation that sex with another human being killed her desire stone cold dead.

Now, as she turned thirty, she was forced to contemplate the word frigid. *Frigid*. How she hated the way it sounded, and the bitter betrayal of body by mind it implied. The condition – she could think of no other name for it – had swung through her life like a goddamn wrecking-ball. She adjusted the rear-view mirror and stared at her reflection. It always seemed to her that the pupils of her eyes were blurred – as though painted with a thousand dots of insecurity and self-doubt. Was this what her boss could see? She felt a wave of indignation. If Isaac had been more of a gentleman, it would have been her on that plane with him taking the call that Jim Gabriel, somewhere in the heart of the Blue Ridge Mountains, had a draft to be collected.

She hadn't bothered asking why the manuscript could not be sent electronically. Everyone knew that Gabriel did not do electronic mailings, just as he did not do computers or interviews. Gabriel's first and only novel had won him the Pulitzer Prize and had been hailed as the most definitive American novel of the twenty-first century. His follow-up was three years overdue and he had already resisted several attempts to wrest it from him.

'Does he even know I'm coming?' she had asked.

'Rent a four-wheel drive,' Isaac had suggested.

She had found the rendezvous easily, a small roadside cafeteria with fifties signage. A tantalising smell of pie blew through the extractor unit, but inside she noticed the plastic tablecloths were scummy with dirt. A woman rolled out from the kitchen area in a wheelchair.

'Can I get you something?' The meth abuse was obvious in the white lumps beneath the skin of her face and the fading scabs around her mouth. No, nobody had been waiting for her. Nobody had left her a message.

Hungry, Elizabeth ordered a slice of pie and settled in to wait. The wheelchair lady busied herself at the till, counting the draw. Descending from her cheap cotton shorts, her swollen legs looked like shanks of undercooked ham, yet Elizabeth noticed that, pinned to the telephone board above her, curling snapshots told a story of sons in uniform and daughters with babies. On the scale of normality, this seeming wreck of a woman had scored highly, whereas Elizabeth represented a full stop on the evolutionary curve: a failed human being who could not be relied upon to progress the race any further.

The meth lady's directions to Jim Gabriel's lair had been based on visual landmarks. A fir tree blackened by lightning, a roadside cross of plastic flowers, a succession of beaver dams. At the end of these, as promised, a cabin materialised. What better cliché, Elizabeth thought, a touch sourly, than a cabin in the backwaters. That Gabriel had aped the Harper Lee/Thomas Pynchon style of literary recluses said little for his imagination. As *Of Shadows and Light* had risen to the top of the *New York Times* bestseller list, the author had predictably become the subject of febrile speculation. Depending on whose account you preferred, he was bipolar, manic-depressive, a jerk. He was an isolationist, deaf in one ear, suffering from disfiguring psoriasis, thrice-married and doubtless also an enthusiastic eater of road kill.

Whoever he was, he did not answer her knock on the door. She heard noises not too far off and, feeling much like a hairbrush salesman or someone collecting for the wives and children of dead cops, she picked her way through the this-tles and daisy weed sprouting around the side of the cabin towards the back of the property.

She recognised him at once. Four million books sold secured you a larger than average photo on the walls of the marketing department of American Fortress Ltd. The portrait was a blow up of his author photo. Unlike Pynchon, everyone knew Gabriel from this postage-stamp likeness. He was a thickset man, with a thatch of grey hair and the heavy, sloped shoulders of an American footballer. His face was curiously asymmetric. An over-wide forehead, eyes sloping downwards, a nose that hooked left. Taken individually, his features were interesting, but together they lent him the crude appear-ance of a criminal photo-fit as described by some overzealous victim of a bag-snatching.

He was slumped in an outdoor chair, a rough-hewn sling-shot in' hand, pinging stones at a line of beer cans. On the grass beside him stood a half-empty bottle of bourbon. At his feet lay a dog. It was a terrible creature, with a large goitre pushing out its neck and an equally distended belly – the kind of dog who needed the outdoors to absorb its smell of impending death.

'Hello,' she said and stopped. She saw at once that he was drunk. She knew before he even opened his mouth that he was going to be difficult and cantankerous, and that she would probably leave empty-handed. She knew too that failure would only reinforce Isaac's poor view of her capabilities.

Gabriel raised his slingshot and felled a can.

'Hello,' she repeated self-consciously, then, remembering his alleged deaf ear, ventured closer.

'What do you want?' he asked over his shoulder.

She gave her name. Gabriel grunted.

'They said you would meet me at the café,' she said.

'They said you would call.'

'I did call.'

'Ah.' He put down the slingshot. 'Mea culpa, it seems. Sit down, have a drink.'

'Thanks, but I'm not much of a whiskey-drinker.'

'Too bad.' He took a hit straight from the bottle then gazed at the label with boozy fondness.

Elizabeth picked up the slingshot from the grass.

'Think you can hit anything?' He squinted at her.

'Probably not.' She chose a stone from the ground and loaded the slingshot. It missed by a mile. She picked another.

'Addictive, ain't it?' he asked in a faux backwards accent.

'I'm not sure it could occupy me all day.'

'Ah, do I hear the sting of a publisher's rebuke?' He downed the rest of the bourbon and wiped his chin with his sleeve.

It was apparent to both parties that this was the right time for a little subtlety, a touch of sexual charm, but Elizabeth knew what Gabriel didn't – that her sexuality was a tool blunted if not lost altogether – so instead she settled for flattery. No one had pushed the boundaries of the American literary ethos quite like he, she told him. Everyone at American Fortress was excited about the new book. Even to her own ears she sounded flat and insincere. Was life this hard for everyone, she wondered. A chipmunk zigzagged across the grass. From somewhere nearby she could hear the sound of a river and thought how nice it would be to swim. Slip out of her clothes and sink down into the cool, dark water. Gabriel pulled a can of Bud Light from the sixpack and snapped the top.

'It's not ready,' he said.

It had been such a long time since either of them had spoken, she'd forgotten what he was talking about.

'What?'

'The book. It's not ready.'

'Mr Gabriel,' she began, with little conviction.

'I'm drunk.' He dismissed her: 'You'd do better with me tomorrow.'

She slept in the car in the parking lot of the café. The nearest motel had been too far away and, although the meth lady's maternal instinct had been roused sufficiently to offer her a bed, Elizabeth imagined all the wheelchair-related items there might be in the bathroom and died a tiny death at the thought.

The night passed in much the same way as the red-eye from Frankfurt. She dozed off, waking up every so often to turn on the heating and rearrange her arms and legs around seat belts and arm rests.

By nine the next morning she was back at the cabin. Jim Gabriel was sitting at the table eating breakfast.

'Do you remember me?' she asked. By way of affirmation he offered her coffee then cut her a wedge of stale Entenmann's Pecan Danish Ring from the box. He didn't ask where she had stayed the night and she didn't offer the information. A recently opened bottle of bourbon was parked on the table but, she noticed, only a thumb's length was missing. The nearly sober Jim Gabriel was more forthcoming but no less bewildering than his inebriated alter ego. He initiated a discussion about Calvinism which segued into a spot-the-difference between the Amish and the Mennonites, neither denominations Elizabeth happened to be well informed about. After a while, he pushed back his chair and extended a hand.

'Well, thanks for your visit but I need to go out now.'

'I beg your pardon?' Elizabeth remained seated.

'I'm sorry,' he said, 'was there something else?'

She heard herself exhaling. 'Mr Gabriel, you said I should come back this morning.'

Jim Gabriel successfully recalibrated his expression into one of bemusement.

'You said you remembered me,' she persisted.

He shrugged. 'I'm assuming . . . some local event or other?'

'Wait, you think I'm some kind of groupie who wandered into your cabin to have breakfast with you?'

'Happens all the time.'

She stared at him incredulously, then shook her head. 'Mr Gabriel, I'm not exaggerating when I say I've barely slept for three nights. I'm tired. I need a shower and a change of clothes so, please, just give me the manuscript and I'll leave you in peace.' She wasn't exaggerating, but nor was she telling the truth. She felt surprisingly refreshed. She had liked waking at first light and feeling the mist in the air. She had liked the splash of cold river-water against her face.

'Why would you want someone to deliver a piece of work before they're happy with it?'

'So you do remember me?'

'Yes, I remember you. I also remember telling you the book wasn't ready.'

'Then why tell Isaac it was?'

'I thought if I agreed to give him a few pages it might shut him up for another year.'

'Well, it would, so let me take them.'

Gabriel plucked a hat from a hook on the wall. 'I trashed them.'

'You trashed the pages?'

'Actually . . . the entire manuscript.'

'Mr Gabriel,' she picked a pecan off the top of the cake, 'can I be downright rude?'

'Feel free.'

'Does the book even exist?'

'You think I'm blocked?' He looked amused. 'Look, what does it matter if you get it this year, next year or 2025?'

'Why don't you at least let me see some pages, then I can tell him everything is on track?'

'Why don't you tell him that anyway?' he said reasonably.

She sighed. 'I'm not sure he would take my word for it.'

'Why not?'

'Oh, you know . . . he thinks I'm jaded.'

'Ah.' He considered her. 'And are you?'

'Maybe.' she shrugged. 'If I was less jaded, I might have already talked you into untrashing the manuscript and handing it over.'

'Well, too late now,' he said cheerfully. 'Thursday is dumpster day. I took everything over this morning.' Then, when she said nothing, 'I'm sorry.' His left eyelid drooped. 'Really, I mean it.'

'It's okay,' she said. Surprisingly, she meant it, too. She didn't care. She had already decided: she would quit her job and try something new. At dawn, she had found herself toying with life as a hobo or perhaps a move to a different city. Who said change was death? Change was the lifeline of the dissatisfied.

She was about three miles from the cabin when it registered in the corner of her eye. A large metal container by the side of the road. Later, when she thought about it, she found it hard to explain what made her stop the car, and even harder to explain what propelled her up the integrated ladder to peer inside. Maybe she was curious to know whether the manuscript did actually exist, or maybe it was the apparent simplicity of the solution. What she needed was in the dumpster. And lo, there was a dumpster! Now, perched on the top, her legs astride the rim, she looked down on the horrifying still life of human extravagance below. Bottles, food mush, newspapers, clothes, a discarded mattress. Bag after bag, swollen and split, their contents bursting out like intestines from the belly of a dead animal. Still, if Gabriel had thrown out his trash only that morning, his bags might be among the more pristine few lying in the emptier section down at the other end. Gingerly, she began inching her way along the top trying to keep her nose pointing skywards.

It wasn't a good moment for a bear to come lumbering out of the wood, but then, for a nine-stone publishing executive raised in the asphalt jungle, no moment could have been a good one. She kept absolutely still. It wasn't a very large bear and was quite cuddly-looking, with molasses-coloured fur and a pointed face. But when it ventured close enough for her to make out the individual spikes of hair on the ruff around its neck, it appeared to fix its sights on her left leg, which, to her horror, she realised was hanging over the edge of the metal dumpster much like a salami in an Italian delicatessen.

Panicking, she hoiked her leg up onto the ledge of the dumpster but her balance was too precarious and she dropped into the bin with a whimpery little scream.

Her first thought on regaining consciousness was that she had broken her ribs. A rib puncturing a lung would account both for the pain in her chest and her difficulty in breathing. It was by no means the only explanation, however. It smelt in the dumpster. This might sound like an obvious thing to say, but it was true. There was no way a person could ever know how bilious dumpster odour was unless they'd lain in one themselves. Elizabeth gagged, then vomited. Both actions were excruciatingly painful but she knew better than to pass out when being sick. She imagined her death being described on the Darwin Awards where people's fatal exploits were rated according to a scale of idiocy then pilloried on the internet. She lay motionless and concentrated on her breathing. From her position she could see flies and maggots and fishbones and different hues and textures of seepage, but she could also see the corner of a mattress, some eggshells and bread ends and the normality of these leftovers comforted her. She began to feel rather at home in the dumpster – it was, after all, its own little ecosystem, albeit a reversed and decaying one – and she decided to stay for a while longer.

After an indeterminable amount of time, she thought she heard a shout and the noise of an engine. More time passed until suddenly she felt a searing pain in her side and hands hauling her up by the armpits. There was Gabriel, ordering her towards a ladder he had balanced against the inside of the dumpster. 'I saw your car,' he said. 'Are you insane?' But she didn't reply, as it had become increasingly obvious she was.

In the cabin, he put her under the shower, still clothed. She leaned her head against the wall and watched as the dirty, rotten mementos of other people's lives swirled around the drain at her feet. She wondered vaguely how many diseases she'd picked up and whether any of them might be fatal. The problem came when she shut off the water.

'What's the matter?' Gabriel asked, finding her standing on the floor, shivering.

'I can't get my things off.'

He put her back under the hot water then, after fetching a pair of scissors, stepped into the shower alongside her and began cutting through her clothes. The water flattened his hair to his skull. He smelt of alcohol and dog. When he got down to her underwear, he hesitated. 'Just do it,' she said wearily, but his hand was less steady now and she flinched as she felt a blade nick the pale skin of her armpit.

Afterwards, he wrapped her in a towel then laid her on the couch under a blanket. He forced her to drink most of the remaining bourbon from the morning's bottle, but half an hour later, when her hand was still shaking and her breathing jagged and shallow, he frowned at her.

'What exactly did you hit?'

'Don't know really.' She found she had to take an extra breath every time she spoke. 'Ribs . . . head.'

He examined the soft swelling on her temple then, ignoring her protests, dragged the towel down until her left breast was exposed and began pressing the arc of each rib bone in turn.

She felt baby tears welling up. 'Go away,' she said, and turned her head.

For a while she could hear him moving round the cabin then felt the heavy touch of his hand on her back.

'Bend your knees,' he said. She rolled obediently then stiffened as his hand moved to her thigh and, shockingly, a finger slipped up her backside.

'Jesus, what the . . .?' She tried to move but he held her firm.

'Stay still.' He covered her with the blanket again. 'These take time to work.'

She strained for outrage but the emotion felt milky and weak. It was like getting stoned from the ground up. Her head felt too heavy for her neck and as light bled slowly from the cabin, her eyelids shuttered down.

She felt the couch dip and dragged open her eyes. Outside the windows, the curve of a moon hung in the night sky.

'How are you feeling?' Gabriel was sitting beside her.

'Better, thanks.' She tried to sit up but her head was still swimming.

'Want me to read to you?' he asked, and to her surprise she saw he was resting a manuscript on his lap.

She tried to concentrate. She would attempt to retain, process and report back. Gabriel's voice rolled out into the silence of the cabin. She waited for the glittering aphorisms, the experimental thinking, she listened for the diatribe on the inexpediency of mankind. But it was not what she was expecting. Not at all.

His mouth, her lips. A dress, slowly raised. She frowned as the words joined into sentences and the sentences built to paragraphs. What was this? The images washed over her. *His fingers spreading her dark curls, her sweet cunt, pink and wet. He, spent, lying on the soiled sheets.*

Dear God, was this why Gabriel hadn't delivered? Was this what the drinking was about? His features blurred in front of her eyes. Was it possible she was dreaming? She struggled to clear her head. The morphine still held her prisoner in a world from which she couldn't escape. A world of transgressions and dark fantasy, a night-time world she was intimately acquainted with. And still Gabriel read on. There was a story there, one of anger, eroticism. A journey of lust and flesh and how could she help but align herself to it, this . . . odyssey of pornography? A spasm passed across her stomach and her hand moved automatically between her legs. The pressure built until it became unbearable but, try as she might, she could not relieve herself. Something was wrong and her eyes flew open.

Gabriel was standing in the doorway, silent, watching her. Why had he stopped reading? Had he seen? Had he even been in the room at all? Was she awake, was she dreaming? She blinked and found him still there but now he was crossing the room swiftly and stripping the blanket from her body. He knelt down, his eyes fixed on hers. With one hand he gently prised her hand from between her legs, with the other he spread her open, wide, then wider still. Very slowly, almost unbearably slowly, he pushed his finger inside her. She felt at once excited, fearful, unable to do anything but hold his gaze, her body forced immobile by the pain in her crushed chest, her mind trapped between the pressure to relieve her desire and her terror of that very same desire dissipating under his touch. Her hips arched. He slipped his hands underneath her buttocks and, as he lowered his mouth to her, she had the momentary sensation of balancing on an exquisite pinnacle, and then finally she felt herself topple and fall.

It was bright outside the window when she woke. She smelt coffee and, as she listened to him moving about in the small kitchen, heat rose in her belly at the memory of the last few hours. Her insides felt burned and raw and there was an aching, pleasurable emptiness to her body. She might have gained entry to the world's least exclusive club, but she had never felt happier to belong anywhere. Her hand automatically dropped between her legs and then suddenly she froze, once again overcome by terrible doubt.

Elizabeth manoeuvred herself carefully behind the wheel of her rented car. Her chest still felt as though a tremendous weight was pressing down on it but the sharp pain had dulled.

'Those ribs will be sore for a while,' Gabriel said, shutting the door after her, 'but you'll be okay.' It was true, she thought. She was going to be okay. In every sense, she was going to be just fine.

It had not been real. From the moment he'd brought in her bag from the car and discreetly left the cabin as she'd dressed, she'd known – it had been a dream. It had been the morphine; it had been all in her head. How could she believe anything else with Jim Gabriel making her breakfast, grilling toast, frying up bacon, cracking four eggs into the hot fat, all the while asking her how she'd slept, being solicitous about her head, her ribs, but saying nothing? Not a look, a word, the slightest touch to suggest anything of what she remembered happening between them. At first, she'd been disappointed, but she couldn't help thinking – how ironic. Just when she thought her fantasy world and real life could not have moved further apart, they had instead become elegantly intertwined. She looked through the windscreen at the road ahead. And who was to say this was a bad thing? No, she thought, firing up the engine, it didn't have to be a bad thing at all.

Gabriel bent down to the window and held out a parcel.

'What's that?'

'What you came for, I believe.'

She looked at the brown manila envelope in his hands. 'It was never in the dumpster, I suppose?'

'This?' he handed it to her. 'Nope.'

She found she was staring at his hand and quickly looked away, colour flooding her cheeks. 'Well, whatever . . . thanks.'

He smiled faintly. 'Any time.'

She moved the car slowly off. 'Any time,' she repeated, then frowned. Through the rear-view mirror she caught sight of him executing an odd little jig. She put her hand on the envelope on the seat beside her. It was surprisingly warm to the touch. Puzzled, she angled the mirror towards her face. The pupils of her eyes were solid, utterly clear and suddenly a small flame of hope flickered inside her. 'Any time,' she said loudly into the still air of the morning. Underneath her hand, the heat from the envelope began to grow and grow.

Prairie Vole

ROSA MUNDI

This happened two years ago. We are all wiser now – except perhaps Laura. She was a very pretty twenty-two-year-old with a nice figure, chestnut hair and the thick, white clear skin that sometimes goes with it. She was in her final year at college, where she'd been majoring in the Victorian novel. She had a live-in dropout boyfriend with a drug problem and a widowed mother on benefits back home. She was having her rent and college fees subsidised by the Hormonic Institute so she could afford the boyfriend and send money back home every term to help her mother out. All the Institute required Laura to do, in return for $1200 a month, was take the occasional course of pills or patches and report back weekly to me, Head of Research.

The Institute is based on campus in the Science Block, and only five minutes walk from her student accommodation, so there was no reason for Laura to be late on this particular Friday afternoon. It was already five past four and she was due in on the hour. She was keeping me waiting and I am a busy woman. Laura was bright, beautiful and likeable; but also easygoing to the point of idleness. This is often true, more's the pity, of girls with a high Suggestibility Quotient, or SQ as we at the Institute call it. Laura was an 8.3, the median is 5.

Laura was one of a group of six girl students taking part in trials of a new family of drugs. The work was, of course, highly confidential: the potential profits unprecedented. I ran my girls rather as the Cold War spymasters ran their agents.

My name is Dr Melanie Holsom. I like to think that on a good day and with a following, alcohol-fuelled wind I can pass for thirty-five – I have a Louise Brooks haircut, a nice nape to my neck, and some help from cosmetic surgery. Nevertheless, my own time for personal sexual experimentation is running out. A pity. I am forty-nine. Desire does not fade with age I find, it's just that opportunity does. But there are other things in life. I enjoy my job at the Institute, which is the UK subsidiary of a pharmaceutical giant based in Switzerland. And I enjoyed my meetings with the girls. I had their trust and liked to think I was a mother-figure to them.

I called Laura at ten past four to make sure she was on her way to the lab: but when she picked up the phone she was still at home, and from the panting and giggles was mid-coitus. 'Oh my God, Dr Holsom, is that the time? I'm sorry.

I'm on my way. God bless oxytocin! It's all the fault of your pills, you know!'

Now actually Laura was in a blind trial, and the pills she had been taking for the past week were placebos. Sweetened chalk. But, believing they were oxytocin, she was evidently behaving accordingly. She had, as I say, a very high SQ.

Oxytocin is the 'love' hormone, triggering birth and bonding, released during sexual orgasm in both men and women, a subtype of the let's-all-just-be-happy hormone serotonin. Think Prozac, Ambien, Seroxat, add a peaking in female libido, and what we at the Institute call an OOA or oxytocin orgasm accelerator, and you have STROX-Original. Every fuck a wanted fuck: every fuck an orgasmic fuck, and that finally goes for women too. We'd tried it on voles, rats, monkeys, gone to human trials in Sierra Leone, made modifications as a result, and now planned to take it to the market within the year. It was bloody exciting.

We were already working on the STROX-Plus concept – simple but brilliant: serotonin with the oxytocin content reinforced. We reckoned intercourse could now lead not just to orgasm, but to love itself.

While I waited for Laura I looked up Elaine's notes. She was due to report in later in the evening. Elaine's SQ is really low: a 2.3. She's a blonde pocket Venus, aged twenty-three: an atheist, a feminist, a tiny delicate thing with a mordant wit and a distaste for sex. She'd just finished a week's course of STROX-Original while being told she was taking vitamins; it would be interesting to see what she had to say for herself. Together with Dr Jorgensen, of the Department of Clinical Psychology, and in the face of considerable opposition, I had developed the whole concept of SQ scores: what better way to evaluate the accuracy of verbal responses in so subjective an area as personality and libido? There were patents pending.

It occurred to me that I rather fancied Dr Jorgensen. There was something about a formal man in a good suit that made one want to leap upon him and tear it off.

This was a rather unusual thought for me and I wondered if it had anything to do with the little STROX-Plus patch now sitting comfortably under my left breast. I rejected the idea. The effects wouldn't cut in for at least another six hours. The lab teams were working day and night on the problem: a time delay was OK for clinical trials, but not for the average punter. If you want to *want* sex, you don't want to hang about. The great advantage of STROX-Original was that you didn't first have to want sex for it to work. As with Viagra: this stuff made you want to want sex in the beginning, and guaranteed orgasm at the end of it. But you still wouldn't want to hang about.

Laura took only another ten minutes to be out of a sweaty bed and into my lab. I had to hand it to her; she could move fast when she wanted to. Her colour was high and her lush copper hair all over the place. She seemed to be still in a hurry, as students often are – being late is part of their culture – and asked if we could do this fast: she had an essay on Aphra Behn to get back to. I assumed this meant she wanted to get back into bed with her boyfriend as soon as possible. I gently pointed out to her the sense of not being grudging with her time and attention to the Institute: she was not a carefree student but a woman with dependents. She quickly settled down. I switched on the vid-cam.

'So how's life?' I asked.

'It's been so great,' she said. 'I love him *so* much.' Yet it seemed the boy was back on cocaine, had torn up his student grant application form, and given up his job in the coffee bar on moral grounds – the coffee beans weren't Fairtrade. But she was sure he would give up the drug soon. He had promised he would.

'And I believe him,' she said, a little surprised. 'But that's the oxytocin at work, isn't it?'

Well, no, actually, it was her high SQ at work. She was taking the placebo. But a lot of satisfactory sex would indeed increase her normal oxytocin levels: which in turn would increase levels of trust. Girls tend to misinterpret this chemical reaction as love, and that's why it so often ends in tears. Working with high SQs can complicate matters – that's why Dr Jorgensen and I had developed the SQ concept to feed into our results.

I rebuked Laura for having read up on oxytocin – she must have, though not meant to – and she said sorry and bit her soft, red lip and looked contrite. She was so pretty: such a clear firm jawline above a long neck, softened by the auburn cloud of hair, and those troubled, almond-shaped green eyes, searching mine, seeing me as guide, mentor, friend, mother.

We got back to the matter in hand. She reported that sex was running at about twice its normal frequency and quality. Eighteen times in the last week: at night and at length, before sleep, once with him dressed as a woman (her idea), oral sex during the day, and every day upon waking, between the alarm and the last of the 'snooze' reminders, either in the missionary position or with her on top.

'And orgasms?'

'Six in total, but I don't mind.' If she'd been taking the real thing the answer would have been eighteen. 'I love him so much. Only thing is, he says I'm wearing him out. He needs the cocaine for the energy. I'm making it very difficult for him to give up. Do I have to go on taking the pills?'

'Of course not, my dear,' I said. 'Not if you don't want to.' Forget placebos, I could see she was ripe for a STROX-Plus patch and no persuasion would be needed.

The consensus among the Institute's focus groups is that young people are losing the capacity for love. Thirty years back 'love' was cited as a reason for marriage or co-habitation by 76 per cent of under-thirties – now it's down to 23 per cent and falling. I think that's a pity. I remembered how love was when I was in my twenties. I wanted it for Laura as well. You know the feeling? When you will do anything, anything, just because he says so? Or a she, if you're that way inclined. (Which I am, on occasion.) Or even a he and a he? I once had a love affair with two gays: there wasn't much actual sex but a whole lot of approval and a lot of looking. And for a time

I felt part of them, a kind of female extension of the unit they made. But we drifted apart. Two's company; three can be exciting and different for a time, but in the end is neither.

I asked her to strip down to her bra and panties. She did. She was wearing an almost transparent matching set in pale green lace, with the most delicious little gold stars embroidered all over them – La Perla, I thought. Her breasts were quite heavy, round rather than tip-tilted, nipples large, pronounced and brown. Though I usually prefer the little pink variety, today hers seemed most attractive.

'Very, very pretty,' I observed, and she whirled and twirled for me. She was a large girl. It was quite impressive.

She was young and strong; I did not think she was likely to die of sexual exhaustion when she took the real thing. The earlier trials in Sierra Leone, of STROX before Original, had run into some trouble. A high suicide rate during the run – so high they showed up in the national statistics – led to the quick suspension of the trials. My own opinion is that the Sierra Leone government overreacted, since the deaths occurred during the withdrawal period, when placebos had been substituted. It was more than arguable, ethically, that it was not the drug but the withdrawal of the drug that did the damage, but alas, there were political forces at work. So now we were back in Europe, where money, rather than politics, talks. And the drug had of course been modified so the suicide risk was greatly diminished.

I asked Laura to remove the lingerie. She seemed reluctant, but then she had been on the placebo.

'What's your problem?' I asked. 'Just thank God for the Institute, and the monthly cheque which allows you to afford filmy green with gold stars, and do as you're told!' It's no bad thing for these girls to be reminded that gratitude is in order. They get paid very well for very little work. Still she hesitated.

'I need to give you a patch,' I said, 'to neutralise what you've been taking so your boyfriend can come off drugs.'

Still she hesitated.

'Do it now,' I said. 'Or you might find yourself put out of the scheme, out of funds and accommodation and how will you keep your boyfriend? He'll leave you.'

Threats work best with high SQs: bribes with low SQs. It would have been counter-productive to say something like that to, say, Elaine. Laura took off her bra and the full breasts fell free. She stepped out of her knickers, and folded them carefully so as not to snag them. She'd had a bikini wax. The chestnut grove had been taken down to a little heart-shaped decoration pointing down to the clitoris.

'Satisfied?' she asked.

Some girls are even better without their clothes than with them on. She was one of them. But she wetted her full pink lips with her pretty little tongue as she stood and looked as mutinous as her essentially good nature would allow. She had tiny earlobes. I quite wanted to bite them. I controlled myself.

'Thank you,' I said. 'You'd better go in to the surgery and lie down. I need to work out whether you'd be better with a groin patch than with one under the breasts. Yours are really rather heavy.'

She covered her breasts with her hands and blushed, self-conscious and abashed. I enjoyed that, and in so doing quite shocked myself. STROX-Plus had been tested so far on only thirty-two subjects. I wondered quite what was going on in me? This was the first time I had used it. Was it possible that the stuff could exacerbate sado-masochistic impulses in a percentage of subjects? If so, it could wrong-foot the trials.

Old Professor Hinton, our geneticist, and orgasm expert, had explained to me lately that there is such a thing as a masochism gene, prevalent in females and gays. The 'bind me up, whip me, choke me, I love you!' factor. Submission in women is species-survival-friendly, for it gets the oxytocin flowing, and the babies born. A whole lot of social conditioning goes into subduing the tendency these days, but even so, cries of 'No, I will not make the office coffee! No, I will not wash your shirt!' will all too easily fade before the tide of oxytocin into the bloodstream which results from frequent orgasm. And the section of the brain active in masochistic excitement is closely linked to the areas that light up when sadistic activity occurs.

'The surgery, then. I need you lying down,' I said. So she had no option but to walk naked in front of me into the next room. I followed. She was, incongruously, wearing socks and trainers. Her legs were very long: her buttocks high and neat but quite pronounced. I believe that girls these days grow into a different shape than they once did. By contemporary standards, Marilyn Monroe was seen to have long legs: today, they seem positively stumpy.

I asked if she had thought of liposuction on her butt – what had got into me? I could only assume STROX-Plus. She didn't answer but lay down on the couch, on her back. I lifted her breasts and asked if she had implants and when she said no, I looked doubtful, and said either way I would have to use the groin area; I would need to prepare the ground with a neutral substance. I took oxytocin ointment – if you are going to do something you might as well do it thoroughly – and rubbed it in the clitoral area. And, though I was rubbing as gently as I could, she complained that I was being rough, began to cry, and threatened to leave the scheme. I rubbed harder and pointed out that if she did she would not be the one to suffer, but her mother and boyfriend, and why didn't she just enjoy it. She was still reluctant.

I pressed into her groin with my fingers. 'Ouch!' she said, 'that really hurt!' That annoyed me. I told her I was going to call Professor Clifton in to check out her cervix to make sure it wasn't swollen: if so, the neutralising patch would be inadvisable.

She was distressed. 'He's a horrid old man,' she said. 'Why can't you do it?'

'All right,' I said, and without further ado firmly parted the legs and drove two fingers of my right hand into that tender, pulsing warmth. It was as if there was another self down there, another personality, a second Laura, an oxytocin-chrysalis Laura. Perhaps we are all like that.

'You like that,' I said firmly, and felt her back arch in response: the second Laura unfolding her wings.

'I like it,' she said. 'But I hate you.'

Still not quite there. I wondered what it would be like to have a SQ 9 or 10 in the trials. It would cost money to locate them but the Institute was never mean when it came to STROX development. I pushed the two fingers further in and joined them with two from the left hand, then stretched the fingers. She moaned a little: then a lot.

'More,' she said, 'please more. Anything, anything!'

That was more like it. I scraped the pubic area with one of the new skin abraders before applying the patch – a second tiny little crimson heart-shaped sticker where the arrow of her muff suggested. The medication absorbs more quickly if the skin defences have been breached.

I left her to herself and got through on the phone to Professor Clifton who said he'd come round at once. He'd told me he'd been investigating a compound of STROX-Original and Tadafil, the weekend Viagra, and was coming up with some good results. I soothed Laura by telling her about prairie voles. If you feed them oxytocin they fall in love. They stop being promiscuous and pair-bond. Oddly, it doesn't work with montane voles.

'Then I just hope,' said Laura sweetly, 'that I'm a prairie vole.'

When Clifton arrived I took him aside. 'I have an SQ 8.3 here,' I explained, 'now, I should think, rising 8.5, doing what high-suggestibles do, that is to say what they're told: already moving into a STROX-Plus phase. I must advise you that I'm in one too. I need you to observe and take notes.'

Professor Clifton surveyed Laura as she writhed upon the table: well-built, wonderfully white-skinned and smooth all over. He was a scientist of the old Mittle-European school: slack-bodied, though with a shrewd and lecherous gleam in his eye, and without doubt a bloodstream flowing with all the mind-bending chemicals the Institute had available. Age and want of confidence need no longer intervene between a man and his pleasures, and soon it would be the same for women too. Exciting!

'You need to examine my clitoris,' said Laura to Professor Clifton, trustingly. 'Dr Holsom says she wants a second opinion.'

'I've heard about Laura and seen her around,' Clifton remarked to me. 'How could one not notice? An 8.3, you say. Though now we have STROX-Plus I imagine all your hard work on natural SQ incidence will become largely irrelevant, superceded.'

I let that jibe go. I was feeling well-disposed towards all men. The sadistic impulse seemed to be directed towards women only. I must make a note.

'Please, Professor, please, examine me!' pouted Laura, bored by talk, squirming, needing action.

'Fraulein Laura, I am coming!'

I handed him one of the thin non-allergenic gloves doctors use for internal examinations and soon his right hand was inside her. She loved the rubbery feel, I could tell. I wished her all the pleasure in the world. Already the sadistic phase seemed to have worn off: perhaps it was so brief it was not necessary for me to record it? I found myself moving towards Professor Clifton, who suddenly seemed not just another ancient academic but the most desirable, intelligent, sexy man in the world. The next thing I remember is that I had put his left hand into my own cunt and it was searching for my clitoris.

'Get out of the way. No!' said Laura, suddenly. 'I love him. He's mine.' She turned on her front, grabbed the Professor by the knees and tried to drag him still nearer to her, aiming, I fear, for his crotch. I for my part aimed a mighty slap at her bare buttocks and she squealed endearingly. Was that provocation, or the drug?

'I think the STROX-Plus is clearly already working,' observed Professor Clifton, 'in the pair of you.' He had become almost genial.

Now he had found my clitoris he wasn't going to leave it alone. It was rather a relief when the entry buzzer went. From my own intense and pleasurable urge to be physically pro-active I suspected some variant of MDMA had gone into this particular batch of STROX-Plus. We were not always told when the ingredients were modified – and sometimes, of course, mistakes were made.

'That'll be Elaine,' I said, standing on my toes to extract myself. 'She's our low-rater. An SQ 3.2.' I went to the door and opened it. Elaine had ironed her long blonde hair and it hung round her face like a curtain and was irresistibly attractive. I have quite a thing about hair.

'Well timed,' I said, brightly. I started to arrange my clothing, but gave up. 'We were just conducting an experiment.'

'I see you are,' she said. 'Well, Professor Clifton, and you here too! And dear, innocent Laura on the couch! The jackpot! What do you need me for? Isn't a threesome enough for you?'

I overlooked her impertinence. Just another Eng Lit student who did not take science seriously. I saw that she took no pride in what she was doing – bringing to a society riven by grief, stress and sexual frustration the true love which only STROX-Plus could provide. She saw what she did for the Institute as trivial and meaningless, devoid of mystery and significance, just an easy source of income and accommodation, the way out of a student loan. I was sorry for her.

'I just need to check you in, and debrief you,' I said. I led her into the lab, sat her down, and took out my notes. She complied, taking evident pleasure in what she was telling me. I had forgotten to close the door: she could see through into the surgery. But since she'd been on STROX-Original for a week I thought it shouldn't upset her too much.

'My boyfriend dumped me on the first day,' Elaine said, 'because he pulled back the bedclothes and found me masturbating. He said I had insulted him by preferring my hand to his thing. So there wasn't a boyfriend to have sex with, I was too upset to go and find another, and I had to pleasure myself all week. Does that count?'

I looked through her records and found that in the past she had masturbated on average once or twice a month when in a regular relationship, and said, yes, it did.

'Elaine,' called out Laura, her long legs wrapped round Professor Clifton's neck – he, thanks to the efficacy of the new generation of drugs, plunging powerfully on. Laura, I noticed, had lost one of her trainers now. 'For God's sake,' she pleaded, beckoning with a long graceful foot, with perfect toes, 'come and join us! Dr Holsom keeps wandering off. I am so in love I want to share!'

'There is no God,' said Elaine piously and automatically. Atheists tend to cluster at the bottom or top ends of the SQ scale. Their determination not to believe can become a belief system in itself. 'But there is love! I believe in love. *God* is love!' And this from an SQ 3.2, after only a week of STROX-Original.

I had to remind myself that this was merely a sample of one, hardly a viable statistic. But it was a straw in a wind – a mighty wind which might blow all our human miseries away: a world lost to love might yet find it again. I called Dr Jorgensen, our clinical psychologist, and asked him to come over. Dr Jorgensen, who looks and behaves rather like President Putin, whom I have always found rather attractive, is a man to respect and trust.

Perhaps hideous to behold to any but oxytocin-clouded eyes, the old man Clifton and the young girl Laura sat naked on the floor next to each other, hands clasped, gazing into each other's eyes, and breathing words of endearment and adoration. They turned to Elaine and beckoned her. She was already stepping out of her clothes and now, slim and naked except for the cascade of fair hair, she joined them on the floor in a loving embrace, all sweet words and nuzzles. Soon enough it moved to a penetrative phase. Only one penis between two cunts but they managed: and I was about to join in too with the vibrator I kept in my office drawer, to help out – only Alan Jorgensen came in.

I was so happy to see him. I had so much to tell him. I felt salvation had arrived. I registered that the trust element in the STROX-Plus was cutting in, driving out the sadistic impulse, driving up my own SQ levels, normally a rational and sustainable 5. The sadistic phase had been brief, STROX-Plus was safe for the nation, and I thanked God.

He regarded the writhing limbs, the sucking mouths, with clinical interest. 'But surely that's old Professor Clifton? Good God!' And then, 'Perhaps you will get your clothes on, Dr Holsom?'

I realised I was wearing very little and had a vibrator in my hand. I made myself more acceptable. I smiled up at him, helplessly. Dr Jorgensen was looking more like the Russian president than ever: so cool, clean and smart, in his elegant dark-blue suit. I wondered what he'd look like without clothes: a lot better, I imagined, than Professor Clifton, whom Laura, and so far as I could see Elaine too, were now loving so passionately.

'Self medication is getting to be a real problem among staff,' he said, without, alas, returning my smile. 'And of considerable concern to management. I must advise you, by the way, that the new STROX-Plus patches have not, after all, been green-lighted for over-the-counter sales.

Your department should have been notified as a matter of urgency.'

'But why?' I was appalled, even through my erotic haze. The end of a dream, and Dr Jorgensen himself probably something to do with it? Could he want to delay our SQ research to some advantage of his own? But I had already forgiven him. He was so lovable. I loved him as I might a father; I blushed with shame to think of how he had just found me, at what he must have thought. I would dedicate my life to loving him, serving him, repairing my image in his eyes.

Now Laura had detached herself from the tangle of limbs, had thrown a paper sheet over herself for decency, and was walking towards us. She looked magnificent, powerful like a goddess. I felt shame again, shrinking from the realisation of how I had treated her. I longed to apologise, explain that it was the drug, not me. She fell on her knees in front of Dr Jorgensen, the sheet trailing, her gorgeous breasts exposed.

'I love you,' she said. 'I want to be your slave. I want nothing in return. I will wait on your slightest pleasure; I will never show jealousy. Use me or abuse me, I am forever yours.' Her language seemed out of some notional past.

Dr Jorgensen had forgotten me: he was retreating.

'Just tell me you love me,' she begged. 'Just one kind word!'

So the unconditional love would have its conditions. In the background Professor Clifton and Elaine continued in their own noisy, ecstatic, transitory lust.

'Why?' I asked again. I took his arm, I gazed into his eyes.

I would have his attention, one way or another.

'The effects of STROX-Plus are not transitory,' Dr Jorgensen said. Oh, how I loved him! So grand, so elegant, so powerful! He could do what he wanted with me. Anything, anything. I was young again. 'So far as we can see the effects are permanent.'

And he turned and fled from the room.

Postscript

As it happened, an antidote was found which worked in 45 per cent of cases. I was one of the 45 per cent. Dr Jorgensen, alas, seems merely human again, not god-like. Laura remains in her psychotic state of love. Even as I write this I get a glimpse of her lovely hair through the lab window. She follows Alan Jorgensen around, waiting patiently for the kind word he occasionally throws her: a bone to a dog. She crouches outside his door all night, cooks his breakfast, washes his clothes, runs errands for his lovers – and if required joins them in their bed. She does his housework naked. She will not be got rid of.

But she is very lovely. If he occasionally succumbs and lets her service him under the office desk it is not surprising. She is so willing and eager; and he is a man. She never complains, just pleads for love: it can be very irritating but he has trained her to do it softly. She did not get her degree.

It is reckoned there are some twenty others walking round the city in the same state as Laura.

The Professor, only a few weeks after these events, had

a heart attack on the job (not with Elaine) and is dead, brown bread.

Elaine is training to be a woman priest, the effects of STROX-Original, I suspect, being not so transitory as is claimed.

We at the Institute are now working on the development of STROX-Lite, serotonin with the oxytocin levels reduced. I am recruiting a new batch of students with high SMQ scores. SM for sado-masochism. But STROX-Plus will soon be available on prescription, approved by NICE (National Institute for Health and Clinical Excellence) as an alternative treatment for acute and intractable depression in post-menopausal women, so long as the partner consents.

Down on the Farm

SUNSET PROUDFOOT

Georgia crouched in the vegetable garden picking broad beans for lunch. It was a warm morning. The sun had burnt off the early mist, leaving the sky a sparkling cerulean blue. Birds clamoured in the lime trees and two black Labradors lay panting in the shade of an apple tree. Mark had left at dawn, creeping out before she had awoken. They were harvesting the fields behind the house. She had closed the windows to keep out the dust. With the children at boarding school and only Sambo and Sid, the Labradors, for company, she felt very alone.

She filled her basket with beans and wandered back into the kitchen to pod them. Mark would be back for lunch, but he'd be out again before they'd barely had time to talk. It was the busiest time of the year. She shouldn't begrudge him. But the days were long, the evenings warm and balmy, the nights still and beautiful. She was forty-three, in her prime; it wasn't right that she should languish by herself in such an idyll, reading romantic novels and fantasising about strange men making love to her.

Her fingers worked skilfully, opening the cases with her nails, pushing the beans out with her thumbs. They were small and sweet. She popped one into her mouth. She couldn't remember the last time she and Mark had made love. He was so exhausted at the end of the day that he ate in the sitting room, watching the news in silence, often falling asleep before it had finished. During the harvest he worked long into the night, returning to the farm after dinner. She'd sometimes wake up at two in the morning to hear the sounds of the tractors and combines rattling back down the track behind the house. She'd lie staring up at the ceiling, wondering where her life was going, whether there was more to her existence than being a housewife, cooking for a man she never saw.

Mark and Georgia had been married for fifteen years and she didn't doubt that she loved him. But love wasn't enough. She needed attention like a flower needs the sun. She eyed the drying lavender hanging above the Aga; she didn't want to end up like that.

A knock at the back door broke her train of frustrated thoughts. Assuming it was the postman, she shouted at him to come in. She stood up to find the letters to go. But it wasn't Nigel's face that peeped round the door, but a young man she hadn't seen before. 'Oh, I'm sorry,' she said, startled. 'I thought you were someone else.'

'Hi, I'm Luke, one of the farm students,' he replied in a strong Kiwi accent. 'The boss has asked me to get a load of beer for the boys.' He grinned raffishly and she felt the blood rush to her cheeks. He was impossibly handsome. She noticed the lines deepen into the tanned skin around his mouth and temples as he smiled. She noticed, too, that his eyes ran unashamedly up and down her body. She felt a frisson of excitement and wished she wasn't wearing a muddy apron.

'Sure. Hang on, I'll get some.' She strode out of sight into the larder and picked up two packs of four. 'How many are you?' she shouted, feeling a jolt of excitement. She couldn't remember the last time such an attractive man had stepped into her kitchen. Hastily, she took off her apron and smoothed her hands over the creases on her sundress.

'Six, counting Bob,' he said, referring to the mechanic.

When she came out he was leaning against the sideboard, arms crossed, watching her. He wore khaki combat trousers and trainers and his shirt was open, exposing a toned chest and muscular stomach. He ran a hand through sun-bleached hair as thick and unruly as a lion's mane. She smiled at him, handing over the beer. 'Hot today, isn't it?' she said, hoping to detain him a while longer.

'I didn't think England would be so warm. I was warned of grey skies and drizzle.'

'Global warming,' she said.

He shrugged. 'I'm not sure I subscribe to all that. The world's been warming up for thousands of years.'

'Global warming or not, I'd rather have sunshine.'

'Me too, any day!' He grinned again and she noticed his eyes were an unusual shade of green, like moss. 'Well, nice talking to you. Better get back or the boss will think I've got lost.'

'Tell the boss you've been keeping his wife company. She doesn't get much of that at this time of year.'

'I guess it gets pretty lonely, huh?'

'A little.'

'You should come and help on the farm.'

'And do what?'

'Drive a tractor?' He laughed as she pulled a face. 'You're not that kind of girl, are you?'

'No. More suited to a BMW than farm machinery.'

'I can't say I blame you.' He raised the beer cans. 'Thanks for these.'

'Come and help yourself, any time.'

'I will. It's thirsty work out there, especially in this heat.'

She watched him saunter off, then leant back against the sideboard and began to bite her nails. If the farm students were all as attractive as Luke, she should spend more time up there. She put the lasagne she had made earlier in the oven then went to her bedroom to check herself in the mirror. She wished she had taken more trouble getting dressed that morning.

She stood in front of the bathroom mirror and stared at her reflection. She was tanned from spending so much time in the garden. She wasn't a beauty, but she knew she had a captivating smile and pretty blue eyes. She wasn't skinny either, but Mark had always liked her on the curvy side. She looked wholesome, at least. Picking up a bottle of orange-blossom perfume she had bought the year before on a girls' trip to St Paul de Vence, she sprayed her neck and wrists and watched the brown skin on her chest glisten. She knew she had a good bosom.

When Mark turned up for lunch, he didn't notice her perfume, or the sparkle that glittered in her eyes. 'So, how's it going up there today?' she asked, watching him help himself to lasagne and beans.

'It's coming in dry and it's a good yield. We'll finish Deep Dell today.'

'Is the forecast going to hold?'

'I hope so.'

'I met Luke, your student.'

'A good lad,' he said, so busy tucking into his food that he didn't see her blush.

'How many students do you have at the moment?'

'Only two. Both from New Zealand.'

'Where do they live?'

'In caravans on the farm.'

'Isn't that very uncomfortable for them?'

He laughed and tossed her a quizzical look. 'They're young, they'll sleep anywhere.'

She bit the skin around her thumbnail. 'How young?'

'Twenty.'

'That *is* young,' she mumbled and began to bite the nail on her little finger. 'I hope they liked the beer.'

'Thanks for that. A rare treat. They're all working very hard.'

'I can come up any time and bring more,' she volunteered.

'They'd love that.'

'What about lunch? Why don't I make them all lunch?'

'Don't overdo it. Why would you want to make more trouble for yourself?'

'Because I'm very lonely down here on my own without the children.'

'You've got the dogs.'

'Thanks!' she replied sarcastically.

'Well, if you don't mind, they'd love the odd snack.' He looked at her steadily. 'A pretty woman like you floating about the farm, you'll really raise the temperature.'

The following morning Georgia rose bright and early with her husband. She made him breakfast, which she didn't normally do, then returned to her bedroom to take more trouble with her appearance. A little flirting wouldn't do any harm and it would be entertaining for her. She washed her hair, rubbed rose oil into her skin and applied a little mascara. She chose a simple polka-dot sundress that showed her curves and a hint of cleavage, then set about making cookies for the men's break.

At eleven she drove Mark's scooter up to Tin Sheds, where they were harvesting peas. The combines were chomping through the field like dinosaurs with wide mouths and sharp teeth. Luke sat in a red tractor at the edge of the field, feet up on the dashboard, waiting for the combine to summon him.

He saw her and waved. She waved back. 'What have you got there?' he asked, throwing open the door.

'A snack,' she replied, striding over the stubble. She showed him her basket.

'Really? For us?'

'Of course. The boss thought you all deserved a treat as you've been working so hard.'

'Oh, this is nothing,' he said cheerfully. 'At least we're sitting down most of the day.' His green eyes slid down her chest to the soft curve of her breasts, insinuated above the material of her sundress. There they lingered a moment, in appreciation.

Suddenly, the combine threw out its arm. Luke averted his eyes and sat up with a jolt. He started up the engine.

'You'd better get in,' he suggested. 'I've got to move.' Without a moment's hesitation she climbed in beside him, placing her basket behind his seat. 'The grub will have to wait.' She noticed him take a quick glance at her brown legs that stretched out beside him. The dress had ridden up now that she was sitting down, and was open at the thighs where the buttons stopped. He changed gear and brushed the skin of her thigh with the back of his hand.

As the tractor bounced across the field Georgia perched on a dusty ledge, holding on to the metal frame of the window with one hand and Luke's seat with the other. The proximity of their bodies in the hot cabin made her sweat with nervousness. 'I'm afraid the air conditioning's gone,' he explained. 'Bob was going to have a look at it this morning, then one of the combines got a flat tyre.'

'Don't worry, I like the heat,' she replied.

'Not if you are in it all day. The sun pounding the glass makes it too hot, even for me.'

'At least you can open the windows. The breeze is nice.'

The tractor sprung over a hard ridge of soil, throwing Georgia forward. She steadied herself by grabbing his shoulder. 'I hope you're not getting shaken up back there,' he said.

'Like a milkshake,' she replied, removing her hand.

'I like milkshakes,' he laughed. 'I imagine you've been doing this all your life.'

'To the contrary. I didn't grow up on a farm, I just happened to marry a farmer. This is the first time I've been inside a tractor.'

He frowned at her incredulously. 'And how do you like it?'

'So far so good,' she replied with a smile.

He caught her eye in the mirror and smiled back. 'Hand me a beer, will you, before I die of thirst.'

Luke lined the tractor up with the combine, making sure the arm was directly above the trailer, then proceeded to drive alongside while the combine emptied itself of peas.

'If I had your job, there'd be peas all over the field,' she said, opening the can. It made a satisfactory hissing noise then foamed all over her hand. 'Looks like the beer's shaken up too,' she said, handing it to him.

'No worries.' He took a sip then passed it back to her. 'Tastes good to me.' She wiped her hand on her dress. He had a nice mouth, she noticed; full lips and just the right amount of bristle to look ruggedly handsome but not coarse.

His shirtsleeves were rolled up to reveal strong, brown forearms arms covered in downy blond hair. As he turned the steering wheel the muscles flexed and she was seized by the sudden desire to run her fingers over them.

It was indeed hot in that little cabin. She wiped her brow with the back of her hand. 'Gets pretty dusty in here too,' he warned. 'What else have you got in that basket?'

She reached over and pulled out a plastic container. 'Cookies,' she replied, taking one out and handing it to him.

He bit into it, murmuring appreciation. 'You might not be able to drive a tractor, but you're a damn good cook.'

'I made them this morning.'

'Delicious!' They locked eyes in the mirror again and for a moment Georgia was unable to pull hers away. 'You're a good wife,' he said. She felt herself blush and struggled to find something funny to say.

'Does the boss get cookies on a regular basis?'

'All the time,' she lied. 'He likes to look after the people who work for him. Feed them up and they perform better.'

He eyed his cookie with a grin. 'That's certainly true. Men are very easy to please.'

'The way to a man's heart is through his stomach,' she said, enjoying a cool breeze that slipped in through the open window as they drove round the corner into the farm.

'Oh, I think it's a little lower than that!' He caught her eye in the mirror again and laughed. She laughed, too, to disguise the nervous tremor that had just rippled through her body.

As Luke backed the tractor into the barn, Mark walked out with a broom. He was surprised to see Georgia sitting in the cabin and waved in astonishment. She lifted up the basket to show him the cookies and cans of Coke and beer. Luke opened the door to let her out. 'Do you want a lift back to your scooter?' he asked.

'Yes, and you can have another cookie for your trouble,' she replied.

'It's no trouble. Isn't it part of the job to keep the boss's wife happy?' Without replying, she slipped past him and down the steps.

'Darling, you're becoming a land girl!' said Mark, striding up to her.

'I'm getting a taste for it,' she replied, aware that Luke was still watching her. Mark put his hand in the basket and pulled out a can of Coke and a cookie.

'I don't get these at home,' he said, taking a bite. 'I hope Luke's been looking after you.'

'Of course,' she replied, trying to look nonchalant. 'He's the perfect gentleman.'

'I'll take some of these for Bob,' he said, helping himself to a handful of cookies and another can.

'I've left my scooter in the field,' she said, as Luke started up the engine again. 'I'll hitch a lift back with Luke.'

Mark nodded. 'Don't let him drink too much beer,' he warned, watching her walk back to the tractor. Once inside, Luke closed the door and she waved through the glass. The tractor rumbled back out of the farm.

Luke smelt of a heady combination of male sweat and hay. She watched his hands as they steered the tractor up the dirt track. They were smooth with youth and smeared with dust. They reminded her of the age difference between them. It was almost indecent, flirting with a man twenty years her junior, however mature he looked. She dismissed the thought and asked him about his life in New Zealand, gazing at his reflection in the mirror when he wasn't aware that he was being watched. He had dark feathery eyelashes that would have been too feminine on a less masculine face and she was glad his skin was already a little weathered from working outdoors. Life on a farm in his home country had given him the rugged appearance of an older man.

Finally, they arrived back at the field where she had left her scooter. 'So, you're going to leave me now?' he asked.

'I'm afraid I have things to do back at home.' She had *nothing* to do back at home.

'Shame.'

She laughed. 'The boss told me not to give you too much beer.'

'I've got a strong liver,' he replied, staring at her with an intensity that made her flush. 'Thanks for the cookies. Will you make us some more tomorrow?'

'I'll leave these with you to share with the others.'

'That's dangerous. You'll be lucky if they get a taste.'

'I don't mind if you eat them all yourself.'

'Then you'll have to make more.'

He opened the door. Reluctantly, she stepped towards it.

'Hey,' he said, taking her hand. 'Don't be too lonely down there at the big house.'

She caught her breath. The sensation of their touching skin caused her stomach to lurch as if she had just driven over a little bridge. 'I've got the dogs,' she replied.

'You can always come and keep me company. There's only so much radio a man can take in one day.'

'The boss really will think I've gone mad.'

'No, he'll just think you're being a good wife and looking after his employees.' His grin was full of mischief. He let go of her hand and watched her walk down the steps. She hurried across the field to her scooter, knowing his eyes were still upon her. Barely daring to breathe, she hooked the basket over the handlebar and climbed on, showing her legs in all their naked glory. When she looked up, he grinned at her and waved. She waved back. With a racing heart she motored back down the dusty track to the house. The wind blew through her hair, the scent of hay clung to her nostrils, and the possibility of an affair took root.

Over the next few days Georgia was unable to get Luke out of her mind. She walked with a bounce in her step, she dressed with care, she wallowed in the bath dreaming the unthinkable and at night she let her hands roam between her legs to ease the tension there.

Having never considered an affair, partly because the opportunity had never presented itself and partly because it was morally wrong, she now appreciated the power of lust. It was like a bright light that blinded her to everything around it. She didn't care whether it was right or wrong, she just cared about the constant ache and how she was going to relieve it. Mark was so busy he didn't notice the glare that blazed around her, like a lighthouse warning of danger. He didn't notice the rose oil she rubbed into her skin, the scented candles she lit in the bedroom, the pretty satin and lace underwear she wore beneath her clothes. He was oblivious to his wife's growing sensuality.

Georgia continued to take drinks and snacks to the boys. She was careful to treat them all with the same friendliness, deliberately hitching a lift in the other student's tractor so that no one would suspect her of favouritism. Only the increasingly ardent looks that passed between her and Luke would have given them away, had anyone intercepted them.

Then, one evening while Mark was in the fields, she could stand it no longer. She decided to take the dogs for a walk up to the farm. She chose her favourite polka-dot dress and the satin and lace underwear Mark never noticed. The dogs bounded up the drive with enthusiasm, sniffing the ground and chasing the odd hare, while she grew more anxious with the knowledge that she was walking into fire, unable to stop herself. She would risk everything, but that risk only heightened her senses and enflamed her desire to be someone different from the devoted housewife, cooking her husband's meals with homegrown produce and selflessness. She had sown years of servitude, now she would reap something for herself.

She wandered on to the farm as the sun dipped behind

the buildings, throwing long shadows across her path. The dogs disappeared inside a barn full of golden wheat, leaving her quite alone. She heard the sound of sweeping and walked towards it. She knew instinctively that it would be Luke and her heart began to pound against her ribcage. She had the chance now to turn back. So far, she hadn't done anything wrong. She could return to her life and find it undisturbed, or she could walk on and punctuate her life with an exciting adventure. Finding the latter too compelling to resist, she walked on.

She found Luke as she had anticipated, in the barn, sweeping. He had taken off his shirt and his skin glistened with the sweat of his labour. His cargo trousers were smeared with dirt, his trainers covered in dust. She smiled at the sight of his shaggy hair falling over his forehead. With every stroke, his stomach muscles clenched and Georgia was reminded of his youth. She feared she was a fool searching for adventure in the arms of such a young man and she almost bolted. But Luke raised his eyes and saw her standing there and it was too late to turn around.

His face lit up and he leaned on his broom. 'Are you coming to help me sweep?' he asked, grinning ironically.

'You look like you're doing a fine job of it on your own,' she replied, walking closer.

He seemed to recognise the intention in her eyes and grew suddenly serious. 'Or are you coming to keep me company?'

She felt dizzy with the gamble she was taking. 'I'm coming

to keep you company,' she replied softly. Her throat constricted with longing and she swallowed hard.

'Then let me show you a place where we can be alone.'

He leaned his brush against the wall and climbed a ladder up to where the peas were stored in the adjoining barn. She followed, looking round quickly to check that they weren't being watched. Only the dogs trotted in, trailing their noses along the ground, picking up the scent of field mice or rats.

Luke extended his hand. She took it. When she reached the top he didn't let it go, but walked over the mounds of dried peas to the corner of the barn where they would be safely hidden in shadow. She couldn't turn back now, even if she had wanted to – watching his broad back as he strode ahead of her, she knew she was doing the right thing in surrendering her desire.

Without warning, he swung her round and kissed her ardently on the mouth. His lips were soft and sensual. He pulled away a moment to gauge her reaction. She smiled up at him encouragingly, gazing steadily into his mossy-green eyes, yearning for him to kiss her again. Satisfied that his advances were welcome, he wrapped his arms around her and pulled her against him, his lips parting hers so that he could explore her mouth with his tongue.

His body was hot against hers and she could feel the hardness of his excitement pressing against her pelvis. The ache between her legs grew in intensity, melting away any reservations she might have had. In that moment, the present was the only reality. She didn't consider her children or her husband. She wasn't Georgia, farmer's wife, but simply Georgia – on an island of her own.

They fell on to the peas, too tense with desire to laugh at the absurdity of making love in such a place. But the peas were surprisingly soft to lie on, moulding to their bodies like sand. The sensation of a man she barely knew running his hand over her skin caused her whole body to shiver with pleasure. His fingers were charged with an electricity she hadn't felt in a very long time. He wound his hands round her neck as he kissed her, caressing the delicate skin there, taking his time, as if savouring every second of this stolen moment that might never come again. He let down her hair and scrunched it between his fingers, fanning it out about her face like a halo. He said nothing, but the look on his face as he ran his lips over her cheek to her temple then down her neck to her collarbone told her she was the most beautiful woman in the world.

Restraining his impatience to taste her all at once, he propped himself up on an elbow and deftly began to unbutton the front of her dress with the other hand, unwrapping her slowly like a sweet. He parted the dress to reveal her silky body in the dusky light of the barn. He swept his eyes over her breasts, contained in the satin and lace underwear her husband had never appreciated, down her stomach to her thighs, and his gaze left a trail of heat beneath her skin. He grinned with admiration, tracing his fingertips across the undulation of her belly and over her panties to her thighs. 'You're gorgeous!' he breathed, and she parted her legs to let him in. Slowly he slid his fingers up the sensitive skin on her inner thigh to the gusset of her panties where they lingered, feeling the damp of her desire that had seeped into the satin. She lifted her chin, expecting him to slip his hand inside her panties, but he didn't. He brought it up to unhook her bra. She squeezed her legs together to assuage her frustration.

With a knowing grin, he dropped his gaze on to her naked breasts. They were large and soft. He cupped one admiringly, running his thumb over the stiff nipple. She arched her back, silently begging him to kiss her there. She stretched out her arms like a cat, wriggling in pleasure as his tongue licked her skin where it was most responsive. His fingers finally slipped underneath the satin of her panties and she let out a moan, parting her thighs in abandon, feeling the delicious pressure of his touch stroke her there with slow, sensual movements. Riding a wave of desire, she gave herself up to her senses, aware only of what she felt, unable to control her impulses. He slipped two digits into her vagina and she let out a deep moan as he inserted them as far as he could go, in and out, in and out, sliding smoothly on the juice of her enjoyment. Her eyes were closed but she knew he was watching her expression. She was too carried away to be self-conscious.

He withdrew his hand and moved down between her legs, pulling her pants over her knees and ankles, tossing them away. He parted her thighs with his hands, as wide as they could go. As she lay open he feasted upon her with his eyes, taking in every detail of her sex. Then he bent his head and licked her pussy with his tongue, from one end to the other.

She groaned with the excruciating pleasure of it. He slipped his thumb in and out of her vagina while his tongue licked her clitoris with gentle strokes, back and forth, up and down, changing from barely perceptible brushes to strong, thick movements with the whole breadth of his tongue. Her belly on fire, she writhed, lifting her pelvis off the peas, spreading her thighs wider, willing him to continue, the friction of his tongue so intensely pleasurable as to be almost painful. She lost her mind in a dizzy fog of bliss, aware only of the slippery sensation on her clitoris and the pressure of his thumb inside her. Then she came, waves and waves of delicious, warm spasms. She cried out, not caring who heard her as her voice echoed off the ceiling of the barn. He remained there until the last jolt told him she had finished. She went limp, her legs flopped on to the peas, her arms spread out above her head. Sleepily she watched him enter her with his magnificently proud cock. She took a deep, joyful breath as he filled her up inside, as full as she could go. Above her, his face showed the strain of his mounting orgasm. His whole body tensed, the muscles on his stomach and arms grew big and hard, and he closed his eyes to experience the glory of the moment without distraction.

Once spent, they lay entwined, wet with sweat and the evidence of their stolen pleasure. Then Georgia laughed. She laughed with delight, guilt, wickedness and pride, because she had never in her life enjoyed such phenomenal sex. 'You're a goddess,' he said, taking her hand.

'I didn't know I had it in me,' she replied.

'I knew from the moment I saw you.'

'You did?'

He sat up and kissed her. 'You're made to be licked.'

'You're very good at it.' She noticed she didn't blush.

'I like it down there.'

'Will you do it again sometime?'

'Whenever you like.' He kissed her neck. 'Just don't wear panties next time. They only get in the way.'

'Anything to keep the boss's employees happy. I'm a good wife, I am,' she said with a grin. 'Feed you up and you perform better.'

'Too right!' he exclaimed. 'Sadly, he'll never know what a very good wife you are!'

That evening, Mark returned late from the farm. He found Georgia in the kitchen, baking cookies. He grinned, noticing how pretty she looked. 'You'll never guess what happened this evening.' She turned round to face him. 'I was with the boys in the workshop when who should trot in but Sambo.' Georgia's grin petrified on her face. 'Do you know what he had in his mouth?' She shook her head. 'A pair of girl's knickers!'

'Really?' Her laugh sounded very false, but Mark laughed with her, oblivious.

'Yes, the prettiest knickers you ever saw! One of the lads has got his leg over.' He raised his eyebrows with admiration. 'She's a classy lady, with knickers like that.' He moved towards her and put his hands round her waist. 'Makes me think of what we're missing.' He kissed her neck. 'We might have been married for fifteen years, Georgia, but that doesn't mean we don't still fancy each other. Let's have a glass of wine, shall we? Then perhaps we can roll down memory lane.' He pulled away and appraised her face. 'You look beautiful,' he said, narrowing his eyes. 'I've been ignoring you. I'm the envy of every man who sees you and yet I leave you down here on your own. I must be mad!'

She smiled at him, basking in his attention. 'I'd like that,' she said, realising that it was him she had wanted all along.

'By the way, why don't you get some knickers like that?' He raised his eyebrows suggestively. 'They'll really hit the spot!'

Things by Mail

DORA BERGGASSE

This afternoon, you press me to describe you with a solitary word. This afternoon, it seems, you are holding a knife.

This is all terribly unlikely. You have, as far as I know, no fondness for weapons. Further, being a Man of Letters, you know quite well that, nine times out of ten, a single word will hardly do. It's unlikely that you'd ask me. It's unlikely that you'd hold a knife.

But, unlikely as these things are, I've permitted them to develop for the entire afternoon. Why not? Unlikely thoughts of you have become quite commonplace.

Yes. I know. I sound like a pussy and don't think me insensible to that. And don't think I'm unaware that Unlikely Thoughts of You could well form the title of a frightful American ballad. And don't dare think that I'd ever 'do anything about it'. Such as, for example, send you an elegant knife by post.

I would, for a start, be fraught when it came to writing 'dagger' or 'masochistic sex prop' on the postal declaration form. And I'd disburse a small fortune in the service of your fastidious taste. Dude, you're so picky. I can imagine you wielding nothing less than a certified Cossack antique.

It's called a Qama. (I looked it up.) And despite its current function as a *tchotchke*, it's tough and sleek enough for you.

So. I've won the eBay dagger auction. You've overcome your diffidence where weapons are concerned. I am dressed for the occasion.

Actually, I don't look bad. I'm wearing my better bra. And, as you know, my tits are brilliant. You've said as much yourself.

Your forearms feature in my unlikely thoughts. They often do. Your forearms, it must be said, are stalwart and charming. You are not a young man. Nor are you particularly active. Your forearms, however, have held up very well.

Oh, fuck it. All of you is hot. This is hardly a secret. But, dude, if I don't ration this mania, I'll do myself a damage. Let's just focus on your forearms, shall we?

One of them is around my neck. The other, of course, holds the very knife that, by phenomenal dint of luck, inched past both the Royal Mail and your wife undetected. The tasteful hostility of the Qama throws your extensor carpi into relief. This is the part of your forearms that I like best. (I looked it up.)

And there they are. Straining at your skin like puppies about to be drowned in a bag.

Of course, I know how you'd feel about this dog. You despise the simile. You despise it almost as much as you do metaphor. Or first-person narrative.

Be straightforward but detached, you say when you bother to look at my work. *Straightforward but detached.* How could you say this? You know I can be neither as far as you're concerned.

How do you defend those strong forearms of yours, anyhow? Is it the writing? Can you work out your keyboard quite that much? You. With your spare masculine prose.

It's not customary for male authors to have their pictures taken with their sleeves rolled up. This is more the habit of politicians in disaster zones. And in your latest promotional photograph (why did you send me that, anyhow? Are you trying to get me hot?) there they are again. The forearms. And there you are. Looking butch and competent and like you're about to muck in.

You're rather fetching in your author shot. You look as though you've been drinking whisky. You haven't shaved. You don't look healthy.

Has your wife been on vacation?

You look like you could fix anything.

This is as you appear in my unlikely disaster: worn. A momentary bachelor. Tired and capable and strong with your sleeves rolled up.

Tell me now, you say. One word. The knife is at my sternothyroid. (I looked it up.) And I'm wet. Actually wet. I wonder how this happened. Men, generally speaking, *do not* make me wet. Much less, wet through denim. And now I'll have to do some laundry before the missus gets home.

One word.

You smell of whisky. And something else. You don't wear scent so I'm not sure what it might be. It's that Man Smell straight gals get off on, I suppose. Ugh. I've known cock-struck bitches to romp about in purloined male garments after sex. I always thought this the lowest form of cross-dressing.

Dude, I'd never wear your clothes. I'm properly queer enough. Given the chance, though, I wouldn't mind finding out where that smell of yours begins.

One word, you say. Won't be easy for you. You're a walking thesaurus.

Actually, this isn't the first time you've called me a walking thesaurus. We both know you never mean it kindly. It's a childish slight and you only get away with it now thanks to your excellent forearms. And your smell. And the knowledge you *never* use a thesaurus. Or word-processing software.

The words just flow, don't they? You just turn on your PC or you open your beautiful mouth.

Once, you opened your beautiful mouth and said: for a friendship to exist between a man and a woman, a little physical antipathy is helpful.

That is you all over.

You are adept at difficult insults. Dude, I said, you can cut that right out. I know, compared to you, I'm not well read. But I was very fond of Nietzsche in my day. Physical antipathy indeed.

Today, in my unlikely thinking, there is only a little physical antipathy. I can tell, just looking at your straining forearms, you'd probably agree to fuck me.

Not that I'd ever ask.

But I think if I asked you'd probably agree. And I'd have to ask, wouldn't I? Most likely, you'd make me ask again. You'd want to see me gagging for it.

One word, you shout as I struggle to regain my reason and speech. One word, you say harshly as your London accent travels west.

All right. I accede. You can have your word. And here it is. You're fucking inconvenient.

That's two words, you say. And you smile and the knife, as it turns out, is a complete fake. You'd spotted this instantly, you tell me. But didn't want to hurt my unlikely feelings.

You see? That's why I'm so fond of you. Your books are very good, of course. I liked them. Loved them, mostly. As you know.

But I'm fond of you because you're funny. Because you'd never hold a real knife. Because, despite your great talent, you're actually not cruel; you are, after all, very nice. And because you can spot a fake in no time flat.

That may be true, you say. So why, you say, do I bother to communicate with you?

Cut that right out, I say. I adjust my things and we pop out for some tea and argue cheerfully about bad English music.

This is the problem with fantasy as it plays out in a worrywart's mind. Reality is inclined to invade.

If I think about winning the lottery, I always factor in tax and the five grand I owe my sister. If I think about finishing a book of my own, I cannot authorise thoughts of its publication or success. And when I think about fucking you or, more to the point, about you fucking me, a joke or a belch or a late-autumn flu always thwarts consummation.

You're just so inconvenient. You're a lot like winning the lottery.

It's been three years, hasn't it, since I won my inconvenient luxury? My impossible distraction. I can reckon to the minute the time that's passed since you.

I like to think that we became friends immediately. I'm certain that we did.

This must be the case. As we began arguing almost as soon as we'd stopped shaking hands.

And, no, I'm not deluded. I do not think of our first argument as washed over in tints of sexual tension. A la a Rock and Doris film.

Then again. Rock and Doris could prove a model couple for our understanding. With me, of course, figuring as Rock. Me, the born homosexual, credibly swayed by your charm.

Your smell. Your beautiful mouth.

And your forearms. You're hot. For a man nearly fifty. For any man. You're tall and you're hot.

Do I want you? Did Rock want Doris?

You have charged me with 'wanting' you on a number of occasions. You always find it funny. Yes, that's right. I answer. When it comes to you, I'm Completely Mad for Cock.

What did we argue about when we stopped shaking hands? I think it was the perils of fusion cuisine, an essay by Susan Sontag (was it *Notes on Camp?*) and the failure of rock. And, really, we didn't disagree about much at all.

It was the kind of argument where opponents invent their differences for fun. Where the argument exists only to safeguard against repose. And from within this restless flow, things are more easily spoken.

You quickly began addressing me as 'Madam'. *Everybody* calls me that. How did you know?

You speak so beautifully. And your accent, particularly when you've been drinking, is all suety vowels and warm offal consonants. Construed by me into a hot primal stew.

Your voice makes me wet. Dude, men *do not* make me wet.

Once, at a dreadful reggae concert when I was almost seventeen, an older girl in a motorcycle jacket took me behind the stage. She worked for an hour before her entire hand was inside my cunt. Then she let me eat her and use two of my fingers to fuck her (astonishing) ass. This, more or less, is the way women fuck. Men are clean, quick and timid. They're like Ivory soap. Why would men make me wet?

They *do not*. Do you not believe Madam?

Everybody calls me that. How did you *know*? When I asked you, you smiled and didn't speak.

The smile said, 'Isn't it obvious?'

I found this immensely flattering. You had Taken an Interest, I decided. You had Taken an Interest and, with some force, I transposed this into . . .

I know how you feel about the ellipsis. You think it's the lowest form of punctuation. Say what you mean, you told me, and do not submit to literary weakness. Be straightforward but detached, you said. Knowing very well, in the instant you called me Madam and smiled, that I could not be either.

Madam was not my *petit-nom* for long. I became Doll, Honey or, less stickily, You Big Dyke. Whatever you called me I quite easily became.

I baptised you a hundred times in the coarse waters of my high-school French. You are Lapin, Puce, Homme Gros. Mostly, you are Dude.

In your last note I'm simply T. I'm not at all sure how I feel about this. This afternoon, I'm an initial. Just an unresolved letter in an incomplete sentence . . . And I'm staring at the photograph you sent me.

You know, of course, that you revived my interest in beauty? It seems to me you did. In at least a dozen ways, Lapin.

I met you and we argued (but not really) about Susan Sontag and food and, almost immediately, I was charmed by the missus again. She and I returned home and fucked as they do on the internet. And despite the fact that they are very good, the details will be spared you. Because their release will make you slyly suggest that I'm Completely Mad for Cock. You'd say: you're only telling me this, T, to try to get me hot.

And what if I was? What would it matter if, on occasion, I happen to imagine the taste of your hand, the size of your cock, the look of your forearm (the left one, I think)?

You can spot a fake in no time flat. But must you draw it to the world's attention? We might have all been happy with this inoffensive lie.

You. With your forearms. Your eye for counterfeit. Your straightforward and detached gaze that bores straight into beauty.

You revived my interest in beautiful things.

She *is* beautiful, I remember thinking.

Naturally, that night I suspected her of converting her passion for you. I didn't particularly mind. As you know, I'm not the jealous sort. You take a fuck, I reasoned, where you find it.

As it turned out, she thought you were just a nice old duffer. Somehow, she hadn't noticed that you were so fucking hot.

She *is* beautiful. Thanks for the reminder.

So here you are, to remind me of all the things I thought were beautiful.

But it seems I am resisting the temptation to write to you. And I won't text or call. I won't remember the usual times your inspiration ebbs and all your chores are done. I won't whine that you're yet to send me your work for proofing.

When I know you've finished your book.

Oh God. I'm not *in* it, am I? Surely I shan't ever be one of your women? You write like a fucking angel. I should be so lucky to find myself in your text. But I've no wish to be one of your women. So often, Dude, they're really quite flat.

I suppose I could see myself among them. But the thought of being etched in the gloom of your books is almost too much to contemplate. This dark little world of yours might prove every bit as damaging as your smile.

The afternoon, really, is quite something. My missus will be home shortly.

She *is* beautiful. And clever and kind.

I've filed work for the day and the tomcats are voguing in that demimonde disco male felines like to patronise.

The afternoon is something. I should be enjoying it. But, as I get out of bed and away from your forearms and collide with hard evidence that my little life is good, here I am. An initial. Or, if you prefer, an ellipsis.

Whatever the fuck it is, I feel quite abridged. I cannot believe that it's you who can help flesh me out.

You smiled. You smiled. You smiled. And you didn't say a word.

For three unlikely years, I've been curling my toes and failing to find real pleasure in anything that's distant from you. This is terribly inconvenient. Particularly given that you are, most of the time, so far away. There's not a lot of mine you could ever touch.

I will not write to you today. I will not send you a message. I will not.

But if, of course, you were inclined to call, I'd probably pick up.

What I like best, and I'm certain you must know, is talking to you almost as one man might with another.

Would you fuck me as though I were a man if I asked you? Would I have to ask you twice? Fuck my ass. Please fuck my ass. It's not easy to resist. I've been failing to resist this perversion now for twenty years.

Would you? Were I to ask? Please.

As you know, I've the tendency to hyperbole. In this way, I am much like local late-night advertisements for carpet warehouses. I could tell you if only you were here, in this last week, how much and how hard I want you to fuck me . . .

You're right to despise the ellipsis. It is a slovenly leap between half-baked thought and nothingness. An ellipsis is a sin of omission, the lowest form of punctuation. Although you rarely excuse the dash, either. You say there is rarely an occasion where a dash can be legitimately employed. There is rarely a cumbersome sentence not improved by a good fucking cleaving.

When you find the time to edit me, you nearly always break my sentences apart. Sometimes, I make them longer than they need be just for the pleasure of your cruelty. You edit me.

And it makes me wet.

The Come On

RUFFY SANTE-MARIE

So I came a bit early to Liverpool Street Station on the Tuesday lunchtime, and I had a look around, I scouted out the toilets, which were pretty horrible really, not at all a good idea, and then went across the station and through the tunnel of shops and up the stairs to where they have that big circular place, I think it's an ice rink in the winter or a roller rink in the summer, I don't know, there's a café there, and there were a lot of people around, countless people getting their lunches and going towards and coming away from the station, they were all wearing officey clothes, and the only mildly good place I could find was behind a little wall with a set of steps going down to what looked like the cellar of one of the buildings, the kind of place where engineers or whatever would go down to get into the building's central heating system and probably not many people would want to go down the steps otherwise, so that was quite good, but was still a bit exposed, and in any case it was under a CCTV camera, in fact there was nowhere that wasn't under a camera.

And that was about it when it came to privacy, there wasn't much else, at least not that I could find. So I checked my watch and went back through to the main station concourse, which was pretty busy, but no sign of her yet and nothing on my phone, I knew she was getting in on the tube so I went and stood where I could see the people coming up from it into the station, I stood outside the shoe-mender key-cutter place above the fruit and vegetable stall, with that strong smell of old leather and oil in the air behind me, and I was watching the surges of people come through the barriers, face after face after face after face, and the faces made me realise I actually had no real idea what she looked like, I couldn't be sure, because I hardly knew her at all, and I began to be scared I wouldn't recognise her, I mean we'd only met five times in all up until then, and we'd only spent together a total of (I added it up in my head and the people kept coming through the barriers, all of them so possibly her, even the people who were really unlike her, I mean the wrong sex, the wrong shape, the wrong colour, the wrong age, that it made my head spin a bit to think of the blatant anonymity at the heart of all the things I'd been so romantically feeling) three hours then two hours, then five, then seven, then six and a half in the Myhotel (and what a stupid name for a hotel, whose room had smelt of furniture polish so acridly that I'd had to prop the window open with the Gideon's before she got there in case I had an allergic attack, and if it *was* my hotel I'd never have used that kind of furniture polish, and I'd also never have charged that amount of money for a room which had one of those cheap wolf-fur throws from Habitat over the bed, the fur of which kept coming off all over us because it was so hot and because we were covered in sweat, we kept having to pick little shreds of fake wolf out of our mouths and off our hands and faces and thighs). So though we'd known each other for five months, in real terms we'd known each other, all in all, for about half an hour less than the twenty-four hours which makes a single day.

The people kept coming and coming and none of them her, and I was thinking several things at once as I stood there, but most I was thinking how unrecognisable to myself I was. Who'd have believed it, me, sniffing round a mainline station in London for a place to have some privacy with a girl I hardly knew, I mean this was so unlike me, so unlike anything I'd ever done in a railway station before that it made me laugh out loud as I stood there, in fact, maybe this was all happening to someone else and I was only dreaming it, like it used to say in my Girl Guide handbook when I was small, *One night a man dreamed he was a butterfly. When he woke up he remembered the dream. But then he said to himself: What if, right now, I am actually a sleeping butterfly dreaming I am a man?* Why on earth was such a story ever in the *Girl Guide Handbook*? Those writers of that book were more cunning than all that information about how to pass your badges in homemaking and horsemanship and being an entertainer suggested, since it was much more possible than it seemed then, I realised now, to try for all sorts of badges that didn't have names, and maybe for some reason I'd been allowed to enter, in a dream, the body of a different person, someone I'd always wanted to be but never had the nerve to be, the kind of person who scouts around public sites in London for places to have a quick something or other with someone who 1. she hardly knows and 2. belongs to someone else in any case.

Or maybe I was going to die soon and God or the gods or whatever there is up there above the departures boards, above the bright shops on the upper concourse, above the arching, church-like, light-filled, upturned-boat-like roof of Liverpool Street Station, gateway to all things east, above the bank towers and the chic shops and the traffic, and the sounds, and the clouds of the London sky, way up higher than aeroplanes, up past spacemen and spacewomen and space debris, up as high as the kindly-after-all rules of the structure of the universe, had decided to take pity on me and let me experience, quick, before I got snatched away to heaven or hell, a comparable paradise, a bit of illicit, surprising, out-of-nowhere love. I couldn't think of any other reason why I should have been given the chance to be a totally other, totally new person whose insides were all butterflies dreaming of being other than they were.

And another part of the new me was, of course, the old me, complete with my childhood and my girlhood and my womanhood and my life till now, thinking to myself as I stood in the prow of the station how the fact that I liked girls more than I liked boys was really all the fault of the Carry On films, by which, yes, okay, to some extent I mean the obvious, I mean Barbara Windsor and her *Carry On Camping* bra shooting off up into the air, and the way those films (with a saucy innocent kindness that we seem to have lost, now that we're all so know-it-all blasé) taught everyone watching them How To Fancy Girls, as well as How To Be A Fanciable Girl, and even How, later, To Be A Miserable Wife or Longsuffering Long-Term Girlfriend, But One With Quite A Lot Of Unexpected Power, usually in the shape of Joan Sims. But what I really mean is: one particular Saturday afternoon in the late sixties or early seventies, in front of the television in our front room when I was seven or eight, the film on the screen was *Carry On Cabby*, with the actress I now know to be Amanda Barrie but who to me that afternoon was simply, by far, the most eye-catching of the range of beautiful girls who sign up to work for Hattie Jacques in the secret cab firm she sets up to rival her workaholic husband Sid James' firm, as revenge, because he works all night on their wedding anniversary after having promised to take her out and wine and dine her.

GLAMCABS. We're Here To Please. Just Ask For What You Want. Glamcabs has girl drivers who don't drive black London cabs like the men do, instead they drive neat little Cortinas with glowing lit-up hearts fixed on their roofs to show they're for hire, probably the hearts are pink, probably the pointy little Cortinas are too (I say probably because the film's in black and white). Pert and dark and light and deadpan-ironic, like a laconic Una Stubbs (but the kind of girl who'd *never* deign to go round Europe with someone so wipe-clean as Cliff Richard in a London Routemaster, the kind of girl who knew there was a big difference, in milk-machine photobooth Britain, between adult and teen, post-war and *Ready-Steady-Go*), Amanda Barrie, wearing her brand new neat little uniform, with her brand new little lady-cab-driver pillbox hat cocked on top of her head like a glamorous air hostess, or like Peter Pan, goes where no girl has ever dared to go, into the cab drivers' caff, a place filled with men in their thirties who look like they're in their fifties (all the men in the Carry On films look like that, people don't look adult like that any more, not these days, not really).

In she comes through the door, to their astonishment, Amanda Barrie, a lone pert girl in no-man's-land, and asks in her perfect received pronounciation if this is the cab-drivers' café, and when they tell her with their eyes wide that it is, she says, with an expert downward inflection, as if it's not a question, it's a statement, *Well in that case can I have a cup of char and a wad.* Or Amanda Barrie, nonchalant, filing her nails, perched with her long sweet legs on show on the bonnet of her car as her fare gets his suit oily changing her flat back tyre, eager-to-please, nothing else he'd rather do in the world. I blame my whole erotic development on the moment Amanda Barrie matter-of-factly came through the door forbidden to girls and women, I blame it on how beautiful and how impassive and how subversive she happened to be, in black and white in the year 1963, and how she carried herself with such a luxurious discipline even then, only a few years before she'd be queen in her most famous Carry On role – Cleopatra in *Carry On Cleo* – with exactly that same comic mastery of nonchalance, but this time in full technicolor, her shoulders all beaded in milk from the milk bath, gazing at the blonde buxom British serving-girl that Kenneth Williams as Caesar has brought her as a gift as if the girl's an afterthought, *Oh yes. Send her to my bedchamber.*

The people came and came through the ticket barriers. A fortnight ago in the Myhotel the first thing she'd done was put herself inside me. She looked down at my cunt and with a frankness that delighted me said, *Oh it's going to be good fun working this one out.* We were new to each other in the oldest way. She was a rogue, a fox, an urge, a pure pleasure, she had boyish hips and a body with nothing spare on it, she was like a sunlit path on an early summer evening and I went down that path like I was freewheeling on the kind of bicycle that you can go for several miles on with your hands off the handlebars and in your pockets, whistling all the way. All evening it was like coming towards a place I hadn't realised was home, and then we went home, she and I, because the six-and-a-half allotted hours were over for the night, and it was back to our proper lives, the lives with the people we loved, we texted each other from different trains until going through the rail tunnels cut the contact, and all the way home in the summer dark I was thinking of how I knew her but I didn't, how she was a total stranger but I knew her, and how she'd lain on me in one of the breathing spaces we'd taken between exploratory fucks and she'd told me, for no obvious reason, maybe just because it was the thing that was at the front of her mind, how once she'd gone to the Museum of the Moving Image and had tried to get one of the paid actors on the Wild West mock-up film set to tell her about life in the old west, what it meant to be a pioneer, what it was like to dance in the saloon, or say anything other than the lines she'd learnt for the fake shootout scene in the film-set town, and how the woman, dressed in Wild West dancing-girl clothes, had looked straight through her, pretended she wasn't there. So she'd kept going, kept asking questions that got more and more surreal, like *What do dancing girls eat? You have to eat, don't you? Do you keep chickens, for instance? Are chickens in America different from chickens in the old country? What do you feed your chickens on at this point in the nineteeth century?* I was genuinely interested, she said in the Myhotel, and the actor wouldn't answer, kept nodding her head slightly and then looking away. And all this time she was lying with her head on her arms and her arms folded on my chest, and she was there so lightly on me, and her beautiful head so small, and the way she did the looking-away action there on my chest with her own head to show me what the actress had done made me laugh, it was almost more sexy than sex, I thought, there in Liverpool Street Station two weeks later waiting for her, that looking-away that she did in my arms. And when we'd got up and dressed and left the hotel in the going light of the summer night, walked along the road, and kissed under the huge cut-out of Freddie Mercury on the theatre where *We Will Rock You* was playing, and she hurried off to the Underground entrance on Tottenham Court Road, a huge white dog was sitting by itself at the top of the stairs and before she went down into the dark she pointed at it and did a little jump in the air, as if just walking along the street and seeing a dog was simply an exciting thing. That had been sexy too, that had been one of the loveliest things, along with our conversation about how it didn't matter, it wasn't going to matter, if we didn't actually come. Well, it matters to me, I'd said rather cockily, but for some reason neither of us had come, in the end, and it really hadn't mattered, it had been lovely regardless of coming, or maybe because neither of us actually came, in fact it had been equal, and easy, it had been strangely loving and comfortable, I thought, for an encounter between two near-strangers, and in the end we just hadn't needed to come, or maybe because it was too much, we agreed, since it was the first time, and the overload of being so new to each other would probably be too distracting, that was probably it. Even the conversation we'd had about how we wouldn't be goal-orientated or competitive about coming had been sexy. I'd gone home happy.

There was a man walking round and round the station dressed as a potato, the neverending people went round and past him as he gave out leaflets to anyone who'd take them about a new fast-cooking type of oven chip, and I was beginning to worry because we only had lunchtime, it was all the time we'd have, just under an hour, time only becomes time when you know you don't have time. Well, if nothing else

I was learning a lot about time from the whole experience, which was perhaps why I had woken up a couple of days ago and lain in bed in the early morning birdsong thinking about the story of my great-great-grandfather who, according to family lore, got up one morning, pulled his suit on over his pyjamas, pulled his only other suit on over that suit, went downstairs and out the front door and left his wife and his children, ran away to London with an actress, a girl from the famous theatrical Booths (one of whose family members, in another country and another history, shot a president at a play, and whose more recent notorious members included Tony, who played the son-in-law on *Till Death Us Do Part*, and Cherie, who married a very different Tony altogether). The dawn birds sang all round the roof of my house and I lay there thinking, maybe for the first real time, of Mr Parsons, my great-great-grandfather whose first name I didn't even know, who made French cabinets in Newark and Lincoln, ran off to London with the actress, had an illegitimate child with her, then made French cabinets again a couple of years later, after he'd come back home to his wife and his children, something I'd only ever thought about from the point of view of the whole story before with its beginning and its end, its sequence and its consequence, and for the first time, now, I imagined, was able to imagine, the open road of that morning for him, the just-wakened state of his mind, the alert, hopeless, hopeful blindness, and that same watching for the single, still-unfamiliar face in a crowd that must somewhere surely have been part of what happened between them, the actress and the cabinet-maker (did they maybe even come through this station together? Pass through this old upside-down boat full of people, this old church of journeys, in their day?) and the new light of that different morning as he felt for the buttons of one jacket, then for the buttons of the jacket he'd pulled on top of that one, felt so sure that two suits were all he needed in the whole world, other than her.

And how had they found each other, how had they first touched, and who kissed whom, and who opened whom, and was he always a rogue, my great-great-grandfather, and was I descended from a long line of roguish Parsons and was it just that I hadn't recognised my own propensity for rogue till now? Or was it love, I mean did they think it was love, swear it was love, know it was love, till what they thought was love ended and they simply went home? And did love end? For the first real time I could imagine what it was like for him, all those years ago, to stand two-suited, awkward, in his own open doorway, the moment before. (The people passed and passed me by and none of them was her.) And was I, who'd been kissed into such new astonishment in a near-empty bar in Old Compton Street at the heel-end of an August Thursday afternoon two weeks ago, nothing more than a cheating rogue myself, even though I'd been above board about it at home (an adventure, I'm having an adventure), or was I the innocent chick in the mouth of the fox who's told me to climb up and sit on her tongue and she'll show me the world (an adventure! I'm having an adventure!) while in reality the fox is hurrying home to feed her sweet foulmouthed cubs? No, I was lucky, blessed, graced by a love out of nowhere that had singled me out in the crowd. Wasn't I?

In a few minutes I'll turn and see her, she'll be behind me, coming towards me, she'll have come from the other tube exit, the one I don't know about. I'll know her at once. Of course I will. People will pass blankly between us as we stand and see nothing but each other. She'll take me by the hand and take me to the photo booth on the main station concourse. PHOTOVISION. Ready In Three Minutes. In behind the curtain, in a white-walled room that's somehow exactly the right size, she'll be backed up against the little adjustable seat, leaning on it, and she'll take both my wrists in her hands and she'll put them behind my back, gentle, firm, and I'll raise my eyebrows at her and she'll raise her own back at me, and I'll realise she's got both my wrists in her one hand now behind me, and with her other hand she'll unzip me, and it will take her roughly three minutes to make me come for the first time, and there'll be music playing into the photo booth, pop music coming from some kind of a stall beyond the booth, either another shoe stall or a stall selling sweets or fruit, and much later I will have forgotten one of the three tracks which will play while we're in there, but I'll never forget the other two, so apt and funny that it's like a hilarious joke played on us by chance, 'Can't Get Enough Of Your Love' by Barry White and 'If I Can't Have You' by Yvonne Elliman, so that it will be as if time has segued us back to the 1970s and given us back all our teenage chutzpah, and by the time the latter song starts, with its gorgeous build-up then its

sudden falling-away, in the orchestral disco sway and shudder of its opening, I will already have come, out of nowhere,
it will be like my whole body is itself an instant lit-up piece of
expert rhythm, and I will be leaning into her, open-mouthed,
looking at her, her hand still in me, and as the song begins,
with the kind of nonchalance that's clearly always done it for
me, with just a slight forward shrug of her shoulder, a slight
raise of one impudent eyebrow, she'll say without saying anything, *You want to dance?*

We'll be in there for only the length of those three love
songs, roughly nine or ten minutes of airplay, that's all, until
we'll pull back the curtain that's been between us and the
station and fall back out, in among all the hundreds of other
people again, the air'll feel much cooler when we do, which
will mean the photo booth must have heated up while we
were in there, and our time with each other for the day will
be up, and in a few weeks I'll walk past the same photo
booth and realise that its curtain is really very short for what
we'd been doing, and more than a year later I'll go through
the busy station on my way to somewhere else and the
whole photo booth will have disappeared, it will have been
replaced by an automated ticketing machine, a couple of
information boards and the station will look as if no photo
booth was ever there.

I didn't know it yet, I didn't know any of it, let's face it,
there was a lot I didn't know, there was everything and nothing still to come, and everything and nothing still to go. All
I knew right then at that moment was that I'd been scouting

around for somewhere to have something, I'd been being seedier than I'd ever known myself be, and now I was standing waiting to meet someone I hardly knew at a station.

But there can't be many better things in life than being on the open threshold, there can't be many better moments in life than the moment when past and future just stop mattering, and in the act of stopping mattering there's the moment wholly new, where everything matters all over again with a whole new choreography. So I stood in the space between history and hope, I stood at the top of the stairs in the London station in the foul, sweet, ancient, fecund smell of leather and metal. It was a Tuesday, it was lunchtime, it was busy, it was noisy, and I waited for someone I hardly knew, and the people went past and past like people have always passed each other, hundreds and hundreds, unrecognised hundreds, and there was nothing new in what I was doing, what I was doing was older than comedy, older than tragedy, old as the hills. But the old, old city was alive and green and raw with the possibility, yes, the known world, like petals on an old rose, doubled and redoubled, everyone under the sun was possible, and as I scanned each face, then let each face go, then looked to the next one and the next, I thought it every time inside me, unspoken, like the beat of small wings, *Come now, I'm here, come on*.

Country Life

MARMALADE BATES

Fiona: The trouble with removal men is that you have to hide everything. I spent most of last night wrapping my old vibrator in tea-towels, followed by a bedspread, followed by the kitchen curtains. It's worth it, though. Unless one of the removal men has a perverse interest in haberdashery, I think I should be safe.

I covered up the rest of the stuff under a box of Nick's old snorkelling gear. Specifically, several Polaroids of my ex-husband's cock and a book of Edwardian ladies with big bottoms that Nick stole from the university library. They say that moving house is one of the ten most stressful things any adult can do. Now I know why. If there's a ten-car pile-up on the way there, I know exactly what will end up on the motorway strip first. It really doesn't help that my ex-husband signed my name on the front of all the Polaroids.

Nick: Goodbye to bloody London at last. I'm not going to miss it at all, even though Fiona's worried that moving to the country is like going to Antarctica. She doesn't think she'll make any new friends – but if anything, I think our social life will improve. And hopefully our sex life too, of course. Ha ha!

Neither of us have ever managed to have a discussion about this, but three months of no sex is beginning to turn me into a wanker. I've taken the book of Edwardian women with huge arses into the bathroom so often that the cover's buckled. I wonder where Fiona's hidden it? The university will kill me if they know I've got it.

Fiona: Oh God! I knew this would happen. There's another vibrator that I've completely forgotten about and I'm sure it's still in the bottom drawer of my bedside cabinet, in the back of the truck. I've hidden it inside a sock, of course, because I'd die if the cleaner ever found it – but the batteries are new, and if it accidentally turns on in the back of the van the removal men will stop the truck and look for rattling sounds under the bonnet, then one thing will lead to another and . . . I couldn't stand it.

I got the new vibrator on the internet because I was bored with the old one. It's bright purple, enormous and makes a strange whooshing sound. It's like the erect phallus of some alien overlord. You can tell it's modelled on someone from another galaxy because even the veins are on backwards.

This is all Nick's fault, of course. If he got it right in bed a bit more often, I wouldn't need all this equipment at all. We've only been married for two years and we're already giving up. It's worse than it ever was with my ex-husband, and I thought that was as bad as it got.

Nick: All the books I've read about fertility (and there have been a few of those lately) talk about relaxing, chilling out, taking the pressure off and letting it happen. One of them goes on about pasta and red wine a lot, too, but that's no good to us because Fiona just makes funny noises if she sees spaghetti these days – never mind alcohol.

I suppose we've got different ideas about the best ways to get us both pregnant. Mine revolve around lots of food, booze, fresh air and country life – and a fair amount of random shagging. Hers involve fruit salad and making every position strictly missionary, just in case something should accidentally drop out, or drip off. Oh, and she likes to use a thermometer, as well, to find out when she's 'on'. No wonder we don't do it any more.

Fiona: I've got to stop thinking about the removal men, and the purple alien-overlord vibrator. I'm sure it's become the focal point of all my anxieties about other things – like adjusting to the new house. It's easy for Nick to tell me to stop worrying, but he's not the one who has to start cooking in that huge, freezing, sixteenth-century kitchen. It's one of those places that screams 'rat corpse' at you, before you even get in there.

Nick: I fell in love with the house as soon as the university offered it to us. Because it was built in 1590, the lease is offered to people in the history department first, and I just happened to get lucky. Each addition over the centuries has made it more interesting in my opinion.

I think Fiona's going to enjoy putting her stamp on the kitchen, anyway. Maybe she'll start making all her organic jams and marmalades again.

Fiona: Nick's logic is simple. Now that I don't have a job (or any kind of business at all, not even my good old rhubarb jam), I'll relax, unwind and suddenly find myself pregnant. I think he has visions of us buying some ancient four-poster bed and spending the entire winter in it, leaving only to fetch the milk and papers. I'm not so sure. It's going to take more than enforced unemployment to make me relax. And who said that peace and quiet led to pregnancy, anyway? My father always says my mother was the most neurotic woman in London before she had me.

Nick: After the removal men go at last, I start to unpack all my old scuba gear, when suddenly Fiona lets out a terrible scream from the other end of the house.

'Shit! What is it?'

'A dog!' she yells.

'What?'

'There was a bloodhound in our room, Nick! Why did you let a dog in the house?' She grabs my arm.

'I didn't.'

I search every room, while she sits on top of the Aga with her legs knotted together. Fiona has always been terrified of dogs, and nothing I say makes any difference.

I expect the bloodhound belongs to one of the neighbours, and at some point we'll get an apology and maybe the offer of a friendly drink, which is fine by me. Nevertheless, I check all the rooms again, look behind all the doors and then lock everything up, waving the key in front of her nose as evidence so that Fiona feels better.

Fiona: I decide to go to bed early, after all that. I leave some frozen sausage rolls out for Nick (he can't complain because I made them myself) and call it a night. I can't find my nightie or dressing gown, so I make do with one of Nick's old rugby jerseys. I make sure I find the vibrators, though, and put them well out of the way, on top of the wardrobe wrapped in the tea-towels. They're exactly the kind of thing that a dog would run off with.

Nick: What can I say? It looks like yet another early night for Fiona. When we first took out the lease on this house, I had high hopes for our very first night of domestic bliss. She seems to be immune to the romance of a sixteenth-century bedroom, though. When I finally go in at midnight, she's already snoring.

I suppose she thinks she's being clever, hiding her vibrators in a tea-towel on top of the wardrobe. That was probably what all the screaming was about earlier on. Bloodhound, my foot. She just wanted to create a diversion before I reached the box with the big purple thing in it.

I found it ages ago, rattling away at the bottom of our bed. If she ever asked me, I'd tell her that's another reason why I find it so hard to get it up these days. That, and the photographs of her ex-husband's family jewels. She doesn't know I've seen those either.

Fiona: Neither of us could be bothered to hang up any curtains last night, so the next morning I wake up with the sun in my eyes. Then I see that Nick has gone. I suppose he's wandered off for an exploratory walk to the village. Then I hear a strange voice in the corridor.

'Puck!'

What? That's not Nick. That's some . . . strange woman.

'Puck! Greedy, gaping glutton!'

The bloodhound I saw yesterday runs into our bedroom with a bone in its mouth, then sees me, and runs out again.

I am trying to be brave, but it is not working. Dogs have the same effect on me that spiders and snakes have on other people.

Then a naked red-haired woman runs past the doorway, chasing the dog, holding her shoes in her hand. She is followed by a much fatter man in seventeenth-century fancy dress, waddling behind her with a huge erection.

Thank God. There's no dog after all. No terrifying bloodhound. This is only a nightmare – I must be dreaming. I wait for the usual 'click' in my head, so I can wake up.

Despite my best efforts to escape my nightmare, the dog stays put. Then something even worse happens. The jiggling, naked woman runs in, followed by the fat man and they start fucking each other on the floor.

There is a red tapestry rug underneath her bottom. I look twice. It wasn't there last night.

'I will not fail to fulfil your desire,' the man promises, as he sits up and cups the woman's hand around his cock.

She laughs, and nods in the direction of her shoes. 'I cross my shoes in the letter of "T", hoping my true love to see,' she recites.

The man makes her switch hands, from left to right, and hides his cock in her fingers again.

'Handy, dandy, prickly pandy: which hand shall have?' he teases her.

Then she laughs, as he twists her around and fucks her from behind. Her bottom is pert, small and very powdery – as if she has emptied a whole packet of flour all over it.

The woman moans and puts her fist in her mouth while the fat man rides her. Then he suddenly decides to pull out and flips her over. She opens her legs immediately, allowing him to dive inside her with his fingers.

'Thy pond is my delight,' he tells her, kissing her there. Then she starts to pant and moan, as he uses his mouth.

I suppose at some point, they will both look up on the bed and see me watching them – and ask me to join in. Then I will wake up with one of those long, exquisite, unsatisfied aches that I often get first thing in the morning.

The woman is gorgeous. She has curly red hair, pale skin and freckles everywhere – and her moaning is almost musical.

Suddenly she gets up, runs out of the room, and comes back with my vibrators, one in each hand, waving them around as if they are the funniest thing she has ever seen – which, I suppose, is probably the case in 1590.

And then, at last, I wake up. There is only one problem, though. The tea-towel package of vibrators which I left so carefully on top of the wardrobe last night has gone.

Nick: I'm glad I decided to get up early and go out for a walk. If this is typical country life, then I want to live here for ever. No taxis, no drunks, no delivery vans. No screeching brakes, no dog shit, no petrol smell in the air. To actually be able to roll out of bed and walk down to a river, and hear the birds waking up, is the kind of thing you can only fantasise about in London.

I tried to wake Fiona up earlier so she could join me, but she was snoring away, dead to the world. Maybe it's the fresh country air.

Fiona: Bloody Nick. After that dream, I am now completely and irreversibly turned on – and I cannot find either of my vibrators anywhere. I suppose he's thrown them in the bin, in a fit of pique. I should have told him about the big, new purple one, but it just seemed like too much effort. And now the worst thing possible has happened; I desperately need to come – and I can't, at least, not without assistance from Nick. Bastard. Where is he? I was always hopeless at using my hands.

Nick: When I go back to the house, I can hear Fiona moaning in our bedroom and I'm sure most of the neighbours can, as well. She's never been particularly loud in bed, but this is ear-splitting. It also happens to be giving me a serious hard-on, so I don't waste any time joining her. Who am I to reject a modern miracle?

Only one problem, though. When I reach our bedroom, I realise it's not her.

Fiona: I give up masturbating after about twenty minutes of trying. I'm much too used to a quick, battery-operated fix, I suppose. Oh God! How am I going to get out of this one? Maybe, if I just go to sleep, the rest of me will go to sleep as well . . .

Nick: I go into the room to find a pretty, fair-haired maid in a bonnet and gown sitting on a chair with her legs apart and her fingers in a jug of cream, playing with herself. At the end of the room, another maid is beating a dark-haired man on his buttocks with a bundle of twigs. His arse is already covered in red marks. He has one hand on the window, while the other one holds his left leg up.

The man's black wig is still on, and so are his shoes – and he has only pulled his breeches down to his knees. It's flagellation – eighteenth-century style. The room is recognisably our bedroom, but there are things in it that I don't remember seeing before. There is a fireplace, for a start, and a pair of bellows. I'm glad the fire is lit, though; it's freezing.

Fiona: I must have fallen asleep straightaway because the next dream seems to unfold very quickly. A woman who looks as if she has just walked out of a Jane Austen novel is beating a man on his bare bottom with a homemade broom, while another maid, with fair hair, watches them on a chair. Every so often she dips her fingers into a jug of cream and starts playing with herself, groaning loudly each time the broom hits the man. He is tall, dark and slightly sexy – not old and fat like the last one. I never thought I'd find a man in a wig attractive, but the man being spanked in front of me has a certain something. He has huge muscles in his arms and thighs, as if he does a lot of riding.

After he has had enough of the broom, the man puts his leg down hard on the floor, pulls himself away from the window and kneels in front of the blonde maid in the chair. His cock is incredible – dark, big and wonderfully hard.

'I have a great mind to have this coral-tipped clitoris,' he tells the maid, giving her tiny strokes with his finger while he kisses her. Then I notice someone else in the room. It's Nick – who looks as stunned as I feel.

'What are you doing here?' I ask. He hardly ever wanders into my dreams.

'I might enquire the same thing of you,' he grins.

'Oh shut up.'

'What do you think of it so far?' Nick asks.

'I love that man. He's gorgeous,' I tell him.

Then the dark man with the impressive cock ruins every-thing by sinking his head obediently into the maid's lap while she inspects his wig for lice.

'Not so gorgeous now,' Nick says, and laughs at me.

'Kindly get out of my dream.'

'Okay, okay.'

Before Nick can do anything, though, the maid in the chair produces two objects from under her petticoats.

'Cupid and Venus!' she announces, and presents my vibra-tors to the kneeling man.

After that, Nick laughs so hard that I'm sure I'll wake up. And if only I could stop staring at that amazing man kneeling on the floor, I probably would.

Nick: Fiona has been in my dreams a couple of times in the past, but never like this. I suppose it's the sausage rolls she left out for me last night – they weren't properly defrosted.

At some point I realise I will have to come out of this dream, but I'm not sure where I'll end up. Am I still outside the house and did I fall asleep in a field somewhere? Or am I actually back in our bed?

Fiona: Watching the spanked man with his maids reminds me of the early days of my relationship with Nick, when we were both worried about me falling pregnant. It seems ridiculous to think of that now, when we seem to spend our whole lives trying to have a baby. Once upon a time, though, he used to kneel on the floor for me, too. He never called it my coral-tipped anything, though. He just used to call it . . . oh, never mind. I'm sure we'll both remember one day.

Nick: The next thing I hear in the dream is this: 'To hell with 1916!'

I realise that I am in our bedroom again, except it is not really our room, because too many things have changed. A man in army uniform is swigging from a bottle of whisky and unpacking a brown leather suitcase. It must be New Year's Eve, or close to it. There is snow on the windows, and a solitary Christmas card on the mantelpiece.

The soldier holds up two pairs of silk stockings and two pairs of girls' garters, and drops them on the bed. Then he unpacks a nightdress, a string of beads, a pot of Vaseline, a condom and a candle. This is then followed, almost inevitably, by Fiona's vibrators.

I am extremely impressed with the way my unconscious mind is registering so much accurate historical detail. The twentieth century has never been my subject, but the condom is labelled THE NEWEST SHEATH. SILK FINISH. NEVER RIP which seems authentic enough, and there is a copy of the *News of the World* on the mantelpiece with the right kind of headlines on the front page – sex and murder as usual, but 1916 style.

I worry for a minute that something horrible will start to happen in this dream, because there's something about this soldier I do not like. But then Fiona appears on the bed, with my old rugby shirt on.

Fiona: One look at the soldier in our bedroom and I know he has shell shock, or depression, or both. He has bags under his eyes and he hasn't shaved for days.

'I crave for intercourse with women I do not respect,' he tells me, as he holds my hand.

I rub his shoulders and try to ignore the fact that Nick is staring at us. The soldier looks as if he is about to cry.

'I have been too often in Long Acre, Jermyn Street and Half Moon Street.'

'That's okay,' I reassure him, assuming these must be brothels. 'I'm sure you're not the only one.'

'I had a girl in Hyde Park and was fined all of the money I had in my pocket.'

'It's all right.'

'We are fighting and bleeding for England!' he says, look-ing disgusted, and swigs from his bottle of Scotch again.

I take his cap off, and then his jacket, and gently ease him around on the bed, so that he's sitting in front of me. Then I wipe his tears away, because he is crying properly now – and I start to undo his belt.

I want this young soldier. He must be no more than twenty-one, but I really, really want him. And something tells me that he might want me too, despite the fact that I am wearing one of Nick's old rugby shirts.

Nick: If there is one thing I remember about early twentieth-century history, it is the appalling spread of VD among British troops. What the hell does Fiona think she's doing? Or about to do?

In the madness of these dreams, I have just remembered something important – that we are trying to have a baby. If she gets the clap from this bastard, it could be the end of everything, and I no longer care if none of this is real.

Fiona: I can see I have a choice now. The soldier – who seems to need me desperately – or Nick. Something tells me the soldier would come in five minutes flat, but I also know he's young enough to last all night, if I ask him nicely. Anyway. Maybe I could help him. Maybe I could educate him.

The exhausted soldier reads my mind. 'Instruct me,' he whispers and, as I close my eyes, he begins to unbutton my shirt.

When I open my eyes again, though, it is Nick who is pulling off my top, and Nick's tongue which is on my breasts.

Nick: Something about the way the maid was moaning in the other dream, when the man knelt in front of her, makes me want to give Fiona some pleasure too. It's time to wake up. Come on Fiona. You know you want to.

Fiona: I suppose, if Nick's chucked my vibrators in the bin, the least he can do is go down on me. It's so unusual for him to do this, though, that it still feels like part of a dream.

Nick: I am still shocked by how jealous I felt of the soldier. I can understand why some men feel driven to kill now.

Fiona: The steady rhythm of Nick's tongue makes me think of that funny red-haired woman's rhyme – 'I cross my shoes in the letter of "T", hoping my true love to see.'

One soft stroke, one hard stroke. One soft stroke, one hard stroke. If he goes on like this, I'm going to faint.

Nick: This is not a dream. This has to be real. Fiona would never be digging her nails into my legs like this, for a start. And every detail of our room is so clear. The alarm clock by the bed. The bare windows. The sausage roll crumbs on the plate.

Fiona: Just the thought of the young soldier in our bedroom is enough to send me over the edge. Is that disloyal to Nick? Am I allowed to think of my poor young army man, who wants me so much?

Nick: If I tell her about the dreams I've had, I know she's going to lose it completely. All of which makes me think . . . why not?

Fiona: Nick starts telling me his dreams – except that they are mine as well. I'd forgotten how sexy his voice is; it's so low and serious. The perfect voice for a history tutor. I could listen to him for ever while his finger is on my button.

Nick: There are few greater pleasures in life than meaningless sex with the woman you love. Did I make that up, or is it something from Boswell? Or Pepys? I've finished with Fiona's body now. For my next trick, I want to play with her mind.

Fiona: Nick tells me all about the dark man in our bedroom with the huge cock, trembling at the window, while his maid thrashes him in front of the fire. Then he tells me about the blonde maid on the chair with her fingers in the cream.

After that, he shows me something else. He has found both my vibrators, hidden under the sheets. Good old Cupid and Venus. I wondered what had happened to them.

Nick: Fiona must have hidden her toys up the chimney. Or that bloodhound has been dragging them around in the woods. They are barely recognisable. Dark, charred and covered in dirt. The purple one looks practically black now. The other one is so worn away, it's hardly recognisable. They don't even look as though they're made of plastic any more. They look as if they've been dragged backwards through time.

Fiona: Can we really have been sharing the same dreams all this time? Perhaps we've been sharing them with every single person who ever lived in this house. I must ask Nick about it one day. Or maybe we'll never talk about it.

Fun

SYMPHONY MERITT

Lindsay and Rick had been seeing each other for four years and living with each other for three. They loved each other. They liked each other. They fancied each other. But – even at the peak of their passion – it would never have been enough for Lindsay. In any case, that peak had passed long ago. It passed, in fact, pretty much from the moment they surrendered their separate addresses, and separate beds. Nowadays, at the end of a hard day, they would both as soon fall asleep in front of the TV as fall on top of one another. Prefer to conk than bonk, as Lindsay put it, late one night, just as Rick was stretching an arm towards her. It made her laugh, and it did Rick, too, over breakfast the following morning. At the time, though, he'd been offended. He'd retreated back to his side of the bed in an angry huff, which lasted for at least three minutes, before he conked out himself.

They lived hard, Lindsay and Rick. In their own ways. Went out pretty much every night, though increasingly rarely together, and during the days they both had jobs to do. Rick invested other people's money, and managed to make a lot of money for himself in the process. As a result, they lived in some style in a luxurious, modern loft apartment in Canary Wharf with glass walls in the bedroom, a vast, state-of-the-art kitchen that was almost never used, a sitting room as big as a ball-room and a large balcony, which stretched the length of the flat, and overlooked the Thames.

Lindsay allowed Rick to pay for most things. They both preferred it that way. But she continued to work, as a PA of sorts, at one of the big accountancy firms in the City. She stayed there, not because she needed the money. She didn't. She stayed because she enjoyed the break. Because, in comparison with the rest of her life, the quiet, beige-and-grey offices were a haven for her: a haven of restfulness, ordinariness, gentle boredom and glorious, mindless peace. She worked there because, in its own dull way, it was fun.

Although perhaps to use the word 'work' would be putting it a bit strongly. She adorned the place, rather than worked there. She drew a salary. She checked in at nine, always on time and always looking very elegant. To the office Lindsay wore quiet, expensive clothes in dark colours that reflected her dark complexion, but which belied her small salary and her fiery character – and which purposefully camouflaged her glorious curves.

From nine to five, Monday to Friday she sat at her tidy

desk in a small office with two other secretaries, and the three of them chatted, pretty much solidly (with a brief relocation for lunch), until home time. At which point they each went their separate ways until nine o'clock the next morning, when the chatting would begin again. Lindsay never socialised with them in the evenings. Ever.

Because Lindsay, as everybody who knew her very quickly learned, was a woman who liked to compartmentalise. And, though she was endlessly curious about the details of other people's lives, she preferred to play her own cards closer to her own, ample, chest. She knew everything about her two colleagues: what they ate for their breakfast, at what age they lost their virginity and how, and where, and with whom, whether they spat or swallowed, whether they preferred *Ally McBeal* or *Desperate Housewives*, whether they fantasised about Daniel Craig or Robbie Williams or Hugh Grant or Richard Madeley, whether they were superstitious about ladders and whether they preferred it from behind.

But the girls knew next to nothing about Lindsay. They knew she had a boyfriend, and at some point (she regretted it) she had let slip he was called Rick. They knew which celebrities she preferred, and they knew a tiny bit – just a tiny bit – about her own sex life. But beyond that, they knew very little. Lindsay, out of necessity, out of habit, and – better yet – because it was *fun*, was a very private person. In her own peculiar way.

She had her work friends, with whom she talked only about celebrities, holidays and sex. She had her party friends, with whom she only talked about celebrities, holidays and sex. And her other friends, with whom she only talked about sex.

And Rick, with whom she talked about everything and anything except, of course, the truth.

'What are you up to this evening?' Rick asked her. They'd been awake for hours, had already enjoyed one, some-what business-like, shag at half past six that morning. Half an hour later they'd climbed out of their God-sized bed, staggered into to their God-sized, walk-in shower and – to Rick's credit – enjoyed another one, right there in the thick steam under the thundering torrent of warm water. It had been much more leisurely the second time round. It had been lovely.

So, no. It wasn't that they didn't fancy each other any more. Far from it. What was missing between them now, in their luxurious but settled Canary Wharf life together, was the *white heat* of the early days. It's what Lindsay craved, quietly. It was what they both craved, in fact. They remem-bered the days when they used to fuck in the toilets at parties and fuck behind bushes in Hyde Park, and fuck while Rick was on the telephone to his clients, fuck in lifts and in chang-ing rooms, and between courses in fancy restaurants – once even while they were still at the restaurant table. (It was a corner booth, and dark and quiet and very, very posh. They'd been surrounded by fat, guffawing men smoking cigars and miserable looking stick-women, draped in jewellery, too vain to smile or eat. Lindsay, wanting to shake them all up a bit, had moved over and sat on Rick's lap, and things had quickly progressed from there. Too quickly in fact. Lindsay, in the throws of her ardour, had accidentally knocked a glass of iced water over the pair of them, which brought them both back to their senses pretty sharply. The waiter stood back until the two of them had rearranged themselves and then, very quietly, ordered them to leave. Which they did, giggling hysterically. (They were lucky not have been arrested.) In any case, with the God-sized bed forever at their disposal, all that kind of craziness had faded away. Sex, in Rick and Lindsay's luxurious Canary Wharf shag-pad, was in grave danger of settling into a pattern.

'If we don't watch out, you know, Rick, Lindsay had chortled to her boyfriend a week or two ago, 'we're going to become respectable. We'll be buying easy-clean pot plants on mail order in a year or two. I'll be sending you out to buy Tampax for me, and hanging my knickers over the bath to dry!'

Rick had laughed uneasily. 'You'll never be respectable, Lindsay,' he said to her. 'You could mail order any number of pot plants. Have a fucking Tupperware party. Tog yourself up like Miss Marple, for all I care. It wouldn't make any difference. You don't have a respectable bone in your body.'

They hadn't looked at each other after that. A silence had fallen and they'd both put on a little show of being thoroughly immersed in their newspapers. Or, in Lindsay's case, thoroughly immersed in her celebrity magazine, where (thankfully) there were several pages of pictures of Paris

Hilton's handbags to be flicked through. In any case, the moment had passed. Just as it always did.

'Hey.' Rick leaned across the kitchen breakfast bar, where Lindsay, still in her dressing gown, was munching thoughtfully on a warm croissant. Rick pinched her affectionately on the cheek. 'Oi! Anyone in there?' he said. 'I asked you what you were up to tonight.'

'Mm? Oh. Nothing much,' Lindsay said, not exactly looking at him. She took a slurp from her mug of hot chocolate, and thought for a moment. 'I'll be home about midnight, I should imagine. Not that late.'

'Seeing anyone I know?'

Lindsay nodded. 'I'm actually meeting up with . . . Melissa. But you can't come,' she added quickly. 'She chucked in her job yesterday. Plus she broke up with her boyfriend. So she's a bit upset. Naturally.'

'Melissa as in gay Melissa, from the other night?' Rick asked.

'Um. Yes. That's right she had a boyfriend,' Lindsay said, a little quickly.

'So what's she so upset about? I'd have thought she'd be glad to break up with him.'

'She is. It's not that. Anyway . . . she says she's got something to tell me. Says it's a top top, *top* secret . . .' Lindsay giggled throatily – keen to divert him. 'I think we already know what it is, though.'

Rick looked confused. 'Do we? Do I? I've never even met her.'

Lindsay rolled her eyes. 'I told you about her – at the party. Suddenly announcing she was gay. I told you, remember? With the *naked dancing*? And her being so out of it, and the *naked Aussie girl* and everything . . . remember?'

Rick paused to picture the beautiful, blonde Melissa, exactly as Lindsay had described her to him when she came back to Canary Wharf late on Saturday night. Beautiful, blonde Melissa (whom he'd never met, but heard so much about) with pupils the size of saucers, and shirt completely undone, had apparently spent the evening swaying dreamily on the dance floor, her arms coiled tightly round a six-foot naked Aussie girl, who looked, Lindsay told him, the spitting image of Rachel Hunter . . . Rick didn't care much if the story was true. He didn't even bother to wonder. He was just happy to be hearing about it.

'I'd like to meet Melissa one day,' he mumbled. 'And the Rachel Hunter girl . . . why don't you invite them round?'

Lindsay shook her head. 'Can't. Unfortunately, they broke up,' she said. 'The Aussie girl flew back to Aussie-land Sunday morning.'

'Shame . . .'

Lindsay swallowed the last of her croissant and looked across at Rick. He was pulling his jacket on, checking his watch, heading for the door. 'Anyway,' she said, admiring the shoulders, the thick dark hair, the suntanned neck – thinking about their meeting in the shower this morning and maybe, possibly, another meeting later on. She wondered if it would be worth waylaying him for a quick repeat act before then.

And decided against it. 'What are you up to tonight, Rick? Anything special?'

'Mm? Oh. Nothing much,' Rick said, not exactly looking at her. 'Meeting up with Alec. But you can't come,' he added quickly. 'We're planning the stag night.'

'Ahhh! Should be fun . . . See you later, then.'

'Yeah.'

They didn't kiss goodbye. They stole a glance at one another – just when they hoped the other wouldn't be looking. It was bad timing. For a split second, Rick and Lindsay caught each other's eye. And they quickly looked away again.

'Later, then.'

'Later . . . Have a good day.'

And from that moment, until midnight, when they would meet again, in that big, beautiful bed with views overlooking the Thames, they were free, pretty much, to do whatever pleased them.

Lindsay sauntered back into the bedroom to arrange herself for the day. She would not be coming home between the end of work and the beginning of the evening, so she needed to think ahead. She sighed. Also, she needed to do something about Stephen Grange, her boss, who was lascivious enough at the best of times, in his own feeble little way, but whose attitude towards her had changed dramatically for the worse since he bumped into her very late one night last week.

She'd been doing someone a favour, helping out an old

friend, and the creep had been using an alias. How the hell was she to have known? She'd taken care not to look at him. She'd not even spoken. She'd just done what she came to do and got out. And he'd been far too shell-shocked to say a word. Nevertheless, now of course, it was too late.

Whereas before he'd used to lust after her quietly, with nervous, secret, tentative longing, now he literally *licked his lips* every time he set eyes on her. It had been getting steadily more awkward all week, and yesterday had been the worst. He'd shuffled into the office and simply stood by her desk and gazed at her, his groin just inches from her face.

'Is there anything I can do for you, Stephen?' she had asked him eventually.

'Mmm?' He blushed scarlet. Jumped, like he'd been given an electric shock. 'What's that, Lindsay? What's that? God, no. At least – *no*. That is, no. Not really, no . . .'

'Only the girls and me – we're a bit busy. We've got ever so much to do.'

The girls, Tamsin and Maxine, sitting side by side, leafing through *Grazia* magazine, stifled a giggle. They very rarely had anything to do at all, let alone 'ever so much'. It was a standing joke between them.

'As you can see,' Lindsay said, trying not to grin, 'we're worked off our feet. And you're kind of putting us off. Also, I hate to be rude, but we happened to be in the middle of a very private conversation. Tamsin's got personal problems. Haven't you, Tamsin?'

Tamsin nodded. They were actually in the middle of

a fascinating discussion regarding the sex life of Mr and Mrs Tom Cruise. In fact, Tamsin had just been saying that apparently Tom Cruise had a dick the size of —

'Very, very personal.' Tamsin nodded solemnly.

'So unless there's something we can do for you, Stephen,' continued Lindsay, 'I'd be grateful if you could allow us a little . . . *time* and *space* . . .'

'Time and space . . .' Stephen repeated feebly. 'Yes, of course . . . Mustn't get in the way . . . busy girls . . . busy girls . . .' And he had tripped off back his own office.

The three 'busy girls' had almost wet themselves with laughter after he'd gone. But underneath, Lindsay was nervous. She wasn't sure she'd be able to control him so well next time, or the time after that. Really, she needed to talk to him. In private. She needed to make it absolutely clear to him where he stood.

Lindsay flung what she needed for the day into an elegant Mulberry travel case and left the flat in perfect time, as always.

Outside on the street, she hailed a cab, just as she did every weekday morning. Then, a block and a half from the office, she ordered the cab to stop. Just as she always did. She asked him to pull over in the same quiet side street every morning. And every morning, she always checked that no colleagues were near, before climbing out and walking the rest of the journey. She was only a lowly secretary after all. It wouldn't do for her colleagues to see her travelling to work in such style. It would have been embarrassing.

At five minutes to nine precisely, Lindsay pushed through the spinning door that led into the accountancy firm's vast marble foyer. She took a single step toward the bank of lifts at the end of the hall – and spotted Stephen. Staring at her.

Waiting for her, actually. He blushed.

She turned around and walked back through the spinning door, out onto the street again. She waited a moment, rattled, not certain what to do. Except to go back again. But when she returned a few minutes later, he was gone. She took the lift to the fourteenth floor and went straight to her desk. She was annoyed – flustered, even. It was the first time she had arrived late to work in four years.

As Lindsay walked in, Tamsin and Maxine broke off from their ruminations on the state of the Jolie-Pitt union. They stared at her in amazement. Not only was she late, she was scowling. And Lindsay never scowled.

'You all right, Lindsay?' Maxine enquired.

'Fine.' Lindsay snapped. 'Just Stephen and his stupid crush. It's beginning to really piss me off.'

'He's nauseating,' Maxine replied. 'But so long as he doesn't object when we never do any work, who's complaining?'

'He doesn't *give* us any work,' muttered Lindsay. 'So how the bloody hell's he going to object if we don't do it?'

Maxine and Tamsin glanced at each other, disconcerted. Lindsay was never like this.

'You all right, Lindsay?' Maxine asked again, this time with a bit more concern. 'If he's pissing you off, then tell him about it. Tell him to stop. He does whatever you tell him anyway!'

Lindsay just shook her head. She regretted having said anything. 'So!' she said lightly, putting on a good smile. '*Anyway*. Never mind him. Who had sex last night? Who with? Why? Where? Wearing what? And most importantly of all, *was it any fun*? Dirty details, please. Who's first?'

Maxine and Tamsin laughed, relieved to have the old Lindsay back. '*Well* . . .' began Tamsin, leaning towards them both. 'It's funny you should ask that. Because last night —'

And then Stephen barged in. He was looking smarter than usual. He was wearing a new suit, with trousers that didn't flap around his ankles, for once, and a new tie – just as nondescript as usual, but without the food splodges down the front. Stephen was neither young, nor old; neither good looking, nor revolting; neither fat, nor thin; not tall or short. He was a just a man. The boss. Somebody for Lindsay, Maxine and Tamsin to laugh at. Until last week, he'd barely registered as a living, breathing individual. To Maxine and Tamsin, he still hadn't.

They knew, vaguely, that he was married with two children. Or possibly three. And that he commuted in from somewhere near Basingstoke. Or possibly Kingston. That was it.

'Morning, Stephen,' Tamsin said dutifully.

'Morning, all,' said Stephen, rubbing his hands together. He sounded different. Lindsay noticed it at once. Like a man with a purpose. He never sounded like that. '*Lindsay*,' he said, turning to her. There was a little sheen of sweat on his forehead. Maybe the hint of a gleam behind the spectacles.

'Yes, *Stephen*,' replied Lindsay. Trying to keep it light. 'Morning to you. How can I help?'

'Could I have a quick word?'

'Certainly can,' she said, still at her desk.

'In private.'

'Oh. In private.' She stood up. 'Okay, then. Fine.' And as she passed him he stopped rubbing his hands together and placed one hand on the small of her back.

Tamsin giggled. Which didn't help.

'I think,' he said, closing his office door behind him, 'that we need to talk.'

Lindsay shrugged. She hadn't been prepared for this – not for him to have taken the initiative – and so early in the day. Now she wasn't sure how to play it. 'Talk about what?' she asked innocently.

He chuckled. 'Lindsay, dearest, I think you *know* what about.'

'Not really, no.'

'Oh . . .' He tipped his head to one side and smirked down at her. It was faintly disgusting. '*Come now*,' he murmured.

'Don't tell me to "come now". I haven't even the faintest idea what you're talking about.' Lindsay snapped. '"Come now" yourself.'

The smirk remained. 'I assure you, Lindsay. I've been doing nothing but. Ever since that most extraordinary night . . .'

'And I assure *you*, Stephen,' interrupted Lindsay, her irritation making her forget to feign confusion any longer, 'there was nothing *remotely* extraordinary about it to me. In fact, I can hardly remember it at all.'

But he didn't seem to hear. He took a step towards her. She took a step back. 'All day . . . and all night. I've been thinking about you in that little hotel room, Lindsay. I can't stop. I can't stop. I can't keep my hands —'

'Oh, for God's sake.'

'I had no idea, Lindsay . . . not the foggiest.'

She shrugged again. 'Why should you? It's got nothing to do with you.'

He laughed. Took another step towards her. Again, she stepped back. 'It had a lot to do with me last week!'

There wasn't much space between them now. She couldn't shuffle any further back, not without falling over his desk, and yet still, he was edging closer, edging closer to her all the time, until she could smell the soap on him. Lux. She could smell the coffee on his breath.

'But it has nothing to do with you any more, Stephen,' she said gently, deciding it might be better to change tack. ' Listen, Stephen. I know what you want . . . but you can't have it. Okay? I'm sorry. It's just not on offer. You need to understand that. I can't help you.'

'You helped me last week.'

'And I never would have done. Never. Not if I'd known it was you. So please. Go away. Go back to your wife.'

'But I don't want to,' he whined. He sounded shrill and childish and yet still somehow threatening. His tone, his manner, the way he continued to edge towards her made

Lindsay want to run, and she would have done. She longed to run, but he was blocking her in. 'I don't *want* to go back to my wife, Lindsay,' he said.

'Then go back to my friend. She can help you.'

'She's boring. Not like you. I want *you*.'

'Well, you can't have me. I told you. It's impossible. So please, Stephen. Try to forget it. Try to forget it ever happened, okay? And let's both of us just get back to work.'

'But that's all I'm asking, Lindsay!' he cried. 'For you to get back to your work!' and with that, he lunged; he pressed his mouth onto hers and grasped at her breasts. She lost her balance, staggered back onto the desk. He moaned with contentment and, just for a second, Lindsay froze. Taking her stillness as some kind of assent, he moaned again, louder this time. His hands began to move. Impatiently, he tugged at her skirt. And then, suddenly, he stopped. Looked up. His left arm still pinned her to the desk, but there was a flicker of alarm in his eyes.

'This is a business thing, right?' he said. 'I mean. Like the other time. It's business. I'm going to pay you and everything. More – even more, if you want. Because of you coming to the office and everything.' He laughed, a phlegmy laugh, fugged up with his own desire. 'It's like door-to-door service. Or whatever. Door-to-door . . . Turn around, Lindsay,' he said abruptly. 'I want to —'

Quick as a whip, Lindsay pulled up her knee and shoved it into his groin. He cried out, staggered away from her in agony.

'Bitch!' he gasped, wiping his eyes, bent double in pain. 'What was that for?'

'What was that for?' Lindsay straightened up and looked at him in amazement. 'What was that *for*?'

'I said I was going to pay you,' he said.

'And I told you I wasn't interested.' Carefully, calmly, Lindsay smoothed her skirt and rearranged her hair. She glanced at Stephen, still bent double; still, clearly, in a great deal of pain. 'Don't do that again,' she said. 'Okay?'

He didn't reply.

'I happen to like my job here in the firm,' she said. 'And I would really like to stay here. And I think you would too. So. I'm going to walk out of this room. Now. And I'm going to pretend this never happened. All right?'

Still, he didn't reply.

'Stephen. Do you understand what I'm saying? You have a lot more to lose than I do, if this little incident became public. You have a *wife*. And *children*. Do you understand what I'm saying?'

'Screw you.'

'I am going to walk out of this office, and in five minutes *you're* going to walk out of this office, and we're both going to continue exactly as we did before. Are we agreed?'

'*Fuck you*,' he grunted, hands still cupped over his balls. Lindsay noted a dribble of spit hanging loose from his lower lip. '. . . Come back here, Lindsay. Come back here this minute, or I swear, I'll tell your boyfriend. I'll tell *Rick*. I'll track him down. And I'll tell him exactly what kind of a dirty little whore you really are.'

She blinked. Breathed deeply. Smiled. 'Don't be silly, now. Out here in five minutes, Stephen,' she said softly. 'Just like it never happened . . .' And she left the room.

Lindsay checked her diary. Not that she needed to. She knew what appointments she had tonight; one at five-thirty, one at seven-thirty, and one at nine o'clock. Same times, same place, same games as usual. Same men. They were regulars. Lindsay kept a little flat in Blackfriars, filled with toys. She'd been entertaining her five-thirty there every Thursday night for a couple of years now. The seven-thirty, she'd been seeing for even longer.

The nine o'clock appointment, however, was a little different. He'd visited only once before. Exactly one week earlier. Tonight would be his second visit. And she was look-ing forward to it. In fact she'd been looking forward to it all week, ever since he called to book again. Now, with only a few hours left, she could hardly contain herself.

Last week – the first week – he'd come staggering into her little apartment, tall and dark and as breathtakingly sexy as he always was, with a recommendation from one of her favourite clients. He'd said his name was Alec. He'd been a bit wrecked – or a bit wired, anyway, and strangely distracted. It was lucky. It meant Lindsay got a good look at him, before he could take a good look at her.

She dimmed the lights – quickly – and dived for the box of toys, re-emerging a little while later with a dark mask that covered her eyes, and a head of long blonde hair, and an accent that could have been from anywhere. What did it matter? He didn't care. She stood behind him, wrapped a soft silk scarf around his eyes, and led him to the bed.

And he didn't speak, and she never knew if he knew then, or if he didn't, or even if he'd always known . . . but he never said a word. He took off the blindfold when he stood behind her, and he bent her gently over the bed, and when he fucked her, he said nothing: not a word. There was perfect silence between them, and all the white heat of the early days, only more: much, much more.

Afterwards, with the lights still low, he left £300 on the table by the bed and wandered out into the darkness, back to Canary Wharf. And then he'd waited. They'd both waited. For tonight.

After the Funeral

BUNTY B. ROAD

It was the laugh that did it. A completely inappropriate laugh ringing around the chapel while they waited for the memorial service to begin. Lizzie recognised it immediately. A school-boy's impulsive bark, with a slightly gravelly timbre, just like his speaking voice. Her head snapped round before she had even told it to, and there he was – Mark le Broyeux.

And while most of the congregation had also turned to see who had perpetrated this inappropriate act of mirth, it was her face he was looking back at.

Maybe it was the stupidly long black feathers on her hat that had attracted his gaze, she thought. She had worried they were a bit flashy for a funeral. But then she forgot the hat. Mark was still looking at her and he was smiling.

The blue eyes. He still had those dark-blue eyes. Eyes that she had always felt could look right into her. Lizzie's stomach lurched, just as it always had around him. And areas a little south of the stomach. Here we go, she thought.

He grinned broadly and she gave him an inhibited wave. People were looking. And it was a funeral.

'See you after,' he mouthed, nodding and raising his eyebrows enthusiastically.

Lizzie nodded back and turned to the front of the chapel as the first impossibly sad bars of Mahler started to play. She tried not to beam with delight.

He was wearing glasses, she realised as she stood up. Then, as the coffin was being carried past her, all she could think about was how marvellous Mark le Broyeux looked in heavy black-rimmed spectacles. And how the navy cashmere overcoat she had somehow managed to take in during that fleeting glance made his eyes look even bluer.

Lizzie let out a loud involuntary sigh. Bella, standing next to her in the pew, squeezed her hand, clearly thinking the emotion of the moment had got to her best friend. Lizzie squeezed back, feeling guilty. It had. Just not the emotion Bella imagined.

And hadn't he been wearing a polka-dot scarf? That would be so like him. A little cheerful note for such a lowering occasion. She desperately wanted to turn round for another look, but forced herself to keep her mind on where she was and why.

But her brain had its own ideas, as it always had around Mark. What would everyone do, she wondered, if she quietly left her pew and walked back up the aisle to the one where he was standing?

She would politely push her way along his pew until she was next to him, *Excuse me, excuse me, I'm so sorry* . . . Then she'd pull out the needlepoint prayer-cushion and kneel on it as she quietly opened that navy coat, unzipped his fly and took his cock into her mouth, without even touching it with her hands.

It would become hard between her lips, she knew, jumping like a freshly landed fish. And when it was a steel rod, she'd swirl her tongue luxuriously around the end, taking more of it into her mouth and then moving her head faster and faster by tiny degrees, increasing her suction at the same rate.

She couldn't help smiling as she imagined the feather on her hat waving merrily in time, until Mark would suddenly grab her head and gasp as he came into her mouth. 'Holy shit!' he would cry out as his cum squirted down her throat. Then perhaps the whole congregation would applaud them both.

'Let us pray,' said the vicar.

Henry would have loved that, thought Lizzie, staring down at the order of service, but not seeing it. Henry, who was now installed on trestles in front of the altar. One of her oldest friends – and one of Mark's too, of course.

She had forgotten that link, but now she remembered – if it hadn't been for Henry, she would never have met Mark. After forty or so years she had to strain to remember the exact circumstances, but hadn't they been at school together? Yes, that was right – Stowe. And then Henry had been at art college with Lizzie, and they'd all ended up at the same twenty-first that summer so long ago.

She had no idea now whose party it had been, but she still clearly remembered the moment she had first met Mark, so handsome in a dinner jacket, his cheeks pink from dancing, shirt collar open, black tie hanging loose.

It wasn't love at first sight, but there had been a sense of instant recognition. Because underneath all that public-school bluster, she had seen something else. The something that had made him, in the years since, not a boring banker, as everyone had expected, but a quietly well-known literary novelist.

That was the quality that had attracted her to him right from the start. The depth. The insight. That and the dark-blue eyes. The sportsman's physique. The joyous laugh. And the conviction that he would be an astonishingly good fuck. She'd just never had the chance to find out and there had been times in her life when she thought that fact might drive her insane. The terrible frustrated wondering what his cock might be like.

It was funny really, she thought, as Henry's brother went up to read the eulogy, how she'd kept in touch with tricky, touchy, tetchy Henry all these years, but had lost Mark. She had always liked Mark so much more. Too much. That was the problem, that was why they'd lost track of each other in the end.

In all honesty, she'd lost him on purpose, because it was just too confusing feeling like that about someone when you were married to someone else and so was he. It had varied over the years who either of them had been married to, but one of them always was.

And here he was again in his cashmere coat and his heavy-rimmed glasses and with those penetrating eyes. His hair, once so dark and glossy, was silver now, his face lined and loosening around the jaw, but he was still able to reduce Lizzie to an obsessive pervert with one smile and the promise of more to come.

But more of what? That's what she'd never known. From that first moment when they'd roared with laughter about a joke he'd made and then she had topped, there had been a bond, but it wasn't romantic. Not at first. It was a meeting of minds, which grew – for her, at least – into a longing for a meeting of gonads.

But, in all those years, she had never quite known whether he felt that way about her. She thought that later maybe he did, but she was never sure enough to act upon it. Or single enough.

Not that he had ever teased her, or led her on, and he had certainly never made anything like a move, but she did know he was always very pleased to see her. As he clearly was today. There was a certain way his eyes flashed when he saw her. Surely that was a sign of simple sexual attraction. But she'd never known for sure.

There had been that one night, though, about twenty years before this funeral, she realised in amazement, when she'd felt closest to it. They'd been seated next to each other at a friend's fortieth birthday party and when everyone else went off to dance, they were left alone in the darkest corner of the marquee.

They had talked and talked, as they always did, but this had been different. The eye contact was unbroken for so long, everything else in the room ceased to exist, and their heads seemed to get closer and closer.

Lizzie had really believed he was going to kiss her and felt quite dizzy with it, too intoxicated to care that her husband, Tom, was somewhere at the party, until someone had sat down at the table with them, brandishing a bottle of champagne, and destroyed the moment.

Shit, thought Lizzie, remembering suddenly, it had been Henry. Poor old dead Henry. She had always suspected he fancied Mark as much she did. Now she'd never know that either.

Not long after that party they had spoken on the phone for the very last time. It had been an ill-advised call really, made by Lizzie after two large glasses of heavy red wine, while Tom had been away for work.

She had made out she was just casually phoning a dear old platonic male friend, to suggest lunch and then on to an exhibition that would interest them both. But really there was nothing casual about that call.

She'd had enough, she'd decided, with the confidence brought on by the second glass of wine. She was going to meet him for that lunch and she was going to tell him. She was going to push him against a wall round the back of the Whitechapel Art Gallery and kiss him so hard his head would spin.

Then, if he kissed her back – and she was fairly sure he would – she was going to guide his hand up her skirt, where he would find that her black opaque stockings ended at her thighs. Forty-three-year-old thighs that were still smooth and firm, and she knew that once he had felt their soft silkiness, his hand would be drawn inexorably up underneath the edge of her knickers to find her secret lips, hot and slick with desire for him.

Would they have fucked right there? wondered Lizzie, as they sat down for a reading. Up against the wall. They were just the right relative heights for that, she knew, from the one – unbearably heavenly – occasion she had slow-danced with him. As long as she had worn high heels – and she so would have. Pointy, shiny, black high-heeled boots. She wriggled in the pew a little, thinking about it, as flickers of desire teased her clitoris.

She crossed her legs and squeezed them together, con-tracting her pelvic floor in flutters, as she imagined him entering her in one push, fucking her hard, the brick wall rough against her head.

She squirmed a little more on the wooden bench, as she felt her G-spot swelling, wondering if she might be about to come and if anyone would notice if she did. Bella turned and gave her a questioning look and she sat still again.

It would have been pretty damn sexy, she thought, her mind immediately turning back to her and Mark and a dark alley in Whitechapel, as the vicar droned on about 'dear friends'.

But she'd always hoped that, if they did ever get together, the first time might be a little more romantic than that. Maybe they could have gone away somewhere together. Isn't that how people had affairs?

She had no idea. She'd never been unfaithful to Tom – or to her first husband, Conrad. She really wasn't the unfaithful kind; she was a hopeless liar for one thing. But even the thoughts she had about Mark made her feel guilty. Not to mention the dreams. The amazing sexual dreams from which she would frequently wake in the throes of a crashing orgasm, hardly able to believe that Mark wasn't actually there.

They were so extraordinarily vivid, she had finally come to the conclusion, that night when she had last called him, that she might as well do it for real. And when he'd picked up the phone she had distinctly heard the unmeasured pleasure in his voice when he realised it was her. It was out before he'd had the chance to temper his response and it was the clearest indication she ever had that he might have felt approximately as she did. Not just platonic fondness, but wild, romantic, sexual love.

They never did have that lunch, though. As they rang off after what had seemed to Lizzie an intoxicatingly warm chat, they had agreed to arrange the date by email over the next few days. But before they could do it Mark had met his second wife at a dinner party.

When someone is officially single, as he was then, that's

how quickly it can happen. And when you are officially married, as Lizzie was, you can't really protest.

She was even happy for him, on one level. If she couldn't have him – and it seemed she couldn't, dammit – she hated to think of him being lonely. Especially as she was, in spite of it all, really happy with Tom. It was so greedy of her to want Mark so badly when she already had such a lovely man. And two gorgeous children. She hated herself for it.

So that was when she made the considered decision not to pursue him any more, even as a friend, via phone, email, or even Christmas card. She just didn't trust her own feelings. It was hard enough hiding them from her husband and from Mark himself, but she knew she could never hide them from another woman. Better to leave well alone.

Twenty years and no contact. Lizzie marvelled at her self-discipline, as the organ struck up for another hymn. Although the dreams had never entirely stopped. And now, here he was again, in the flesh, and his effect on her completely undiminished. Her heart – and her cunt – clearly hadn't been keeping track of the time.

The rest of Henry's service was a blur, although she continued to sit down and stand up in all the right places and had collected herself enough by the end to give his partner, Eric, a big hug and make him promise to come and stay as soon as possible.

He looked shattered, she thought, poor lamb. Hardly surprising. He and Henry had been together for as long as she had been in unrequited love with Mark le Broyeux, which was, she calculated with a shudder, now over forty-five years.

And there he was, as she stepped out of the chapel, the bright winter sun flashing off those unfamiliar spectacles and, judging by the expectant smile on his face, waiting for her.

They hugged. The hug of old friends. Upper-body contact between two people who have just lost someone they'd both known since they were nineteen. A hug of shared memories and mutually recognised mortality. But as he pulled back and looked deep into her eyes, in that way of his, without really loosening his hold, was there also something a little bit more? Or was her heart still playing its old tricks where Mark was concerned? She hadn't been able to tell when she was twenty-seven, or when she was forty-three, and she couldn't tell now.

Bella came over, also delighted to see Mark. She had known him as long as Lizzie, after all, but never as closely. They kissed and the three of them spoke about Henry, until Bella broke away to greet someone else in those strange, muted cocktail-party exchanges that happen at funerals.

Lizzie turned tentatively back to Mark, expecting to find him also about to move off towards another friend, but he was still there and looking at her.

'Come and have a drink with me,' he said.

'Now?' replied Lizzie, thinking how stupid it sounded as the word came out of her mouth.

Mark nodded. 'Eric's not having a wake or anything today. He's going to do something big in town in a couple of weeks.' He paused for a moment and a poignant smile she remembered with a lurch, flickered around his mouth. 'We could just slip away.'

'Okay,' said Lizzie, realising that they could. She'd come down alone on the train; it was nobody's business how she left.

He had a car parked around the corner, a sporty two-seater. Lizzie was impressed. The royalties must still be coming in nicely, she thought, as she threw her hat in the back.

Mark sat for a moment before starting it up, as though he was considering what to say. 'I'm staying down here for a while,' he said eventually. 'I've always liked this part of the country and I'm going to stay on and do some writing. I'm in a very nice hotel. Shall we go there?'

Lizzie nodded. She didn't care where they went. She was still in shock that they were together.

'Did you ever learn to drive?' he asked her as they set off and she was immediately touched that he remembered that little quirk of hers. She never had passed her driving test.

Lizzie wondered if she was blushing and changed the subject to Mark's books, until they were pulling up on the gravel in front of a magnificent red-brick William and Mary house.

'Splendid, isn't it?' said Mark, as she gazed up at it.

She nodded, but neither of them made any move to get out of the car. Lizzie didn't want to break the hum of atmosphere that had built up and she was fairly sure he didn't either. She felt as though they had been transported back to that tantalising moment at the party, twenty years before.

'So tell me, Lizzie,' he said eventually, his eyes locked on hers, as they had been that night. 'Are you still very married these days?'

'No,' she said, gazing back at him. 'Tom died three years ago.'

'Oh, I'm so sorry,' said Mark. 'I hadn't heard. He was a great guy. That must have been hard.'

'What about you?' ventured Lizzie, her voice threatening to go squeaky on her. 'Are you very married?'

'Very not, as usual. Seems to be my default state.'

'What happened?'

'Tina?'

Lizzie was puzzled. 'I thought her name was Polly.'

'Oh, there was a Polly, but she turned out to be a bolter.' He laughed, but there was a tinge of bitterness in it. 'Then after that there was Tina, but I didn't marry her. She left anyway. Another bolter. I do seem to specialise in them, so now I'm all on my own again.'

We both are, thought Lizzie. For the first time since they'd known each other neither of them was attached. It seemed as though Mark realised it at the same moment.

'Lizzie,' he said quietly. 'I don't think I want that drink any more. I don't want to be around other people.'

For a terrible moment Lizzie thought he meant he wanted her to leave.

But then he looked at her with his most penetrating gaze and gently took hold of her right hand. It was the most intimate gesture he had ever made to her and she was so surprised she almost stopped breathing.

Still looking into her eyes, he raised her hand gently to his face and brushed his lips tenderly against her black leather glove.

'Will you come up to my room with me, Lizard?'

Lizzie smiled and blinked. That was what he used to call her. Lizard. She'd forgotten. She was glad she was still wearing the large dark glasses she'd put on in the churchyard. They gave her something to hide her feelings behind. And there were a lot of feelings to hide.

Mark's room was enormous and beautiful. It had four long windows looking out over a Capability Brown landscape and a huge four-poster bed hung with yellow silk curtains. Was this it, she thought? Was this really it?

She went over to the window, as a nervous distraction, and looked out at the view, terrified even to dare to believe this might be the moment she had anticipated for so long. And then, as she felt his arms go around her from behind, the vista she had been gazing at turned into a blur.

He enclosed her in his embrace and nuzzled into her neck, kissing it gently. For Lizzie, the entire world ceased to exist apart from their two bodies. She turned round in his arms and looked up at him, her hands framing his beautiful, familiar cheeks. He'd taken the glasses off.

'I love you, Lizard,' he said quietly, looking into her eyes, right into her, that way he did. 'I've loved you for nearly fifty years and fancied you rotten too. Please, can I finally kiss you?'

Lizzie wanted to laugh, she wanted to whoop and yell and run leaping round the room. Mark le Broyeux loved her. Mark le Broyeux fancied her. She really couldn't believe it, but at the same time she did. How could he not have loved and wanted her, when she had loved and wanted him so very much for so very long?

She said nothing and put her lips to his. Her eyes closed and as she felt his tongue slide against hers for the very first time, it was – astonishingly – just as good as she had always imagined it would be.

She had sometimes wondered over the years if it wouldn't perhaps be a disappointment if the thing dreamt of for so long ever actually happened. What if he had been a horrible kisser? She'd had a few of those over the years. But he wasn't, he was a wonderful kisser. And here he was kissing her. Like he meant it.

After that Lizzie stopped having conscious thoughts. She was lost in the physical abandon of Mark's mouth, his closeness, the smell of him and the feel of his chest, as he shrugged off his coat and she unbuttoned his shirt.

She felt like Edmund Hillary, planting his flag on Everest, as she put her hand on Mark's shoulder. The muscles were still there. The skin was soft and a little loose, but underneath the defined muscles of his shoulders were still there.

She could remember the precise moment in his garden years before when Mark had put a cup of tea on the table for her, wearing a singlet – he'd just come in from a run – and she'd seen those muscles move beneath the skin.

161

She had fantasised about Mark's shoulders so many times while Tom had been making love to her and now she couldn't believe she was finally touching them for real. She pulled down his shirt and gently sank her teeth into one.

'Ouch,' said Mark, playfully, as he unbuttoned her dress and pulled it open. He cupped his hands around her breasts and lifted them, lowering his face to flick his tongue over her nipples through the lace of her bra.

'Oh, my,' he said. 'Your beautiful breasts. I can't believe I'm finally touching them.'

He pulled her dress off her shoulders and gently lowered her bra straps down her arms, so he could free each breast. Holding one in each hand, he kissed them gently and then sucked quite hard on her nipples.

'Gorgeous,' he said.

Lizzie looked down and saw his head against the crêpey skin of her décolletage. Her breasts looked sad and sunken to her and she felt suddenly self-conscious that he was looking at them in daylight.

'It's a shame you didn't see them forty years ago,' she said, immediately wishing she hadn't.

'I did,' said Mark, starting to laugh. 'Why do you think I've been obsessing about them ever since?'

'When did you see them?' asked Lizzie, wondering if she had done something embarrassing while drunk. They'd been terrible binge-drinkers in those days and she knew she hadn't always behaved with the greatest decorum. She had been an art student, after all.

Mark stood up and put his arms around her again, pressing her breasts against his bare chest and moving against her, teasingly, slowly. 'Don't you remember that time at Henry's parents' place, when we all went swimming?'

Lizzie nodded. Of course she remembered. She remembered every time they had ever met in microscopic detail.

'Well, I accidentally came into the pool room while you were in there. You didn't see me because you had your T-shirt over your head, and I had a front-row view of your breasts in all their splendour, which has comforted me on many a lonely night since.'

It was at least forty years ago, but Lizzie clearly remembered the door slamming suddenly that hot afternoon while she had been changing into her bikini. She had thought it was one of the younger kids fooling about and had been more concerned after she came out that she couldn't see Mark anywhere. She thought he'd been so revolted by the idea of seeing her in a swimsuit he'd done a bunk.

'What happened to you that afternoon?' she asked him. 'You disappeared for hours.'

He laughed. 'It's very hard to hide an extreme erection in swimming trunks. I had to disappear to recover myself.' Lizzie put her head back and laughed, shaking her head slightly.

'And now,' said Mark, taking her hand and leading her towards the bed. 'The really amazing thing is, I have one similar.'

He wasn't kidding. Over the years Lizzie had seen Mark's shoulders, his legs, his toes, and his back. She'd enjoyed checking out the muscles of his forearms, his elegant fingers and the outline of his buttocks, but she'd never seen his penis.

She wondered how many hours of her life she'd spent wondering what it might be like. What if it was tiny, or weird in some way? Maybe that was why he had been so noncommittal with her, she had sometimes thought. But it wasn't. As she slowly undid his fly and pulled down his trousers and boxers, she saw that Mark's cock was as gorgeous as the rest of him.

Just as she'd imagined in the church, she took it in her mouth and ran her tongue over the head.

She loosened her mouth around it and blew gently, then alternated flicks of her tongue with stronger swirling. Finally she gripped the shaft firmly with her hand and lowered her head so that his entire cock disappeared into her mouth and partly down her throat. Then she began to move her head up and down.

'Holy shit,' said Mark, emitting a long groan. 'You better stop that.'

'Why?' said Lizzie, looking up at him, his cock still in her hand.

He had lifted his head up from the pillow and was looking down at her with something approaching amazement. Lizzie gently tongued the end of him, at the point where the foreskin was attached to the head. 'Don't you like it?'

Mark grinned at her and half sat up, pulling her up to him.

'You dirty girl,' he said, chuckling. 'You beautiful, dirty girl.'

And then he rolled her onto her back and in one smooth movement climbed on top of her, opening her legs with his knees. Lizzie gasped as she felt his fingers gently probing, sliding up and down on her smooth wetness. She thought he was going to enter her then, but he slid down the bed and thrust her knees wide apart with his strong hands.

For a moment he stopped and just looked at her. 'Beautiful,' he whispered and lowered his head.

At the first stroke of his tongue against her clitoris, Lizzie let out a moan that took her entirely by surprise. It got better. He alternated holding his tongue flat against her in a slow slide and making smaller lighter circles with the point, and when he put two fingers inside her and started to apply gentle pressure with the same rhythm, Lizzie could feel her orgasm start to rise.

'Mark,' she gasped, grabbing his head and pulling it up. 'I'm, I'm, I don't, I want . . . now.'

He smiled and pulled himself up on to his knees. He took hold of his cock and stroked the length of it a few times with his fist while he looked down at her. She groaned and put out her arms to pull him to her.

She felt his fingers part her lips as he put the very end of his cock against her, then her eyes snapped open as she felt the first push of him inside. It was, she realised, the pivotal moment.

She'd had his cock in her mouth and his tongue inside her,

but this was the moment she had waited nearly fifty years for. Mark le Broyeux was fucking her.

As he slowly pushed himself inside her he lifted up his head and looked deep into her eyes in that way he always had, but more so. He didn't break his gaze as he pulled nearly all the way out again and then pushed gently back in. A tear slid from Lizzie's eye and he kissed it tenderly from her cheek, but he didn't stop moving.

And then everything dissolved into the rhythm and the sensations, until Mark's movements became more urgent and as he pushed and pushed the feelings in her grew stronger and the wave started to build until suddenly it crashed. She moaned as he carried on moving and it crashed again and again.

Mark collapsed on top of her and then rolled to one side, panting. Lizzie just lay there completely still, letting the pleasure course around her bloodstream. She looked up the yellow silk canopy over the bed and smiled. It definitely beat a wall in Whitechapel, she thought to herself.

She turned to look at Mark's face. His beautiful face. Very lined now, eyelids like prunes, some hair growing in his ears, lobes getting longer, eyebrows a bit random, but all still beautiful to her.

She looked down at herself. Her breasts spreading to either side. Pubes grey. Stomach a post-natal catastrophe. But she didn't care.

Mark smiled gently at her and stroked her face.

'Hello,' he said softly. 'Have we met?'

'We have now,' said Lizzie.

The Peacock

HARRIET PETERS

Flanner says every man is allowed one vanity. My husband's vanity is his peacock.

'It's such a stupid ol' bird,' I complain to Flanner as he slips my blouse from my shoulders. 'It doesn't lay eggs. It doesn't even cluck, just screams once in a while. What the hell is it *for*?'

Flanner likes to take my husband's side in such matters. It makes him feel better about the fact that he's poking his wife. 'Mary,' he says, 'Not everything has to *do* something . . .' He slides my blouse down my upper arms without unfastening all the buttons, exposing my breasts. My arms are trapped against my body, so he helps each breast gently over the taut edge of the blouse then bends his head and kisses each nipple, slowly, drawing them out in turn. 'Is this *doing* something?' he asks as he lifts his face.

He has a point. Flanner is a handyman. We employed him to fix the leak in our water tower. He will only get paid when the job is done, and then but a few dollars. My husband works harder than you would think a man could work, rising before first light each morning and going straight to the cow shed without so much as a cup of coffee. And me? Well, we have no other help on the farm, apart from Flanner's occasional visits, so the house, the hens, the vegetable patch, the herb garden (which brings in a little each month at the Saturday market), the cooking, the laundry . . . all these and much more are mine. When I was a girl I had beautiful hands.

And then there is the peacock, the rangy, mangy peacock that sits on the fence in our yard and won't even spread his tail feathers. I catch my husband staring at that peacock sometimes, with a blank, hungry look on his face, willing it to move. The peacock belongs to my husband and Flanner belongs to me. He is my vanity. I like him to fuck me hard and simple against the armoire, so that I can look over his shoulder and see our reflections in the mirror that sits on the chest of drawers directly opposite; his face buried in my neck, my fist clutching a handful of the hair on the back of his head, my solid legs around his waist . . . When he loses control, throwing his head back and thumping against me, I watch him losing control, watch myself lost in his loss of control, and I wish the whole town of Indigo, South Dakota, was here in this room, watching us, seeing how beautiful we are.

It began a month ago. My husband hired Flanner one market day. We have to have a handyman once in a while on account of how the dilapidations on the farm occasionally get too much for one man. We never seemed to keep on top of things, Abel and I. Our barn door always hangs from the hinges, our fences always sag – it's the same in the house. No matter how often I sweep the prairie dust or scrub the sink with bleach, I feel the dirt of our lives lies over us like a thick blanket.

Well, that was how I felt at that time. I had stopped looking at myself in the mirror, at that time, but I knew that my sand-brown hair was already showing strands of white at the temples. How have I come to this, so quickly, and without even a child or two to show for it? I used to think, occasionally. Well, that last bit was easily explained. My husband had not laid a finger on me since our wedding night.

I must have seen Flanner around town before but I only got a proper look that day he came to us. Abel was over at the barn. I saw Flanner approach, trudging slowly up our lane early one morning. I went out onto the back step, wiping my hands on a cloth.

He stopped just short of our steps and looked up at me. He was a squat, powerfully built man, slightly shorter than me, with a large crooked nose and small dark eyes – the cumulative effect was somewhat hawk-like. His face was slightly wrong in some indefinable way. He did not smile.

'Mrs Hanson,' he said with a nod.

I indicated the barn with the cloth. 'My husband's in there.'

As Flanner turned to go, I observed the thick rope of muscle across the top of his shoulders.

I hardly spoke to Flanner for the whole of the first fortnight that he worked on our water tower. I watched him sometimes, stripping to the waist to climb the tower, a hammer jammed in his trouser belt and a row of nails in his teeth. The sun didn't seem to bother him. The only time I ever saw him lose his concentration was when the peacock, standing in the middle of our yard, let out a sudden scream. I happened to be at my kitchen window, and saw Flanner startle and drop his hammer to the ground, where it struck his toolbox with a clatter. The peacock was startled in its turn and rose slightly, flapping – it was a weak flier – until it wheeled and perched on the fence to the left of the tower, long tail draped over the fence, its tiny head turned, regarding Flanner with one round, suspicious eye.

Flanner cursed and climbed down from the tower to retrieve his hammer. As he straightened, he saw me watching from the kitchen window. Our eyes met. He stared at me, and I stared back, neither of us smiling. That is all. We stared at one another.

A weekend passed by and on the Monday I expected Flanner to walk up our track early, as he did each morning. But Abel came over from the barn and ate some fried bread with eggs for breakfast and there was still no sign of Flanner. I kept my voice light as I said, 'Is our mechanic coming over today? He's usually here by now.'

Abel shook his head. 'Saw him in town Saturday. Got some other job he has to finish.'

'Oh, Abel,' I said crossly, snatching his plate from him and dropping it in the sink with a clatter. 'Why, you should have told him to finish our job first. We've been waiting long enough to get that tower fixed.'

Abel never could stand an argument. 'Well, I suppose so.'

'Why didn't you insist he came?'

'He'll come back soon enough,' Abel said, rising from his chair. 'I guess I had better not keep you from your chores.'

All that week, Flanner did not come, and I realised I was waiting for him, and that's when I started pressing myself up against the sink, my hands turning dishes over and over in the warm soapy water, imagining Flanner coming up behind me and bending me forward, one hand in the hair on the back of my head, the other raising my dress. That's when I began brushing my hair of a morning, instead of just twisting it and fastening it with pins. That's when I began looking in the mirror.

He showed up the middle of the following week. There he was one morning, on my doorstep. I had given up waiting for him by then and gave such a start when I turned and saw him there.

He stared at me, then said, 'I am sorry, Mrs Hanson. I didn't mean to give you a fright.'

My breath was coming a little fast and I could sense the rise and fall of my chest, and sensed that he sensed it too, although he stayed in the doorway on account of his dusty boots. I was annoyed he had the advantage over me, not just for startling me but because all this week he had known when he would see me again whereas I had had no idea when I might see him.

I turned away, muttering, 'Half our water reserves gone by the time you finish, Mr Flanner . . .' It was a feeble thing to say. When I turned back, he had gone.

For the next couple of days, he worked without once glancing over at the house. Some time after noon, he would descend the tower and sit in its shade and eat some bread and cheese from his knapsack. Once or twice, he went over to the barn to talk to Abel, and one afternoon I ran upstairs in time to see them both striding out across the cornfield, our two dogs snapping and jumping around them, off on some joint task or other. Then I went down to the kitchen and sat at the table and looked at my dirty fingernails and felt unhappy. You are a fool, Mary Hanson, I thought.

That day, at the end of the afternoon, he finally came over. I had been hanging laundry in the yard and was walking back across the veranda with the empty wicker basket in my arms. Just before I went into the house, I heard him say, 'Mrs Hanson.'

He was holding his boots in his hand. He held one up. The lace was broken.

'I wonder if I could trouble you for one of your husband's bootlaces,' he said. 'I have a spare at home but my truck is broke so I'm on foot. I can bring a new one tomorrow to replace it.'

'Mr Flanner,' I said, 'I'm sure we can spare you a bootlace. Which colour would you like?'

He looked down at his boots and said, 'Any colour, I guess. Would you have an old one? I wouldn't want to waste new on these boots.'

I went to my box of spare things, beneath the stairs, then returned with a new pair of brown laces. 'You may take these and you will insult me if you replace them,' I replied firmly. Abel and I were not wealthy people, but I had a feeling we could afford a set of bootlaces more easily than Flanner. Abel was even talking about getting a wireless set.

I extended my hand and, as he took the laces, our fingers brushed.

He turned and sat down on the step and I stood by the kitchen door, waiting while he laced the boots. When he was done, he rose from the step, nodded once without looking at me, then asked casually, 'Will you and your husband be going on Friday, then?'

Friday was the town social. It happened four times a year; all the farmers from the outlying farms would meet up at the Old School Room on the edge of town, which was little more than a barn, and some fiddlers would come over from West Indigo. The women would all bake and Grey Harper, who had the biggest truck, would do a run into town for crates of beer. The women loved it, of course, for we got to talk to each other, and dance with each other too; the men often stayed at their tables drinking beer from dark-brown bottles and muttering, like men do. But even those who were not social felt obliged. It was where you got to find out who was selling their barrow or who might have hay to spare. Anyone who thinks farmers are not a competitive breed should come down to our social once in a while.

I drew breath to answer, but Flanner had finished lacing his boots and rose from the step abruptly and strode off across our yard.

He didn't come the following day, nor the one after, which was Friday. That morning, once I had cleared up the break-fast things, I set about roasting four large trays of squash with cream and cinnamon – Elizabeth Quincey was picking me up at three and we were going down early to help the other women set up the trestle tables. They all liked me to do the squash on account of how I added some herbs from our garden. Abel was out mending fences on the far border and would drive himself into town later, so I was alone in the house, alone with my thoughts.

The heat had not abated and having the oven fired all morning was not helping. My blouse stuck to my back. My thighs were clammy. I would have to wash myself before I slid on my dress for the social – my best yellow cotton with the tight waist and the laces that pulled the bodice in a ruff but looked as though they could be untugged nice and easy. I wore it four times a year. When the trays of squash were all ready and covered with tea towels, I ran upstairs to get my bowl and then ran back down and filled it at the pump in the yard. I tipped two whole bowls of water over my head before I filled it a third time and took it back upstairs.

In the bedroom, it was dark. The shutters were closed against the hot sun and very thin, bright-white strips of light gave the room a close glow. I unbuttoned my wet blouse and hung it over the back of a chair, then slid out of my skirt. My cotton slip was soaked through as well. I pulled it over my head and, as I did, caught sight of myself in the small mirror on its stand on top of the chest of drawers. I tossed the slip on to the bed, and approached the mirror. There I was, a large woman, full breasted, not pretty but handsome some might say, in a dim light such as this. My hair was darkened by the water from the pump. There were beads of sweat on my upper lip. I could only see myself from waist up, so I watched my face as I parted my legs slightly. To reach down between my legs, I had to bend forward slightly and rest one hand on the top of the chest of drawers to support myself. My face was close to the mirror and I could observe in detail how my lips parted as I slid my fingers in. I was already wet. I stared into the mirror, and pictured Flanner standing behind me, further back in the room, watching as I watched myself. I withdrew my fingers and began to stroke the soft flesh outside, very lightly. When I felt myself begin to rise, I pushed my fingers in again, to delay the moment. My breath condensed against the glass.

I was still there, naked, against the chest of drawers, breathing hard, when I heard the screen door bang. A voice called up the stairs, 'Coo-eee! It's only me.' Elizabeth Quincey. 'Coo-eee!'

I lifted my head. 'I'm just dressing, Elizabeth, I'll be right down!'

She came to the bottom of the stairs and called up. 'You want me to come up there and help you, honey?'

'Er, no, thank you, Elizabeth. I can manage!'

Flanner arrived late at the social. The Old School Room was already full but despite the noise and the crowd I spotted him as soon as he came in the door, and I saw that he was looking around. I was still serving food, and I concentrated on performing the task with a smile. He would see me soon enough.

It was busy and time passed quickly, so it may well have been an hour or more before Flanner came and stood before me, holding out a plate. When he did, I confess I felt a rush of disappointment. He was wearing a checked shirt but the colour did not flatter him. He had combed his hair and it lay too flat on his head. I realised that the real Flanner was not quite up to the Flanner I had pictured in my mirror. I only managed a sentence or two of small talk and soon he turned away. Good, I thought, as he walked off. I am cured. It was a strange thought to have. Cured of what?

After I had helped serve some of the other dishes until the line had diminished and most were fed, I piled my clay trays and took them out to the backyard to clean them. I put them down by the garbage box and then lifted them, one by one, to scrape any trace of leavings. A couple of stray dogs were snuffling around the garbage, hoping for scraps, and I waved the spoon at them and hissed, but half-heartedly. Even a stray dog is entitled to a social, after all.

As I rounded the corner of the back of the Old School Room, I heard voices. I stopped, and stepped back into the dark. Two men were behind the school room, pissing against the wall, and I had recognised one of the men as Flanner. 'Do your duty, then . . .' he was saying, and by the conversation that followed, I gathered that Flanner had been teasing the other man, a wheat farmer by the name of Crake, that as the best dancer among the men, he was having a busy night of it.

'It sure is hard being fair on 'em all,' Crake said, as they buttoned their flies. 'I have to say there are some of those wives in there that I'm a little keener on doing my duty with than others.'

'What do you reckon to Abel Hanson's wife?' Flanner asked casually.

'Well,' said Crake, after a pause, 'I sure do like a woman who puts her dress under a bit of strain.'

There was a silence, which I could feel filled by their grins, their nodding agreement, their summation of me. *Flanner*, I thought angrily. That's all I am to him, a passing remark to be made as he pisses against a wall.

Back inside the hall, I strode over to Abel, who was seated at a table, sharing a beer with old Crake's son, a thin boy with hair that grew over his eyes. 'Where's the truck parked?' I snapped, still holding the clay trays.

'I want to put these in it.' Old Crake's son looked down at table.

Abel muttered, 'Plenty of time for that, ain't there . . .?'

I could not help myself from taking out my anger at Flanner on Abel. 'Well, I don't know how long you're planning on staying but I've been here all afternoon.'

Abel sighed. 'You want me to take you home and come back, darlin'? I ain't really done here yet.'

Now he had called my bluff, I was panic-stricken. I had hardly spoken to Flanner all evening and now somehow I had to communicate that I hated him. 'No . . . no, it's all right, I just wanted to . . . put these in the truck, is all,' I finished lamely.

The Crake boy got to his feet. He was taller than I remembered. 'Let me take those out to the truck for you, Mrs Hanson,' he said, his head still bowed. 'They look mighty heavy.'

'Why, thank you,' I said. 'That is gallant of you, for such a young man.'

The Crake boy gave a charming laugh, tossed his hair, glanced at my husband and said, 'I'm twenty-three years old, Mrs Hanson.'

He took the trays from my grasp and turned to go.

Abel took a slug of his beer. 'You tired, darlin'? You still want to go?'

'No, I guess I'd better do some clearing up first.'

'Hell, go and dance. You've been working hardest of all, I seen you.' Well, that much was true.

Abel got to his feet. 'I don't think that boy even knows which truck is ours. I better go and make sure he doesn't go donating our crockery elsewhere.'

As I walked back across the hall, I saw Old Crake and Flanner standing by the dance floor, regarding the dancers with amused, appraising expressions on their faces. I strode up to Old Crake, slowing my walk as I did and pushing my body forwards, so he could see precisely how much strain my dress was under. 'Why, Mr Crake,' I said, giving him my broadest smile. 'I hope you weren't planning on taking a rest just yet. You know you're the best dancer in the room.' I glanced up and down Old Crake's tall frame. For a man well into his sixties, he was well preserved. I ignored Flanner.

Old Crake returned my smile and gave a slight bow. I lifted a hand and he took it, and led me to the dance floor as the fiddlers struck up the next tune.

I danced with abandon and after three tunes it was Crake who pleaded for mercy. 'You forget there, Mrs Hanson,' he said, leaning a heavy hand on my shoulder and shouting into my ear to be heard above the band. 'I'm an old man here!' I leaned towards him and put my mouth close to his neck. 'Mr Crake, you and I both know you're not nearly as old as you make out.'

Flanner was watching us. I could feel it.

I put one hand flat on Crake's chest, my fingers splayed. 'Now, how about we have a drink?'

Crake slid his arm about my waist and pulled me in tight against him, digging his bony fingers into my flesh a little more than was strictly necessary. 'Mrs Hanson, you sure are in a party mood, all right.'

As we strode together around the edge of the dance floor, I saw Flanner standing stock still where he was, staring at us, his face expressionless.

Close to the dance floor was a table of men I knew, local men, Abel's friends. As Crake and I approached, the nearest two seated jumped to their feet. I sank as if exhausted into a seat, flapping my hand in front of my face and laughing.

'You all met my new lady friend?' said Crake. 'I'm going to go get her a beer!' The men grinned. One of them pushed his beer across the table at me and leaned forward. 'You want a suck on *my* beer while you wait for the old man?' he said. It was toothless Parker, a man I normally wouldn't bother to pass the time of day with. I stretched across the table and placed the flat of my hand on his cheek.

'Why, Mr Parker, you sure know how to treat a girl.'

The men all laughed as I took a wild swig from the bottle. They were drunk and enjoying my coquetry. They would have enjoyed it a darn sight more if I had been one of the young, pretty things gathered in a corner, but they could never have behaved in such a fashion without getting a reputation. For me, meanwhile, it was absolutely fine. Who would think that solid Abel Hanson's solid wife would mean any harm by it? I put down toothless Parker's bottle and pushed it back to him.

'Here,' said the man sitting next to him, 'try mine . . .'

'I'd like to try them *all* . . .' I said, and took another wild swig. Before I knew it, there was a glass of whisky in front of me. I lifted it, toasted their grinning faces, and threw it back in one. The man sitting next to me shuffled his chair a little closer and lifted his bottle in my direction.

'Say, Mary Hanson, you want to try mine sometime when we have a little privacy?'

'I think this lady has probably had enough.'

The smiles on the men's faces died. I looked around. Flanner was standing next to the table, staring at us all, with a set, hard look upon his face. The men glanced at each other, unsettled by the change of tone.

I looked up at Flanner and said in a derisive, sing-song tone, 'Well, Mr Flanner, you could always pull up a chair if you like . . .'

At that, Flanner reached out and grabbed my upper arm and with one swift movement raised me from my seat. The men sat back, surprised, and toothless Parker half stood. Flanner nodded brusquely at him and said, 'Mrs Hanson, your husband is waiting in the truck. He asked me to remind you of that, and take you out to him.' The men relaxed and sank back in their seats.

'Well, goodnight y'all!' I said merrily over my shoulder, as Flanner, still grasping my upper arm, pulled me through the crowd towards the door.

Once we were outside, he hustled me past the group of teenage boys lounging on the steps and pulled me unceremoniously to where the cars and trucks were parked in a nearby field. He marched me over to his, wrenched open the passenger door and pushed me inside. He slammed it shut behind me, then strode round to the driver's door.

We drove in silence, me leaning against the door and staring out of the window. It was a starless night, pitch black outside. The whisky had kicked in, spreading around my body, through my head. If I closed my eyes, the world began to spin.

After half an hour's driving, we approached the end of our track, but instead of turning up it, Flanner carried on past. I sat up a little. 'Where are we going?' I asked, meekly.

'Up to the ridge,' he replied.

'Abel . . .' I said.

'Your husband left an hour ago with the young Crake fella,' Flanner snapped.

We passed down the lane up to the ridge, then took a turning. Flanner stopped the truck sharply, pulled on the handbrake, then jumped out, slamming the driver's door behind him so hard it made the cab shake. He turned, kicked the truck door viciously and swore. Then he took a few steps away and was lost in the darkness. I wondered for a moment if he had strode off and left me, but then I heard a match strike and saw the flare of a flame as he lit a cigarette.

I stayed in the truck for a few minutes, watching the dim shape of him smoking in the dark. After a while, I opened my door and got down carefully, then walked round to him. As I approached, he threw the cigarette into the dirt and ground it with his foot.

'Why are you so angry with me?' I asked gently.

He reached forward and grasped both my upper arms this time, bringing his face close to mine. I could smell the smoke on his breath, the sweat beneath his shirt, even a hint of the herbs I had put in the squash when I baked it that afternoon, all layered with menthol, a mouthwash scent, clean and hard.

'Because,' he said, his voice even, 'if you are going to be unfaithful to your husband with *anyone*, Mary Hanson, it is going to be *me*.'

Several things happened at once. I felt my knees buckle, the combined effect of the whisky, tiredness perhaps, the soft night air around us and the grip of his hands on my arms. At the same time, his lips were against mine and his tongue was in my mouth and his arms around me and I felt myself sinking down, down, so that I was lying in the dirt with him on top of me. He raised himself slightly, then pushed the fingers of one hand into the hair at my temple, to hold my face immovable, then his mouth descended on mine again, and the kiss was so long, so drawn out that, for all I knew, half the night had passed by the time he pulled away and rolled off me, lying on his back at my side.

We were silent for a long while, looking up at the starless sky, then he said, 'I've wanted to do that for years.'

I rolled on my side and propped my head up with one hand. 'Years?' I asked sceptically.

'Oh, yes,' he said. 'I've wanted to kiss you like that since I saw you unloading those trays of lavender at the store – you know, the ones you used to sell all tied up with ribbon.'

My lavender experiment had been an abject failure. Wrong kind of soil, I guess. I haven't tried to grow lavender in six years.

We were silent for a long time, lying next to each other. I may even have dozed off. When I awoke, Flanner was breathing in my hair. He kissed my cheek. I turned my face to him. He smiled down at me. Who would have thought that serious, hawk-like face could have such a smile? As he smiled, he reached out and stroked my cheek with the back of his hand, then let the hand wander down across the expanse of flesh above my neckline, then travel over the top of my dress and come to rest on my left breast. My body arched towards him. He bent his face to mine, kissed me briefly on the lips and said, 'I think we'd better get you home, Mary Hanson.'

Our house was in darkness and our truck was nowhere to be seen. In the shadow of the home I shared with Abel, the mood between Flanner and me changed. We sat in silence for a while. Eventually I said, 'Night, then,' and climbed down from the truck without waiting for a reply.

The dogs lifted their heads as I mounted the porch and, sensing it was only me, lowered them immediately. Inside, all was in darkness. I drank a glass of water from the jug by the sink and then went straight upstairs, pulling off all my clothes and dropping them on the floor. I fell into an instant sleep.

I woke as Abel climbed into bed, the bulk of him making the mattress undulate. I sat up suddenly. 'What . . .' I said, bewildered.

Abel lay down with his back to me. He reached a hand backwards and patted my thigh. 'Sorry,' he said. 'Go back to sleep.'

How late it must be, I thought, as I lay down again.

In the morning, I woke up to the smell of coffee. I went downstairs to find Abel sitting at our small kitchen table. The screen door was open and the morning light flooded in. Abel had filled the red enamel coffee-jug that we normally keep for the rare occasions when we have guests. It sat steaming in the middle of the table, two cups on either side.

He glanced up at me as I came over, and then sat down at the table. I felt a slightly sick, hollow feeling. Was he going to question me about last night? If he suspected Flanner, what would happen? I sat down and he poured coffee into the empty cup in front of me. He put the jug down and, still without looking at me, said, 'Honey, do you remember when I brought home the peacock?'

About once a month, Abel went to the city for the weekend to do business with the buyers who bought our stock and to bring me anything I needed for the house. Sometimes he came back with new seeds. The lavender had been his idea. It had been about a year ago that he had returned with the peacock. When I asked him where the hell he had got such a thing, he told me he had won it in a card game, but my feeling was that it was a story he'd made up so's I wouldn't give him a hard time for wasting money.

I nodded.

'Well,' he continued, 'I was telling Sonny Crake about that last night, that's why I was so late. I was driving him back and we parked up by the ridge for a smoke. He was real interested in the peacock and I told him next time I went over to the city, I would maybe take him with me.'

Then, Abel did something extraordinary. He laid his hand on my arm. It was the first time my husband had touched me like that, deliberately, since our wedding night eight years ago. On that night, he had lain on top of me and, as soon as he had entered me, his cock had shrivelled and shrunk until it was no more than a sliver of raw meat, and in all those eight years we had not tried again, nor had we ever mentioned it to each other, not once.

Abel was staring at me. 'Would you mind, Mary, if I took Sonny Crake to the city with me?'

All at once, all the harshness and irritation I had felt towards my husband over the years melted away, and I thought that perhaps to understand a person all you needed was to know what they wanted, what they secretly wanted, and then you could never feel angry with them again.

I took a sip of my coffee. Abel did not move his hand from my arm.

'If you was to start going to the city more often, I might get a bit lonely,' I said slowly. 'I might have to ask a friend over to keep me company.'

'Well,' Abel said, 'I think you'd be entitled.'

He removed his hand from my arm. We finished our drinks in silence.

'Thanks for making me coffee, Abel,' I said, as I rose from my chair.

'You're welcome, honey,' he replied.

Flanner comes to me often now. Sometimes we cannot wait until Abel goes to the city, and he comes to me in broad daylight, when we could be interrupted at any minute, and he bends me over the sink when my hands are in the suds, just as I fantasised. I told him everything that I fantasised about, and he has made it his business to see I get to feel what each fantasy is like in real life.

One afternoon, when Abel is away and we can take our time, he takes me up the stairs into the hot dark of the bedroom and tells me he has finally remembered to return Abel's bootlaces. He gets me to lie down diagonally on the white sheets and ties my hands to the bedpost above my head. He touches me until I cry out and then he is suddenly up, upon me and inside me and I am lost in him and him in me. I close my eyes and hear the peacock shrieking in the yard and think that, even though that bird has never spread his tail feathers for Abel, he was worth whatever was spent on him, for we all of us need our vanity. Our desires are what make us human and allowing the desires of others makes us most human of all.

Percussion

QUAVER COVERDALE

The apartment block was one of those buildings that had sprung up in the 1960s; functional and rectangular, it was anonymous architecture that utilised every square foot within its four walls. The walls were thin – plywood sandwiched with air and glorified insulated foam – separating the occupants visually and psychologically, but also ensuring a certain kind of audio-voyeurism.

This building had peacefully occupied the corner of a main street leading down to Bondi Beach for over thirty years. Tenants moved in, made love, had children, moved out, died within the building, died outside it, grew roses in the two long flowerbeds that ran heroically along the walls, banged their furniture against the entrance hall doorway, chipped at the cheap paintwork and rode the small steel elevator up and down the six floors for decades. Lives delineated by small rustlings, sudden thumping and the occasional muffled shouting match – the whole range of audio minutia that gives shape to suburban existence. Then in an unexpected property boom, the building was suddenly renovated. The façade was transformed, balconies extended, a basement excavated and an underground car park constructed. The straggly rose bushes were pulled out and replaced with palms, rusty steel sandblasted, glass glazed, ceramic tiles replaced by marble. But the internal walls stayed the same.

Meredith Harrowgate lived in 5b, a one-bedroom apartment with a balcony that boasted a slim sliver of beach view, with her husband Clive. Clive, a stocky balding man in his mid-forties, was the chief financial officer for a legal firm. His original training was in accountancy, which was evident in his obsession with numbers, an obsession Meredith had once loathed, then tolerated, and now found amusing. Besides, tolerance is one of the foundation stones for a good marriage and over the years Meredith's tolerance had evolved into a quiet unassuming love, even if the marriage was, well, a little monotonous. The headquarters of Clive's company were in Brisbane and this meant that Clive travelled a lot. His extended absences were also one of the foundation stones of the Harrowgates' relationship.

Meredith, a tall willowy thirty-eight year old, had once had ambitions to dance. She now worked as a freelance copywriter specialising in the short pithy descriptions of properties required by real estate agents. Meredith had fallen into this line of work by accident, when the Harrowgates sold their first property themselves. Her description had read as follows: *Compact Victorian terrace house, two bedroom, obscenely large sitting room and seductively secluded garden, could provide sanctuary to both the urbane and the ambitious.*

Meredith's imaginative adjectives attracted not only potential buyers but the realtors too, and she'd been employed ever since. In fact, Meredith was working on her biggest commission so far – a series of ads for a new high-rise city apartment block – when the new tenant of 5a moved in. She was halfway through a sentence – *An architectural triumph that arcs into the sky* – when the removal van pulled up outside the building. Ducking down behind the potted palm she kept on the balcony, Meredith watched as the removalists unloaded a large bed, a deckchair, a dining table, four chairs, several wrapped canvases and what she could only imagine might be a large bass drum and several cymbals. She was just about to phone the strata management to complain about having a musician for a neighbour when a classic silver E-type Jaguar roared up and parked alongside the removal van. The driver climbed out.

Even from two flights up, without her reading glasses, the man's sexual magnetism was obvious to Meredith. He was tall and slender and moved with an unself-conscious grace. He was wearing an expensive-looking suit, his shoulders were broad and, if anything, his hips were a little too narrow for his frame, but Meredith found that endearing. He had black hair, high cheekbones, a full mouth and an aquiline nose that saved his face from prettiness. If Meredith squinted she could just make out the light colour of his eyes – blue, she thought. A European, she concluded, watching him argue with the removalists, his hands (large, she noted with a certain satisfaction) flying about him dramatically. Only when he disappeared into the building did Meredith return reluctantly to her copywriting.

An hour later, stumped by the challenge of describing a two-tier penthouse with a 360-degree view over the CBD, she went to the fridge, poured herself a glass of pomegranate juice (as she did every day at twelve) and wandered back out onto the balcony.

Leaning against the corner post she craned her head to see the sea. The view was comforting; her way of escaping what she secretly felt was the smallness of her life. Her ambition to become a contemporary dancer had translated into taking the occasional tap-dancing classes; she was a copywriter not the novelist she had dreamed of becoming; and the one-bedroom apartment she now lived in was nothing like the large terrace she'd always fantasised about. Then there was her husband.

In her younger days, Meredith had always had a weakness for good-looking younger men. Verbal foreplay, intellectual discourse, displays of power – physical or material – had never impressed her. She liked to do the chasing and the seducing. It was a control thing, she told herself as she gazed out at the tiny strip of blue shimmering on the horizon, remembering her past conquests. But then came Clive. Clive had chased her relentlessly. Whenever her latest conquest hit an emotional wall Clive was there, stoic, funny and out-spoken about his desire to commit. After the tenth young lover departed, leaving her with nothing but a bad case of gravel rash, to her astonishment Meredith found herself attracted to the accountant. Even more astonishing was the first night they made love. Clive turned out to be a four-erections-in-one-night kind of guy – even in his mid-forties – and he was hung. They were married within a year. Meredith considered herself happy, and when her friends asked her she was most emphatic about it. But, in truth, lately Meredith had become a little bored.

A bee, spiralling up with a breeze, buzzed about her face. As she brushed it aside she caught sight of the adjacent balcony – the one belonging to 5a. She leaned over to get a closer view. Her new neighbour was lying naked on the deckchair she'd last seen being unloaded from the removal van. He appeared to be sleeping. His head was turned to one side and she could see the sharp curves of his cheek-bone and his aquiline profile. There were tiny beads of sweat on his upper lip. He was astonishing, the perfect model of a Renaissance male, Meredith concluded, as her eyes ran down his smooth broad chest to the undulating curves of his pectorals, the muscular stomach taut even in repose, then down to his cock, which lay unfurling against his thigh, the apex of the composition Meredith told herself, as though she was observing him with the cool eye of the artist and not the hot and increasingly bothered eye of the voyeur.

Perfectly symmetrical and straight, the penis boasted a

thick shaft, the head of which lay heavy and smooth. It was one of the most finely formed Meredith had ever seen, and she considered herself a connoisseur in these matters. She watched transfixed as – almost in response to the warmth of the sun – the cock began to stir and thicken like a beautiful underwater plant, growing larger and larger. Fascinated, she watched it grow to its full impressive length, now rising up from the belly, the slim hips and muscular thighs of its master only emphasising its size, the tip glistening in the sunlight. Meredith glanced back up to her neighbour's face but he was still asleep. Somehow she sensed that his erection was a pure and sensual response to life, to the sun, the jasmine-scented breeze and, perhaps, to his very youth.

Even more interesting was her own physical response. It was if Meredith herself were touching the soft velvet skin, rubbing the tip of it along her cheek, the rich pungent smell of his balls triggering in her a primal lust. She imagined running her face and tongue up from his crotch over the taut rippled stomach to the muscular curves of his chest, her fingertips tracing that full compliant sleeping mouth as, already wet for him, she would mount him . . .

Suddenly the phone rang from inside her flat. Startled out of her erotic reverie, Meredith stumbled back into the potted palm. Terrified she would be seen, she ducked down and crawled back into the flat on her hands and knees. It was Clive, telling her he'd be flying back from Brisbane early. Inspired, Meredith suggested they try out her new lingerie that night. Troubled by her sudden enthusiasm, Clive guiltily checked his diary, convinced he had forgotten their anniversary. Back at her desk the newly inspired Meredith found the copy for the new high-rise flowing freely. *The primal ambition of this shaft of glass and steel soars up into the sky, almost as if it were impetrating the very heavens themselves,* she typed furiously.

That night Meredith surprises her husband by walking in front of the television wearing nothing but a quarter-cup red satin corset, crotchless pants, black seamed stockings and high patent-leather pumps (by Chloe). Resigning himself to sacrificing the pleasure of watching the Rabbitohs finally win a match, Clive allows himself to be dragged off to the bedroom. He likes to think Meredith is inspired by his newly shaven head – he'd decided it was sexier to have tiny stubble over his naked pate. Tragically, Meredith is imagining an entirely different scenario. Once inside she leads him by the penis toward the wall nearest the bed: Clive still clad in his suit with his cock sticking out like an errant mast, as thick and sturdy as its master.

Clive starts to slip off his shirt but Meredith stops him. She likes him like this, as if his clothed body is a blank canvas she can project upon. Groaning, she kneels and takes him into her mouth, circling the thick shaft with her tongue, feeling the hardness of him, the promise of which has her already wet. Clive leans back against the bed, the tensions of the day beginning to evaporate as pulsating pleasure radiates from his crotch. Meredith climbs up onto the bed, her arse towards her husband. The sensation of the stocking tops gently cutting into her thighs is exquisite, as is the air on her naked pussy, revealed by the crotchless pants. Clive grabs the orbs of her arse. Sinking his fingers into the flesh, he separates her, buries his face into her. This is an act of worship and love but also of lust, for Meredith is still Clive's fantasy muse, the siren of his wet dreams. He tongues her arsehole then moves down to her clit, fingering her as she shivers in ecstasy. Somewhere in the apartment block Meredith hears the sound of a door slamming. She's convinced it's next door. She moves over to the bedroom wall, with Clive still licking and crawling after her.

'Take me from behind,' she commands now, standing with her back to him, palms on the wallpaper and, most importantly, ear pressed to the dividing wall – the bedroom of 5a being behind this very partition. Clive tries to oblige but finds that with her shoes on Meredith is too tall for him. He pulls two books from the bookshelf, *Pride and Prejudice* and *The Fishing Guide to the Rivers of New South Wales,* which are about the same width and height. He places these beneath his feet for leverage, it works, and slowly he eases himself into her – marital paradise, he thinks to himself. As Clive pounds his way to an orgasm Meredith presses even closer to the wall. To her delight, a whole aural extension to their lovemaking opens up. She can hear the bedroom activities next door. It is like being underwater, the sound muted but clear enough for her to know what's going on. She hears groaning – or is it her own? She hears a woman's short screams of pleasure intermingled with the low grunts of a male, *her* male, Balcony Man, Meredith's own private sex god. For a moment she is furious that another woman is making love to her fantasy, but Clive's groans jolt her back to reality. Tentatively, and in rhythm to Clive's thrusting hips, Meredith bangs against the wall with her hand. Three short raps. Then she waits. She hears the sound of furniture being dragged, the thud of a body pushed against a wall – her wall – directly on the other side of her, then female groans. A second later, three short raps answer her own. Is she imagining this? She peers under her armpit at Clive's labouring face. He appears oblivious to everything but the sensation of cock in cunt and the precarious business of staying balanced on the two volumes beneath his feet.

Meredith (good wife that she is) emits a couple of low moans and a few pants as encouragement then, her heart pounding in sudden anticipation, she thumps the wall again, this time four raps evenly paced – a moment later she is answered. Somehow the volume of the thumps suggests to our heroine that the thumper is a male, and therefore the mysterious European neighbour whose tumescence had fascinated her only hours before. As she listens to the shrieks, the low murmuring of an excited man, the chords of distant music, she visualises the lovemaking in 5a. She imagines that it is his hands which are pressed against the wall in the exact same place she is leaning, that the woman he is fucking is on her back, her feet hooked over his shoulders as, kneeling, he penetrates her, playing teasingly with her clit, slowly drawing out her orgasm the way Meredith would like him to do to her. It is this fantasy that sweeps our heroine to orgasm as she imagines, with her hot burning ear pressing against the wall, that it is his body, his hard slender hips mirroring her own. She imagines his thick cock filling her blissfully, her clit hard against the shaft, his large, beautifully formed hands cupping and pulling at her erect nipples, his chiselled jawline and cheek pressed into her bare shoulder, his perfect teeth sunk into the back of her neck. Clive and Meredith come together. Something they hadn't done in years. Thrilled with his own performance, Clive steps off the now dented tomes and sinks to the floor.

'Jesus, we're good,' he murmurs in a stupor of self-satisfaction before falling, snoring, into a post-coital nap. Closing her legs, Meredith presses her ear back against the wall – the bedroom of 5a had gone strangely quiet. Curious, she raps an SOS. A minute later, her rapping is answered with the exact same reply. This, she decides, must be Fate.

And so it was that the Harrowgates' sex life blossomed over the next few weeks. Meredith now adopted only positions that incorporated some form of contact with the bedroom wall – a foot, an elbow, a hand or even a knee – any part of her body with which she could, unnoticed by Clive, thump messages to her co-conspirator, who unfailing answered in kind. It was their secret sex language, the tongue with which our heroine envisaged a whole parallel love affair involving illicit daytime trysts on sun-filled balconies, intense conversations in another language (a Spanish/French/Portuguese fusion that was entirely invented, as Meredith herself was mono-lingual) in which she would always have the epiphany that here was her soulmate, the one who truly understood her hidden artistic nature. The only cloud to mar this burgeoning fantasy was her neighbour's promiscuity. At first Meredith was appalled by it. Then she decided that his seemingly insatiable quest for variety was in fact a desperate search for the right woman – a woman who could guide him into a true fusion of sex and intimacy, who would liberate him into higher, more spiritual realms of concupiscence. That liberator was, obviously, Meredith herself. (As we all know, there are few creatures more capable of delusion than a woman in lust.)

She was convinced that they had developed their own secret code, a language of meaningful raps. 2-3-3-2 meant they were about to begin lovemaking; 2-1-1-2 meant the lovemaking was okay but not great; 1-2-3-4 meant orgasm was imminent (important because Meredith liked to time her climax with that of her neighbour). Clive pretended not to notice, but being the numbers guy he was, it was hard not to. At first he thought it might be rats in the skirting board but even he realised rats weren't that intelligent. He was just thank-ful to whoever or whatever it was that had ignited his wife's erotic imagination. The sex was fantastic. This arrangement could have gone on for years but fantasies – particularly those that are easily accessible – have a tendency to manifest.

And so it was that one day Meredith, overwhelmed by

the need to let the sea breezes refresh her sense of purpose, stepped into the lift to find her fantasy figure from 5a already there.

They stood awkwardly side by side, facing the steel door of the lift. Meredith could smell his sweat, his aftershave; she even sensed the heat emanating from his bare sun-warmed arms. She didn't need to look at his face to see the long eyelashes, the full mouth, those eyes which she now knew to be green, the long tanned fingers resting against his hip. Just standing beside him was impossibly arousing, Meredith thought. To look at him would be fatal. Resigned, she gazed at the numbers lighting up as the lift descended. She could have stood there forever in an erotic miasma, but between floors 2 and 3 she heard a distinctive rap – 2-3-3-2 – their signal to begin lovemaking. She turned and the man was smiling, his hand still rapping out the code. Remembering a trick from her adolescence, Meredith reached into her handbag for a piece of cardboard. She found an old business card, folded it then jammed it between the old-fashioned buttons of the lift. It came to a noisy grinding halt and, without even a hello, he pulled her to his lips.

There are some who describe kissing as the most erotic act there is. Meredith had never been one of them, but here, now, with this beautiful stranger's tongue circling her own, his hands pulling at her clothes, reaching for her nipples as she tears at his belt, kissing suddenly makes sense. The man is an artist; his full lips make their way down her neck, over her breasts, her belly, and then, kneeling, he flings her skirt over his head and, parting her nether lips, sucks at her clit as she watches their reflection in the polished steel wall. It is both erotic and empowering to watch this beautiful young man servicing her, worshipping her. She pulls him to his feet, and he lifts her up against the wall, his cock nudging against her, hot against her clit, playing for a moment before thrusting into her. The size of him makes her gasp, the scent of him, the smooth softness of his young skin a dramatic contrast to the hardness inside her. He rides her until they are both coming, their screams reverberating in the lift. Still without a word between them, they sink exhausted to the floor.

Ten minutes later they walk out of the foyer. They still haven't spoken – to do so would be to break a spell, an illusion. Without a wave or even a gesture, he begins walking to his Jaguar while Meredith sets off for the beach. Just as she passes his car she breaks into a little tap-dancing routine – 2-4-4-2 – a great orgasm. Then, smiling to herself, she continues on her way. As she turns the corner she hears his car horn replying in kind – 2-4-4-2.

That night in bed Clive casually remarked that he'd met the new neighbour from 5a.

'He's from Spain on sabbatical with the Australian National Orchestra. Goes back tomorrow. Pity, really. We could have watched soccer together, he's a Seville supporter too.'

'Really?' Meredith tried to sound disinterested. 'What's his main instrument?'

'Drums, you know, bass drum, cymbals, anything that

involves drumming or rapping on things. I guess that explains the rats then.'

Meredith sat up and glanced at her husband. She wasn't sure exactly what he was referring to but thought it wise to play along.

'I guess it does.'

And they grinned at each other, as innocently as fellow conspirators.

Just Lie Back and Think of England

MINXY MALONE

She was nursing her cup in both hands, a wintry gesture, despite the warm weather. Outside, the garden was drunk on its own juice but she was as brittle as her evening biscuit. Sipping on her hot cocoa and nibbling on the noisy digestive, she felt ambushed by a sudden pang of desolation. Loneliness, hung around her like a fog. Even though it was spring, her life, of late, was endless January – chilly, bleak, predictable. At her age, even the anaesthetising comfort of sleep was starting to evade her. Every night she would wake, gnawed at by worries: her children and their disastrous marriages; her grandchildren and their wild ways; her cantankerous husband. It hadn't been a happy marriage, she post-mortemed. At any rate, he'd always been an abrupt and unimaginative lover. She was not sexually experienced, but had a vague feeling that the act itself was supposed to last longer than it took to run the Derby.

She glimpsed her reflection in the dressing-table mirror and sighed. Her face was becoming a burden to wear. She felt like some ancient ruin, her body a historic monument of abandoned, unremembered nooks and crannies . . . She glanced down at her legs, akimbo atop the satin bedspread and half expected them to be as mottled and mouldy as some weathered Victorian tombstone. She was pleasantly surprised to see them pale, unblemished and still shapely. But it didn't make her feel any less painfully the drip of time and the hourly toll it took on her flesh.

Ah well, she rallied. A child in the war years, she'd learnt to compartmentalise her feelings, blocking off anything unpleasant as though she were a stricken ship sealing off the damaged decks in order to keep on sailing. Another go at the crossword, a flick around the telly dial, a dab of face cream, return to page 157 of the latest unthrilling thriller then, hopefully, some slumber.

Except that it was then that she saw the man. He was standing in the darkest corner of the room by the open window, as though he always stood there – a devoted sentry. She gave a gasp, small and shocked. She scrutinised his face as he emerged from the shadows. Was it someone she knew? But no – he was an intruder. The security people had installed new and better locks, but they didn't take into account the new and better intruders. Her eyes darted in the direction of the panic button. She had to distract him for long enough to reach it. She heard her own voice, piping, false, mock heroic.

'What on earth do you mean, barging in here?'

Unnerved, she rearranged her nightgown more carefully than her husband arranged the strands of his comb-over.

'I'm sorry,' said the stranger. 'I just couldn't think of any-one else to talk to.'

Like all women, she'd thought about prowlers many times and always imagined blind terror. But she shocked herself now by remaining outwardly impassive, her only concern a possible weapon.

'To talk?' she said, slowly lowering her newspaper, breath-ing steadily, buying time.

'I've admired you,' he volunteered, 'for so long.'

She'd expected him to speak roughly, but the interloper had a silken, mellifluous voice. If one had to put a colour to it, it would have been deep sea-green. She thought of her hus-band's drilled belligerence and barking tone – and winced.

Worry and hard work were etched onto his handsome fea-tures. He looked beleaguered and baffled – which reminded her, ridiculously under the circumstances, of the name of some law firm or other. Although rumpled, the smell of him was sharp and clean – tobacco and soap. He was only in his forties, she guessed, lean and muscular. If he were an area of London, he'd be described by newspapers as 'up and coming'.

'What do you want?' she demanded in her beige voice, the voice she used on underlings.

The muscles in the man's throat thickened and knotted. 'I'm so sorry to intrude. Do you mind if I sit down? I've been walking all day and I'm totally knackered.'

'If you must,' she said loftily. She sat even more upright, with a rigid, imperious grace.

He slumped on the end of her bed. The brown corduroy coat resting across his denimed lap took on the faithful demeanour of an old dog. 'It's my life. It's unravelling. It's the small humiliations that erode your soul,' the stranger said gently.

She opened her mouth to say something authoritative and condescending, but no words came out. The raw pain and genuine emotion in his voice had wrong-footed her.

'You try not to care but then the coldness settles in permanently like a snow drift. And then you get used to feeling cold.'

The aloof implacability with which she usually dealt with the world was inexplicably evading her. 'Yes' was the word she was flabbergasted to hear coming out of her own mouth.

'I've worked so bloody hard all my life. Worked at being a good man. Provided for my family. Now, I've one kid in rehab. The other's just gone down for welfare fraud and I've had to remortgage our home to pay the legal bills.'

She was taken aback to find herself nodding sympathetically. 'If only we could keep our children umbilically attached. To protect them from their own stupidity.'

'And now the old woman has run away with her Pilates instructor. The missus is Spanish. We got on well . . . until I learned to speak Spanish that is.'

She felt all the rounded vowels, all the cold homilies in her throat like a gag – and amazed herself by smiling instead.

The interloper smiled back at her. It was strangely companionable.

'I can't believe I made it into your room. Climbing over the garden wall, I thought I'd set off the Working-Class Detector which I'm pretty bloody sure your old man's had installed. Am I right?'

Another small smile escaped from her normally pursed lips. She mentally reprimanded her body to behave, not to deviate from procedure. What was undermining her was that despite the stranger's attempts at humour, sadness was obviously devouring him. His face flickered and tensed. He tried to shake off the melancholy, like a wet animal attempting to get dry. It was oddly endearing. She astonished herself with an impulse to pat his head.

The stranger crackled open the cellophane on a packet of cigarettes and offered her one first, a gesture of friendship. And, telling herself she was stalling for time by keeping him calm (after all, the poor man's children were drug addled and in prison, his wife had abandoned him for some fitness pseudo and the bank were foreclosing on his home – there really wasn't a condolence card to cover all that), she accepted. When he leaned toward her to light the cigarette, an understanding passed between them, an understanding that there was no malice in his mind. His eyes, she now noticed, were brown and glassy, like those of her favourite nursery teddy.

'I have so many people to take care of. Responsibilities. Like you do. But who takes care of us? Who takes care of *you*?' the visitor asked baldly.

Before she could answer by rote, with her face set in its rehearsed expression of polite disdain, she felt something crack open inside her and the stranger saw straight through to her heart. 'You're lonely too,' he said. 'Disappointment and loneliness can attach themselves to a person, kind of like a perfume.'

Yes, she realised. And he could smell it. But just because she often had the demeanour of an Easter Island statue, didn't mean she did not have feelings. Passions. Urges, as her sports mistress used to say. Her face flushed – which she put down to the fact that she'd obviously drunk one too many gins before dinner and one too many nightcaps after. He hadn't touched her, but he had a charged presence. She suddenly knew that he wanted to touch her. And that he would. She put out her cigarette to buy more time.

When he asked to kiss her hand, she felt a mix of dread and anticipation. She had a fleeting moment of panic, but it subsided at the touch of his lips on her fingers – warm, soft, comforting.

He reverentially kissed her other hand now, as though she were the Pope. Despite her alarm, she felt herself shiver at the moisture from his mouth and her pulse gave a little unfamiliar quickening of lust. She was caught in a cross-current of feelings – outrage, curiosity, arousal. She could not suppress the feeling that the mystery caller had a sixth sense – he knew what she was thinking. His lips curled into a hungry smile and there was craving in his eyes. There was something carnal about him, but it was not incompatible with sensuality. Once she'd allowed herself to think of the uninvited guest as attractive, desire burrowed down and took root inside her. The green smells wafting up from the garden were sharp, warm, wet and delicious. She was a woman of education and sophistication, but she also adored nature, the raw, untamed, energetic spontaneity of it.

'Can I touch you?' She felt the urgency and appetite of his voice in the pit of her stomach. 'Only with your permission,' he added, his voice like velvet.

Over the course of this unexpected encounter, she had changed from a hardy perennial, into a delicate floral thing that needed water, air, warmth. She experienced a little quiver at the heat coming off his broad-shouldered body.

Moonlight was flickering in through the leaded glass of the window. Her locked bedroom door yielded a sliver of weak light from the hallway. She felt the illicit thrill of complicity. An ache, a longing spread across her skin. 'Yes.' There was that word again.

With his calloused, almond-shaped fingertips, he stroked her arm, then her legs, then her back. She stretched like a cat, even though she was more of a dog person. This feline arch surprised her, as did the fact that she was newly aware of muscles she'd long forgotten, as the nerves in her skin jumped at his touch. Her breathing became deeper and her movements slowed to match his tender strokes.

He leaned forward and put his lips to hers for no more than a second.

'Can I lie down with you?'

He was looking at her with such yearning. There it was, on his face, an expression she hadn't seen for so long – desire. She was poignantly aware that this would never happen again in her life and how nobody would ever know of their convergence. If he said anything about this stolen moment, she'd deny it. And who would believe him? The heat, the low light, the privacy, conjured up a fantasy in her that they had Brigadooned into another erotic dimension.

She startled herself by pulling him into a kiss – the slippery softness of her lips providing her answer. Feeling the contours of his unfamiliar musculature, she simply let her body take her where he wanted her to go. She slid her arms out of the satin lining of her nightgown, her soft flesh emerging from lacy collar and embroidered cuffs. There was no inexpert fumbling. He found her nipple and put his mouth around it. Encouraged by her soft moans, his lips moved lower, as he mapped out unexplored erogenous zones. The man is a carnal cartographer, she thought, realising simultaneously that she would actually never have to think again because her head was emptying faster than a garden party that had run out of Pimms.

'Your skin's as smooth as vanilla ice-cream,' his deep voice drifted up to her.

And then she was trapped under him. Pleasurably trapped. It had been so long since she had felt the weight of a man. He was heavy and hot, and it should have been claustrophobic, but her body rocked against his, independently of her better judgement. He moved with such deliberation that when he finally entered her, it was as natural as breathing. And, like the heroine of some paperback romance, she yielded to him, moving against his body until she was flooded with heat. She closed her eyes as he slid deeper into her. He steadily quickened his pace, pushing down harder. The rhythm he built up in her twisted tighter. The excitement she felt was close to pain, which made her bite his ear lobe. When she tightened her grip with her thighs, he crushed his head against her breasts to suckle once more. Her body went rigid, then pulsated with pleasure. He pressed her down and she heard the gasp of her breath. She clung to him then as though he were the last lifeboat on the *Titanic*, as every nerve in her body shimmered.

And then he shuddered, holding himself still, like a cellist allowing the last draw of the bow to reverberate. He collapsed, the full dead weight of his body winding her. She lay there, savouring the unanticipated pleasure . . .

'Well, I definitely didn't lie back and think of England,' she finally stated, dry-mouthed, as he rolled away. 'I think one could do with another ciggie, don't you?'

As the stranger threaded himself back into his clothes and lit up their cigarettes, she studied his fleshy mouth, brown eyes and rugged, sun-kissed features. A builder, she presumed. Or a gardener. Out of habit, she nearly asked him, 'And what do you do?'

With one arm propped behind her head on the pillow, she sucked ravenously on the cigarette and let the smoke play around her mouth, reminiscent of the movie stars of her youth. 'You realise that this never happened? And that I must press my panic button. Otherwise how could I explain your presence? You are no doubt on some CCTV footage somewhere,' she sighed resignedly. 'But I'll make sure you're not prosecuted. Just let off with a warning. And, young man . . .' the Queen said, between gratifying puffs.

'Yes, Your Majesty?'

'You need never again feel humiliated or inferior. Not with crown jewels like those.'

The intruder smiled with his eyes for the first time. 'I knew I'd feel better after I'd talked to you, Liz.'

The Queen laughed. Oh, how her flunkies would be flabbergasted by his informality. 'And, sweet man?' Her finger was poised on the panic button.

'Yes?'

'Thank you.' And there was no beige in her voice at all.

Do You Remember Paris?

PATCH O'GILBY

This is the story of one night in Paris. You know Paris, don't you? You remember Paris? I do. There's a little street – there's always a little street, of course there is – no doubt there is also a café, a bar, a family-run place with a nice man called Patric, who has deep-but-still-sexy wrinkles reaching out from the corners of his tired eyes to the beginning-to-grey hair. Patric is only forty-three, but has worked nights for twenty-five years and the smoke from his wife's cigarettes has caused him to squint, etching solid time between eye and hairline. Patric will make the perfect cocktail, your perfect cocktail, your too-dry, showing-off (he is French – he is Parisian – he knows a little more Noilly Prat would be far more success-ful), your ever-so-dry vodka martini – one olive, no twist. He knows your taste, you love this, you adore having a local.

There is his wife Annisette, with the astonishing breasts

and the always-cool hands and the French woman's narrow hips, who kisses each guest as if they are long-lost friends and counts her family's income in return visits. She is very good at kissing strangers as if they are family. I am very fond of Annisette, though I do think she should eat dinner sometimes.

I am very good at kissing strangers.

There is a little street. It is not far from the Gare du Nord. Which is useful for those of you, of us, who travel on the Eurostar, who make our way between home (me) and work (you) beneath the Channel, sous la Manche. The street runs – narrowly, sideways – between Montparnasse and Pigalle, north and west of those squat, wide shops that sell clothes destined to tear and fray after one strong wash, shoes with heels born to snap, garments for the people who can't afford fair-trade fabric, whose empty purses and thin wallets force them to put their trust in man-made cloth. This is a narrow street linking wider roads of summer heat and winter chill, and girls-not-women and older men, Australian backpackers and young Americans wishing Bowie still cared. That part of town. In summer. In heat. July though, before the offices are entirely empty, at the point where businesses are just beginning to close and those who can leave the city to the tourists. To me, on the arm of you.

You are not a tourist, I am not visiting the Louvre, Tour Eiffel, Notre Dame, Pére-Lachaise. I am visiting you, in this hotel, close to the Gare du Nord. (I know you would have preferred me to set this in St Germain; it is far better suited to your Jean-Paul/Simone fantasies. But the truth is this hotel was cheaper. I live in London, I understand a river division economy.)

So. There is a little street. A hotel. An hôtel. The hotel began as a boulangerie – that is, it was once a bakery. Here, in this courtyard, men, and no doubt women, worked through long nights. I suspect there were more men than women though – baking has always had that work-through-the-night macho, don't you think? Men make good bakers, they are not susceptible to the vagaries of the moon, those old wives' tales of when a woman may bake and when she most definitely should not. Beyond that too, the more macho the man the more likely he is to embrace the suffering of early shifts, cock-crow rise, while most women, many women, I, embrace the mattress. And the sheet. The duvet. The blanket. You. I embrace you. Did. Would do again.

Sorry. Getting ahead of myself. Not for the first time. So, you do remember Paris? Maybe we should forget. Should. Ought. Variations on the imperative intended to help me forget. I remember.

There is this street, this hotel that was once a boulangerie, with working men, men's hands, fat-fingered men's hands, heavy adult men's hands, carefully and softly but equally forcefully folding butter into flour into water into – with heat, with time, with air – croissant, brioche, pain aux raisins, pain aux chocolat. Fueillette. Puff. The olde English 'paste'. Flake. Flakey. Flakier. Flakiest. We all have our layers.

This hotel that was a bakery now has cold, empty ovens where the owners store excess crockery and too-big pans. It has a messy, slightly overgrown courtyard at the back and, on the other side of that courtyard, a tall, wide house. I think the nice women have husbands, partners – there are men there who look like they belong in the back rooms, behind the counter – but they do not run the place, these men. The nice women who now own this collection of buildings and the courtyard and path in between have reinvented the house at the back as a range of rooms, each one individually decorated, and none of them in grey or black or beige or taupe.

This is Paris. Paree. Here they don't care that Manchester thinks London loves minimalism, that Leeds wishes it were Manchester without the setting sun, that Birmingham still tries so hard, so bloody hard. Here they paint in Egyptian blue and Moroccan orange and Lebanese red. This hotel is colour-drenched enough to feel at home in Sydney or Sienna or San Francisco. And we are in Paris. Every room has an old, deep wardrobe and a high, wide bed, with a clean and acceptable bathroom, a square of soap wrapped and ready in a dish, but nothing else that smacks of 'boutique' and every extra detail confirming the suspicion that the women at the desk, which was once a boulangerie counter, will leave you alone. Leave us alone. Thank you. No, thank you.

Thank you.
    Again?

What?
Say it again.
Thank you.
Good girl.

The bakery shop front, the part of the shop the customers used to visit, with tiled floor and walls, windows of art nouveau glass, that's where you have breakfast. Where we had breakfast, three mornings in a serried row, but not the fourth. Not the fourth. Breakfast that was handed to us on a paper plate. (Handing myself to you on a plate.) Fresh croissant from down the road, a dollop of jam, they don't ask which you prefer: I like apricot, you prefer strawberry, we were given raspberry. Maybe it was sign. Though we ate it anyway, too sweet already and eating it anyway. Beside the jam, a fat chunk of yellow unsalted butter, as if there wasn't already enough in the bread.

Butter. Coffee. Café au lait. Ready mixed. Yes, it probably is Nescafé. But this is the European Nescafé, not the British one. We know they have a different blend; it is supposed to be a secret, like the various flavours of Fanta for different continents. It is not secret. It is just different. It isn't bad, it is another drink. It is what they say it is. It is Nescafé.

(Do you see how I remember Paris? The detail, the warp and the weft of Paris? How I remember you?)

And so.

Three nights. Four days. Three times you and I were there together. Just one night at a time, until the last day, that day, the day we spent the illuminated hours together. You had never seen the courtyard in the daylight before. I think perhaps you were a little disappointed. In the daylight. Not me, not me and you. How could we ever disappoint? Each other maybe, it was always inevitable that we would disappoint each other, but as a couple? As yet another couple sneaking away from home, from family, from real life into the waiting arms legs hope hunger want and satisfaction of each other? The path of one couple, like any other couple, heading for their expected failure where lust is beaten by betrayal of trust – this is what every affair begins and ends already understanding, the only variable is time. I did not ask what you knew, but I knew it would not last. That was not how we disappointed each other. Those couples do not disappoint, even when we are one of them, following the age-old plot of desire; decide go with it flow with it fuck with it push aside the barriers of what we should not have been doing and get on with doing it anyway. As much a ritual as a kabuki bow, Pierrot and Pierrette painted-on kisses, make-up tears. Yes, we were that much of a cliché. But not any more, we are nothing like those traditional illicit couples now, are we?

Wait, I'm getting there.

That first night there was a storm. Well, there was rain. And a little wind. Lot of wind, I wanted a lot of wind and lashing

217

rain and lightning. You would have seen the courtyard better in lightning. I don't like thunder though, so perhaps all I really wanted was an excuse to hide beneath your coat, your arm – have you hold me closer, save me from the rain. You could not have held me closer.

You were there before me, waiting for me. I had given you the address and you said you would find it. Why should I doubt your ability to find a simple, stable hotel, when you had already found me with such a clear sense of purpose, aim, direction? Have you always been a hunter?

You were waiting in the room, perched on the edge of the bed. You did not want to get in first, did not want to make it yours when it should be ours. That's what I assumed. Not what you said. You have never said much. You save words, I spend them. One of us is richer for it. As always I made my choices about what you were thinking. It made it easier for me, to assume an understanding of your desire. Easier then.

Waiting on the edge of the bed, that bed with the heavy, white sheets and blanket. No duvet. I said before I liked to hug the mattress, the duvet. With a blanket it is more a matter of wrap and twist and tuck. Tuck me in the way my mother and father used to, rip off the covers the way no parent should. Rip off my covers.

The first morning we had breakfast, there were two young women sitting at the table next to us. They were from an iden-tikit mould of perfect, fashionable lesbians. They both wore black – thin women in tight black. One had Louise Brooks hair and a gash of red lipstick, the other high Cuban-heeled boots and a young-Elvis quiff. If they weren't from New York they should have been. They could not keep their hands off each other, were smoothing perfect skin and stroking perfect hair and then I saw that one of them had a suitcase behind her chair. They were saying goodbye and I forgave them their teenage touching in bodies of thirty. You and I did not touch in public unless we were on an unlit street or a hidden alley of discretion. I believed our touching to be the more intense because of its very holding back. Belief is always a choice.

We did not hold back in those heavy sheets. You and me together. You on me. Your lips on mine, hips on mine, weight of mine on you. You know I love that – loved that – didn't you? The feel of you on me, the heaviness of you on me. You used to worry you were too heavy for me. Worried you were too heavy. Worried it was not comfortable for me with you there, here, there. It wasn't. And even when it was, uncomfortable, it wasn't. I wanted it, that, you. That thing you did, so many things you did. I list them now. It puts me to sleep, it keeps me awake, it holds me with you and – even when you are no longer with me – it does still. I do it still. Like you did. In my head. My hands. My head.

You holding me, my hands above my head and you holding me with one hand of yours and the heft of your hips against mine. Pushing me into the bed. The floor. The wall.

Me on your back and your skin beneath my fingers. I could sip your skin with my fingertips, taste the idea of you before I felt the flesh, held you in my mouth. Now too, though you are far from my touch, I taste the sweat, slick, smooth skin of you. The skin that covers the rest of you. The rest of you. I wanted it all. We did not rest.

Me at your feet and looking up to the smile you couldn't hold back whenever I was there, at your feet, when you knew what was to come. I was to come, you were to come and you didn't always want to, sometimes wanted me face-to-face beside you, often wanted me above you, but there, in that mockery of tradition, you still adored me. That smile. Knowing and wanting and demanding and every teenage fantasy come true. I was that for you, I know I was. You said I was. (I believed you.)

You on your knees. You were good there. I was glad you were good, it was a pleasant respite, and we were so skilled at all these positions and we gave and took and always, always I gave that little bit more – because I wanted to. I love to give, I know the power of giving. I know the strength in being the one who is in charge – leading the action, making it happen. I thought I was making it happen. And you let me think that, or it was true. Then. For a while.

You and me in the dark of that alley down behind Patric and Annisette's bar. So close to the noise of your neighbours, so far from my home, so dirty and rough and your hands readier than I was and it hurting and that we both wanted it to, to hurt both of us, the youthful vigour we don't really have any more, the desperation to fuck do it now make it happen make it now don't wait until the bed and the sheets and the clean and the light, here here now fuck God now right now and yes and yes this wall and yes this street lamp and yes the insistent drip drip of a broken drainpipe and some stinking cat's piss and dear God the blissful fuck made purely dirty. And open. And the chance of being seen.

There was always the chance of being seen. Not recognised, not me at least. But seen, yes. I didn't mind that. It was you who needed to be careful of others' vision. Others' views. How they saw you. See you. Then. Now. How I loved to see you. Look at you. Look at you looking at me. I have never been so naked as when you looked at me.

Paris plage. You thought it was silly, I thought it exciting. It was both: childish and entrancing. Three nights, one day. We went to the beach. You'd suggested a brisk walk, a strong coffee, a long lunch. I wanted the beach. I got what I wanted, then, briefly. I was used to getting what I wanted. I thought it would always last. The getting, not us. I knew that wouldn't last.

We were dressed all wrong. You in your suit, that perfect cut, perfect line, that beautiful linen suit with the smooth silk lining. Me in an old pair of jeans and a little top I'd grabbed from one of those squat shops on my run from the train to the hotel and you. New (cheap) knickers and bra too. I always ran when you called. Your night suddenly free and an hour for me to get the train. No time to pack – I'd lock my door and rush to you from wherever I was. I'd been cleaning my windows. You said come as you are. I always did. I left friends at dinner, hurried from a meeting, was rude to my mother's aunt, forgot to feed the cat. In a way it was lucky we only had those three nights – I'd have lost it all given the chance. Thrown over every one of my futures for your call.

I don't regret this, never have. Three nights, one day. Many, many phone calls though. Fucking the sound of your voice with a touch that isn't yours. Reaching for you through the generosity of Edison and Bell. Good men.

Dressed all wrong. You in that beautiful suit and me looking like your maid, your servant, your daughter. The thin T-shirt material of the cheap knickers and bra was close enough to a bikini for me to peel away the window cleaner's jeans, the shoddy new top. You removed your jacket, rolled up your fine sleeves, took off your shoes and we dipped our toes in the sand, in the water. Dipped our toes in how it felt to be here together, in sunshine. The illicit affair makes vampires of us all.

The flavour of your skin. It is something to do with the cleanliness of your clothes. They smell laundered, not dry-cleaned. They remind me of childish clothes – cotton dresses, already slightly dated when my mother bought them for my sister and I – but the sunshine and just-pressed scent, that's what does it for me. I don't suppose you have a washing line though, do you, in your family home, the four-bed apartment two floors up? It must be to do with the soap you use, or other products, something the maid sprays on when she irons. (You have a maid, I find it amazing, funny, that you have a maid.) Perhaps it is a skin-care product. You have wonderful skin, but I don't know what products you use, if any. I have never been to your bathroom, your bedroom, inventoried the secrets of the private cupboards you share with your family. Yet now, in my mouth, there is the smell of the taste of your skin, of you. And I am hungry for that. Still hungry for that. Even at fourteen I preferred the excess of bulimia to the denial of anorexia. I would always rather have than have not. Have had, than not.

Do you want to know what happened? Why I changed my home number, bought a new mobile, ignored the cards, refused the next summons and then the next? Why I did not come again? Okay. This is what I did.

I came, without your call. It wasn't to surprise you, it wasn't really about you at all. It was for me. You were not my only reason to go to Paris. I have always been fond of the city, feel more for it than a tourist's pleasure, a voyeur's joy. Even before you, I thought I knew the city well, had been there several times for my work – remember when I had my work, my own work? – on other occasions for pleasure. You and I first met there, after all, and I was no stranger to the stations, the metro, the taxi drivers' whims. Other than London, where I live, and that distant city where I was raised, it is probably Paris that I know best.

As I said, I knew we wouldn't last always. You would never leave her for me, that life for mine, my city or your city for our home. So even back then I was preparing, unconsciously perhaps, but readying myself for the day, week, month when the call did not come. I showered and washed my hair, shaved my legs, took time to fill my bag with the things – book, water, pen, paper – I so often left behind in my rush to you. Dressed appropriately for both travel and arrival. And came alone.

I was not spying or hunting. I would have been happy not to find you or to catch a glimpse. To have seen you with your work colleagues, your family, your real daughter, from a far distance. I did not need to put you in that homely focus. I would have greeted with equanimity the sight of you grabbing a quick lunch while discussing business on the phone. Enough to watch you leave the office and throw your briefcase into the passenger seat, drive away from the staff car park. I wanted one look, one small view, and then the rest of the day would be mine. I would visit the cafés I went to before you, light a candle in the Madeleine, a church you find both oppressive and ostentatious, give a few euros to one of those over-keen Polish students busking for the Louvre queue, their le Coq-taught mime funny to me, tedious to you. I just wanted to go for a walk. With myself, so my skin would feel mine again. I promise you, I was doing this for me, about me. I actually wanted a day in the city that wasn't about you. You and me.

You and her. You did not meet her at the Gare du Nord, for that I am grateful. You did not take her to our hotel, for that I am grateful. You took her to a secluded path on the south side of Montmartre and from there to a private garden where the two of you fucked on well-watered, carefully cut grass, close to a small bay tree in a midnight-blue pot. Her dark, curly hair looked good against the green and the ceramic gleam.

I have never thought myself a tourist. Was never much interested in looking, watching, before. I stared, took it all in. Absorbed the view. She was beautiful, of course. You would not have been with her otherwise, I think. She was not like me. Shorter, finer, though slightly curvier perhaps. A little, very little, curvier. (I wonder if I had known you liked more curves would I have eaten more? Maybe not. As I said, the taste of you filled me, fulfilled me.) She was leaning over you, into you, and then your bodies turned together, twisted in time, a rhythm that cannot have been purely accidental, brand new. A rhythm that knew itself too well, knew you too well. She did. I did.

When she turned her head to face me, eyes not seeing, seeing nothing but you, that was the second surprise. Patric and Annisette's daughter. She is nineteen. Nineteen. I don't know why this shocks me. You have a family and a career and live out the role, all those roles, do them well. I don't know why, when I know what you and I had, that it should seem so bad for her to be so young. I wonder if I would have answered your plaintive phone calls and messages the day, week, month, later if she had been a grown woman like me. A grown woman like you. But I couldn't. Didn't. Stood and watched the two of you, your reaching into her, scratching the back of her neck, her smooth, rounded young girl's upper arm with your perfectly manicured nails. Wanting you and watching. You reached inside her T-shirt. A teen-ager in a T-shirt. I know your hand was cupping her breast, cupped mine.

My own hand under my own top. You pushed your tongue against her lips, her lips parted, mouth open, tongue touch, tongue taste, opening wide, hips swayed. Mine too. I was there with you. Am there with you. You touch her, touch me and I am touching me in that street that looks into the garden where the two of you lay, fuck, lie.

But you are in a garden and I am in a street. And when I can bear to break my gaze, away from that break in the edge of the fence, away from you and her, from you on her on you on her, I see the man watching me. Watching me touch me as you touch her. He reaches into his pocket and for a moment I think perhaps he is about to return to me the three euros I gave the Polish mime, that I have been his show as you were mine. But men in back alleys tend not to pay for the street theatre they come to view.

I could hear the two of you talking, whispering sweetly to each other. I know your whispers were sweet. You speak well, in several languages, and your words are always the same. And she is not a child, and neither am I. So I came home. I do not eat strawberry jam and I do not travel to Paris through that fast tunnel, simply because I can, and I do not come to you. Except now, as I speak of you, touching my skin, touching me. Touch me. I do.

The Convenient Gardener

STORM HENLEY

I suppose I was something of a sitting duck. My two children were in knee-socks, happily and variously occupied at school with projects about Ironbridge and Marine Animals on the Verge of Extinction. My husband parked his skinny arse in the same seat, at the same time, every day as he commuted to his office in Canary Wharf. And there I was, jogging on the spot in Holmes Place, buying clothes I wouldn't wear, for parties I no longer went to, drinking more pinot than I should, all the time slowly atrophying on the vine of life. Until one stormy day in early May, when a fortuitous gust of wind changed everything.

'That back wall's down,' informs Steve, chomping on his toast and pointing his crust at the French windows. 'That was one hell of a storm.'

'Mmm,' I reply, barely bothering to raise my gaze from the obits page in the newspaper.

'That's a professional job.' Steve nods knowledgeably, his mouth full of toast on a spin cycle. 'There's no way I'm wasting my weekend putting that back up.'

'Sure,' I say. 'We should get a builder.'

'That's not a builder's job,' Steve corrects.

'Oh?'

'I think you'll find a gardener will do. And they're cheaper,' he adds, as he picks up his shiny black briefcase and heads for the door. 'I'll leave it with you, right?'

'Fine.' I exhale. Why is it that I get all the shitty jobs round here?

'Oh, by the way,' he pauses on the threshold, 'I'm not in tonight. I've got a business dinner with the boys. Bye, kids!'

'Bye, Dad!' they reply over their bowls of Cheerios.

He's gone, the children follow soon after, and I am left alone for another long day of gym appointments, the school run and reading my horoscope in an afternoon bath. Except, of course, there's that back wall to fix.

I don't know what it is that makes me pick Pavel out of the Yellow Pages. Maybe it's because he has the biggest advert? Or perhaps it's the mention that 'No job is too small or too menial'? Either way, it speaks to me, which, it transpires, is more than he could do. Standing on my doorstep forty-five minutes later in his thick coat and heavy boots, it quickly becomes apparent that Pavel's repartee is limited to 'Yes', 'No' and 'Very fine'. But I don't particularly mind; he comes with a long list of gushing recommendations from local ladies, a spade, a bucket and his own thermos of black tea. He is quiet and convenient and perfect for the job.

On the first day we both studiously ignore each other. The rain drizzles down, Pavel keeps his coat on and pulls his woollen hat further down over his head, while I read the newspaper, take phone calls from my girlfriends and plan a dinner party for ten in three weeks' time. Worried that he isn't entirely to be trusted not to rip off the contents of my house, I only leave him alone for half an hour while I go to collect the children. And when I return, he's gone. That evening, when Steve comes home, he is less than impressed with the work so far.

'The bloke's done bugger all!' he exclaims, pressing his nose against the french windows and looking down the lawn. 'All he's done is laid out a few bricks and he's already covered the decking in mud and cluttered up the side return with all his bags of sand and cement.'

'He's not exactly speedy,' I agree.

'Have a word,' sniffs Steve. 'Give him a nudge or we'll have to find someone else.'

So, the next morning, it is with a certain bristling sense of injustice that I march down the garden. Overnight, the weather has changed dramatically. The sun is shining, the air is warm and the birds have decided it's pleasant enough to sing. Spring is definitely here and the sap is rising.

Pavel is bent over his bricks as I approach. It is the first time since his arrival that I've actually bothered to look at him. In his late twenties, his legs are long, lean and muscular;

his buttocks slim and firm as they point towards me. He is in good shape.

'Excuse me,' I say. He stands up and turns around. Jesus Christ! His topless torso stops me in my tracks. The pale skin, the gently rippled stomach, the definition of his pectoral muscles, the strong, masculine curve of his shoulders and the thin line of hair from his navel to the top of his trousers . . . It's all I can do to stop myself gasping out loud. He smiles, runs his rough hands through his thick dark hair and looks at me with pale-blue eyes.

'Yes please,' he says.

My thoughts exactly. I smile. 'Umm, would you like a cup of tea?' I say weakly, biting the inside of my mouth, trying to calm the sudden rush of sexual longing that courses through my veins, making my stomach tighten, my heart beat urgently and the crotch of my tight jeans fizz with desire. He looks at me quizzically. The way his top lip curls makes my cheeks flush.

'Tea?' I try again, making a drinking gesture with my slightly shaking hands.

'Oh,' he nods towards his Thermos. 'I'm very fine.'

'Yes, you are,' I say, smiling at him. 'Very fine indeed.'

I walk back to the house almost unable to breathe. Should I make some coffee? Calm myself down? Go for a run? A swim? Or have a shower and frantically play with myself to relieve this terrible, burning ball of sexual tension lodged in my stomach? But in the end, like a Stepford Wife on remote control, I simply reach for my secateurs and gardening gloves and join him in the garden.

For the next hour and a half I snip away at my *Hydrangea heteromall a*, removing burgeoning bud after burgeoning bud as my mouth grows increasing dry and my labia swell with lust. But I can't keep my eyes off him. The line of his back as he leans forward, the light on his shoulders, his strong arms, his rough hands, the wrinkle of his skin over the hard muscles of his stomach. The way his trousers hang off his hips. I cross my fingers, bite my lip and pray quietly to myself that he isn't wearing underwear.

By lunchtime, as he sits in the sun, tearing the thick white crusts off his hearty cheese sandwich, I can't take it any more. So I disappear upstairs and vigorously finger myself off with my chamois leather gardening gloves. I tear off my top as I look out of my bathroom window, rubbing my rock-hard nipples against the cold windowpane. It doesn't take long. I am wet with longing and my gloves are rasping and coarse. I'm not sure if he sees me. He glances up at the house when I cry out as I come. But that could just have been wishful thinking.

The afternoon is unbearable. I stalk him round the garden, pretending to tame the gaudy gush of pink flowers sprouting from my voracious *Clematis montana*. Giddy with desire, I tweak and tug away at the pale-pink blooms while I watch his strong back bend over the piles of bricks and his large hands place them gently on top of the wall. He's working up quite a sweat – up and down, mixing the cement, slathering it across the bricks. I can see shiny silver beads across his shoulders and if I move a few steps towards him I can catch the sweet, high smell of his musk.

Then, as I walk towards the green compost bins at the back of the garden, my arms laden with fresh fronds of *Montana* that I have inexplicably scythed down in their prime, Pavel brushes past me. I'm not sure exactly why he comes so near, but he rubs himself against me. I shiver with excitement and for a fleeting second imagine I feel the hardness of his rigid cock against my thigh. It is a stupid thought, I know. I grip my cuttings even tighter, hold my breath, get a grip of myself and, throwing back my long blonde hair, I walk ever more purposefully towards the bins. After all, what would a deliciously lithe twenty-something gardener want with a forty-something housewife like me? I take the lid off the bins. The smell of rotting vegetation explodes forth. I push aside some sticks and grass and tip in my trimmings, compacting it all down with the palms of my gloved hands. I then bend forward to pick up the lid. I don't manage to straighten up before I feel him rub himself up against me again. This time there is no mistake. He is hard and urgent, ramming his erection against the base of my spine. The force of his taut, toned body pushes me up against the wall. My heart is beating faster and faster. Flushed with an urgent longing, I want to turn around and pull his trousers down to get my hands on his fantastic cock.

'No,' he mumbles in my ear as he pushes me harder against the wall. His soft tongue teases the side of my neck, while one hand goes up the front of my shirt, under my bra, and cups my right breast. He pinches my nipple between his thumb and forefinger, rubbing his stiff shaft more urgently against my back. He slips his other hand up under my skirt

232

and between my thighs. I can't breathe. I close my eyes. My cotton pants are wet with excitement. My hips squirm in desperation. I don't know how much more my clit can bear. It is swollen to bursting, like a ripe redcurrant.

'Just fuck me,' I moan, my right cheek rubbing against the brick wall.

He moves my pants to one side with his weather-worn fingers and slips two digits inside my welcoming pussy. In and out he slides them. His skin is like sandpaper. He gathers rhythm and purpose. He tweaks my clit, arousing it some more.

'I can't wait any longer,' I urge, almost shouting.

Finally he releases his cock from his straining flies and, pulling my underwear down to my knees, thrusts into me.

'Oh my God!' I cry, as I collapse against the wall. It is huge and hard and perfect. At first he pumps away with long deep thrusts. But he soon gathers speed and the faster he rides me the more I ride him back. Quicker and quicker. Deeper and deeper. My face rubs against the wall, chafing my cheeks. He comes seconds before me. His final thrust pushes me flat against the wall. My own shuddering climax makes me grip the trellis, sending frissons of shaking delight all the way along the fragrant, purple pendants of my *Wisteria floribunda*.

'Angela? Is that you?' comes the clipped tones of Julia, my next-door neighbour. Her 'fun' jumper and sensible hair are preceded by the arrival of her rose-coloured marigolds. 'Are you okay?' she asks poking her long nose over the fence.

'Absolutely fine,' I reply, inhaling deeply while I discreetly try to pull my blouse down over my breasts. My pants are down by my knees and warm cum is seeping between my thighs, but Pavel had pulled down my skirt as he withdrew, so Julia is none the wiser.

'The whole trellis was shaking,' she adds, leaning further over.

'Really?' I smile, glancing down to witness Pavel tucking his decidedly more pliant cock back into his trousers. 'I was doing some gardening.'

'Oh?'

'Yes,' I add. 'I have employed a new gardener.'

'What a good idea!' says Julia. Pavel zips up his flies and stands up from underneath the fence. 'Oh!' Exclaims Julia, a little taken aback. 'I didn't see you there!'

'This is Pavel.'

'A gardener,' marvels Julia, taking in his bare torso, curled lips, light-blue eyes and thick dark hair. 'How fabulous!'

'Isn't it?' I smile

'How often is he coming?'

'Every day,' I reply.

'Good, good.' Julia seethes with irritation as she turns away. 'Oh,' she says, looking back over her shoulder. 'You seem to have scratched your face.'

Julia happily swallowed my 'gardening' excuse for the cuts to my cheek, Steve, however was a little more circumspect.

'You mean you did that trimming back the clematis?' he

asks at least three times over the fish pie and peas I'd reheated for his supper. 'I find that hard to believe.'

But quite frankly I don't care because the real explanation – that I'd been taken roughly from behind over some bins at the bottom of the garden while inhaling the sweet smell of rotting vegetation – is so far beyond the realms of his imagination that it doesn't matter. All I can think about, and all I am interested in, is what time Pavel will turn up again tomorrow.

It is almost 9.30 a.m. and I am beginning to lose hope. I have checked the kitchen clock about forty times in the last half-hour and still he hasn't shown. I've managed to persuade my friend Anthea to take the kids to school for me again, just in case he rings the bell while I'm out. But he's supposed to be here by now. I pace the sitting room, biting the pink polish of my manicured nails, burning with frustrated desire. What if I've overstepped the mark? What if he doesn't come? What if that was it? What if he was just using me? But much more importantly, what if I never got fucked like that again?

The doorbell goes. Thank God. My stomach tightens as I go to answer it. I open the door. And there he is, dressed in his loose, thick trousers, his white T-shirt pulled out of his waistband, mud already clinging to his heavy work boots.

'I am sorry,' he says. 'The lady at number twenty-four needed her bush trimming.'

'Oh,' I say, a little put out and also slightly surprised that he can actually speak that much English. But the prospect of more al fresco sex is too tempting for me to be sidetracked by such trifles.

'Come in,' I smile, pressing my breasts together with my elbows. 'That wall won't lay itself.'

Pavel smiles sweetly and walks down the garden. He barely manages to get his work tools out before I have my hand down his trousers and his own hard tool in my mouth. And I swear I have never seen anything quite so magnificent in my life. Long and thick and unyielding, it's a pillar of perfect youthful tumescence and utterly unlike the flaccid marital offering that occasionally gets shoved my way after some boozy work dinner or festive office party. Crouching by my blooming *Iris pallida*, I lock my lips around his pretty purple head and suck on it like a lollipop. I can hear his breath shortening as my tongue runs up and down his shaft. I look up to see his toned stomach tighten with pleasure as I take him further into my throat. His arms out, he leans, Christlike, against his rake and spade for support. I see the whites of his knuckles as he clasps the handles and shudders to a rushing climax in my mouth.

'Yoo-hoo!' A pink marigold waves over the fence. 'Only me!'

Shit! Not again, I think as I'm forced to swallow before standing up.

'Morning, Julia,' I say, coughing slightly before wiping my lips with the back of my hand and quickly pulling a black pubic hair out of the corner of my mouth. 'How are you?'

'I see you've got your hands full there!' she grins.

'What?'

'It must be hard to keep someone that fit and young busy in such a small garden,' she jokes. 'If he has any spare time, I wonder . . .'

'Don't worry,' I smile. 'I can think of plenty of ways to keep Pavel busy.'

'Well, if you're sure,' she says, placing the point of her elbow over my fence, looking like she's ready for a long chat.

'Quite sure,' I say. 'And if you'll excuse me, Pavel was just about to talk me through some problems with the back wall.'

'Don't mind me,' says Julia, looking Pavel up and down over the top of her turquoise-framed reading specs. 'I'm just admiring the view.'

I tap Pavel on the shoulder and indicate for him to follow me inside. Julia's interest irritates me. Also her lascivious looks make me uncomfortable. They remind me a little too much of my own.

However, once inside the house my discomfort soon vanishes. And any doubts I'd had that the sex with Pavel was simply an open-air fetish soon melt away as he lifts me up onto the kitchen worksurface between the cooker and the sink and pulls up my skirt. He runs his hands up the length of my thighs and with one swift movement rips off my pants. He then combs back my pubic hair with his long, muddied fingers, pulling my engorged labia apart. He looks down and licks his lips.

'Very fine,' he nods. 'Very fine,' he says again before he runs the tip of his tongue around the edge of my cunt. The effect is electric. A shock springs right through my body, making me throw my head backwards, hitting the shelf behind me. I am sure it hurts, but my body is in the throes of so much pleasure, it disregards the pain. His tongue laps and licks the folds of flesh. It is incredible. He probes and teases and, just when I can't take any more, he slips his fingers inside me and brings me to another screaming climax.

I let go a long, sated sigh and look down at his mop of thick black curls between my thighs. I ruffle my hands through his hair. He looks up and smiles. His lips are wet; his breath smells of me.

'Thank you,' he smiles.

Every day for the next week Pavel and I fuck each other like rabbits who've just discovered birth control. My day goes something like this: Pavel arrives between nine and ten in the morning and we immediately have sex. In the hall, on the stairs, the sofa, over the kitchen table. He never gets into the garden itself until somewhere between eleven and twelve. Then he makes some sort of attempt at working on the wall. This ploy keeps Julia entertained and Steve off the scent. Although I have to say he must have noticed something is up. I am so good humoured I'm positively hysterical and I am also so highly sexed at the moment I even made a pass at my own husband. However, the resulting lame bout of intercourse, where he flapped around on top of me like a slowly asphyxiating plaice, only made me make that mistake once.

The afternoons are more languid. Pavel takes his time bringing me to orgasm. Sometimes he simply kisses me, playing with my breasts and caressing my curves, until I beg him for sex. At other times he lies next to me on a blanket, running his hands up and down my thighs, inserting flowers into my pubic hair. And, very occasionally, we return to the bins and the wall for a swift rogering from behind, where this whole affair began.

But then, on Friday, something awful happens. We fuck in the hall and the stairs, the *Clematis montana* gets given a good shaking but he can't delay it any longer. Pavel lays his final brick and finishes the wall. He looks at me and I look at him, and we both realise that it's over. I want to hurl all my weight against the goddamn thing and push it over – anything to make him stay.

'Don't worry,' he says, putting his hand up my skirt and patting my naked backside. 'You will think of many little jobs and many little things for me to do so that I can come back.'

'Absolutely,' I nod determinedly.

'Just give me a call.'

Two days later I spot him coming out of number thirty-eight. I nearly run after him. I nearly beg him to take me over the bonnet of the green Mini Clubman parked in the street. But I don't. He hasn't returned any of my calls. All the jobs I try to book him for are apparently too menial after all. Instead I knock on the door of number thirty-eight. A flushed middle-aged woman answers.

'I am terribly sorry to bother you,' I say. 'But I have just noticed a young man leave your house.'

'Oh, Pavel,' sighs the woman. 'He keeps all the ladies in this street happy.'

'Really?' I say.

'Oh yes,' she smiles. 'Just take a look at their gardens.' I look up and down the street. The front gardens are immaculate, as though the BBC1 *Ground Force* team have only just left. 'He's such good boy.' She smiles again. 'And so convenient. He keeps everyone's bushes trimmed.'

Twice Shy

BUNNY PRINCESS

My top drawer was open and pants, bras, filmy knickers from Freya, crotchless lace scraps from Myla and angry-looking red bras from Agent Provocateur were frothing out. I was searching for something suitable for this afternoon's assig— what? Assignation, or assignment? I mentally settled for assignment. It sounds more professional.

Reaching my hand towards the back, I drew out what I had been looking for in a lucky dip: a black bra in stretchy Lycra from trusty M&S and a pair of black briefs that almost matched it, that is, if you looked at the black panty-set with your eyes half closed. I put them on. Then I took the specialist spare pair I had ordered, folded them into a square, and dropped those in too. Just in case.

I stomped to the Tube. Central Line. In my bag, along with the special prosthetic underwear, I had put all the usual things: mobile, keys, Tampax, Oyster card, wallet, Lancôme cranberry lip gloss, to make my teeth look whiter, and *Vogue* to read on the Tube – as my present to myself, something I had bought in advance in much the same spirit as my mother would console me for missing some treat by saying, 'Darling. I'll make it up to you, I promise,' and never, in the end, did.

I got out at Tottenham Court Road. It was a sunny Sunday afternoon in Central London. Noisy, dirty, with the pavement pockmarked and spotted – as if it were a grungy Damien Hirst-style installation – with dingy, white rounds of flattened gum.

Tourists were disgorging from the mouth of the Tube station only to disappear down the long, straight gullet of Oxford Street, and were milling around aimlessly, talking Italian in loud voices, swigging from water bottles, doing all the annoying things that tourists do without apparently being aware of it, like the woman on the train who talks for the entire duration of the journey into her mobile in a loud voice all about last night and her boyfriend, to a girlfriend one senses she never actually sees.

I threaded through them with unconcealed impatience and made my way past the theatre where Ben Elton's rock musical about Queen has been playing for longer – it seems – than my children have been alive.

My children. I suddenly checked them off in my head, as if to do so would ward off danger. I knew that it was too late to prevent anything humiliating happening to me. But then, that was the box I had ticked myself, and it was far too late to change my mind.

One son was watching a Chelsea match with his father. His twin brother, who unaccountably supported Arsenal, was at a friend's house, while my teenage daughter was at home with her friend Bella, both no doubt adding pictures of themselves to their Bebo pages. (I prefer not to think about it. Last time I checked, Flora had posted a self-portrait wearing a croptop, pants, and bunny ears. Flora is thirteen).

Trying not to think about my daughter being groomed – actually, trying not to think of her and her budding sexuality at all – I marched purposefully down Tottenham Court Road, past music shops and bookstores and sex shops, towards my destination in my knee-high black boots, my bare thighs swishing together slightly under my tight black pencil-skirt. It had been carefully chosen to suggest a woman who had managed to remain in touch with her mojo, her moxie (words I freely use in print, but never actually say out loud) but not necessarily grappling with it on a permanent basis.

This is the look I strive for when I'm out on the job. Not my day job, of course – I'm a psychotherapist – but my part-time gig: agony aunt/sex columnist for a US magazine called *Mary Jane*. A magazine for women that men read when they find it lying around. Thankfully, it's the sort that you *can* leave lying around. My job is to report what's Out There sex-wise. Sometimes I sample it for them. Sometimes I don't.

I like the public-service element of the job but today's

appointment, I sense, might be taking things a little bit too far. Especially for me.

When I started work at *Mary Jane*, I laid down two ground rules. As firmly as I could. 'I won't write about anal sex,' I had told the lissom blonde editor, Viv, her long legs clad in a pair of white sailor-trousers and a navy Chanel cardy over a plain white tee, as she giggled openly at my prissiness.

'My mother reads *Mary Jane*. So does my dad, when he can get his hands on it. Need I go into detail? Women are equipped with a perfectly serviceable orifice already. Please, I don't want to have to write about riding the dark horse. I don't want to make weak puns in order not to offend your middle-aged, Spanx-wearing readership about . . . bringing up the rear.

'And, secondly, I won't, ever, write about physical chastisement. Spanking. Whatever you call it. Mmm? It's for saddos. I for one find it a major-league turn-off, and I've yet to meet one single, normal, healthy woman who has ever given it a moment's thought. I hope I have made that absolutely clear.'

That conversation ran through my mind like a bubbling stream as I rang the bell to Soho House. I swear I could almost hear Viv laughing like a drain as I spoke.

'I'm here for, er, the spanking lesson,' I said quietly to the pair of black-clad women in immaculate maquillage who sat at a sleek black desk, punching numbers into phones, and buzzing-in members of the celebocracy to snort coke, and telly people to do deals.

To their credit, neither raised a perfectly groomed eyebrow.

'Oh yes,' said one, neutrally, as if I'd asked where a treatment room to have my vegan nail polish reapplied in the spa was.

'It's in the private room. Upstairs.' She gestured towards a staircase.

Little tea-lights had been placed all the way up the minimalist, narrow ascending passage, which seemed to be detached in some clever way from the walls on either side. It was very dark and secretive here in the club after the public glare of the sun outside, and as I climbed, I sensed the pulse of the day change and quicken, and my heart started to beat under my ribs, and I started to feel warm and flushed in my clinging cashmere jersey.

I had no idea that in a matter of minutes, I would be feeling even hotter without it.

Bunny Princess's sex column in the March issue of *Mary Jane* magazine (reprinted with kind permission of the publishers, Hurst Corp.):

So, readers . . .

What on earth am I doing on a lazy Sunday afternoon, standing (in only my bra and pants), while a young man in a kilt lashes me with a bullwhip, cracking the leather and rope so fast and so skilfully that he can both break the sound barrier and lightly graze my left nipple at the same time?

Good question. Before I answer it, I have a sham-
ing confession to make. I've never been big on spanking
myself. I've always sworn not to write about it. I've never
fantasised about anyone flogging my backside – funny,
that – with a cane. I have no yearning to be placed over
teacher's knee and taught a lesson I'll never forget. The
only time I've even come near to being spanked was
when I was at school and I was offered the choice of the
slipper or not going home on an exeat (this was a very
traditional boarding school, as you might have gathered)
and I innocently chose the slipper. It sounded cosy.

The headmaster went a bit grey after I informed him
of my decision. He liked, generally, to beat his charges
bare-bottomed. But his charges were boys, not girls.
There were only two girls in the school: me and Steph, a
strapping wench who liked nothing more than a violent
game of hockey on an icy February afternoon.

He assumed, silly man, that as a fluffy little female,
I would choose not to see my parents, even though they
lived abroad and I only saw them a couple of times a
term, simply to avoid the stain, the pain, of corporal
punishment.

He was wrong. He had boxed himself into a corner.
Soon, he would be calling me, an eleven-year-old girl
into his study, asking me to remove my attractive, elas-
tic high-waisters, asking me to touch my toes, before he
set about my buttocks with a carpet slipper. I almost
laughed when I saw his face sag at the grim prospect.

Later that day, I found myself seated alone in my form-room, completing a Latin grammar test. He had bottled out.

But would I?

Well, it is true that I paused outside the door saying SPANKING SALON. I debated briefly with myself whether I would enter, fulfil my professional obligations to you, or slink home, tail safely tucked between my legs, rather than horse-whipped. I took a deep breath, and pushed the door open. Try anything once, I told myself. Except Morris-dancing and incest. I am a reporter. This a job. Indeed – this is my job.

A silence fell as the door swung open. I stepped in, and halted. I raked the room with my gaze, just to see what was in store, before taking in the scene. Carefully presented couples in variations of black, denim, cashmere and leather sat on chairs in a circle. Several pairs were wearing buttery suede trousers the colour of shortbread. I wondered whether that was a secret Masonic signal – how spankers revealed themselves to each other.

A table was littered with cuffs and chains, and crops and cuffs, and switches and other bridlery and saddlery. Now, I like shopping as much as the next girl, but none of these retail items were my thing at all. Frankly, even though I gravitate towards stalls selling hand-knits and macramé bags at village fêtes, I easily resisted the pull of the cat-o'-nine tails, and imagined I would never find regular use for that black, mean-looking designer sjam-bok, however beautifully tooled.

In the middle of the room, encircled by participants, a slim young man in a kilt and biker boots, with dra-matic slash eyebrows, and a tight T-shirt that showed off his broad shoulders and narrow waist, was holding a whip. Now, talk about beautifully tooled. He was much more my thing.

There was also a dominatrix-type woman of breath-takingly curvaceous, wasp-waisted proportions whose chair was slightly forward of the circle, denoting her position of power within the group.

'Ah,' the young man said, pointing the whip at me as I stood uncertainly in the doorway, as if they had all been expecting me.

'Our volunteer.'

Before I can slip onto an empty chair, he holds out his hand, and leads me into the middle of the circle. Everyone looks at me with interest, as if they have paid for this floor show and are determined to get their mon-ey's worth.

'So, how much prior experience have you had?' I am asked (everyone else there, it turns out, is either well into whipping or has completed Spanking Skills 1).

'None at all,' I squeak. 'I'm a novice.' As soon as the words fall from my lips, I realise my mistake.

There is an intake of breath around the circle, and the kilted man gives a significant glance to Jessica Rabbit, the woman in vertiginous, teetering heels, with a tiny waist, long black locks, white skin and a lush red mouth. She pivots, and pouts at me.

A novice! I can almost hear them thinking. And novices must be . . . broken in, I sense, just as a thick steak has to be tenderised before being slapped on the barbie. My heart begins to hammer and I look around, searching for my escape. Do I tell them that I'm here as a journalist? To write about the spanking lesson? Or do I keep schtum?

Any minute now, I am going to be whipped in front of a roomful of strangers. Unless I speak up. My mouth drops open, the words of my abject confession already taking shape, but it's too late to stop now.

The man in the kilt comes up to me and looks me up and down. He has a well-defined, rosy mouth, a straight nose, and almond-shaped eyes. His hair is dark and thick and spiky.

'I'm Cobra,' he says. Something inside me says, You've got to be kidding, what's your real name? I bet it's Timmy, or Jeremy, but I am distracted. Cobra has reached to my waist and draws my jersey over my head.

I am standing in just skirt, boots and bra.

'I'm Bunny,' I say.

Then he undoes my skirt, and draws it down to my knees. Obediently, like a child, I step out of it. I keep the boots on.

So now I am standing in boots, black pants and black bra.

With his warm hands on my white shoulders, he guides me into position. 'Stand still,' he commands.

Crack! *cracks the bullwhip, and the leather length encircles my torso, like a slithery, stinging hug.*

Crack! Crack! *Cobra the dominant is working up a slight sheen. He flexes his taut arm further back, as if he really intends me harm. The leather whip unfurls like a snake towards me, hissing through the air.*

Then it hurts. *I am smarting, and when I look down, I see a red line, like a belt, appear faintly around my hips. 'Ow,' I squeak. But he ignores me. He knows exactly how much he didn't hurt me, and I am squeaking too soon.*

He does it again. Crack!

'Stop,' *I beg. He raises an eyebrow, and drops his arm. 'Sit,' he says.*

I return to my seat, unharmed: and unwelted. The dominant had been kind. But later, we are paired off for role play (oh, you know, stable girls, naughty maids, army majors – the usual) and he comes up to adjust my technique as I am striking the bethonged buttocks of a pole-dancer with a – I can't believe I'm writing this – riding crop.

'Your arm's too stiff,' he complains, taking the crop. 'Bend over, Bunny.' I bend over. But he pulls me straight and, without asking, without so much as by your leave, he removes my skirt. I step out of it obediently, like a small child with Mum in the changing room at the swimming pool.

Then his hands come back to my body and, without saying anything, he pulls down my specially chosen sporty black knickers, arranges me over a chair and starts, very expertly and with an unmistakable zest of cruelty, to stripe my bare buttocks with a riding crop, just allowing the pain to burn and then simmer and then gently glow and prickle before striking me again.

I have never been beaten by anyone before on my bare bottom, but of one thing I am clear. Cobra is a true master of his craft.

'That's enough,' I say, after a short while, anxious that I am showing a high pain threshold and soon he will have me screaming for mercy, but embarrassingly, anxious that everyone will see how much I seem to be enjoying it.

So, I hear you ask, does this Miss Whiplash recommend?

Well, I reply, it's what turns you on, of course. But, after having been expertly flogged by a professional dominant in front of a roomful of total strangers, I can tell you that, for me, spanking held, if nothing else, a . . . novelty value at least.

As for you, I'd say, if you're remotely interested, it's like everything else. There's no harm – well, it depends how hard you work at it, of course – in giving it a go. See you next month. The bruises should have subsided by then, I hope.

Copyright © Bunny Princess

After I was thrashed, Cobra and Jessica Rabbit toasted my progress with champagne. I put my clothes on, embraced my newfound friends, promised I would visit Cobra in his dungeon, where he flogs bankers to within an inch of their lives while their trophy wives are having their hair done, and went home.

But something had been kindled inside me. At the club, I'd felt almost ashamed by how much I enjoyed the anticipation, followed by the release of pain, followed by the high of the after-burn. After all, this was the one fetish I had sworn I would never even try at home, let alone in Soho House with a bunch of abuser-friendly sadomasochists on a quiet Sunday in November.

It was so exciting, back there, that I even worried at one point – I think it was when the delicious Cobra was intent on my rear end – that any second, the squirming, itchy, lustful sensation that was building, as swish followed swish, and wriggle followed wriggle, would lead to me making a prat of myself. Nor could I ever admit, not to Viv or my readers, that after I'd been soundly thrashed, I accepted Cobra's invitation to whip him next. How could I tell the readers of *Mary Jane* that I'd done that?

But I did. I took the crop, while Cobra leaned on the back of the chair. With one practised action, he flipped up his kilt, so I was presented with a pair of perfect, muscular, jutting buttocks. I paused for a second to admire his bum and his fine legs, felt sad that I couldn't see his beautiful cock, which I felt sure from the flush in his cheeks would

be beaded at its eager, rosy tip, and then did what I was
told.

'Harder,' he kept saying, as I built up a head of steam
and began thrashing him with all my might, feeling mighty
relieved that nobody I knew was in the room, and nobody
knew me. 'Harder, Bunny! Get your arm right back, and go
for it.'

No wonder that when I got home, I was still on fire. During supper, I flung pans, and complained about having to do
everything myself. I was most unmaternal. I snapped at the
children about mess and mugs left around, before heading to
my study to write my copy (I like to write it when it's fresh)
and that, of course, only made things worse.

I was dying for release; I couldn't waste something this
hot and strong. But I didn't know how to convey . . . my need.

I didn't know what I wanted. I prowled around, beside
myself. What I had had was so good, it had to keep. Obviously, I couldn't say so, wouldn't say so, in so many words, in
print, but the spanking class was a revelation. I was – for the
first time in *years* – hornier than a rhino's face. But no way
was I going to admit it. Not even to Heck (short for Hector).
He'd laugh at me. So would Viv. If I ever admitted I found it
a huge turn-on – let alone reveal that to the growing readership of *Mary Jane* – I'd never hear the end of it. So I lay in
bed, my hands trailing over my breasts and between my legs.
I idly picked up a magazine that was lying on the floor, and
read the contents page. It was *GQ*, so I read my competition – the female sex columnist. Her copy was called 'A Bug's

Life'. I skimmed it and realised that there was, after all, no law that dictated female sex columnists should be committed prudes.

My breath quickened as I read it:

'I found myself telling him to fuck me properly in the arse. All the way in. The next time, he did. A finger, at first gentle, then firm: then came the condom, coated with lubricant, filled with his erection. I was on my knees. He lowly pushed against my anus, through the tight ring of muscle, and penetrated me, first with only an inch or so of cock . . . I wanted more, and he fucked me properly, this time, sliding all the way in.'

I heard Heck come up, to brush his teeth, so I quickly read to the end:

'Girlfriends, if you're reading this, think again. This is what you want. You want his fingers in your pussy, while he's putting lube over your arse, into your anus. Take the largest vibrator, turn it up to high, and slide it into you. Ask him to massage more lube into your arse, and follow that with his erect cock, penetrating through your anus, stretching the sphincter' – I heard the bathroom door – *'Then tell him to fuck you, all the way. Then harder. If you won't, you don't know what you're missing.'*

I slid the magazine under the bed, and waited for Heck to join me.

'So how did it go? I can't wait to hear – do tell me,' Heck begged, as he came to bed at last.

'Oh,' I said, snuggling up to him, and pressing my hot little naked body to his. 'It was okay. A bit disappointing, actually.'

I trailed my fingers over his thighs. His penis lay sleepily coiled, like a mollusc. But me – it felt as if someone had anointed my pussy with liquid lust. By now, I was throbbing between my legs and was trying not to moan out loud, because I was too proud, and too coy, to admit the dual reasons for my arousal. I was, after all, on record about it.

I was still feeling the striping across my buttocks, and seeing Cobra's proud male ass in my mind's eye, and burning.

'Oh, come on,' he protested. 'You can't get away with not telling me. I demand you tell me.'

So I told him about being bullwhipped in my panties in front of strangers, and of being thrashed on my naked buttocks, and then, the *pièce de rèsistance*, when I took the crop to the perfect globes of Cobra, under the watchful tutelage of Jessica Rabbit.

By the time I'd finished, Heck's cock was straining against my hand, and I could feel his glans pumping, and his balls had tautened to cluster at the root of his penis, like coconuts on a palm tree.

I levered myself so that I was on top of him, and his bright hard gaze looked up at me. His long lashes were swept back, and his blue eyes penetrated my soul and seemed to scour me for what I really wanted.

I mounted him immediately, just so that I had the release of something hard and throbbing inside me, and rode him, pitched forward so the angle of his penetration was deep and lashing.

I came almost immediately and fell onto his chest, panting. But he wasn't finished, not by a long chalk. My description of the afternoon's flogging had lit kindled something within him too, something fierce and brutal.

'Turn over,' he ordered.

I flipped, like a dying mackerel, so I was lying face-down. Then I heard him open the drawer next to the bed, and I felt something cold glisten on my anus, where I was already wet from my orgasm. He anointed me carefully, and then placed his rock-hard penis against my closed rose. Straight away, it unclenched, as if it was waiting for this, and only this.

He pushed in an inch, and I felt a ring of pain flare. But as soon as I complained, he stopped pushing, and then the pain eased, to be replaced by an absolute determination to hold all of his thick, throbbing cock inside my anus.

'Hold on,' I said. I opened my bedside drawer and removed my vibrator. I went high onto all fours, and inserted it deep into my vagina, and placed it on high.

I had to fight off an instant orgasm, so I switched it off but left it snugly in place. Heck resumed his position and thrust his cock halfway in – four inches – and left it there. I moaned. It felt – so incredibly, hornily bad; so wrong, but so good. I thought I would pass out. But I didn't want to miss a second. He started thrusting in and out, slowly but rhythmically. I switched the vibrator on.

His breathing was becoming jagged and his actions rougher. I was on the point of the most thunderous orgasm of my entire life, and as I heard him cry out, I let myself go.

In the morning, I had an email from Liz, the editor of *Mary Jane*.

> Dear Bunny,
>
> Loved your copy about the spanking salon! I've sent it upstairs and Nick, the managing editor, totally loves it too. So thanks for that.
>
> Can we discuss next week's assignment? Now you've broken your taboo about spanking, do you think it's time to cross the next Rubicon? The AS piece, which I've been on at you for YEARS to write and about which you are so strangely prudish!
>
> Come on, Bunny – you owe your readers no less! Otherwise, I'll make you write for the seventh time this year about the decline in female libido and what wives can do to spice up their intensely dull sex lives with their run-to-seed husbands, and make you try each new technique in turn.
>
> Consider yourself warned.
>
> Let me know. Liz.

I deleted the email and went downstairs, pausing on my

way down only to remove the pair of padded pants, which I had ordered as a precaution, from my bag and lightly drop them in the bin, with a satisfied smirk playing across my lips.

Breaking the Rules

POM POM PARADISE

'Tonight's the night,' she sang quietly as she traced the gloss applicator round her lips and pouted at her reflection. She inspected her face closely for any telltale smear of foundation, knowing it would destroy the illusion that the look she'd just spent the past half an hour achieving was 'natural'. Dropping her robe to the floor, she unclipped her straight, naturally blonde hair, long enough to tickle her nipples, and cupped a breast in each hand. They were nicely rounded and pert, tweaked upwards by a cosmetic surgeon two years previously, and her stomach was washboard flat thanks to not having kids and a diet that consisted mostly of steamed food that tasted of cardboard.

She was thirty but looked closer to twenty-five, with large dark-brown eyes and thick lashes, a perfectly straight nose, courtesy of Mother Nature, and a full mouth covering the even, white teeth, courtesy of 'Mother Fucker', as she'd called him shortly after receiving his iniquitous bill for veneering and bleaching.

When she was a child, her mother's battle cry had been Helena Rubenstein's assertion that there were no ugly women, only lazy ones, and now, maintaining and enhancing her looks had become a way of life for her too. She was only five foot six – nothing a pair of killer heels couldn't fix – and perfectly in proportion, with slim, sexily muscular thighs that tapered to shapely calves. She felt sorry for those with 'cankles', where the calf and ankle are indistinguishable in thickness, sentencing them to a life spent in trousers or knee-high boots, but hers were finely turned and could be displayed to great effect. If it wasn't for her height, she could probably have been a model.

'Go get him,' she murmured quietly, before padding through to the bedroom.

She was pretty sure he'd be there tonight so she had chosen her outfit carefully. To him, the chase was clearly everything. She guessed he liked women whose sexiness was understated, not obvious – the Royal feMail of the dating world: someone who promised much but with no guarantee of delivery.

Selecting her sheerest pair of black stockings with lace tops, she hooked them up to her suspender belt and inspected herself in the mirror. Like most women, she found them an impractical but deadly weapon in the armoury of seduction. From plumbers to paramedics, chartered surveyors to property magnates, even presidents . . . whatever their skill or intelligence she marvelled how, throughout history, so many powerful men had been brought crashing to their knees, both physically and professionally, by the sight of some black nylon and a few poppers.

She smiled at the predictability of it as she selected a black balconette bra, prettily teasing the ornate lace so it showcased her breasts to maximum effect, before gingerly edging up the matching black pants that were held in place by two perilously flimsy, sheer side panels.

Next came her favourite black silk shirt, with its inviting softness and distinctive chrome buttons, the third one being ideally placed to reveal enough of her cleavage to appear unintentionally sexy rather than one centimetre lower and desperately exhibitionist. Then the black crêpe de Chine pencil skirt, tailored to tightly follow the contours of her firm bottom, ending just above the knee, and finally, the patent black Yves Saint Laurent stilettos with a six-inch metal heel that screamed, 'Fuck me, but don't fuck with me'.

It was a warm night so she abandoned the idea of a coat and attracted several admiring and some downright lascivious glances as she sashayed her way to the nearby bar where she'd first noticed him two nights ago, sitting alone in the far corner, occasionally chatting to the staff but otherwise seemingly comfortable in his solitude.

With thick black hair in a half-inch crop and startlingly blue eyes, he looked like a movie star version of a war hero: broodingly handsome with a determined jaw and wide, strong shoulders. Wearing an expensively tailored suit and a crisp, white shirt, he'd exuded the faint arrogance of the wealthy, an assumption borne out when he flipped open his Louis Vuitton wallet and pulled out a black American Express card.

An image suddenly flashed in her mind of his face, just inches from hers, contorted in the agony of ecstasy, his shoulder muscles straining to bear his weight as he lay on top of her. Stopping for a moment, she closed her eyes and took a deep breath of the warm night air. If she wanted to seduce him, she knew she had to stay in control.

The first night she'd seen him, she'd popped in at the tail-end of a long jog, her face sweating and devoid of make-up, her hair scraped back in a ponytail. He'd barely glanced in her direction so she'd quickly surmised that his kind of woman was one whose appearance shouted, 'game on'. This was confirmed the following night when she had watched him idly studying the curves of a young flame-haired woman wearing what her brother always described as a 'barbed-wire fence' dress, serving its purpose but not restricting the view. As the woman ordered drinks, 'Brad Fit', as she was now mentally referring to him, had leaned forward to say something and the woman had thrown back her head in a throaty laugh, exposing the smooth paleness of her throat before hanging on his every word as she idly twirled a strand of Titianesque hair around her finger. You didn't have to be Desmond Morris to know she found him very sexy indeed. But seconds later, another man appeared at her side to help carry the drinks and the woman was gone, leaving him alone again.

Checking her reflection in a shop window, she smoothed down her skirt and made sure her shirt collar was turned down neatly. Tonight was Friday and she was almost certain he'd be there. If so, *this time* she planned to be the one catching his attention. A few steps further and she was pushing open the door to the bar, reeling slightly as the noise and intense heat hit her.

It was packed with braying City types, the men in ubiquitous pinstripes and clichéd red braces, the women resembling delegates at an Alice-band convention. Craning her neck to see over them, she felt a thud of disappointment as she noted his usual seat was occupied by a blond surf-dude type in a baseball cap and a T-shirt that read I LOVE ANIMALS: THEY'RE DELICIOUS.

All this bloody effort for nothing, she thought mutinously, wincing slightly as she felt one of the suspender poppers digging in to her leg. Sighing, she stood motionless for a few seconds, like a Covent Garden performance artist affecting a statue position amid a maelstrom of passers-by. One drink, she decided, the alternative being to slope away sheepishly, like a strippergram who's turned up at the wrong venue.

The queue at the bar was three-deep and it was at least ten minutes before she nudged her way to the front where, above the optics, a sign fashioned like a gravestone read: THE DEAD BARMAN: GOD FINALLY CAUGHT HIS EYE. She stared unblinkingly at the nearest one while, to her right, a large red-faced man in a grey suit waved his arms like an air-traffic controller as the staff studiously ignored him.

'Nightmare, isn't it?' he boomed at her. 'If I ever get bloody served, can I get you a drink?'

Outside every slim woman there's a fat man trying to get in, she thought wearily. Smiling enigmatically, she shook her head, not wishing to appear rude but anxious not to engage with him either. From past experience she knew that one drink would lead to more and, undoubtedly, at some point between now and closing time, a bumbling attempt on his part to slobber all over her.

'Lighten up, love, it's only a drink.' His expression had hardened slightly, enough to suddenly make her uncomfortable about drinking alone.

She was about to fight her way back through the crowd when someone behind her touched her forearm.

'Forget it mate, she's with me.'

She turned, following the voice. It was *him*, wearing the same suit, but this time teamed with an aquamarine shirt that enhanced his strikingly blue eyes.

'Yeah, whatever,' muttered the other man, glaring at her before turning his back on them and resuming his mission of getting served.

'Bet his family tree's got no branches,' muttered Brad Fit, pulling a 'duh' expression then following it up with a killer smile. 'Now I've saved you from his clutches, I'd better buy you a drink for authenticity.'

She nodded gratefully, glancing with practised ease to his left hand. No wedding ring and no giveaway pale indentation of one having been recently removed either.

'A white wine, thanks.' She pointed towards the back of the crowd. 'I'll wait back there.'

Finding a small table, she rummaged in her handbag and pulled out a compact mirror, hastily checking her lipstick and hair. She felt an adrenalin rush of nerves and breathed deeply to try and calm herself. Normally cucumber-cool when meeting new men, this rising apprehension was alien to her. But this was no ordinary mortal, this was a love god in human form. As he pushed his way through the melee towards her, two glasses held aloft, she was able to study his face for the first time. His eyes were even more piercing close up, with flecks of yellow that gave him the look of an innately dangerous big cat, currently in repose but liable to pounce at any time. If she was lucky.

'There you go.' He set down her wine.

'Thanks.' She smiled and extended her hand. 'I'm . . .'

'Sssssh.' He placed a finger against her lips. It smelt deliciously musky. 'Being strangers is much more fun.'

Her skin tingled with anticipation as his eyes travelled seductively down her body, widening slightly as he reached her feet.

'Now *those* are "fuck me" shoes,' he said casually. Again, the image of them having sex flashed through her mind. Jesus Christ, she thought, I need to get a grip here.

Two glasses of wine later and the only grip on her mind was that of her French-manicured fingers encircling his cock. They'd talked about music, films and politics, but her train of thought had been interrupted several times when she'd glanced down and seen the large bulge straining against his trousers. Now, fuelled by alcohol, she'd given up all pretence of normal conversation and was openly staring at it. He followed her gaze and grinned.

'See what you're doing to me?'

He rested his hand near the hemline of her skirt, his thumb slowly circling her flesh. She felt the familiar warm spread of wetness in her pants as he ventured further and felt the lace of her suspenders, letting out a low groan.

'Stockings.' Now he was actually fucking her with those eyes. 'Are you meeting someone?'

She dragged her gaze away from his crotch and shook her head. 'Was,' she lied. 'She rang and cancelled while you were at the bar.'

It sounded pathetically unconvincing but he didn't seem to notice. Or perhaps he didn't care. He leaned forward, his face so close to hers she could feel his hot breath on her cheek.

'Stockings for a girls' night out. You're my kind of woman.'

He moved his chair closer and she felt the muscles of her groin contract with raw lust. She wanted to grab him and push her mouth against his, but with a man like this she knew it was important that *he* came to her. So she stayed unflinchingly still. Seconds later he obliged, his mouth reaching hers, gently tugging her top lip with his teeth before flicking his exploring tongue inside her mouth. The fine hairs on the back of her neck pricked to attention and it took a superhuman effort for her not to spread her legs right there in the bar and put his hand where she wanted it.

Now his tongue was running across her lower lip, his eyes faintly mocking as he toyed with her, like a bird of prey gently pecking at a mouse before devouring it in one go. As he started to kiss her neck, her insides went on to spin cycle, the roughness of his chin igniting her nerve endings, like hundreds of tiny fireworks exploding at once. Then he started to nibble her ear, occasionally inserting his tongue.

'Hmm, you can't beat aural sex,' she murmured, hoping humour might allow her to regain a little control. He stopped and afforded the remark a passing nod and a quick smile before resuming the look of a beautiful devil.

'Do you live near here?'

She knew the question was as loaded as the trouser torpedo now visibly pointing in her direction.

'I'm in a hotel round the corner.'

'Perfect. Let's go.'

He stood up and grabbed her arm, lifting her with him before placing his hand on the lower crevice of her back and propelling her towards the door. His arrogance in assuming she would have sex with him was breathtaking, but she didn't care. In fact it suited her needs. He wanted to fuck her and that was all she needed to know.

Out in the street, he nuzzled her neck, his tiny bites prompting a pulsing ache between her legs. His left hand was rubbing her thigh through the thin material of her skirt, dwelling on the suspenders.

'I'm going to fuck you senseless,' he whispered.

Her palms now sticky with sweat, she deliberately con-
tracted her pelvic muscles in a vain bid to get some relief
from the dull throbbing of her clitoris, but, if anything,
it made it worse. She had never known anything like it,
this primeval, animalistic urge to fuck that was so strong
she wanted them to do it right there in the street, like two
dogs.

'Here's the hotel.' The words caught in her throat as she
grabbed his hand and led him through the small foyer to
the waiting lift. As the doors closed, he pressed her against
the wall, his hand yanking her shirt and bra to one side as
he lowered his head and began sucking and biting an erect
nipple. She slid her knee between his legs, moving it back
and forth across his rock-hard cock.

The lift jerked to a halt, momentarily bringing her to her
senses. She pushed him away, hastily rearranged her clothes
and stepped out to an empty corridor. Her room was right in
front of them and her fingers were already curled round the
key inside her handbag. But she paused a moment, pretending she couldn't find it, needing a few moments to think.

Her plan had never been to actually fuck him. It was
against the rules she set herself. She'd just wanted to flirt
and perhaps play around a little, before saying she wasn't the
kind of girl who went all the way on a first date.

But sexual frustration was bubbling inside her and she
knew the minute she put that key in the door, there was
no going back. He wanted to fuck her senseless, as he'd so

succinctly put it, and she felt overwhelmed by the urge to fuck him right back.

She had opened the door just an inch before he placed his palm flat against it and shoved, using his powerful body strength to push her into the room. Booting the door closed, he used his left hand to press her against the wall while his right dropped to the hemline of her skirt, yanking it up so it bunched around her waist and stayed there. His mouth bore down on hers, rendering her immobile and freeing his hands, one to grip her buttock, the other roughly tearing her pants before he jammed his fingers into her, sliding them in and out. The pleasure was all-consuming and at that point, any will she had to stop him was abandoned, smothered by her need to feel him inside her.

She tugged at his trousers and boxer shorts, pulling them down until his cock sprang out gratefully into her waiting hands. Caressing it, she admired its size and smoothness. Fuck, she thought, even his bloody *dick* is gorgeous.

Moving his mouth away from hers, he tore apart her shirt, sending two of the buttons clattering to the wooden floor. She noticed him bend his knees slightly, manoeuvring himself into position.

'Wait,' she panted, using his cock to gently tug him further into the room until they were alongside the double bed. 'Here.'

Pushing her backwards on to the pure white duvet, he used his knee to spread her legs while removing his shirt with a sleight of hand that suggested he'd done it many times before. She stared admiringly at his broad, tanned shoulders and hairy chest, which tapered to a thin, downy line that crossed his taut abdomen and led tantalisingly to his groin. Following it with her tongue, she edged her way slowly down towards his cock before working her way up it with small butterfly-kisses. Reaching the top, she circled her tongue around its rim, as if licking a melting ice-cream, smiling triumphantly to herself as she heard his low groan of pleasure.

She was about to push him fully into her mouth when suddenly he pulled away and buried his head between the soft flesh of her thighs, nibbling and licking everything but her throbbing clitoris. She pushed her pelvis forward, desperate for the feel of his tongue, but he would only flick across it, causing a brief explosion of desire before deliberately retreating, abandoning her on the brink of ecstasy.

Unable to bear it, she started to masturbate, but he pushed her hand away and stood up, lowering himself onto her while using his teeth to grip the underwire of her bra and tug it above her breasts. Moving from one to the other, he gently bit at each nipple, the tip of his cock poised for action, nudging against the flimsy lace barring its entry. She felt his hands near her groin, then the sound of lace ripping before he thrust his hips forward and she felt a searing pain tear through her followed by waves of ecstasy as he moved in and out.

As she moaned with pleasure, she felt him shifting slightly, see-sawing his hips until his pubic bone touched her clitoris, then rhythmically swaying from side to side, rubbing, stimulating until she felt the familiar rush of warmth spreading from her groin through her entire body. As the climax surged through her, she let out a cry of raw abandonment.

Subtly pressing her cheek against the bedcover to sap up the moisture, she turned to face him again, lifting her stockinged legs so they were wrapped around his back, her metal heels digging into his flesh.

'Do you want me to fuck you harder?' he panted.

Not waiting for an answer, he upped the pressure, barely breathless as he muttered, 'Is that good? Do you want more?' She nodded, digging her nails into the firm flesh of his back as she pushed her hips forward and her clitoris connected with his pubic bone again. After a few more well-placed thrusts, another orgasm powered through her and he simultaneously growled, 'Fucking *hell*' before rapidly pulling out and ejaculating over her stomach, rivulets of semen running down her sides from the overflowing pool in her navel.

He'd left ten minutes later, muttering something about an early flight the next morning, the piercing eyes that minutes earlier had seemed so invitingly sexy now cold and detached.

After he'd gone, she lay back on the bed and stared at the ceiling, replaying every second of their Olympian fuck and feeling like an empty husk, her mouth dry and sore from his teeth mashing into it. She felt spent, battered and bruised, but she gently caressed herself to an easy third orgasm with thoughts of him powering in and out of her before falling flaccid by her side, a glistening, panting Adonis whose heady smell of musk, fresh sweat and sex she'd wanted to bottle and keep for ever.

'We must do this again sometime,' she'd said matter of factly, breaking another of her rules. But she couldn't help herself. This man was like the worst kind of drug, a quick high followed by the low of feeling like a spent force, with aching limbs and the will to even breathe almost sapped out of you. But the all-consuming rush of pleasure as he'd fucked her had far outweighed the crash of the aftermath and she wanted him again. And again.

'Sure,' he'd replied casually, scribbling a number on hotel notepaper and handing it to her. 'Give me a call sometime.'

Sometime. That vague word uttered by men the world over as they leave the side of a new sexual conquest. What does it mean exactly? Tomorrow? Next week? Or 'you'll never clap eyes on me again'? It wasn't a situation she'd encountered before. Usually, the men in her life fell into two categories: those she met through friends and got to know gradually, perhaps dating a few times before starting a proper relationship. And those she met in bars or clubs and flirted with, perhaps sharing a passionless fumble before demanding they leave. Never had she wanted to see *those* men again. Until now.

Sighing, she sat up and placed the piece of paper next to the phone, glancing at it occasionally as she moved around the room collecting her clothes. Gathering up her shoes, skirt and suspenders, she laid them on the bed and walked across to the door, stooping down to gather her shirt buttons before scrutinising her torn pants and throwing them into the bin as a lost cause.

Tugging on jeans and a sweatshirt, she extracted a wet wipe from her bag and ran it over her face, removing the make-up that still bore the smudged imprint of their passion. The delicate skin around her mouth was red-raw from his stubble, so too were her inner thighs. She closed her eyes, trying to recapture the ecstasy of the moment his cock rammed into her, but she couldn't. From now on, she knew no one would ever satisfy her as brutally and wholly as he had. Sitting on the edge of the bed, she took a deep breath and picked up the piece of paper again, studying the neat slanted writing. Reaching for the phone, she punched in the number.

As it started to ring, she felt a swell of apprehension rise in her chest. What would she say if he answered? It was a landline number, so surely he couldn't have got back home that quickly? She hoped not, she just wanted to check it was genuine before deciding what to do next.

Click. Someone had picked it up. Her heart skipped a beat.

'Hello?' It was a man's voice, but he sounded foreign.

Shit, she thought, I don't even know a name to ask for.

'Um, hello, sorry to bother you, but does anyone live there except you?'

'No one live here,' said the voice, probably Eastern European she now deduced. 'This is dry-cleaners.'

Slamming the receiver back on its cradle, she stared at it uncomprehendingly for several seconds, before shaking her head slowly and emitting a small snort of resignation and disbelief.

'You bastard,' she muttered out loud. 'You absolute, Grade-A fucking *bastard*.'

Picking up the piece of paper, she folded it carefully and tucked it in the side pocket of her handbag before walking across to the TV cabinet and lifting down the small overnight bag resting on top of it. She opened it to reveal a compact digital movie camera, positioned so its lens pressed against a small pinhole, externally disguised by an elaborate dragon motif embroidered down the side.

Lifting out the camera, she pressed rewind for about one minute, then play. The tiny screen fired into life at the exact moment she'd cried out with joy during the first orgasm, and she watched intently as she twisted her face to wipe away the tear. Sighing heavily, she rewound it to the point where they'd burst in the door and he'd torn at her clothes, then deleted what came after before carefully placing the camera back in the bag.

Scanning her mobile for the number she needed, she pressed it to her ear, staring forlornly into the middle distance. On the third ring, it was answered.

'Hi, it's me. How's the weather in Barbados?' She listened for a few seconds, idly scraping her finger across a denim snag on her jeans. 'Sounds lovely. Look, sorry to ruin your holiday, but I'm afraid you were right.'

She let out a long, sad sigh of regret, not for the person at the other end of the phone, but for herself and the gut-wrenching realisation that although he'd affected her so deeply, to him she'd been just another fuck.

'I came very close to having sex with your husband last night and I have all the evidence you asked for.'

The Poodle Dog

KITTEN MONTAUK

'Oh, Mr Collins! I have never seen such a grand place in all my life!'

Jack Collins smiled as Brigid, awestruck, looked around her. Her wide eyes drank in the elegant smocked wallpaper, the French ceiling mural, the fine linen tablecloths and the polished cutlery, which reflected the dazzle of the chandeliers. She observed with lively curiosity the passage of the uniformed waiters, starched napkins laid over their forearms, transporting hot platters protected by great silver domes. Her cute little nose with its one sweet freckle at the tip sniffed at the air, aromatic with cream and butter, venison and liver. Gaping at the fine, rich fashions of the lady diners, she glanced down at her own, hand-sewn outfit with a touch of self-consciousness. Jack Collins could not have been more pleased. Brigid's naive enthusiasm was as appealing as her waist, cinched so tightly into its corset he could have spanned it with his hands. It was as charming as her eyes, bright and sparkling as Frisco Bay on this perfect spring day.

'Best meal for a dollar you can get in this town, Miss Callaghan,' Jack Collins proclaimed, as though he'd had something to do with it. His adopted town made him swell with pride. 'San Francisco really knows how to put on the dog,' he added.

It was true. Gold had lent the town shine and flash. You could see it in such high-class establishments as the Palace Hotel, where Society arrived in fancy broughams to sup in the glass-domed dining room before going to see an opera at the Alcazar, 'the most elegant Moorish Theatre in the world'. Not that you'd find Jack Collins at the opera. Vaudeville was more his style.

There were plenty of men like Jack Collins in San Francisco. If Frisco had come up since the early days of the gold rush, it was still a wild town, rough as guts. It was also a forgiving town, one that gave a man the kind of second chance he'd never get back in Iowa. Jack Collins had grabbed a third and fourth as well. His fortunes had risen and fallen as precipitously as the Bay City's streets. He'd done well for himself in the gold rush, less so with his investments. At least he hadn't been as foolish as some he'd met in his panning days – men so thoughtless of the future they had boozed away half their takings and had the rest picked from their pockets as they slept it off. Jack Collins' real genius had been to take passage out to that other wild town of the Pacific,

Yokohama, where he developed an eye for curios and silks and a knack for trading them. After a sad little episode with a Japanese sing-song girl and a series of tragic ones with a variety of Western harlots, Jack Collins lost his taste for whores and developed a hankering for virgins.

Virgins weren't easy to come by in Frisco. If the town was teeming with men with secret histories, quick fists and big ideas, it was also full of fast women ready to kick up their heels, drink a man under the table and dig the gold the men had mined. Even Frisco's heiresses were known to chase a fire for the firemen, and everyone knew how Society matron 'Big Alma' had come to her mansion on Pacific Heights, or they had a pretty good idea. In the kind of circles Jack Collins travelled in, a virgin, especially a young and pretty one, was a rare prize. Most of the ones he heard about were on auction Saturday nights at Madam Carrie's Brothel – and then again the Saturday night after that. Jack Collins was not fool enough to fall for that one. Girls from good families, meanwhile, were scarcely going to look at someone like him, even if he had made a reasonable packet with his business.

Jack Collins ran a tidy little store selling jewellery and treasures from the Extreme East in a neighbourhood that may not have been the wealthiest one in town, but was respectable enough. One morning, a Mrs Callaghan came into the store with her lovely daughter Brigid. It did not escape Jack Collins' notice that Brigid was ripe as a summer peach and just as juicy. The awkward manner in which she fiddled with the buttons on her gloves, the way she blushed when directly addressed and her shy, darting glances got him going right then and there. He wanted her badly. He also knew that virgins could not be rushed; anyway, there was no joy to be had in rushing them.

So he had taken his time. Mrs Callaghan left her card, so he sent her a note, thanking her for her custom and asking after her delightful daughter. Had she liked the ivory hairpins? Jack Collins fretted over his penmanship and his spelling. He needn't have worried. Mother and daughter visited the shop again soon after, and a pleasant acquaintance was struck up. When some weeks later, a blessed opportunity left him alone with Brigid for a few minutes, he whispered an invitation to lunch. She looked startled. Roses bloomed in her cheeks.

'Mother says one must never go to a restaurant alone with a man,' she demurred. 'Only fancy women do that.' The phrase 'fancy women' caused her voice to tremble adorably.

'Surely,' he persisted, 'it is different when the man has no ill intentions and is a friend of the family, as I hope you and your mother consider me by now.'

Brigid looked down at her hands. 'I could ask her permission,' she said. 'But I doubt she would grant it.' She twiddled the pink satin ribbons on her skirt. She looked up, saw his disappointment and bit her lip. 'Or perhaps . . .'

'Perhaps?'

'Perhaps,' she said, her words tumbling out, 'perhaps I could just tell her I was taking tea with cousin Mary.'

Jack Collins smiled. The luck of the Irish was with him, or at least, luck with the Irish.

The day of their date finally came. With one hand lightly resting on Brigid's slender back, Jack Collins guided her through the front door of Le Poulet, the famous French dining establishment on the corner of Eddy and Mason Streets.

'How do you pronounce the French name?' she asked him.

'Poodle Dog. That's what I call it. Me and everyone else. The poodle dog is French too, after all.'

Brigid looked bewildered when, instead of seating them at one of the tables, the head waiter beckoned them to follow him to the back of the restaurant. Jack Collins smiled reassuringly.

'Downstairs is just for ordinary diners,' he told her. 'We'll be taking lunch in one of the special rooms upstairs. I think you'll find it even more to your liking. And that way there will be no danger of any of your mother's friends seeing us. I would hate for you to get into trouble.'

Brigid nodded, though the way she bit her lip as the elevator cage rattled upwards made Jack Collins think it was not such a good idea to remind the lass she was going against her mother's wishes.

The elevator came to a juddering halt at the third floor. The operator levered open the clattering doors and the pair stepped out into the quiet of a luxurious foyer decorated with voluptuous statuary. An attendant led them to one of the dozen or so doors leading off the foyer. When she first saw the room, Brigid blinked with delight. 'Why, it's beautiful!' she cried, clapping her hands. The furnishings – table, chairs, chaise longue – represented the height of turn-of-the-century fashion. On the table sat a silver epergne piled with dried fruits and sweets, on either side a scrolled silver candelabra set with beeswax candles. The candles' honeyed scent mingled with the fragrance of the fruit and the spray of jonquils in a Chinese vase on the little side table to make for a heady, almost intoxicating atmosphere. Heavy velvet curtains were draped over the window and across the back wall. The attendant handed Jack Collins a thick menu from which he swiftly ordered champagne and food.

When the waiter left, Brigid skipped around the room looking at the curtains and the epergne and the chaise longue in turn, exclaiming over everything with a gay, girlish innocence. 'And look at this!' She sat down in a rocking chair. 'I have heard of these!' Experimentally, she pushed with her feet. As the chair tipped backwards she gave a startled little cry. The hem of her skirt floated up, revealing a trim pair of ankles and pink-ribboned bloomers, and she brushed it back down with a mortified giggle. She then tried out the chaise longue, and the sight of her lithe, curvaceous body in its fashionably strict bindings wrestling to get comfortable made Jack Collins' breath grow short.

'Oh, Mr Collins, this is truly the height of luxury! I cannot wait to tell Mama all about it. She would love it. I wish we had asked her to come as well – I feel badly for deceiving her.' Brigid's eyes went suddenly moist and her sweet mouth fell into the prettiest little pout Jack Collins had ever seen. When a tear dropped out of one of those blue eyes, he offered

his handkerchief with a look of concern. She accepted it
gratefully and dabbed at her eyes. 'I'm sorry, Mr Collins, you
must think me such a daisy.'

'Not at all,' he reassured her, and made bold to pat her other
hand, which rested in her lap, a site of intense interest to him.
He thought it would be marvellous if someone could invent
a machine that allowed one to peer beneath the layers of a
woman's skirts and petticoats and bloomers, straight through
to the holy of holies. He imagined Brigid's, the hair downy,
the lips pink and swollen and moist as they must be if she
were feeling even a modicum of the excitement he was experiencing, her tight and unexplored love canal blocked – for the
moment! – by its precious hymen. The rosy bud of her little
asshole, the plump smooth cheeks of her ass. He spread his
fingers wider so that they encased her delicate hand in its soft
white glove, at the same time pressing down with thumb and
pinkie ever so lightly on the plump thigh beneath her skirt.
For a long and thrilling moment, she did not move. Her fine
young bosom swelled above the line of her corset. As though
protecting her breast from his gaze, she slid her hand out from
under his and placed it there. He left his hand on her thigh.

'You must be accustomed to ladies of far greater sophistication than I, Mr Collins. I hardly know what to do or say.'

Another tear threatened. Murmuring a string of reassur-
ances, Jack Collins reluctantly removed his hand from her
leg in order to clasp the hand which lay across her bosom
in both of his. The skin of her décolletage was radiant
with warmth and smoother than silk. He patted her hand,

devilishly tempted to lower it towards his lap, where already turmoil and tumescence were taking hold. A knock on the door made them both jump.

'Who could that be?' she cried.

'It must be the waiter,' he replied soothingly. Jack Collins had been caught once before at the Poodle Dog by a young lady's father. It had not been pleasant. He had since taken the precaution of enlisting the attendants' cooperation by dispensing generous tips beforehand.

It was indeed the waiter. He pushed before him a linen-draped trolley on which a bottle of champagne rested erect in a bucket of ice with two glasses. There was also a platter of oysters and plates of other delicacies. Ascertaining that nothing else was required for the moment, the waiter left the pair to lock the door behind him.

'Champagne, Miss Callaghan?'

'I don't know if I should,' Brigid replied in a small voice. 'The priest in our church has often spoken out against the Demon Drink. He says that more often than not it leads to mischief.' She watched him pour two glasses, her expression equal parts worry and curiosity.

'My dear Miss Callaghan, surely you do not fear that I should lead you to mischief?' His eyes full of it, he handed her a glass.

She hesitated a moment and then accepted the champagne. 'Oh, dear Mr Collins, I hope you do not think that is what I implied! I am so young and foolish and you are so much older and wiser. You must teach me things.'

'Nothing would give me greater pleasure, Miss Callaghan. Now, to your health.'

They clinked glasses. Brigid took a tiny sip of champagne. She wrinkled her nose at the taste but then with a brave and unexpected gesture, tipped the rest down her slender throat.

'Oh!' she giggled. 'So *that* is the taste of the Devil! It's rather pleasant. Of course Mother would be shocked to hear me say that.' She burped daintily and immediately covered her mouth. 'I am so sorry! You must think me terribly crude.'

'Not at all,' Jack Collins replied smoothly, using the opportunity provided for another comforting stroke of her hand. 'In the cultures of the Extreme Orient with which I am acquainted, that would be a sign of appreciation.'

'Oh, Mr Collins, do tell me more about the Extreme Orient! You must have so many tales. I think those Japanese women – what do they call them, the geishas? – must be very beautiful.'

'Not as beautiful as a Rose of Tralee,' Jack Collins said, topping up Brigid's glass.

'Mr Collins, you know the Irish ballads!' Her eyes admired him over the rim of the glass.

'I know an Irish rose when I see one.' He was very smooth, was Jack Collins. 'The geishas are quite enchanting, though I must say I cannot find blackened teeth an attractive feature in a woman. I much prefer perfect white pearls such as your own.'

Brigid blushed. 'Oh, Mr Collins, you flatter me. I shall

quite lose my head, if you continue. But blackened teeth? Do they really do that?'

'Yes, it is considered most comely over there. Quite strange, really. Please, Miss Callaghan, do try an oyster.'

Brigid took another sip of champagne before setting down her glass. Looking closely at the tray of oysters, she tipped her head to one side. 'I have never had an oyster before. However does one eat such a thing?'

'Well, I would suggest first removing your gloves.'

'Oh, of course!'

Brigid tugged at the fingertips of her gloves and gently pinched them upwards. She eased them off slowly. Inch by inch, the pale, unblemished flesh of her forearms, wrists and delicate young hands revealed itself to Jack Collins' aroused gaze. Finally, with a little sigh, she pulled the gloves off completely and lay them down by her hat. Impulsively, Jack Collins reached for her hand and kissed it from the back of her fingers to her wrist. She gasped and pulled it away.

'Oh, Mr Collins!' she cried in a panicked voice. 'Whatever are you doing?' Tiny tears made her eyes shine. 'I knew it was wrong to come here without Mama. I fear I really must go now.' She was reaching for her gloves and hat when Jack Collins dropped to his knees before her. She looked at him, startled.

'Oh, Miss Callaghan, overcome by your intoxicating beauty, I forgot myself. Please do forgive me.' He reached into his pocket and pulled out a fine gold bracelet. 'Please, Miss Callaghan, do accept this small gift as an apology and token of my sincere esteem.' He pressed it into her hand, and closed her fingers around it.

Brigid's jaw dropped as she examined the gift. 'Oh, Mr Collins, I have never owned anything so fine. I couldn't possibly accept this from you. It wouldn't be proper.'

'Please, Miss Callaghan. It's nothing. I should never forgive myself if you don't.'

Brigid bit her lip. She did not resist when Jack Collins fastened the bracelet around her wrist. She turned it this way and that and then gazed upon her worldly benefactor in wonderment. 'Thank you. I don't know how I could possibly repay such kindness.'

'Just stay and dine with me, my dear Miss Callaghan. Shall we have those oysters?'

He poured out more champagne while she picked one of the oysters off the tray and squeezed some lemon over it. 'Go on. You'll find it most agreeable.'

Dubiously, she raised the oyster to her lips and stuck her tongue out to lick it. 'It's salty!' she exclaimed.

With an expression that flickered between curiosity, pleasure and revulsion, Brigid sucked the oyster's meat off its shell. She rolled the slippery muscle over her tongue and into the centre of one cheek and then the other until, having thoroughly explored the oyster's clotty texture and unusual taste, she tipped her head back and swallowed. The sight of the little bump working its way down her pale and slender throat was rather too much for Jack Collins, whose urgency was already straining his buttons.

'Did you find that agreeable?' he asked, his voice near to cracking.

'I should think I have never swallowed anything quite as strange and exciting,' she said, licking her fingers. 'May I have another?'

By the time she had eaten three, and washed them down with more champagne, roses had bloomed anew in her cheeks and her eyes reflected the sparkle of the drink. 'I wish there was music,' she exclaimed suddenly. 'I feel like dancing.' She began to hum a popular waltz.

Emboldened, Jack Collins held out his hand. 'May I have this dance, Miss Callaghan?'

'Of course, Mr Collins.'

One hand on her waist, and the other holding her delight-fully bare hand, he spun her laughing around the room a few times and then, sensing an opportunity, pulled her close. When she smiled at him, he lowered his face to hers. He felt her tense. Yet she did not resist as he kissed her smooth fore-head, her pert nose, her downy cheeks. Experimentally, he pressed his lips upon her own. He had just tasted their lem-ony warmth when she squirmed out of his grasp and threw herself down upon the chaise longue. Burying her face in the dusky pink tasselled pillow, she began to sob. He approached her cautiously, cooing apologies, blandishments and com-fort. Her face still in the pillow, she shook her head with such violence that a hairpin came loose. One long silken rust-coloured lock of hair came tumbling down upon her exquisite neck. Jack Collins stood helpless, fingers nervously palpating the air above her quaking shoulders until at last she turned and raised one tear-stained cheek and shining eye in his direction.

'I have never allowed a gentleman to kiss me before,' she cried. 'I fear I am ruined!'

'Miss Callaghan, you are anything but ruined. And I am sorry to be so forward, but please believe me when I say I am no bounder. I must confess my true and deep feelings for you – I love you.'

Jack Collins ventured this last statement with fervent sincerity. It was true. He loved all beautiful virgins. The fact that he rarely sustained that emotion much beyond the deflowering was quite besides the point.

Thence followed a cavalcade of sighs and glances and trembles of lip and hand and shoulder. Jack Collins could only stand by as every nerve in him burned with anticipation. He thanked Jove that he was experienced enough to stay cool even as his blood ran hot. 'My dear Miss Callaghan,' he said. 'May I offer you another token of my great esteem in the hope you will forgive me, my darling, my sweetheart?' He extracted from his pocket a second gold bracelet, heavier and more exquisite than the last, this one set with a sprinkling of rubies.

When Brigid saw the bracelet she sat up again and dabbed at her eyes with a handkerchief, forcing a smile as he fastened it above the first. 'No one has ever called me such sweet names. Except dear Papa, when he was alive, of course. He was called to his Maker when I was very young.'

Which is lucky for me, Jack Collins thought. 'Here,' he said, offering her a refreshed glass of champagne. 'This will make you feel better.'

She took the champagne and sipped at it thankfully. Casting a glance at her tinkling bracelets, she looked up at Jack Collins with a perplexed expression. 'But how is that you, a mature man of the world, could love a naive and silly girl like me?' Her voice had a touch of the coquette in it, and she blushed as though taken aback by her own flirtatiousness.

Jack Collins smiled and sat down next to her once more. That turn in voice was exactly what he'd been waiting for. The scales had tipped. 'In all my days I have never met such a beguiling young lady as you, Miss Callaghan, and that I swear. I look at your sweet, sweet lips and it is torture to know that I must wait, perhaps forever, to kiss them again.'

Brigid looked at her hands, which were lying in her lap. She fiddled with a ribbon. 'It is torture for me as well, Mr Collins. I should like to kiss you very much,' she confessed in a whisper. 'Oh, how loudly my heart beats!' She put a hand on her breast, which was heaving, and gave Jack Collins an imploring look. He bent his face to hers once again. Her lips trembled but they did not retreat from his. Gently, he pulled her close, crushing her breast against his chest. Her lips were tense, tight and stiff. He knew to be patient. He caressed them with his own, nibbled gently at them and, as they began to relax and soften, he teased them apart with his tongue. He could feel her hold her breath as his tongue began to explore her mouth and play with hers. At last, the flame was ignited and she eagerly kissed back with tongue and lips. Again suddenly, she pulled away, panting for breath. Her eyes filled afresh with tears and her whole body quivered.

'What is it, my angel?' Jack Collins asked.

'It's just . . . it's just that I am feeling things I have never felt before and am so very frightened. I have never even been alone with a man before. Oh, if Mama —'

'Shhhh.' Jack Collins put a finger against her sweet lips. There would be no more talk of her mother.

She nodded, pleading in her eyes. 'Please, Mr Collins, do not think me a fast woman.'

'My darling sweetheart, I would never think that.' Jack Collins reached into his pocket again. 'And Miss Callaghan, I should be ever so pleased if you would call me Jack.'

She smiled sweetly then. 'Jack. And you must call me Brigid.'

'My dear Brigid, may I demonstrate once again my affection with a paltry gift?' Tenderly, he slipped a gold heart-shaped locket over her head.

She felt its weight. 'It is so heavy!'

'Such is the weight of my affection,' said Jack Collins, his hand across his heart.

'Oh, Mr Collins. I mean Jack. Darling Jack.'

They shared a long and melting gaze, and then he fell upon her lips again, which he found were now soft and yielding, and it was not long before her tongue began to respond afresh to his own. This was fine kindling for his fire, for he felt her desire blossoming. Her hands, hesitant and faltering at first, found his neck, which they stroked with all the tenderness of youth. When he reached up into her fine, soft hair she pulled her face away, but only for a moment, while she released her hair from all its pins. Shaking her head, she let her hair tumble in great beautiful reddish curls down over her back and shoulders. The movement thrust those excellent firm breasts towards Jack Collins once more and this time, when he went to kiss her, he did not linger on her moist and open mouth but brushed his lips down over her rounded chin and onto her soft neck, occasioning the most delicious little sighs from her. He had begun to ease her down upon the chaise longue so that his body could press upon hers when again she stiffened and pulled away. Confidently, he eased yet another treasure from the chest that was his pocket and slipped it onto her pinky – a fine jade ring from the East.

Progress with a virgin was never smooth. It was full of stops and starts, tears and hesitation, promises and pledges, sighs and trembling. There was always the chance that she would pull away, close the gate and bar the door and that risk, for Jack Collins, made it all the more thrilling. It was in the knowledge that he might be rebuffed at any moment that he eased her out of her bodice, where sheer emotion might have led him to rip it off. With practised fingers, he loosened the laces of her corset, which soon joined the bodice by her hat and gloves. Soon she wore nothing but her chemise, bloomers, stockings, shoes and gold. Shyly, she wrapped her arms across her chest.

'Are you all right, my darling Brigid?'

'I feel . . . chilled.'

Jack Collins strode to the back wall and swept aside the velvet curtains to expose a cozy and well-appointed bedroom with a sturdy double four-poster. This revelation naturally led to more tears and doubts and gifts and promises but at last Brigid allowed herself to be gathered up in Jack Collins' strong arms and laid gently down upon the coverlet.

He liberated her feet from their narrow boots, which he placed neatly by the chair before returning to kiss the sole of each stockinged foot. Her eyes were closed, her mouth opened slightly and her bosom, now unbound, jiggled attractively under the thin material of her chemise with every move. Loosening the ribbons on her bloomers, he pushed them up her plump thighs, unfastening the ribbons which held her stockings up. He then slowly teased her stockings down her shapely legs and plucked them off her feet.

When he disappeared for a moment after that, Brigid opened her eyes. Seeing him return with a basin of warm water and a flannel, she quickly closed them again. Setting the basin on a bedside table, Jack Collins set about bathing her feet as though she were an Egyptian queen and he her Nubian slave in the sort of Oriental fantasy so popular at the time. The occasional tickle and kiss to the soles of her feet was rewarded with a voluptuous squirm and adorable fit of giggling, but it was an open-mouthed gasp which greeted him when he placed her toes in his mouth and licked the spaces between them with a wet, fattened tongue.

'Oh!' she cried. 'Oh! Oh!'

He parted her legs. She was still wearing bloomers, but in the fashion of the day they were split for the convenience of relieving oneself under layers of petticoats. And through this split, Jack Collins finally glimpsed that holy grail, the vestal temple, softly haired, pink, fat and dewy as a summer meadow at dawn. Brigid raised her head and with a wide-eyed trusting look that made Jack Collins feel quite incapable of sustaining the pressure in his trousers a minute longer, pulled her chemise up over her head.

Her exposed breasts were so pale they almost glowed in the semi-darkness. Their nipples, the colour of peaches, stood up flushed and swollen with unmistakeable arousal. She crossed her arms over them but Jack Collins eased her hands away and bent over her to kiss and suckle at her bosom, unbearably excited by the knowledge he was the first man ever to do so. At the same time, he hastily shucked off his trousers. Dressed only in her bloomers and her new jewellery, which by now included a pair of Japanese pearl earrings, another ring and a necklace, Brigid shrieked to see the upstanding, swollen and fearsome rod that he was now pointing at her, and physically recoiled. Cooing, stroking and speaking sweet words of comfort and encouragement, Jack Collins finally coaxed her into touching and then stroking it with her hand. But the risk of spending himself prematurely was too great. He suddenly withdrew himself from her by now enthusiastic grasp and surprised her by crawling up the end of the bed, yanking down her bloomers and burying his face between her legs.

Brigid really began to struggle and shriek and moan now. 'Mr . . . Jack . . . dear . . . you mustn't . . . oh, oh!' Her head thrashed from side to side, and beads of perspiration appeared on the down of her lip. She placed one hand on her breast and with the other she pushed weakly at his head. Jack Collins had no intention of listening to any protests now.

Sucking on her clitoris until it was red and swollen, he licked the pink lips of her delicious virginal quim and ran his fingers over the wet, fleshy opening all the way back to her asshole. He entered her with his tongue and pinched her slippery flesh rhythmically between his fingers. She kicked and strained beneath him, panting and squealing for mercy. His cock was painfully swollen and while it flashed through his mind to introduce her to the infinite delights of fellatio, he feared he might explode before he had a chance to taste the ultimate pleasure of defilement.

So, giving her a last fat lick, he scrambled up on all fours above her and, urging her not to be afraid, knocked gently at first against her maiden door. Then, unable to control himself a minute longer, he thrust past the barriers. To the accompaniment of a marvellous symphony of screams and cries and whimpers and sighs, Jack Collins went to that mythical land where no traveller had been before. Her tight fluid passage gripped him like a vise as her fingernails raked down his back, her toes curled and her back arched up against him. He fastened his mouth around one buoyant nipple, held her thick hair with his hand and bucked like a bronco-rider until he felt the semen pour out of him in a hot stream. He collapsed then upon the fair girl and, as the tension drained away, would have fallen fast asleep right then and there were it not for her sobbing.

The subsequent discovery of drops of blood on the sheet and between her thighs caused further hysteria.

This was ever the problem with virgins. It took gentle caresses for which he no longer had much heart, promises he had no intention of keeping, lashings more of fine champagne and a few additional gifts – a Japanese lacquered box and fan – before Brigid's tears were dried and she had promised never to tell her poor mama what had transpired that day, for all their sakes. He helped her to dress, lacing her corset and watching her pin up her hair with a pair of jewelled hairpins, which he was relieved to see had helped restore her smile. She clung to him as they prepared to leave the room and then, straightening up and adjusting her hat, bravely walked out with him as though nothing out of the ordinary had ever transpired between them.

Downstairs, the mâitre-d' of the Poodle Dog bowed and thanked Jack Collins most kindly, for he was a good customer and a good tipper. For that matter, so was Brigid Callaghan, professional ingénue and frequent virgin, but the maitre-d' knew that she and 'Mama' would see to him, and generously, later. The women particularly appreciated the provision of a thimble of chicken's blood, strategically placed. He hummed to himself as the pair passed onto the street.

The song he hummed was a popular one, and it went like this:

Dry martini then another,
Then she telephones to Mother,
She'll take dinner with her brother,
    Out in 'Frisco;
If in Poodle Dog a crowd,
disturbs your nerves with noises loud,
    Out in 'Frisco;
You will go just one floor up,
And in privacy you'll sup,
Close beside your Buttercup,
    Out in 'Frisco;
Or if in the elevator,
In parlance of the waiter,
    Out in 'Frisco;
You more quiet wish to be,
You will ask to stop at three,
Just to see what you can see,
    Out in 'Frisco;
There you'll find the rooms en suite –
and the 'outfits' hard to beat –
    Out in 'Frisco.
But if your conscience becomes rife,
Because it's another fellow's wife,
Just remember this is life
    Out in 'Frisco.
When you finally cash in,
And you end this life of sin
    Out in 'Frisco.

They will gently toll a bell,
Plant your carcass in a dell,
No need to go to hell —
    You're in 'Frisco!

The One that Got Away

PENNY RICHMOND

There's always one, isn't there? The one that got away . . . Or should that be the one that gets away with it? It depends . . . Anyway, mine was a boy called Nathan. Some of his friends called him Nat when we were at university; though I never did – I thought it made him sound like an insect with an irritating bite.

Still, if I'm honest, I should have known there was something slightly irritating about Nathan. Actually, that's an understatement. He was clearly faithless and vain and he knew that a large number of girls lusted after him from a distance. But when he chose me – bestowing himself upon me, like a blessing – I forgave him everything.

And I fell for him from the start: his dark hair that fell in a tangle of silky curls; his amber-coloured eyes and caramel skin; his beautiful cheekbones and his body . . . his body was just about perfect. Six foot two, with broad shoulders, narrow waist, muscular torso, and long, strong, powerful legs: all of which made him look like a man, even when he behaved like a little boy. I was twenty, he was a year older, and we were at a party on a wintry night – the tail end, as people were leaving, the cold air coming in like a wake-up call from the open front door – when he smiled at me and said, 'There's always been something unspoken between us, don't you think?' I just nodded, mutely, and melted into his arms. I thought I was the luckiest girl in the world; I thought I'd died and gone to heaven. I should have said goodbye and gone home to my own bed, but instead, I let him lead me to straight to his.

'I need to get some sleep, otherwise I won't be able to work tomorrow,' I said, weakly, trying to surface from his kisses.

'Who cares about tomorrow,' he murmured, 'when we're enjoying tonight?'

Of course, that was also the problem; that he wouldn't see further than the immediate present. But I was young and foolish, so I ignored the fact that we couldn't really talk to one another; that there was a kind of blankness behind his lovely eyes, and that really, he lived for the moment, and if I was in that moment, fine, but he never promised me a future. Which is fair enough, I suppose – we were both so young, why should either of us make promises? But I couldn't help myself. I needed a tomorrow. I wanted him to promise that he would meet my family one of these days; I needed him to tell me that he loved me, like I loved him.

He never did, of course. He said things like, 'You're

gorgeous' or 'I really like being with you'. But he never said he loved me, because he probably never did. The strange thing is that I put up with that for three years – three whole years of him not making any promises, three years of him telling me that he had commitment issues because his parents were divorced. I'd nod, sympathetically, when I should have said, 'You know what, Nathan? My parents are divorced, too. But that doesn't mean I don't want something different for myself.'

We were sort of living together by then, except not really. It was my flat – I'd started renting it when I got my first job at a glossy magazine, after leaving university – but Nathan spent a lot of time there, although officially, he still had his own place. Well, I say 'his own', but it was a basement flat in his mother's house. And that should have been a warning to me, shouldn't it? Along with everything else. Men should leave home as soon as they have the opportunity, especially when their mothers are bitter middle-aged women who drink too much, and think that no girl is good enough for their darling only son. Nathan's mother was called Amelia, and she used to be a model – which she told me at every opportunity. 'I used to model for your magazine,' she'd say, when I started working there, 'and don't you forget it.' As if I ever could.

Amelia hated me, just as she had hated all of Nathan's girlfriends, except the weird thing was, as soon as he broke up with them, she started behaving as if she'd always liked them – almost encouraging him to go back to them. He seemed blithely unaware of her emotional dysfunctions, even when she got drunk one Sunday lunchtime, and told me that I was a gold-digging bitch. Which was absurd, given that I was the one who paid the rent and all the bills for the flat, while Nathan spent his salary from the advertising agency on Prada suits and cocaine.

The pathetic thing is that I carried on putting up with this because we had great sex. I'd like to say I now realise it wasn't *that* great — because having reached some form of emotional maturity, I can see that our sex life was based on adrenalin and anxiety (mine) and illicit pharmaceuticals (his). And there would be some truth in that observation, but it's not the whole truth. We had great sex *despite* our hopeless relationship; our bodies somehow fitted together with astonishing ease; just the faintest scent of his skin (smoky and soapy at the same time) made me long for us to be naked alongside each other, beside and inside and tangled up together; and he responded to me with as much passion as I did to him. Shame about everything else . . .

Eventually, I was forced to acknowledge that he was never going to make me happy, aside from in bed, and even then, it wasn't exactly happiness that I felt, more a kind of wild abandon that sometimes bordered on misery, so that I'd find myself crying in the dark, but he never saw my tears, because his eyes were closed. And when he came back to the flat one night and told me that he'd just had sex with his secretary in the cupboard at work, halfway through their Christmas party, I finally snapped.

'That's it,' I said, feeling so angry I wanted to hit him, and the rage was making my head hurt. 'It's over.'

'Babe,' he said, 'she doesn't mean anything to me. It was just one of those stupid things – that's why I told you, because it's so unimportant – it didn't mean anything more than a kiss.'

'It might not matter to you,' I said, 'but it does mean something to me, and a kiss means something, how can you say it doesn't? I can't do this anymore, I just can't do it . . .' I was sobbing by then, and the strange thing was that he looked shocked, as if he couldn't understand why, and then he was trying to kiss me, to brush my tears away with his lips. But I knew that if I let him, we'd end up in bed together, as always, and that would be that – I'd be doomed to life as his doormat.

So I made him leave, and then I sat and cried for hours, and finally fell asleep for a little while, and when I woke up in the morning, I felt like I had a huge heavy weight that was crushing my chest. I rang up my sister and said, 'I'm so unhappy; I've broken up with Nathan.'

'Thank God,' she said. 'He's a total shit. You're better off without him, you really are.'

I knew she was probably right, but I still felt that everything had gone wrong; and I carried on feeling that dark weight in the bleak mornings that followed, and they turned into weeks, and then into months; yet slowly, slowly, the sense of being crushed – of being a nobody without Nathan in my body – began to fade. Not that I stopped hoping that he would see the error of his wicked ways, and ring me, begging for forgiveness, saying that he loved me and couldn't live without me; but I knew that this was a fantasy, as remote a possibility as him finding God and becoming a curate.

Eventually, about a year afterwards, during which time I heard not a word from Nathan, I started going out with someone else – a boy that I'd known since college. He was nice – we could talk to each other, and he was kind, but the sex was friendly, rather than fabulous. When I told my sister that it was a bit underwhelming after Nathan, she said that I needed to see a therapist. 'Your problem is that you associate physical pleasure with emotional pain,' she said. Which seemed slightly glib an analysis – the sort of cod psychology that appeared in the magazine where I worked, as a matter of fact. But I suppose she was right, to a certain extent; not that I was ready to think about it then.

The relationship ended without any great recriminations – we sort of drifted out of romance and back into friendship, simply by sleeping together less and less. So when I went to Paris last week, I was officially single – and had been for several months. It was a work trip of the kind that I rarely go on, a brief outing that sounds glamorous, but usually isn't. Someone had to represent the magazine at a launch of a new perfume by one of the big beauty companies – an important advertiser – and under normal circumstances, the beauty editor would be there, in all her fragrant glory. But the day before, she came down with food poisoning (which was unfortunate, given how little she actually ate), and her deputy was on holiday, much to my editor's annoyance. 'For God's sake,' she snapped, casting her eyes around the office. 'Why is there never anyone useful here?'

Her eyes came to rest on me, a junior member of the features team. 'Olivia,' she said, with a sigh. 'You'll have to do.'

I knew better than to say, 'Do what?' I simply smiled and said, in a way that I hoped sounded eager yet efficient, 'What can I do to help?'

'We need someone to go to Paris tomorrow afternoon,' she said. 'It's an overnight stay, and then you'll need to be back in London first thing, ready to write a short piece.'

The last time I'd gone to Paris was with Nathan, as it happens, and I felt a bit melancholy on the train, remembering that weekend, and wondering whether I had been too hasty in splitting up with him, or if I was destined to live alone. But as the Eurostar pulled into the Gare du Nord, a wave of optimism swept over me – it was a chance to escape the office, after all – and the hotel room was infinitely more glamorous than my flat, with parrot-green velvet chairs and silvery cushions and pearl-grey walls. It had clearly been booked with the beauty editor in mind – a suite to befit her status – and on a little mirrored side-table there was half a bottle of champagne and a porcelain plate of tiny pale-pink macaroons, all of which I enjoyed immensely. I spent a long time lying in the bath, floating in rose-scented luxury, and then got changed into my favourite pair of red satin high heels and a little black dress that I'd bought in a seconds shop, but that fitted me like a sheath, as if it had been made

to measure. When I glanced at myself in the mirror, smoothing the material over my body, the reflection that smiled
back at me seemed mysterious, just for a few seconds, and
somehow more alive, pulsing with a kind of feverish anticipation. I turned away, almost embarrassed by what I had
seen, scooping up money and keys into my bag in a flurry of
practicality. Then I went downstairs, as instructed, to meet
a tremendously chic French publicist, her scarlet cupid-bow
lips matching her perfect manicure; and she shepherded me
into a taxi, to take us to the Rodin Museum.

The perfume was called 'The Kiss'; hence the extravagant event at the museum that housed the original sculpture.
Heaven knows what it had cost to hire for the evening, but
here we were, being served champagne cocktails and caviar
on the terrace, as the early summer dusk settled over Paris,
and the sky dissolved into a luminous transparency. There
must have been a hundred of us – about half were journalists
from around the world, including some exhausted-looking
women from the Far East, drooping from jet-lag, and the
rest were people who worked for the beauty company, the
marketing and sales executives, I suppose. I didn't know
anyone, apart from the French publicist, and she was busy
with the grander beauty editors, from American *Elle* and Italian *Vogue*. But I didn't mind – it was like finding myself in
a scene from someone else's life – and I slipped away into
the garden, which was beautiful in that very formal, Parisian
manner, with clipped hedges and perfectly trimmed lawns
and a fountain falling gently over a large stone pool.

I was standing alone, looking down into the dark opaque water, when someone came up behind me, so quietly and swiftly that I hadn't time to spin around before feeling a hand on the small of my back. 'Olivia,' said a man's voice softly, and I turned to see him, and there he was . . .

'Nathan,' I said, my heart pounding so loudly that I thought he must be able to hear it. 'What are you doing here?'

'I might ask you the same question,' he said, raising one eyebrow, slightly teasing, in the most familiar of ways.

I didn't answer – I felt too confused, and I hoped that the twilight would soften the blush that was rising from my neck to my face. 'I moved to this company last year,' said Nathan. 'I work in the advertising department – and what about you? I didn't see your name on the guest list.'

'I'm a last-minute replacement,' I said. 'Our beauty editor couldn't come.'

'But you're still working at the same magazine?' he said.

I nodded, and he smiled at me. 'How long has it been?' he said. 'Eighteen months?'

It was two years since we'd split up, but I wasn't going to tell him that I still remembered the precise anniversary of our separation. I just nodded again, stopping myself from staring at him, though I took in every detail, his curls looking a little neater and shorter than before, trimmed to the collar of his white shirt, no tie, but his suit was dark and expensive, and he was clean-shaven, with a faint aroma of lemony soap and cigar smoke.

'You look lovely,' he said. 'Why don't we ever see each other?'

'Because you had sex with your secretary,' I said.

'Oh, her,' he said, a flat dismissal in his voice, a hint of moodiness. 'I don't see her any more, either. And I've got a very fearsome dragon of a secretary these days.'

'How disappointing for you,' I said.

I saw him glance down, very fast, to my left hand, which was bare of an engagement or wedding ring. 'Isn't it extraordinary to find ourselves here again,' he said, sounding warm and provocative, the trace of sulkiness gone. 'Do you remember that weekend?'

It wasn't very much of a coincidence – we'd come to the Rodin Museum together, as students, during our time in Paris, like hundreds of thousands before us, and stood in front of 'The Kiss', amidst all the other tourists, as you do. But I remembered it, of course. I remembered feeling uncertain and oddly alone, even as he'd taken my hand in his, whispering into my ear that he wanted to spend the afternoon in bed with me; and I also remembered the tautening excitement of that uncertainty, and how it mingled with the lust I felt for him.

'How could I forget?' I said, and then immediately regretted my words, because a pleased look flickered across Nathan's face, an instant of smug self-satisfaction. I didn't like it – and I didn't like myself for slipping back into the habit of pleasing Nathan – so I started walking away from him, back to the throng on the terrace.

'Don't go,' he said, but I carried on walking, trying not to wobble in my satin stilettos on the gravel path, realising as

I did so that I was already slightly drunk, after several glasses of champagne on an almost empty stomach (the canapés were fashionably small in size and quantity, and the macaroons had been doll-sized). Nathan walked beside me, and when we got to the doors that led from the garden to the museum, he steered me past a gaggle of Japanese journalists, towards one of the side rooms.

'Look,' he whispered, '*Le Baiser* . . .' And there they were, still locked together, just as they had been last time we were here, just as Rodin himself had left them, contained or imprisoned within the stone, the marble figures frozen in their moment of naked passion, the woman's arm around her lover's neck, his hand resting on her thigh.

'She reminds me of you,' he said, and then he brushed his fingertips against my cheek, very softly. 'I miss you . . .'

I could have been as cold as the marble woman, or simply shaken my head at him, or I could have told him that his words were clichés, just as Rodin's statue had become a cliché. But I didn't; I just found myself silently re-reading the inscription on the plaque next to the statue, keeping my eyes on those words, until Nathan slipped his arm around my waist, and led me away.

What happened next seemed to proceed with graceful inevitability. We went into the room together where the party was in full swing, and though Nathan was called over to join a group of his colleagues, just before the presentation of their advertising campaign began, I knew his eyes were still on me; it was as if a thread were pulled taut between us again, never slackening or snapping, even as we moved in different directions.

The ad campaign was shown on a big screen in the main hall, and it was just as you would expect: a slick three-minute film made by the most sought-after Oscar-winning director, with a Hollywood star in the lead role. That's the way per-fume ads are done these days – at vast expense, presumably in the hope of making even vaster profits. But for all that, I found myself being swept away by the fake romance of the campaign – for it was beautifully shot, with a Parisian backdrop that was suffused with golden light, and at the end, the Hollywood star – who supposedly wants to escape from the gilded cage of celebrity – runs through the gates of the Rodin Museum to meet her lover in the garden, where they kiss as if their lives depended on it. As I watched the ending – an apparent re-enactment of Rodin's 'Kiss', except these lovers remained fully clothed in couture – part of me felt cynical, because I knew that the celluloid figures were as unreal as the marble ones. But even so, I felt the oddest of sensations, at least in this context, which was the pricking of tears in my eyes.

Afterwards, Nathan came over to me. 'What did you think of the ad?' he said, trying to sound offhand, though I could tell he wanted my approval.

'Suitably emotive,' I said.

'You always were hard to please,' he said.

'Me? I thought I was too easy – a complete pushover.'

He laughed, and shook his head, and then when I turned

to walk away from him, he followed me. The rest of the party went past in a blur, him introducing me to people he worked with, me smiling, being charming, being charmed. It was dark outside when we left – a velvety night, with no moonshine or stars, just the gleam of streetlights and flashes of neon as we streaked past in a taxi. Nathan reached out and took my hand while we were sitting on the back seat, and started stroking my palm with his thumb, tracing feathery circles, so light I could barely feel his touch.

We were staying in the same hotel – his company had booked most of the rooms for the night – and we went up in the lift together to the fifth floor, where I was staying, and he followed me along the corridor. 'I'm not asking you into my room,' I said, as I reached into my bag for the key.

'Why don't you come and see mine, then?' he said. 'It's on the top floor – it's got a wonderful view of the city.' He took my hand again, and pulled, very gently. 'Please,' he said.

So I went with him, and we looked out over the Paris rooftops – absurdly romantic, like a fairytale scene, the iris-blue air seeming to beckon me to take flight out of the open window – and I felt so light, as if I could float away, high above the rooftops. But then he kissed me, pulling me close to him, insistently, urgently, gathering me back to him, and it was so easy, to tumble into bed, to slip down into all that we remembered. 'Darling,' he whispered, 'I love being with you . . .'

Afterwards, as we lay on the expensive linen sheets, he ran his hand down my spine, and then rested it on my thigh. 'Your beautiful body,' he said. 'There's no one else like you . . . I wish it could be like this forever.' Then he fell asleep, as quickly as he always used to do, like a child; and I could feel the weight of his hand on me, getting heavier as he sank deeper into sleep.

I was still wide awake, but I felt oddly frozen, as if the bulk of his muscles were keeping me from moving, and all the sensual fluidity of a little while ago – the suppleness of our bodies as we came together – had ebbed away, to be replaced by this cold heaviness. And as I lay there, I thought of what he had just said to me – the closest he had ever come to a declaration of tenderness – but instead of feeling soft and relaxed beside him, I remembered what I had read on the museum plaque next to 'The Kiss'. I hadn't noticed it before, when I'd first gone there as a student with Nathan – or maybe I had, and managed to forget it, instantly – but when I saw the inscription this evening, it seemed impossible to ignore. The figures were of two doomed lovers from Dante's *Inferno*, and originally designed for Rodin's monumental bronze, 'The Gates of Hell'. Which meant that his sculpture – supposedly the embodiment of eroticism and romantic love – was in fact conceived as a depiction of eternal anguish and damnation.

So, I couldn't stay there in bed with Nathan, could I? Even if I wasn't going to end up in such a dramatic form of imprisonment, I knew this was a dangerous place to be – a sort of limbo, neither coming nor going, just captured by him, by his body. And while one captivating night was all very well, I didn't want to stay like that forever.

I took a deep breath, and slid my body away from his, and his hand fell heavily from my thigh, on to the bed beside him. He sighed a little, in his sleep, but didn't wake up. Lying there, he looked almost vulnerable, so I leant over, and kissed him, very softly, on his cheek. Then I got dressed and left a note on the pillow.

'Goodbye,' I wrote, 'with a kiss . . .'

A Blast from the Past

TUTTY MONMOUTH

'I'm bored,' I groan down the phone to Kate.

'Of work? Of Dave? Of life?' asks my best friend.

'The lot,' I grumble. 'It's all the same.'

'Sorry, zero sympathy. I'm nothing but envious that you've been happily married for two years. Try hauling your cookies on a new blind date every Friday, only to have your, already extremely low, expectations dashed as you meet men who look like Quasimodo and have Homer Simpson's IQ. Or try internet dating. Or speed dating.' Her voice rises, just hinting at how desperate she sees her situation to be.

I know, I know. In my head and heart I know that I'm far better off in a stable, happy relationship that might occasionally tip towards the humdrum, than still be putting it about waiting for Mr Right and only finding Mr Just-About-All-Right. I know it in my head and heart – it's just a little bit south of my stomach that I sometimes feel restless. Dave *is* my Mr Right. He *can* be clever, funny, thoughtful and sexy – when he turns his mind to it. It's just that we've been together long enough for him to believe he doesn't *need* to be any of these things on a regular basis. We've been together seven years now. Seriously, I'm beginning to believe in the seven-year itch. Slowly, I'm turning my mind towards who is going to scratch it.

'Maybe it's because Dave and I work together, as well as live together. I get a bit fed up of him always being *there*. And everything always being the same. There's no variety, no challenge,' I comment.

A tiny bit of me is wistful for those weekends on the pull that Kate still experiences. There's nothing quite like that feeling of expectancy and excitement as you push open the door of a trendy bar and you're hit by the smell of fags and booze and by the noise of confident, irresponsible chatter. I remember the slight thrill of stumbling across gangs of mysterious men in dark suits. Men who have just been paid and, for that night at least, are all about flashing the cash as they force their way through the crowds, towards the bar and ultimately into some woman's psyche and bed.

Bars are quite an aphrodisiac, even if you are half a couple. Before Dave and I got engaged and started saving for the wedding and then the house, we used to go to those over-priced joints two or three nights a week. Then we'd come home and rip each other's clothes off. I think it was something to do with the loud music. Thudding, pulsing, pumping into our brains and then rushing through our bodies, hovering between my legs and around his cock. I'd always want to dance, even when there was no space. I'd fight a powerful need to whoosh and swirl, carving out my own private dance floor – which wouldn't have been the appropriate thing to do in those deeply stylish bars – not at all cool. I understand stripping. Music does equate to sex. It pounds and devours and replenishes and ultimately relieves. I prefer to make love to music, rather than in silence. It helps create the mood, whichever mood I want. Swift and frenzied or leisurely and seductive. To be honest, I'd have it any old way at the moment. Dave and I don't go out much at the weekends now. One or the other of us always cries out, 'I'm too knackered.' Not sexually, you understand – if only. Knackered with work, and commuting, and bosses, and stresses, sadly.

'Jane, you're pathetic,' Kate says affectionately. Her no-nonsense approach has been earned after nearly fifteen years of friendship. Her frankness and fondness go hand in hand.

'Maybe.'

'Look, you know that you're mad about each other. It can't be constantly hearts and roses – that is such an unrealistic expectation.'

I'm not after hearts and roses; I'm keener for stockings and massage oil. That's the sparkle that's been doused with familiarity.

'How's business anyway?' She asks, in a blatant attempt

to change the subject. I know she thinks I'm being self-indulgent.

'Fine, you know. It's just hard to get overly excited about selling car insurance.'

'You do okay on commission and you never used to complain. You said working in a predominantly male environment was hot,' points out Kate with a reasonableness bordering on the annoying.

'Well, it was until Dave and I clicked, shagged and married.' Getting married was the nail in the coffin as far as my harmless office flirtations were concerned. Suddenly I disappeared. 'Now there are no sneaky sparks darting over the water cooler while loafing around with colleagues.'

I cast my mind back and trawl through a number of flirtations and dirty, fast liaisons. Readily supplied by working in a male-dominated environment I shiver with delight at the memories. I admit I miss the ego boost.

'My heart bleeds. I don't get the same opportunities in the beauty spa. Any men I come across are as gay as a maypole and just want me to wax their backs, sacks and cracks so they can impress some chunk of hunk.'

I giggle at the thought. 'Does it impress, having hairless balls?'

'Don't know; it's a mystery to me. Men are. Straight or gay. I suppose it must attract, else they wouldn't keep coming back; I mean, the pain must be off the scale. Anyway, aren't you going on some sort of conference soon?' she asks. 'That'll be a bit different, a change in routine at least.'

'Yup, in Brighton next week. Three days and two nights. I'm thinking of shaking off Dave and snogging someone inappropriate,' I say flippantly.

I don't really mean that but I want to shock Kate. Or maybe a tiny, tiny part of me does mean it and admitting as much shocks *me*.

'A more sensible approach would be to talk to him about how you feel,' she says.

'I don't do sensible.'

'No, you don't, do you? How could I have forgotten that?'

It's the usual corporate dinner thing: big, indecorous and reckless. Everyone's really going for it and, now I've given Dave the slip, I can too. Drunken, not-too-fussy men stand in hungry gangs trying to attract women by shouting loudly and shoving one another around. Sometimes I think we're still in the school playground and that's where we'll always stay. Flushed, these guys reel about, their words and thoughts becoming hazy. The women are sweaty and surprisingly keen as they too have been enjoying way more than the odd glass of wine on the company expense account. Tomorrow will be all about embarrassed, reluctant glances and hideous hangovers but no one cares about that right now. I find my table and name plate, sit down and pull my face into a professional, polite smile.

It's him. It takes me some seconds to place him. As soon as I acknowledge him in my mind, I acknowledge him in my knickers too. A delicate, woozy sensation, at once tingling,

317

exciting and unnerving. I met him years ago. Sometimes it seems like another lifetime. I wasn't expecting to see him here tonight. I hadn't expected to see him ever again, let alone find him sitting at my table. It's been such a long time. He gives me a slow, wide grin and his grin hits me between the legs. His eyes strip me naked. I can almost feel my slinky top drop to the floor. His eyes are sparkling green with golden flecks running through them. Suddenly I think of sunshine dripping through the leaves of a dense forest and me running through said forest – naked of course. All domestic thoughts scamper to the dark recesses of my mind. I have no intention of airing them tonight. He has fine, transparent skin and high cheek-bones. He is reasonably buff but not so it's intimidating. I'd say he's well-defined: athletic but not bulky. He's been working out. He looks at me and his eyes level me. It's as though he knows all about me; all my secret, horny, unfaithful intentions. A nuclear explosion of emotion and instincts sparkle and splinter inside me; they lodge in my head and tits. My G-spot and heart sing as one. I'm quivering.

The familiar masses around us blur into one indistinct and unimportant smudge and we're left alone in our togetherness. Together in our aloneness. I *have* felt lonely recently. I hadn't realised quite how much until I find myself languishing under his familiar but forgotten gaze. Lonely is a terrible thing to feel when you are married. I decide in an instant that I'm going to have him. Stunned and messed-up by undeniable lust, I can't ignore the attraction between us.

I can almost smell it. I'm sure I'd be able to taste it. I have to stop myself licking the air between us, for fear he'd think I am insane.

'I didn't expect this.'

'Nor did I, but take your pleasure where you find it.'

I don't know how he knows about my recent thoughts of discontent but it seems that he does. He must sense it and he's going to take advantage.

'So, Titch, want a drink?' He is already pouring me a glass of red (my preferred choice). That and using my nickname creates a tangible intimacy. Something I've been lacking at home recently. I search around my head for his nickname. I do vaguely remember he had one. What was it? It was something to do with his huge member, I recall that much. Donkey? Studley? I've got it! Stuffin. As in Stud Muffin. Or, I suppose, the other sort of stuffing. God, we used to laugh at that. Calling out 'Dave' during orgasm (fake or real) is so pedestrian in comparison.

We flirt to an unprecedented level. Within minutes I fall back into my flippant and frivolous ways, which were second nature before I married, but have seemed redundant and superfluous of late. I suddenly feel like I'm up there with every great seductress in history. I am as mysterious as Cleopatra who bathed her sails in spices so that, even from a distance over the seas, her scent attracted her warrior, Antony. I am as irresistible as a dark and doe-eyed heroine from a black and white movie. He does want to come up and see my etchings. Frankly, he just wants to come up.

I am Mrs Robinson and my graduate wants me to roll off my stockings. To hell with the consequences.

I am straightforward and direct about my intentions and yet I'm slippery and vague when he tries to rush to pin down the deal. Our starters haven't even been devoured; I've no intention of giving it up yet although he's already hinted that we'd catch up better in the privacy of one of the conference hotel's bedrooms. I manage to be direct and yet coy – a good bet but not a sure bet.

He is also full of challenges and inconsistencies but they don't infuriate or frustrate me; rather, he has the safe familiarity of an ex-shag but the tremulous expectancy of something approaching a new and unexpected level. He pours me another drink.

He talks about his job, which is the same as mine, therefore deadly tedious, yet somehow he manages to appear dazzling. He has funny customer-related stories to tell and I'm in peals. Dave and I do the same job and we are more or less at the same level. Actually, I got a promotion in my grade last year which he didn't get, so technically I'm more senior. He said he was really pleased for me but I noticed that, after that, we stopped talking about work. It can get a bit tricky. Besides, what's the point, since we both do the same thing day in, day out? Cold calling, following-up leads, upgrading existing insurance deals; it's not like either of us work for the UN. But tonight I see that Stuffin can talk about our dull job in an amusing, interesting way. I wish these conversations could go on between Dave and me over the dinner table;

perhaps if they did I wouldn't have started to refer to Dave as 'Dull Dave' in my head whenever I think of him.

Stuffin makes quite a wedge on commission because he has the gift of the gab and he's undoubtedly a charmer on the phone. He is in the flesh; that much is definitely true. I'd forgotten just how charming.

'Not that it matters how much I make, because my wife spends it as fast as I can earn it,' he comments. I bristle and cough into my wine. I'm uncomfortable with his grumble about his wife. I don't want to hear it – not tonight.

I need to change the subject. Sex comes to mind. His too, apparently.

We remember the things we have in common and discover some new things too. He confesses that he fantasises about three-in-a-bed scenarios, although he's quick to point out that he's only interested in a two-women-one-guy scenario.

'Sexist pig,' I comment. Then more seriously I ask, 'You're kidding, right?'

'Four tits, choice of holes, an abundance of flesh. It's every man's dream, isn't it?' I think I must look a bit concerned because he breaks into a grin and then reassures me. 'It's a fantasy. Relax. Truthfully, I'd probably never have the guts to go through with it, even if —'

'The missus said it was okay?' I finish his sentence.

'Exactly. Even if she gave me her blessing, I'd no doubt bottle. I'm sort of old-fashioned in that one particular way. I like the woman I'm with to know that she's my focus.'

It's a pretty bizarre comment under the circumstances.

I blush and reach for my wine. He stretches to help me and we touch hands. I swear I feel fireworks going off in my G-string. Quite a feat, because it's a very small piece and can barely hold my newly waxed bits.

'I've just had a Brazilian,' I blurt.

'No way.'

'Way.'

'Why?'

'For a change. To be, I don't know, tidy.' I thought that area needed a little attention, a little TLC, but I can't bring myself to confess as much.

'Did it hurt?' he asks.

'A pain like no other, baby.' I laugh.

He laughs too, he picks up his wine glass and as he takes a gulp he mutters, 'I'll make it worth your while, sweetheart.'

I scree indecorously and then push away my plate. Really, I haven't got an appetite, at least not one for food. The evening zooms by in a flash of bright images and vibrant, overpowering smells. Expensive colognes shield perspiring bodies, the smell of poached Scottish salmon and hollandaise sauce becomes indistinct from the taste of metallic mass-catering trays. I can't decide what I can taste, what I can smell and what I can touch, see, hear. Stuffin is all. His presence overpowers every one of my senses and I can't, or won't, steady myself. The crowds around me are tremendously loud; laughter and exhilaration bang up against random lust and all-round expectation. Packing a suitcase has mysteriously led to a loss of sense of self and propriety for many, many more people other than me. It seems everyone in view has abandoned their inhibitions.

We continue on our exploration of sexual fantasies. I tell myself we're only talking, what harm can it do if I tell him what's really on my mind? Dave and I normally talk about stuff like changing electricity suppliers or whether we should retile the bathroom. With Stuffin I am able to be quite a different woman.

'I'd really like to do it al fresco,' I giggle into my champagne (bought by Stuffin – a frivolous, expensive indulgence and twice as tasty because of that).

'I'm sure that can be arranged,' he says with a cheeky wink. I gasp and pretend to be outraged. I mean, I ought to be outraged. I'm a married woman. Married women don't behave like this, I tell myself. But I'm not convinced. The fizz of excitement that is scuttling through my body suggests, married or not, this is exactly the way I ought to be behaving. I feel more alive and magnificent than I have for months and months.

'I'd like to do it at my mum's,' says Stuffin.

'What?' Now I *am* taken aback.

'It would just be so naughty to slip out after the roast lamb and before apple pie. Excuse myself and then have dirty, fast against-the-wall sex in her cloakroom.'

'That's actually quite weird,' I laugh, somewhat hesitantly.

'It would be so risky. The idea of banging you against the wall and all her little bowls of smelly soaps jumping off the shelves is just too exciting. The fish and mermaid ornaments would be scandalised.'

I laugh out loud because that proves it: boys never grow up. I'm enjoying the thought that sex can be fun again. Recently whenever I've thought of making love to Dave I've counted it along with chores such as putting on another load of washing or tidying up my sock-drawer – something I really ought to get round to. I take another swig of champagne; it punches the back of my throat. The fresh, addictive dryness of a million bubbles dancing excitedly on my gums makes me confess.

'I'd like to be tied up.'

'Then I could cover you in cream —'

'No – champagne.'

'Then I'd lick you clean.' We both fall silent for a second to consider the idea. 'I'd like to join the mile-high club,' I add.

'I'd like to have sex in every room in my house.' Stuffin says, 'I'd like to see you in very scanty panties, suspender belts, stockings – the works.'

'Can't manage that tonight, I'm afraid.'

He grabs my arm. Nearly pulls it out of its socket and we dash from the dining room.

'In there,' he orders pointing to the room that the conference delegates are meant to retire to for coffee after dinner. As we leave the dining room dessert is being served. People would be filtering through in no time. It's very risky; maybe we should go to my bedroom. Stuffin seems to be reading my mind.

'In there,' he commands again. Clearly the risk factor is an attraction to him.

There are coffee cups lined up in neat rows, two huge urns of boiling water and plates of chocolate mints. But I know that it isn't caffeine that's on Stuffin's mind. Barely pausing to check for privacy, he slams me against the wall and urgently and repeatedly kisses me. It's frantic, and hurried, and amazing. He grabs both my hands and pins them above my head as he pushes his body into mine and kisses me hard. He barely has to restrain me; I'm rooted. His kisses are strong, dark and engulfing. It feels as though I've never been kissed before. Or, if I have, they were poor dry runs. I feel his cock stiff and large against my leg. He kisses me in all the usual places, pulls up my top to press his mouth to my stomach, waist, breasts, my neck and shoulders, head and hair. But he finds the less usual places too: my eyelids, my eyelashes, my nose. I kiss him back, and lick and suck and consume. He inches up my skirt, his cool fingers dance across my flesh. By the time he slips his fingers inside me, I am drenched by my own excitement. Ice-cold fingers on red-hot flesh, I come immediately – spurting out on to his hands. The exquisite release sends shocks plunging up my spine. With one hand he teases me, with his other he scrabbles with his flies and then almost instantly sinks into me. I stare into his glinting eyes and he stares back, never losing me. Not for a second. It feels astounding. It feels imperative. It feels right.

He's soaring, he's filling, he's plugging. He completes me.

It's over in minutes. But at this exact moment I know this will never be over.

'Again,' I mutter breathlessly.

He nods. 'Not here. Outside.' I smooth down my skirt but all my attempts at grooming are wasted as I'm sure there is a big neon sign over my head announcing, 'I've just been stuffed by Stuffin'. My lipstick is smudged into slutty streaks across my mouth and chin, my hair is scrambled where before it was neat and sleek. I pray we don't get spotted.

'Come on.' Again, he leads the way and I love that he takes charge. At best, I'd describe Dave as compliant – he always allows me to take the lead, whether that's booking mini-breaks or initiating anything in the bedroom – at worst, I'd describe him as lazy and apathetic. None of the above is attractive. Stuffin grabs my hand and pulls me through the reception, seemingly oblivious to the curious looks we attract; his determination and confidence is an undeniable and irresistible turn-on.

'Over there.'

He points towards Brighton's pebbled beach. It's pitch black now. I hope the cloak of night will protect my modesty because I get the distinct feeling Stuffin isn't giving it that much thought. He's clearly hungry to tick off my al fresco fantasy and, giddy and exhilarated, all I want is more.

My throat is dry and tight and my hands are clammy. I feel nervous and delighted all at once. We fling ourselves on to the pebbles and immediately start pulling at each other's clothes – swiftly, expertly undressing one another. He tugs my spangled top over my head and flings it to one side. I don't even care that it's not machine-washable and that extravagant display is going to cost me a trip to the dry-cleaners. I'm naked from the waist up and my skirt is bunched up to my hips. He takes off his jacket and shirt and is wearing his trousers on one leg. I treat myself and allow my eyes to slowly fall from his face, down to his broad shoulders, his ever so slightly rounded stomach, his evident passion and finally his legs, which are strong and hairy. I lie facing him. After an unhurried viewing, I return my eyes to his face and find that he is staring at me as though he's never seen me before. Without any sort of shyness, but with bold delight, I wait as his eyes fall from my lips, to my tits, to my mound. Suddenly he lunges and kisses me there. Slowly, so slowly he kisses and licks and nibbles, until I whimper with pleasure. Gently I lie back. My flesh – naked and exposed – is occasionally jabbed by a rough pebble. No doubt my back and buttocks are going to be covered in dirty telltale bruises tomorrow but I hardly notice the discomfort, let alone care about it, I'm so involved with what he's doing to me. Stuffin is concerned and wiggles me onto our now damp and crumpled clothes.

I can smell the sea and feel invigorated and high on it. Bit by bit, little by little his tongue explores my body. When I think that I can't take any more and that I'll explode with wanting if he persists in his gentle exploration, he suddenly plunges. He dives, he shoves, he seizes and pulls until I cry out with a violent mix of pain and desire.

I am worn out with rapture, but I can't let it all be one way.

I don't want to appear lazy. He's already come once tonight and I'm not certain of his recovery rate but I have to give him the opportunity. I push him onto his back and kneel over him. He makes me feel so sexy, an undeniable expert. He groans, writhes and slithers beneath me. I grab hold of his cock, tugging up and down, swiftly and expertly until he quivers and becomes breathless, finally he yells out. A terrifying howl that definitely must have alerted the more conventional lovers – those who are walking along the pier – to our secret whereabouts.

'Shush,' I giggle as I scramble to find my top to cover my moist tits just in case anyone comes to root us out.

He pulls me to him and says, 'Just hold me for a while.'

My hair is damp with exertion and is glued to my neck. My tits are wet with his kisses and my stomach and thighs with his love. We hold each other closely, until our breathing relaxes and we inhale and exhale in unison. His hands smell of sperm; I do too. But I feel clear and cleansed. His face radiates with elated, confident ruddiness. He seems so deliriously certain of everything. I hope I'm mirroring him. I imagine I am.

'I am the luckiest man on the planet, do you know that, Titch?'

'You can call me Jane again now,' I say with a contented sigh.

'I fucking love you, Jane. You are the perfect woman. How many other wives would have had the guts to admit that things were becoming a bit predictable and instigate this whole "let's pretend we've just met" thing?' He shakes his head with genuine respect.

'Not many, Dave, not many.' I smile to myself. 'All the fun of a real affair.'

'Without any of the messy bits.'

We can hear voices, probably teenage boys, and they seem to be getting closer. I doubt they are hunting us out. Probably looking for somewhere to swig their cans and smoke, but I don't want to be part of their teenage education. We scramble to our feet and dress quickly.

'My top will have to go the dry-cleaners. Can you drop it in? I'll pick it up. You'll probably have to take your jacket too,' I tell him.

He laughs. 'Red alert: wild abandon disappearing,' he teases.

'Well, at least until you take me on holiday. We still haven't ticked off joining the mile-high club,' I point out.

'True. Well, in that case I'll pop into the travel agents when I drop your top in at the dry-cleaners,' he says as he leans in for a long slow kiss that hits me south of my stomach.

The Rehearsal

CASSIUS PRIORY

Charlie was sobbing. She'd been rifling through her boyfriend's bag when she'd found a poem – a love poem – scrawled on the back of an envelope in several tortuous drafts. 'Rob's in love with someone else.' She clutched Nell's hand. 'He's admitted it. Said it's been creeping up on him for some time.'

Nell had never had a boyfriend who wrote poetry. Did Rob write poems often? Had he written them for her? But under the circumstances, she knew these questions would sound heartless. 'You poor thing,' she said instead. 'The bastard! How could he?' And she put her arms around her friend and felt the soft, feathery tickle of her skin, so fine over her sharp bones.

Charlie was the most beautiful girl in their year. There were other girls on the drama course, some more obvious, more perfect – one pre-Raphaelite Swede with a porcelain complexion, a French girl with a pouting, bee-stung mouth – but Charlie had glamour. She was tall and angular, with fine, pale skin and chestnut hair as wispy as a child's. She dressed carelessly in shades of slate and lint, colours Nell would never have considered, but she looked marvellous, as if the secret, the real secret, of her beauty lay within.

'What will you do?' Nell asked her as she wiped her eyes. 'I mean, about the flat. Will one of you . . .?'

'He's moving out; he's getting a van this weekend and he's taking his things.' Charlie's nose grew red and her eyes, already swollen, spilled over with new tears. 'I'll be living on my own.'

Nell looked away. It gave her an unexpected flash of pleasure to see that even Charlie, the enviable Charlie, could look unattractive when crying. When Nell cried her whole face puffed up, her neck turned blotchy, her ears grew red and she'd do whatever it took to hide herself. Unless, of course she was acting, when her tears, unreal, were made of lighter stuff and would trickle – just one or two – down the side of her face. This wasn't always what was wanted. 'You're a milkmaid,' a director had bawled at her during their first-year production, 'not a lady. Get a hanky out. Let's see some snot!' Nell had blushed a deep red, right down to her cleavage, which was shown to great effect in yet another square-cut bodice trimmed with white.

Beside the many beauties in their year, Nell felt small and plump as a pony. She had straight dark hair and a freckled face and so far, four terms into the course, had been given nothing but wenches and servants to play, although once, when she'd complained, she'd been cast as someone's aged mother.

'Nell?' Charlie had hold of her arm. 'Listen, I've got an idea. Why don't *you* move in?'

'Me?'

'Please! It will be such fun! You can move in on Sunday, right after Rob takes his things. Or before. Or any time. You can have the spare room.'

Nell bit her lip. She'd have to give notice where she was. Although not much, and at Charlie's she wouldn't have to endure those late-night talks outside the bathroom with her landlord, always inexplicably wandering round the house in his open dressing gown whatever time she came home.

'Okay,' she said. 'I will. I'll do it. The week after next.'

'Thank you.' Charlie wiped the tears from her face and Nell watched as the colour in her cheeks subsided and, with one small smile, her beauty was restored.

Charlie lived on the top floor of a house in Willesden. From the outside, it looked unexceptional – the window frames peeling a little more than most, the glass in one panel of the front door boarded up – but once inside the full scale of the dereliction hit you. Damp, decay and a deep, heady stench of rotting wood. Charlie ignored it. She kicked shut the front door, swept up two flights of stairs, past the abandoned flats on each landing and onto her own floor, where the radio was playing low, a battered sofa was draped in creamy shrouds of cotton and bunches of dried flowers stood on low tables among scattered photographs and abandoned mugs and the occasional beautiful object – a blue glass bottle or a gold statue of a god.

Nell had visited several times. Had gone back with Charlie after college to go over lines, had sat in the foam comfort of the armchair, encased in its white throw, with the gas fire blasting and Charlie, even in midwinter, slouching in a pair of combat trousers, her bare feet tucked under her, her smooth, pale arms and prominent collarbone shown off to their best advantage in a boy's school vest. Until now she'd never really noticed the spare room – had only seen the room Charlie shared with Rob, its low white bed, always unmade, the layers of antique lace at the windows, the clothes – flea-market dresses and a dun-coloured trenchcoat – hanging from pegs on the wall. But today Charlie continued up the stairs to a small room in the attic. It had a window to one side with a view over the garden, and a gas fire built into the chimney breast, cracked across the middle. There was a bed and a cupboard and the raised pattern of the wallpaper was just visible through a coat of magnolia paint.

Nell dropped her bag and sat down on the edge of the bed. Charlie crouched on the floor and lit a match and the fire fluttered, flickered and attempted to catch. 'Are you sure it's safe?' Nell asked, vaguely remembering some warning of her mother's about the dangers of gas fires, but Charlie blew on it a little to spread the flame and said she'd slept in here often after rows with Rob and she'd always left the fire on all night.

'Bastard. Bastard.' She crawled across the bed. 'Thank God he's gone. You wouldn't believe what a wanker he was. You know he was so vain? He was obsessed with his ears. Said they stuck out too much. He was always holding them back and asking what I thought.'

Nell pictured Rob and laughed. She'd met him three or four times but he never remembered her. He was one of those men who only noticed women who were beautiful. Fuckable, is what he'd probably have said. 'Now you mention it I did notice his ears,' Nell said in revenge. 'Has he considered surgery? You could offer to reset them yourself.' And they lay on the bed laughing up at the ceiling, their fingers entwined. 'So . . .' Nell added after a while, 'what now? You're free and single. It's been two long weeks. Anyone you've got your eye on?'

Charlie sighed and rolled towards her. The flames from the fire threw shadows over her pale face and then suddenly she was crying. Her face creased up, her fists pushed against her eyes as if to stop the tears. 'Bastard,' she said. 'How could he? I thought we were so in . . .' She choked on the word 'love', and flicked the tears angrily away, while Nell watched her, intrigued, thinking all the time, if I were a man I'd never leave her. What's the point of anything if men leave girls as beautiful as that?

'He's an idiot,' Nell said gently. 'He'll regret it, that's for sure.' And, impulsively, she put her arms round her friend and kissed the side of her face. Charlie, sniffing, pushed herself against her. Her face, still damp, nuzzled into Nell's neck, her shoulder pressed hard against her breasts, and they lay like that, breathing shallowly, until the room was almost dark.

Eventually they got up and moved into the kitchen where, wordlessly, Charlie set a pan of water on to boil.

'Can I do anything?' Nell looked around.

'No, no.' Charlie was chopping an onion now. 'This is your welcome dinner; go and sit down.'

Nell went into the sitting room and waited, listening to the radio, which spun out dreamy, drifty tunes, interspersed with a murmur of chatter, too low to catch. The fire was on in here too, hissing soporifically, and Nell sat down in the soft foam of the white-armchair and waited.

Eventually, Charlie came in with two plates of rice. The rice had been fried with slices of bacon and green pepper and a few scratchy sprigs of parsley. She put the plates on the floor and came back with a bottle of white wine and two glasses, which she filled to the top. 'Cheers,' she said. 'Here's to freedom.'

The food was disgusting – oily and a little under-cooked. 'I'm so sorry,' Charlie winced. 'Please don't eat any more,' and she pushed her plate as far away as she could and took a huge gulp of wine, as if to take away the taste.

Nell ate some more, out of politeness, and also because she was ravenous, and then abandoned hers too.

'You know who I do quite fancy, if I had to choose someone

from college . . .' Charlie lit a cigarette. Nell lit one too and curled back into her chair. This was definitely better than her old room where, once she was home, there was no one to talk to except the gloomy landlord or his spotty teenage son.

'Who?' she said, picturing the entire year seated in a semicircle.

'Well, if I had to choose someone, just for a fling . . . I think, if I was forced, I'd go for Dan.'

'Dan?' Nell felt her stomach falling. 'You're joking!' Heat rushed to her face. 'But you know how I feel about Dan. You know I've been besotted with him since day one!'

'Oh my God!' Charlie put her hand over her mouth. 'Of course, I forgot. I'm so sorry. Forget I said anything. Please!' She looked at her and creased her eyes, pleading, and, just in case that didn't work, she poured them both more wine.

'Anyway,' Nell said gloomily, thinking how Charlie could get Dan with one quick look, 'he's going out with Beth. God. Why are there no decent boys in our year?'

Her stomach still felt hollow but the blood had drained away from her face and now she was cold. She wrapped her arms round her legs and stared into the fire.

Charlie stretched out on her sofa. 'I really am sorry.' She looked over at her. 'I suppose I've spent too much time thinking about myself.' And when Nell didn't respond she said, 'Hey, why don't we make a plan? To seduce him. For you, I mean.'

Nell frowned. 'But how? He's with Beth. They're always together.'

'Well . . . Hang on, I'm going to run a bath. I always think better in water. Come on.'

The bathroom was off the corridor, beside the kitchen, and when the bath was full and the strawberry smell of the bubbles had filled the room, Charlie slipped out of her vest. She had no bra on and her breasts were small and pale with rosy nipples, hardening with cold. She had no knickers on either. She just stepped out of her trousers and kicked them to one side, and Nell saw that the hair between her legs was so fine and sparse it barely covered her. 'Ow, ow, ow,' Charlie said happily as she climbed in, 'it's hot.' And soon, a pink glow had spread across her face and chest and the strands of her hair stood up prettily from her face.

Nell sat on the edge of the bath and trailed her hand in the froth of bubbles. Charlie closed her eyes and lay back. 'Hmmm,' she said and when she opened them she caught Nell looking. 'Get in, why don't you? It's lovely in here.' And she moved her long legs to the side as if to show her just how much room there was.

Nell turned away to take off her clothes. She had on tights and a denim skirt, boots and several layers of vests and T-shirts. She struggled with them in the narrow room, the steam making the walls and floor shimmery with wet until she was naked and uncomfortably aware of the dark, thick triangle of her own hair, the heaviness of her thighs, and the great weight of her breasts as they were released from her bra. There seemed so much of her, although she was shorter than Charlie by five inches at least. Charlie bent her knees against the bath edge and Nell slunk down into the water. It felt good. The heat and the sweet smell and the shiny feel of her friend's thigh up against hers as she slid in. She leant back against the end, propped her head between the taps and smiled.

'So,' Charlie grinned. 'How do you get Dan into your bed?'

Nell didn't answer. She had no idea. It had never occurred to her that it was up to her. Fate, she'd always imagined, would decree.

'How about,' Charlie mused, 'we ask him back here to rehearse a scene. After college. Then we'll go to the pub to discuss, come back here for supper, I'll open wine, you can show him round the flat, and when you get to your room . . . pounce! Hang on.' Charlie rose from the water, her body gleaming, dotted with foam. 'I'll be right back.'

Nell heard the music turned up loud from the sitting room and Charlie appeared again with both glasses and a new bottle of wine. She slipped back in. 'So?'

Nell lifted her glass and took a quick cold slug. 'Let's do it,' she grinned and, although her head was spinning, she raised the glass again and drained it.

'You know something?' Charlie was smiling at her. 'You're gorgeous.'

'No!' Nell protested, disbelieving, thrilled. But she didn't repay the compliment, because she couldn't have said it without blushing, couldn't have watched while Charlie skimmed the foam off the water and rubbed it under her arms, across her neck and over her rose-pink breasts.

Dan had a sweet, buffoony smile and a dark, tousled head of hair. That was his charm, really, and the fact he was faced with almost no competition from the other boys in their year, who were either gay, or obsessed with perfecting juggling skills, or quoting Shakespeare sonnets in low, sonorous voices. Most of the girls had boyfriends in the year above, unfairly popu-lated with heterosexual, possibly even talented, men or, like Charlie, they'd looked outside college for their love affairs. But since the first day of the first term Nell had been in love with Dan. She'd waited, smiling occasionally, brushing past him in the queue for lunch, until one afternoon she realised she'd waited too long, because there was Beth, holding his hand, waiting at the bus stop with him, wearing his scarf. Occasionally, it was true, they split up, but within days there was a stormy reconciliation and there they were again, sheep-ish, tousled, late for college.

'Dan.' Nell caught him in a corridor.

'Hello.' He gave her that wide, soft grin, and shuffled slightly. He wore his trousers low on his hips and when he yawned, which he did often, he showed a glimpse of flat, smooth stomach.

Nell spoke fast before she lost her nerve. She told him about the scenes she and Charlie were rehearsing, how they needed a man for the, she hesitated, male parts, and she sug-gested Tuesday. Next Tuesday. After college.

Dan shrugged. 'Okay.'

'A friend of Charlie's might film it,' she threw in, to make it more enticing.

Dan nodded, as if it was all the same to him. 'See you then.' And he moved off, awkward, along the corridor.

'The deed is done!' Nell hissed to Charlie as they stood at the bar for ballet, risking the hawk eyes and vicious tongue of Olinka, the dance instructor, who'd once tapped Nell's stomach with her stick and loudly requested that she pull it in. Nell's cheeks still burnt when she thought of it and she would have liked to have taken that stick and beaten Olinka with it, and shouted into her ear: 'I want to be an actress not a fucking freak of a ballerina!' But instead she'd stood at the bar with tears of humiliation in her eyes, dreading the moment when they'd have to leap and twirl diagonally across the room.

On Monday night, Nell and Charlie lay in the bath. Charlie had dotted the room with vanilla-scented candles and Nell added some musky essence, twice the recommended amount.

'So what will we rehearse?' Nell murmured. 'Shouldn't we have pages or something?'

Charlie sank under the water and came up, sleek as a seal. 'Oh, we can read a few pages of . . .' she hesitated. 'I'll find something. Don't worry.' She rubbed shampoo into her hair and sank down again, pushing her body hard up against Nell's end of the bath, her legs bent, her thigh against her shoulder. There were tiny bubbles glinting in her pubic hair and it occurred to Nell she could move her hand a matter of inches and slide it between her legs. The thought jolted such a spasm through her that she gasped. It was almost painful, the ache of desire, pushing against her, sharp as a knife.

'Sorry,' Charlie laughed, as she came up, and Nell slid down too, to hide her scarlet face. She kept her body pressed against the bottom of the bath but there was nothing she could do to submerge her breasts which hovered above water, the nipples hardening. To feel Charlie's hand just graze against them, she allowed herself to think, to feel her mouth cover each in turn . . . but she came up as if nothing was different and vigorously scrubbed the hard skin of her elbows with a flannel.

'Right.' Charlie was standing up, rising above her, stepping out. She wound her hair into a towel and left the room. Alone in the bath, Nell felt deflated. She washed under her arms and between her legs, desultory and workmanlike. And with the day looming so close, she began to dread it. The ridiculous idea of the 'pounce'.

Nell and Charlie stood on the steps of college, pretending not to watch, while Dan and Beth said goodbye. Beth clung to Dan and Dan whispered, at unnecessary length, Nell thought, into Beth's ear. Nell turned her back and rolled her eyes and wished she could think of something to say to pass the time, when eventually there he was, loping towards them, his bag hanging carelessly from one shoulder, his trousers lower than ever on his hips. Just then a bus swung round the corner. 'Quick!' Charlie yelled, and they ran towards it, shrieking and free.

They raced up to the top deck and sat in a row at the front, where Charlie, her eyes glittering cruelly, began to sing in perfect imitation of Samantha, a big-boned redhead whose ambition was to go into musical theatre. 'I'm just a girl who can't say no. Can't seem to say it at all.'

'Agony.' Dan was laughing. And Nell reminded them of hulking great Kevin and his rendition of 'Somewhere Over the Rainbow'.

'I thought I was going to die.' Charlie clutched her stomach, and they dissected every minute of that afternoon's music class, every flat note and clumsy move, weaving themselves tight into a net of their own superiority until they were on the corner of their road and they clattered down the stairs, shrieking, 'Stop, wait!' and leapt off the end of the bus as it slowed.

'A drink first? Or rehearse?' Charlie asked and, without waiting for an answer, pushed open the door of the pub. They started with lager, a pint each for Charlie and Dan and a half for Nell, who sat between them at a corner table and explained about the scene they would rehearse and how, when they were ready, a film-school director would shoot it, and show it, probably, to anyone and everyone who was important so that, basically, the three of them, before they'd even finished college, would be stars! As Nell talked, Charlie pressed her arm against hers, and then as they drank, drink after drink, moving from lager to spirits, she wove her arm around her shoulder and twined her finger in her hair as if to present her to Dan as a tender, longed-for thing of beauty or, possibly, Nell found herself hoping, to claim her as her own.

It was almost ten when they tumbled out through the door of the pub. 'Which way?' Dan asked, unsteady, and Charlie linked his arm and snaked her other round Nell's waist. 'Isn't she lovely,' she whispered to him loudly. 'Isn't she fucking gorgeous?' And when Dan stuttered and mumbled she pulled Nell towards her and kissed her on the lips. Nell's mouth opened in surprise and Charlie's tongue slid in, firm and narrow, hot as whisky, her lips as soft as down. As she kissed her, deeper and deeper, she pulled Dan round to shield them, and slid her free hand up under Nell's jacket and rubbed, hard, against her breast.

'Bloody hell,' Dan muttered.

Nell was reeling. She wanted Charlie's hand against her skin, she wanted to unclasp her bra and push her breasts into her mouth, to kneel on the ground and slide her tongue along the length of her thigh, up, slicing and tickling the perfect, pale-pink curve of her slit. She wanted to feel her shiver, feel the wetness release as she teased her, but Charlie had taken control and was leading them both towards the house.

'Bloody hell,' Dan said again, as the door slammed shut behind him and the splintered boards and broken banisters revealed themselves. He covered his nose against the smell of damp and gas, and paled a little as he followed them up. At the first landing he took hold of Nell's hand, but her passion for him had faded and the touch of his skin felt clammy and foreign.

'Boys and girls,' Charlie called from the kitchen, 'wine or beer?' She appeared with both and led them towards the sitting room.

A dark shape appeared in the hall. 'Hello.' It was a man's voice, low and amused. 'What time do you call this?'

'Rob!' Charlie stood and stared at him, until, with one hand, he reached out and took her wrist and pulled her roughly into the bedroom. The door clanged shut behind them and Nell and Dan stood alone in the hall.

'My room's up here,' said Nell, cold suddenly and nauseous from no supper, and she led him up the small flight of stairs to the attic.

Dan sat on the bed while she attempted to light the fire, blowing on it as Charlie had done while the flame guttered and ran and refused to catch. 'Is that safe, do you think?' Dan asked. 'Gas can be dangerous.' And she threw him a withering look before giving up. Their backs to each other, they took off their clothes, or as many of them as they dared, and climbed into bed where they lay side by side until eventually Dan said. 'Do you mind if we don't? It's just Beth . . . she'll mind.'

'No, it's fine. Sorry.' And they turned away from each other and tried to block out the moans and grunts of Charlie and Rob as they crashed about in the room below.

The next day, Charlie's door was firmly closed when Nell

and Dan got up for college and later, when she arrived home – having endured a day of searing headaches and accusing looks from Beth, and all Beth's friends – Charlie was lounging, smoking on the sofa. 'Can you believe it?' She tossed over her pack of cigarettes. 'He's back for good! I hope you don't mind. I mean, you can stay till the weekend, of course, but then you're going to have to find somewhere else.'

Nell stared at her. 'But . . .'

Charlie crawled across the carpet to her. 'He's dumped her. Isn't that great? He's said he's sorry.' She grinned. 'Said it about ten times in fact. My God – how was last night?'

'Last night?'

'Dan? How was it?' Her face was starry with expectation.

'Great.' Nell gathered herself. She even smiled. 'Really good.'

'So, aren't you going to thank me?' she pouted. 'For getting you two together?'

'Oh yes. Of course. Thanks.' Hurriedly, Nell got up and went into her room where, unsure what else to do, she kicked her foot so hard against the fire that the cracked pieces fell out onto the floor leaving nothing but the gas pipe and two camel-humps of wire.

Pas de Deux

QUINCEY PARK

London 1896

I should never have said yes, but you can't expect to be thinking quite straight in the circumstances. I mean, the hansom was lurching about so much you'd have thought the horses were as addled as the cabby was and I was worrying about hurting Esmond – I've got sharp teeth, Ma's always said – and whether my mantle was getting dirty on the floor. So I said yes, or rather I just nodded a little, being a bit squashed and not in a position to speak, and after the half a couple of days later the callboy banged on the dressing-room door with a note for me.

No one took much notice. It was a Wednesday, about halfway through January, and everyone was tired after the matinee, and from knowing it was only Wednesday. Hot too, with snow like a quilt on the roof of the theatre and all of

346

us ballet girls crammed in with the gaslight on all day. I'd left getting ready a bit late. I pulled the note open and then picked up the spoon I was heating my mascara in and held it over the gas again while I read.

Darling Pearl,

I hope you will like the apartment. It is in Gordon Square, No. 15, and you are to arrange it just as you please. I'm sure your mother will have no objection, when she realises how much closer you will be to your work. The house is run by a most respectable lady, a Mrs Mundy, and she will oblige with cooking and cleaning as we choose. You may send your things there whenever is convenient for you: she is expecting them.

I have to go to Birmingham on business for my father, but hope to be back by Saturday, when I shall escort you there. Until then, I shall look forward to taking my dearest girl in my arms.

Your loving

Esmond Straker

P.S. Of course, if the flat is not to your taste, you must tell me and I shall take a different one.

Well! I'd never thought he'd take me up so quick on a word I hadn't even actually said. I dropped the spoon and all the mascara splattered across the table.

Gertie jumped. 'You stupid cow, Pearl! Look what you made me do!'

'Sorry, Gert,' I said. Luckily I'd only my tights and head-dress on and no dress yet to get mucky, or there'd have been a fine for me. But Gertie had a great stripe of grease-paint like a Red Indian down her cheek, instead of the tiny little dot in the corner of your eye that makes them sparkle. I started to giggle but then the five was called and we all had to bustle about to be down on time. It was the beginning of the run – *Cinderella* – and an awful lot of chorus work. None of us had time for thinking except getting the numbers right. Not that I can ever think of anything when I'm danc-ing, even if I want to, not properly. Not even if it's just a few steps while I'm minding the copper in the scullery. I used to dance with my brother Johnnie when he was a baby but he got too heavy, though for years he'd put his arms up and ask. Ma always said, 'Don't feel bad, Polly love. He'll have to learn that there'll be some things he'll never do, not after the fever in his legs, and dancing's one of them.' Pearl's only my stage name, you see, I'm Polly, really, short for Margaret, but Esmond liked to call me by it.

Where was I? Oh, yes, *Cinderella*. It was a good engage-ment but, oh, how I did ache by the end of the week. And I didn't know the other girls well, so none of them warned me, even if they could have. I suppose Maisie might have, but she'd taken the day off to have a bit of bother dealt with in Hammersmith, and in the event she was poorly afterwards and was off for the rest of the week. 'Fancy her letting him put it up *there*!' Gert said. 'In her mouth or up her arse, but not *there*, the silly bitch.' Gert was silly too, saying it in the wings, because Mr Carlton heard her and soon it was all round the place. He was the second Ugly Sister that year, though like Mr Leno said he wasn't any good – no spark – and a couple of weeks later he was given his notice, and Gert said serves him right for eavesdroppping.

Anyway, Esmond. You see, when a gentleman spots you from the stalls and sends up his card from the stage door, everyone knows what's what. Of course there's always some poor chit in her first engagement who doesn't know how it is, and thinks it's Love. But if you survive that, then you've learnt a lesson worth learning. He buys you dinner and escorts you home in a hansom cab, which makes a nice change from a not-very-hot pie and the last bus back to Stepney. And in return you give him a good time, as and when. Since you enjoy that too, and he enjoys his dinner, everyone's happy. Even your Ma's happy if she sees he's behaving himself, and she doesn't think too hard about why you leave home in the morning when the show's not till eight at night. If you're clever you can even tuck away a bit of cash against when your knees start to get stiff and your face lined and there isn't a place for you even in the back row. We all know that's coming.

Don't get me wrong, Esmond was a pet: not much older than me and lovely looking – tall, a proper gentleman. When he smiled at you he really meant it, that was what was so nice. It made you mean it back. And he was generous with it.

On Saturday we ran late; there was some trouble with the limes in the matinee. The limelight crew were all over the place, and the gas men too, and there was a big delay going into the transformation scene. In the end the matinee came down so late that the management sent sandwiches in, there not being time to go out to eat before the last show, so we didn't come down till gone eleven. And I always like to have a good wash before I get dressed, even if I do have to queue for the sink. Esmond was waiting among everyone else at the stage door and we pushed our way out through schoolgirls wanting autographs, and gentlemen callers, and the gallery still pouring down the stairs. In Drury Lane itself it was almost as crowded – all the toffs milling about in evening dress, and tarts and newspaper boys and pickpockets and matchsellers.

I explained about the limes. 'Let's go straight home,' he said in my ear, and I nodded. I was wide awake, the way you are after a show, whether it's good or bad. 'It's not far, but we'll get a cab. I asked Mrs Mundy to leave us a cold supper.' There wasn't a cab to be seen, though, just a wicked little wind that seemed to come straight off the river and whistle along Waterloo Bridge and get in under your skirts and into your throat, however tight you buttoned up your mantle.

'We'll find one if we walk towards Charing Cross,' said Esmond. 'You're not too tired?'

'No,' I said, though I was. 'It's not so bad now the snow's made them give up on the early show. And it's lovely to think I haven't got to get all the way back to Stepney.'

'That was just what I was thinking,' he said, and I could tell what else he was thinking too. The pavements were emptier along the Strand. We talked about the show, and the flat, and what he'd done in the afternoon – playing tennis, and then taking a train out to Harlow to see his old tutor from school, who was getting on and loved a visit. Then he'd dropped by his club and seen some friends. 'But I was killing time, really. Waiting for you.'

I had one hand in the chinchilla muff he'd given me for Christmas and the other in his, tucked into his pocket. He had lovely hands, Esmond, and his gloves were fine enough that I could still feel his fingers: not broad, but long – and clever too. I thought about his clever fingers and felt myself warming up. He felt it too, looking down at me, and I didn't try to stop myself smiling and my tongue showing just a little, just touching my bottom lip, as if I wanted to lick his. That look came into his eyes, and that made a little wanting stir in me, and just that minute a four-wheeler came towards us and Esmond hailed it.

As soon as we were in and trotting up Wellington Street he took me in his arms like he always did. The fur of his coat collar was soft against my cheek and warm when I pressed into it. He was so much bigger than me that being held by him was like a nice kind of drowning: his mouth on mine and me sinking into him, warm broadcloth and starch and that gentleman's smell of cleanness and toilet water. He undid my mantle, a little bit clumsy, and his mouth tasted good, rich with a little bit of whisky, so I began to explore it, all warm and wet to my tongue. His hand slid in and between the edges of my jacket until through the muslin of my blouse, he found where the hard edge of my corsets pressed into the soft curves of my titties. He suddenly breathed out through his nose and I knew that he was hard and wanting more and I was just wondering whether to change from kissing him on the mouth when the four-wheeler stopped with a jolt.

It was ever such a smart house; even though there was no one to see us I was glad I'd done up my mantle and straightened my bonnet. There was even a lamp in the hall, which Esmond said was lit all night for the convenience of residents, and the stairs were carpeted. It wasn't like trying to slip in at home and not wake the children, but Esmond was talking quietly and I could feel all the other residents asleep behind their nice shiny doors. He explained how Mrs Mundy lived in the basement and there was a woman who did the cleaning, and I could order a meal to be ready whenever I liked. When we got to the apartment door – *our door*, he said, squeezing my hand – he unlocked it and then he turned to me and scooped me up, awkward but laughing, and I was laughing too because he was so sweet and clumsy, not like a ballet boy, but so happy and so was I. He carried me straight through the sitting room and put me on the bed, mantle and boots and bettermost bonnet and all. Oh, it was a lovely bedroom; there was a nice little fire in the grate and a big brass bed, very soft and with the biggest, puffiest silk eiderdown I'd ever seen. The carrier had delivered my trunk from home and it was standing by the window, all ready for me to unpack.

Esmond pulled off his overcoat. 'I'm sorry, my darling, you must be famished.'

'No. Like I said, we had supper given us at the theatre.'

I undid my bonnet's ribbons and tossed it onto the chair. 'Wouldn't say no to a glass of wine, mind.'

He bent over the bed and kissed me, just a peck first, but I nipped his bottom lip and he laughed and it turned into a lovely long one. At last he straightened up and went into the next room. I lit the gas lamp and took off my mantle and unbuttoned my boots.

I'd taken off my bodice and skirt by the time Esmond came back with two glasses of wine. He was in shirtsleeves, collar and tie off, and stockinged feet. He gave me a glass and kissed me on the mouth; I could taste that he'd had a drink already. 'To us!' he said, and we clinked. As I drank I untied my petticoat and let it drop to the floor so I was standing there in nothing but corsets and stockings and my prettiest open drawers. I put a hand to the top of my corset and began to undo it, my titties spilling out as the hooks parted.

For a moment he was quite still. Then, very carefully, he took my glass and put it and his own on the table, turned back, and pushed me down onto the bed. I fell into the eider-down and all the pillows and laughed up at him. He pounced on me, catching my ankle then sliding his warm hand up my leg. He ran his finger round my garter – of course, I wore sus-penders for dancing, but he loved the way a garter looked and felt, so I often put them on. The lace of my drawers rumpled about his wrist as he went up, deeper. He reached the top of my stocking and the soft, real skin of my thigh. I love it when a man does that; I get that hot shiver that means you know it's going to be good.

He heard my gasp and pressed his mouth back onto mine, tasting more strongly of wine. He was beginning to smell of man and my back began to curl, pressing me into him. He stopped and reached down to his buttons, all fumbly. I helped him, feeling his cock inside his drawers, and then it sprang out big and hard into my hands, and suddenly I couldn't have stopped him even if I'd wanted to. He didn't try to get undressed, just pushed my knees apart and entered me so quick that I cried out. But even though I wasn't really ready, it was good too, the way he pressed in so deep, again and again, the cloth of his trousers harsh between my thighs, and his slight stubble scraping against my jaw. My back was already curled round to meet him, but it wasn't enough, bending my legs up wasn't enough; I wanted him deeper.

As he pressed in again I lifted my legs and crossed my ankles round his back.

His eyes flew open and he stared at me but he didn't see me. It was that blind stare that makes no sense because the only sense he knows is his cock deep in your cunt, and when it's someone you like it's magic, the way that stare makes you want them so much. All he can do – all either of you can do now – is push together and apart, again and again, until his back arches and his head comes up and just in time he pulls out and seizes you again, so that his cock's pressed between his belly and yours, and with a shout he comes.

When I awoke the fire was almost out. We'd snuggled under the eiderdown but hadn't got properly into bed and Esmond was lying on his front, dead asleep. I was awake, but the blankets under me were scratchy and I was beginning to ache, as I always did. My fanny was a bit sore, too. All I wanted was to be was asleep properly, between sheets, in my nightgown. I slid out and got undressed, quite glad for once that Esmond wasn't watching. The washstand was beautiful – flowery china with gold on the edges – though of course the water in the brass can was long cold, so I just did face and hands and wiped my belly clean. I pulled a nightdress out of my trunk and cleaned my teeth, wondering how everyone was doing at home, whether Alice would manage the little ones in the mornings or have to get Ma back from the shop, whether Nellie would refuse to go to school, whether Bert would be able to carry Johnnie all the way there without being late . . . oh, all sorts of things. At least while *Cinderella* was on and with Esmond so generous I'd still be able to send quite a bit of money home.

I climbed back into bed carefully, so as not to wake Esmond, and it was like climbing into a cloud made of linen and lavender and goosedown – just heavenly – and I lay down feeling as if all my aches would float away for ever.

I was woken again by Esmond's cock prodding me in the back. For a moment I thought it was still night, then I realised the curtains were so heavy and rich that the daylight could hardly get round the edges.

Esmond kissed the back of my neck. 'Good morning, Pearl darling.' His left arm was round my shoulder and when

I turned my head to kiss his wrist good morning he started to play with my nipple. My heart sank a bit, because it was lovely and warm in bed but the last thing I feel like in the morning is a bit of fun, not till I've got up and got myself moving and had a cuppa.

'Isn't this lovely,' he said in my ear. 'We haven't got to go anywhere or do anything, just enjoy ourselves. I knew this was a good idea. Wasn't it, darling?' And he slid his right hand under me so that he could go on playing with my titties, while his left stroked my flank. Then he pulled up my nightdress and pushed his fingers between my legs and began to stroke me there. 'Isn't this a good idea, darling?'

I nodded. It felt nice, of course it did. And I'd get used to it, wouldn't I? Get used to Ma and the little ones being the other side of London, get used to explaining to Esmond that I did want to see them even if it meant spoiling a Sunday, get used to being able to tell, even if he didn't ask, to it being bloody obvious what Esmond wanted.

All of this – the thick carpets and the silk eiderdown and Mrs Mundy downstairs waiting for orders – all of this was for me, because he was such a gentleman, because he always wanted me to be happy and comfortable. But they were also for him, so he could have what he wanted in comfort, whenever he wanted it.

I rolled over and wriggled down the bed, quite quickly, past the smell of myself on his fingers. I had to shove the bedclothes aside so I could breathe while I slid my mouth over his cock. I don't think he'd been expecting me to do that just then. I heard his breath whistle out through his teeth, and I set to work circling my tongue around the ridge and pointing it into the little 'V' at the front, which I knew he couldn't resist. He couldn't resist me stroking his balls either, or the muscle behind them, and soon he was groaning and I almost didn't stop sucking in time because, though he loved it when I swallowed and it's less messy when you're somewhere you shouldn't be, I really, really don't like the taste.

Living so much nearer the theatre paid off, though. I was less tired and I danced better, like I'd found again what my old teacher Mrs Le Maître called my *ballon*. When Maisie was better she was only fit for the back row and quite happy to be there, poor cow, but instead of shifting everyone up Mr Greeley put me straight into her place. And a week after that one of the girls in the front eight sprained her ankle jumping down the stairs on a bus just when the driver whipped up the horses, and I got the place. We had a benefit club so she got sick pay and I didn't feel too bad about it, and I couldn't pretend the extra couple of shillings in my wages weren't welcome, because all the chorus work meant I was getting through the shoes and stockings like you wouldn't believe.

The way they staged it that year, the front eight were partnered almost all the way through the show. My partner was a boy called Joe, who I didn't really know, what with the *Cinderella* company being so big and the front eight being a cut above the rest of us. Not that you'd have called him a boy in any other trade – he was older than me and just the right amount taller and built like a proper tough – just that they always *are* boys, same as we're all girls, even the ones who are married with half a dozen children. Of course some of them are boys in the other way too, but then there are some girls who aren't far off the street either. Takes all sorts, and who knows what any of us would do if we had to?

Anyway, like I said to Esmond when I told him I'd be out all day on Sunday, I needed every minute's practice I could get, and a costume fitting as well. In the front eight there's nowhere to hide.

The theatre was almost empty. We trailed up echoing stairs to the room at the top we'd been assigned. It was dim; the daylight was going and, even with the mirrors crookedly lining the walls, the skylights didn't seem to throw much light around. But they'd lit the stove and it was quite cosy, with Signorina Benelli putting us through our paces and Mr Gordon the pianist thumping away at the numbers while he read in a newspaper about a body found in a trunk. Joe turned out to know what he was doing, and after half an hour I'd got the first number off pat, except for a step where we turned opposite ways on the off-beat, on *pointe* with our arms crossed, and it had to be fast or you landed on the wrong foot at the beginning of the next bar. Three times I got the grip wrong and nearly wrenched his arm out of its socket.

'Stupid bitch!' he said, rubbing his shoulder. 'Do that again and you'll not get off the ground for the rest of the week.'

'Sorry,' I said.

He reached and gave me a hug. 'Don't worry, girl. It'll come.'

A couple of hours later I *jetéd* into his hold for about the hundredth time but we were both pouring with sweat and trembling with being tired and his hands slipped as he grabbed for my waist. I fell off *pointe* and crashed to the floor. I didn't twist anything, thank God, but my banged elbow and my knee stung and there was a ladder in my stocking where the suspender had pulled it. I must have been wearier than I thought because I could feel myself starting to cry.

'Take a ten minutes, ladies and gentlemen,' said Signorina Benelli. 'Is a boy in the house? I call him. We have tea.'

Joe and I sat on a property sofa that looked like it hadn't been mended since before the Crimean War. And the tea, when it came, tasted like it had been sitting in the stage door-man's pot for a month, which it probably had. But between the two it did the trick. I began to feel better.

'Haven't seen you doing the rounds,' Joe said. 'You new, Pearl?'

'My real name's Polly. No, but I was in *A Gaiety Girl* for the whole run, so I've been out of circulation. They say there'll be more of them. Would you do one? A musical comedy?'

'If I could get it. Been on the halls mostly, outside the panto season. Chance would be good, if it's a long run. Dream come true.'

'Maybe.' I drank some more tea and thought of Esmond and the apartment, and tried to work out why I didn't agree with Joe. 'I don't know, though. On the halls, it's up to you which houses you play and how many, if they'll have you. You can call your soul your own, even if things do get a bit thin sometimes. And there's always the panto season. But musical comedy . . . It's good money and may be a long engagement, but you're tied to the one show till the notice goes up, and then that's it. Finshed. Nothing.'

St Mary-le-Strand struck five. Signorina Benelli looked up. 'Eh! Is that the hour already?'

'Only engaged till half-past,' said Mr Gordon, folding up his newspaper.

'We're due in wardrobe at seven,' I said, 'and I wouldn't mind a wash first.'

'We do just the last section,' she said, and I went to the rosin box and had a good grind – soles a little, as well as toes. Didn't want to slip again, that was for sure. The more tired you are the more damage you do. 'From letter "H", Signor Gordon,' Signorina Benelli was saying. Joe and I got ourselves into position. 'Ready?' Mr Gordon started to thump away. 'And *one*, and *two*, and *three*, and *four* and . . .'

It wasn't a hard routine, showy but not tricky. Except there was one lift, the last one, where I jumped off *pointe* into the lift which was more like a dive. Joe had to grab me between the legs, and it took a few tries. Some girls it works best if the boy grips them under the thigh but I always feel safer if his hand's plumb centre. Once Joe'd got it right I found that his thigh was just right, too, for the arch of my back and my arse tucked nicely into his groin. We were lovely and solid, we could have held it for hours.

'And hold, and . . . Yes,' said Signorina Benelli. 'Is good.

And rest. Thank you, ladies and gentlemen. See you tomorrow.' Mr Gordon pushed the score into his case and left too.

I wiped my face down with my towel. 'You going to wash?' asked Joe.

'I suppose. Don't fancy the dressing room, though. It'll be freezing.'

'Do it here, if you like,' he said, pointing at a sink in the far corner. 'I'm going to.'

'Well —'

'I'll go outside and wait on the landing, if you like, and the other way round.'

So we did: me first, like he said, and then him. There was even hot water in the kettle on the stove, and the boy'd left a bit more coal in the scuttle. 'You want a sandwich?' I said, when we were both clean and had changed out of our practice things. It didn't seem worth getting all togged up when we were due in wardrobe, so I just had my undies on and a robe over the top and he was in trousers and a shirt but no collar and tie – it was warm enough that neither of us wanted a jacket. I pulled the packet of sandwiches out of my bag. 'Ham or cheese? Oof, I'm tired! Mind if I lie on the sofa?'

'Thanks,' he said, taking a ham one. 'Go on, get comfortable. Plenty of room for me at the end. Little one like you doesn't take up much space.'

We munched for a bit and I wiggled my toes. When I'd finished my sandwich I lifted one foot to give it a massage. If the front eight's harder work than the back row, it's your feet that take the worst of the punishment.

'You want me to do that?' said Joe, just the way Maisie or Ma would've, and I stretched my foot out to him. He held my foot over the instep and ran his thumb up the sole, just firmly enough not to tickle. It was lovely, just right, better than Maisie even, because his hands were stronger. Then he began to dig into the ball of my foot, and pull each of my toes, firm and gentle, the way you pull a horse's ears, and then the other foot too, and they stopped feeling like they'd been walking on red-hot stones, and went warm and soft like the rest of me.

He did both feet and when I opened my eyes he was smiling, but I could tell by the sag of his shoulders that he was tired too, and we still had a long wait till wardrobe would be finished with Mr Leno and could see us. 'Do you want to put your feet up too?' I asked him, shifting myself towards the back and onto my side. There was plenty of room on that sofa; you could have got half a dozen ladies on it in the days of crinolines and still had room for a pug dog.

'Go on then,' he said, just the way I do to Johnnie if he wants to get into bed with me. Joe wriggled himself along next to me and then lay down. 'So what d'you think to Ma Benelli?'

'She's all right.' He stretched his arms above his head and then winced. 'That your shoulder? I'm sorry.'

'I'll live. You learnt quick enough. You're good all round, aren't you?'

It's always nice to be told, but then he moved and winced again. 'I'll give it a rub,' I said. It was the far shoulder and he rolled towards me so I could reach it. He was really strong, which didn't surprise me because ballet boys *are* strong – they have to be – even though they dance like they're not, and some of the men who want them would rather they weren't. Only I'd never lain beside a ballet boy feeling his breathing all quiet and his big muscles gone easy and soft, and smelling his skin carbolic-clean.

I don't remember asking myself if he was one of those, and by then I knew he wasn't, not really. We fitted together so nicely, so easily, even when we were that tired. His hands were in the small of my back and his mouth matched mine so neatly that I laughed when our tongues met, except it came out as a kind of hum, like music sounds sometimes when you're dancing and it's really got into you. I felt his smile under mine. The muscles in his back shifted as he touched my breasts, gentle and firm, just right like he'd held my aching feet. And when I ran my hands down his back I felt the lovely tight grip of his arse as we got closer together, fitting together again the way it was when we danced . . . yes, we fitted together.

Honest to god, I didn't think of it till then. And even when I realised what was happening – what would be nice . . . what I wanted . . . I don't think I really believed it would happen. It wouldn't be right, because of Esmond. Only I was soft with tiredness, and Joe was so sweet.

He pulled open the ribbon of my chemise and bent his head and licked each of my nipples with his tongue, making a sound as if they tasted good. I was enjoying the way his hair grew short and crisp round his ears and up the muscles on the back of his head, and then he dipped his head and tasted my titties some more, little nips with his teeth, but gently, as if he couldn't resist. He was moving on down me, pushing up my chemise and kissing my belly till I was long-ing for more, burying his face in my bush so that for a while my mind drifted with him. Then he curled into me, not with his fingers but with his tongue, so wet and hot that I didn't shiver, just melted. I even felt his tongue fitting right inside me; it was like electricity, only warm and gentle and I felt a surge inside me so that I moved under his mouth without meaning to.

Then he stopped as if I'd broken the spell by moving, and I wished I'd kept still. He was sliding upwards between my legs, and the weight of him was on me, not all of it but enough, and the warmth of his chest was on mine. He raised his arm and wiped his mouth on his shoulder and then he kissed me, and though he tasted a little of me he tasted more of himself.

'Polly?' he whispered. 'Beautiful Polly. May I? I'll be care-ful.' I nodded, though I knew he'd have stopped if I'd said no. It was like that, him and me. So I didn't have to say no. He slid into me as easily as a hand into a glove, only so much better: close and perfect, like a beautiful, expensive present he was giving me, though by his face you'd have thought it was me giving him the present.

For a moment we just lay, enjoying it. And then it wasn't enough, because even the tiniest movement seemed to light fireworks inside us, and we were greedy, Joe and me, we wanted to keep moving, keep lighting those fireworks, keep trying to catch them as they soared, one after the other in the skylights above us, again and again, thigh against thigh, mouth against mouth, dancing in the air, in the sky, among the stars, until they burst in my head, and I knew dimly that only then did they burst for him too.

We lay together, still fitting; he wasn't heavy on me, and I didn't want him to move. There didn't seem anything to say. But then, it's not easy to put words to such things, any more than the name of a step – *ronde de jambe, pas de chat, tourne en l'air* . . . Any more than any of them, really, can tell you what it feels like.

Roma

OLIVIA PAINSWICK

In an Italian restaurant in west London the conversation, inevitably I suppose, turns to Rome. Restaurant recommendations are swapped. People coo about the Pantheon. 'Is the extravagance of St Peter's an appropriate earthly tribute to God?' asks someone clever. I sip a glass of Barolo while my date talks about a jazz bar in the Trastevere. My free hand rests on the table next to my plate. He picks up my hand and squeezes it as he says, 'September is a great time to visit Rome.' I smile. He smiles back and I realise I might have accepted an invitation.

'The trick with the Colosseum is to join one of the guided tours,' says one of his friends. 'Otherwise you'll be queuing for days . . .'

'I think that place is spooky. All those people who went to their deaths there, chased by lions.'

'Or dwarves with clubs,' adds Mr Clever.

'*Morituri te salutant*,' says the man holding my hand.

And suddenly I remember standing outside the Colosseum feeling as though I was about to die.

You were the man holding my hand that afternoon. Our romantic weekend in Rome. We held hands on the early plane from London and whispered plans for our afternoon 'nap' in the suite you'd booked on business rates. We arrived too soon to get into our hotel room so we walked straight to the Spanish Steps. I took a photo of you there. I still have it. Your eyes are half shut but you're smiling.

I remember that, shortly after I took that photo, it started to rain. We sheltered in the doorway of an English-style tea-shop, surrounded by other tourists. You put your hand up my shirt under the watchful eyes of twenty or so Russian matrons on a walking tour.

When the rain stopped we ran across the Piazza di Spagna to Via Condotti, still holding hands. You took me to La Perla. You almost took me *in* La Perla. In the changing room, you made a bra of your fingers around my breasts as I tried to choose between peach and pink lace. You pressed your pelvis against my buttocks and told me you were going to come in your trousers. The red-haired sales assistant, with perfect English, stood right outside the cubicle the whole time and somehow managed to look nonchalant when we emerged, both smirking and slightly ruffled.

I persuaded you to buy a yellow jacket in Brioni. You

looked so good in it I found myself getting jealous. I imagined other women seeing what I saw and I considered telling you to buy something else. Something like an anorak.

When we returned to our hotel, the room, thank goodness, was ready. The manageress accompanied us in the elevator, not knowing that, for you and I, an elevator was an opportunity for a kiss. I blew you a kiss behind her back. She took forever showing us how to work the air conditioning. When at last she left us alone, I ran a bath while you unpacked. You didn't believe it but I found your compulsive neatness sexy. Like a boss lusting after the tidy secretary in her glasses. Your habitual control made the prospect of your eventual loss of control that much more exciting.

You climbed into the bath behind me and heaped scented bubbles on my shoulders. You blew them away and kissed the wet, bare skin you revealed. You told me you were happy to be there with me, in Rome, in the hotel where you'd once stayed with your ex-wife. I pretended that didn't bother me. I leaned my head back against your chest and you stroked my cheek as though I were the most precious thing in the world.

Still damp from the bath I lay on the wide white bed. You knelt between my legs and dipped your head to kiss me from my belly button down. We made love quickly and slept for three hours in each other's arms.

That night we ate at Osteria del Pesce. Our Italian wasn't good enough to order properly and we ended up with two plates of raw red shrimp. We dared each other to choke one down. I could barely swallow for laughing at the faces you pulled. The waiter brought us something tamer. Something cooked. We drank pinot grigio – more than usual, to wash the shrimp down. As we walked back to our hotel that night, we passed the Pantheon and I thanked however many gods there are that I was in Rome with my lover *and* my best friend.

You fell asleep with your mouth on my shoulder, your breath tickling my skin.

To wake up beside you was always the best start to my day. But the following morning in Rome was exquisite. Woken by the bells of the Trinità dei Monti, my back warmed by the early May sun through the window. You were still asleep. You had your back to me. Your brown skin looked so good against the white sheets, I couldn't resist touching you. I let my hand rest between your shoulder blades for a moment, the way I did whenever you had a nightmare. Somehow that always seemed to work, bringing you close enough to waking to escape the monsters.

I got up to pee. On the way back to the bed, I paused in the doorway between the bedroom and bathroom, just taking in the picture of you to file away in my favourite memories. You stirred and looked up at me. A slow smile spread across your face. You started to get up.

'Stay there,' I said.

I'd promised you a massage. I'd promised *myself* I would give you a massage. The opportunity to touch you was always as much a pleasure for me as it seemed to be for you. It was a rare chance to nurture you in a way that you wouldn't refuse, like you refused my terrible cooking.

I poured the scented oil into my hand and started at your feet. Your perfect feet. I stretched your toes apart and pressed my thumbs into your heels. I moved up your calves, well defined from playing tennis. You sighed; they were stiff from playing tennis too. With two hands I kneaded each of your thighs. My fingers dug deeper into your flesh; you moaned appreciatively. With long strokes, I moved upwards on your inner thighs, brushing your balls with my thumbs on every pass. Then I turned my attention to your buttocks. My favourite bottom. The bottom I admired in a pin-striped suit, in your Brooks Brothers boxer shorts – naked best of all.

'You could stand on any plinth in this city,' I said, bestowing your right cheek with a gentle bite.

I stripped off my cami and prepared for some real work. I poured more oil into the hollow of your lower back. Then, with my hands on your shoulders to help distribute my weight, I placed one of my knees on each of your buttocks. I let my knees slide down towards the bed, leaving you gasping and laughing and begging, 'Again!'

Touching your body always left me feeling hot for you. As I untied the knots in your shoulders, I couldn't help but dip my head to kiss your warm, brown flesh again and again.

'Roll over.'

You did as you were told with a smirk. There was your penis, already erect. You made the usual joke about 'feeling stiff'. I sat astride your thighs and covered my hands with oil once more.

'Stay still,' I instructed. 'I haven't finished the massage.'

But already your hands were around my waist. Then you reached across to the massage oil and poured some onto your own fingers. You slid your hand between our bodies and started a massage of your own.

I tried to move away from you. I hadn't finished working the knots out of your shoulders. I hadn't finished showing you how much you meant to me. But you pulled me down towards you and silenced my complaints with your kiss. I gave up pretending I would ever finish your physiotherapy and instead held your head in my hands so that you wouldn't stop kissing me too soon.

As we kissed, I could feel your hands moving to my waist again. Then, gliding back upwards, you cupped my breasts in your palms. My nipples were already tight in anticipation of the brush of your fingertips.

The cold whisper of a breeze through the open window made me shiver. You pulled me closer. The heat from your body travelled quickly through mine. You rolled me over so that you were on top.

You dipped your head to kiss my breasts. I arched my back towards you, exposing my throat to yet more of your kisses. When it became too much to bear, I wrapped my arms around your neck and drew you down until I could feel the weight of your whole body on mine. I parted my legs around yours and felt your penis resting hard against my pubic bone.

I wanted to feel all of you. I wriggled my hand down between us and sought out your erection. Meanwhile, your fingers had moved to the silken triangle of my pubic hair and quickly found their way inside me. I couldn't help gasping as I felt you make contact with my clitoris, sending sparks of arousal up and down my spine.

I was wet already. Just touching you, massaging you, was enough to do that to me. Now, with your fingers stroking me at last, all I wanted was to have you properly inside me. Not just your fingers. I wanted the most elemental part of you.

I wrapped my hand around your penis, gently moving the soft skin backwards and forwards while my other hand massaged your balls. It wasn't long before you were hard enough for me to tilt my pelvis towards you and slowly guide you inside.

The first penetration always made me sigh. Such a feeling of relief in that moment as my body relaxed around you, and you began to move. I wanted to wrap my arms and legs around you and hold you so close that I started to melt into you. I loved the way you kept on kissing me or buried your face in my neck. I loved the taste of the sweat on your skin when I kissed you back.

I couldn't think straight when you were inside me. The sensation was too big for that. When I closed my eyes sometimes I felt as though I might lose consciousness. When you pushed really deep I felt as though I was sailing over the top of a roller coaster with my heart coming out of my mouth. I felt as though my body had started to tell you all the things

I'd never say – that you were irresistible and fabulous and whenever I saw you I felt as excited and nervous as when you knocked on my door the very first night we kissed. Whenever I was with you, I wanted to be touching you. I wanted to trace your lips with my fingers and breathe in the warm comfort of your flesh. And while you were inside me, I wanted to dig my hands into your buttocks and pull you closer still. I wanted to climb on top of you and look down into your face while you came beneath me and set off a chain reaction of ecstatic laughter in my body. I didn't ever want you to stop.

'Hold me,' you cried out that morning in the Hotel de Russie. I held you as you came. I wrapped my arms around your shoulders and my legs around your waist.

Afterwards, as we lay together, with you still inside me, I felt my body pulsing around you.

'Can you feel me?' I asked.

You nodded into my shoulder. You stayed there for a long time.

I felt loved.

So, later on that night, I thought you were joking when you told me you couldn't go on seeing me. Suddenly you were telling me you couldn't escape the monsters. You weren't prepared to move into the future. You couldn't. My hand between your shoulder-blades wasn't enough any more. You'd messed up in the past and you'd do it again. We had to part before you really hurt me. You couldn't give me what *I* wanted. You told me I didn't know what I wanted. When I tried to express it – when I said that it was you – you told me I was wrong.

So I lay awake all night. The wideness of the bed that had seemed such a luxury was clearly a relief to you. You curled into a ball.

The following day, crazy from lack of sleep, I guess, I suggested that we try to enjoy our time in Rome regardless. No need to go home early, I said. But I felt like dying at the Colosseum. I wanted to throw up while you ate a hearty lunch and drank three glasses of wine.

You held my hand as we walked through the Forum. You kept your promise to kiss me every time we passed a monument. There were lots of monuments. Back at the hotel we got into bed for a nap. You held me like you used to. I could feel your erection against my back. You kissed me on the nape of my neck when you thought I was asleep. But when I turned towards you, to see if I could love you back to me, you told me you weren't going to change your mind. And we argued properly. And you changed our flight to first thing in the morning.

We went to dinner. At Camponeschi on the Piazza Farnese you lifted your glass of Prosecco towards mine and told me you had run out of 'easy toasts'. On the table next to us, a group of Americans were celebrating a golden wedding anniversary. While they made their very easy toasts to love and laughter, I stood up and walked away. I left you with your artichoke and my caprese. I got lost on my way back to the hotel. I passed the Pantheon again and imagined some god I didn't believe in picking up an effigy of you and moving it away from me.

When you got back to our room, you were colder than I had ever seen you. I apologised for walking out on you. I didn't want to embarrass you. You told me you were used to it. Your ex-wife walked out of restaurants all the time. It was the first time you'd ever compared us out loud.

The next day we flew back to London. I left the La Perla underwear in a waste-paper basket in the BA lounge at Rome. I said goodbye to you at the taxi rank at Heathrow. The taxi driver said you must have gone off me, simple as that. Everything else was excuses. Then he told me about his divorce.

And so, half a summer later, I find myself in an Italian restaurant in west London with a man who wants to love me. He wants to give me all the things you said I should want for my life. He can picture me in a white dress and it doesn't make him frightened. He can see his children with my eyes.

He squeezes my hand and I wait to feel something other than the pressure on my metacarpals. Nothing.

He drives me home but I don't let him in. 'I am going to seduce you one day,' he assures me. He plants a kiss on my mouth and lingers there until I have to kiss him back. He wraps his arms around me. My own arms hang limp by my sides. But when he steps back and looks into my eyes, he seems pleased with what he sees there. He's sure that next time he'll be staying the night.

I know I won't see him again.

I walk into my empty house and pour myself a glass of Prosecco. For an easy toast. I sit on the sofa where you and

I shared our first kiss. Which one of us made the first move? When we were telling each other the story, we never could decide. As I remember, we were sitting side by side to begin with, like visiting aunts. The way that I wanted you had taken me by surprise in the Italian restaurant where we'd eaten dinner. I think it was when you made one of your legendary toasts to my brown eyes (which have always been blue).

I remember I tucked my legs up and turned so that I was facing you. You did the same. I stroked your leg through your jeans on the pretence of removing some fluff. You put down the mug you were holding . . .

I remember my relief that you tasted right. We must have kissed for three hours straight that night. Like high-school kids, you'd say later. We undressed only as far as the waist. The following day, I looked like I'd had dermabrasion to my chin. I couldn't wait to do it all again. The memory of your bare chest beneath my hands made me shiver in the queue at the supermarket. I closed my eyes and thought of you lying on top of me, your erection straining at your jeans.

Five days later, we made love for the first time.

'It was always making love,' you told me in Rome. 'I never had sex with you. From the very first time we were always making love.'

I break the silence. You pick up the phone and your voice is like a soft kiss on my ear.

'I think we should see each other,' I tell you.

And you agree.

Dress Code

CASSANDRA BEDWELL

Monday 7 p.m., Barbican Conservatory, London. Ivory lace quarter-cup bra with pink fringe, matching briefs:

She waited patiently, standing quite still. Above her, a fine mist of moisture engulfed palm fronds and dripped down on to leaves as wide and flat as water lilies. She moved slightly, craning her head to glimpse a tumble of purple bougainvillea in a far corner. The path was grainy and damp under her heels. A wan moon peered through broad fronds of *Brahea edulis*, the Guadalupe palm, whose highest leaves grazed the soaring glass roof. Voices drifted over, their owners invisible through dense foliage, but to all intents and purposes she was alone under the chill azure of the night sky. She shivered, beginning to feel cold in her cream suit, which hugged her body but offered little in the way of insulation. Then she detected soft footfalls, someone walking quietly towards her, and her shoulders tensed.

A moment later, his breath was on her neck. His hands gripped her arms and he pressed forward until their bodies touched. He exhaled and held her close for a few seconds, saying nothing as he slid his hands down to her waist. He lingered for a moment, his breath speeding up as he mapped the contours of her body.

'Ready?'

'Of course.'

He turned and shepherded her along the narrow path, palm fronds brushing her shoulders like the fingers of ghosts. On the steps that led out of the conservatory, two men stood close together, one younger than the other. Seeing strangers, they started to move apart, then the younger man caught her eye and a flash of understanding passed between them. He grinned and flattened himself against the railing, his hand on the sleeve of the other man's overcoat, allowing her to pass. She walked without hesitation to the area between the lifts and pressed a button set in the wall. The door opened and a child bounded out, followed by a young woman who started to say something, saw their faces and abruptly turned away. Inside the lift he stood behind her, and she was as still as she had been a few moments before, until it arrived at their floor. The door opened and they headed for the entrance, where he overtook her and strode into the freezing night air. She shivered.

'Taxi!'

He gave the driver an address and they sat side by side in the back, staring ahead. His hand rested on her knee, pushing her skirt aside until his fingers touched her skin. She closed her eyes and moved her legs very slightly apart, feeling the strength in his fingers. After a while, the cab came to a halt at a set of traffic lights. She sat up and glanced through the window, reading familiar street names, and not long after it drew up beside a terrace of white-painted Victorian buildings.

He leaned forward. 'A bit further . . . this is it.'

A revolving door had been set in the ground floor, with a canopy overhead. He got out of the taxi, held the door for her, then took out his wallet and paid the driver. Inside the hotel, a man and a woman waited behind a reception desk, professional smiles already in place.

'Room 119.'

The man handed him the key and a piece of paper. 'Message for you, sir.'

He crushed it in his pocket and guided her to the stairs. On the first floor, they turned right and walked two-thirds of the way down a thickly carpeted corridor. It was dimly lit, with paintings of Venetian masks hung on deep-red walls. No sounds came from the rooms – not even the distant cackle of a television. They stopped outside room 119, light from a discreet wall lamp falling on her sleek blonde bob. She waited as he fitted the key into the lock, opened the door and motioned her to go inside. As she looked round, taking in the antique furniture – reproduction, but with the expensive sheen of solid walnut – he strode across the room and started to close the heavy curtains. They caught, and it took him a moment to shut out the yellow light from a street lamp. When he had finished, he turned and looked at her with raised eyebrows.

'Good,' she said in a neutral voice.

An expression of relief flitted across his face. On a table, a bottle of champagne was chilling in an ice bucket and he set about opening it, pulling the cork with a 'pop' and catching the foam in a tall glass. He filled a second glass and passed it to her, watching as she tasted it. After a few seconds she went to the bathroom, gently closing the door behind her. He moved an armchair, turning it so it faced the door she had disappeared through, and settled in it to wait for her return. Minutes went by and the silence thickened, as though the room itself were braced for what would happen next.

The door opened. She stepped into the room unhurriedly, her clothes removed except for her underwear and high heels. She stood still for a few seconds, then turned a full circle. When she faced him again, he saw that her breasts nestled in an ivory lace bra whose pink fringe feathered upwards, her nipples peeping stiffly through the soft filaments. She stroked the swell of her breasts, then moved her hands down over her belly. Licking her index finger, she stretched the luxurious fabric of her briefs with one hand and slipped the other inside, arching her neck as she touched herself. He gasped, watched for a few seconds, and when he finally broke the silence his voice was unsteady.

'Come here . . .'

He pushed himself out of the chair as she walked towards

him. His hands came up to her breasts and he copied her movements, stroking and squeezing the plump flesh. She pulled away, turning round and leaning against him while he teased her bare nipples between his fingers and thumbs. He pulled sharply upwards and she rose on her heels, relaxing as he let go. He whirled her round to face him again and took a nipple in his mouth, sucking on it as he slid his hand inside her briefs. Her fingers were wet and they entwined briefly with his, then he let go and traced the coarse hair at the top of her legs. He slid her pants down and she cast them aside, still touching herself with her other hand. They moved closer to the wide double bed, heaped with pillows, where she pushed his jacket off his shoulders and unbuttoned his shirt. She undid his belt and fly, stroking his penis for a few seconds before helping him out of his trousers. On the bed, she straddled him and guided him into her. She threw back her head, her breasts overflowing her bra, and he grasped them with both hands. She tilted forwards and they smothered his face, his lips sucking greedily. She lifted her hips until his penis was barely inside her, waited a few seconds and pushed down, repeating the movements and taking more of him inside her each time. At last he reached up and tore off her bra, casting it on the floor. He pulled down and her body bucked as she ground herself against his hips. She cried out, shockingly loud in the silent room, and a few seconds later he came in a series of hot waves. She collapsed forwards and he held her, feeling her breasts flatten against his chest. His penis softened and slipped out of her and they lay still, bound together by semen and sweat. A couple of minutes passed, and their breathing became less ragged.

Abruptly she rolled away from him. Lying on her back, her eyes on the ceiling, she said, 'I must go.'

'The champagne . . .'

She sat up, shaking her head impatiently.

He watched as she moved round the bed, scooping up her underwear. Inside the bathroom, he heard the shower run and got up to get himself some champagne. When she emerged a couple of minutes later, fully dressed, he was sitting on the bed in his underpants. He held up his glass, a questioning look on his face. She looked at him, giving nothing away, and moved to the door.

He said: 'You won't —'

'You know the rules.'

He sighed and slumped back against the pillows. 'Tomorrow?'

'No.'

'When?'

'Wednesday. Perhaps.'

'Here?'

'You'll hear from me.'

She opened the door. Her eyes roved the room, as though she was about to say something. Then she stepped into the corridor, waiting a few seconds as a Sri Lankan maid pushed a heavy trolley past and disappeared from view. He watched the curve of her hip longingly, waiting to see if she would look back. The door closed, and she was gone.

Wednesday 4 p.m., British Museum. Chocolate-brown ankle boots with buckles and three-and-a-half-inch heels:

When she arrived, the gallery was full of schoolchildren, racing up and down and asking questions of two tired-looking teachers. She frowned, checked her watch and was relieved to see that she was ten minutes early. Now the children were gone, herded to another part of the museum, and she was able to look at the exhibits in peace. She stopped in front of the Centauromachy, where human and animal forms twisted and reared in perpetual combat. She leaned closer, examining the detail of a panel that showed a bearded centaur abducting a female figure.

'South metope 29,' she said aloud, sensing his presence beside her. 'A centaur, sometimes identified as Socrates, carrying off a woman.'

He slid his hand under her arm. 'Seen enough?'

'Yes.'

They crossed the gallery, the spike heels of her boots clicking on the floor. She pushed open a heavy door and he noticed that her nails were painted a glossy brown, matching her ankle boots. He waited as she retrieved her coat from the cloakroom, pulling it on as she skirted a group of French tourists. He followed her down the steps and across the courtyard to the main gates.

'Taxi?'

'No need.'

She turned left and he followed, speeding up to match her

swift pace. Not long after, she stopped outside a flat-fronted house with black railings and a wrought-iron balcony. Taking out a set of keys, she identified one and slipped it in the front door. It swung open to a tiled hall with a broad flight of stairs leading to a dark landing. She hesitated for a second, glanced round, and then went to the first door on the right. She opened it carefully and gave a little sigh of approval. Inside was a drawing room, warmer than the hall, with gold silk curtains and flames leaping in an Italianate marble fireplace. Table lamps cast a gentle light over sofas, chairs and book shelves crammed with old bindings. He remained on the threshold as she removed her coat.

'The door.'

He turned and closed it, took off his overcoat and draped it over the back of a wing chair. She stood in front of the fire for a few seconds, warming herself, then bent to grip the hem of her dress. She rolled it up, slowly and carefully, lifting it over her tumbling brown hair and dropping it on the floor. Underneath she was naked, no underwear, her body tilted forward by her spike heels. He walked towards her, his face tight with expectation, and reached for one of her breasts. It filled his hand and he slipped the other between her legs. They moved apart a little as his fingers pushed between her labia, moist to his touch. She used invisible muscles to grip, grip and release, while her hand stroked his penis through the fabric of his trousers. She undid his fly, brushed the glans with her fingers and took a couple of steps away from him.

She turned, the pinkish-gold light from the nearest lamp

transforming her back into a shadowy landscape. He watched for a moment, freeing his penis, and saw her place her hands on her hips. Her waist was tiny and he was about to circle it with his hands when, with an abrupt movement, she bent forward and grasped her thighs with her hands. Her legs made a perfect inverted 'V' in the high heels: an arrow leading to straight to her vulva. He gasped, stumbled towards her and seized her hips, pushing his penis into her. She tottered but steadied herself as he made a series of long thrusts, burying himself in the generous flesh of her buttocks.

She exhaled as he completed each action, pushing herself hard against him. He dropped his hands, trusting her to take his full weight, and cupped her breasts as they swayed in time with his thrusts. She reached for the mantelpiece, bracing herself as he speeded up, and moaned as his semen flooded into her. Neither of them moved for several seconds, then she pulled away and his penis slipped out of her. He tried to take her in his arms but she was already busy, wiping herself and reaching for her dress. She lifted her arms, slid the dress over her head and, shaking her hair free, smoothed it over her hips. She went to a gilt mirror, rearranged her hair and applied fresh lipstick. By the time she turned, her face cleared of smudged make-up, he had dressed and was moving away from the fire.

'Hot in here.' He wiped his brow. 'Who does this house —'

She moved to the door.

'Wait. Tomorrow?'

She shook her head.

'Friday?'

'Maybe.'

She opened the door and frowned, glancing towards the stairs as though she had heard something on an upper floor. She listened for a moment, but the noise wasn't repeated. Her shoulders relaxing, she stepped into the cold hall.

Saturday 7.50 p.m., rue des Francs Bourgeois, Le Marais, Paris. Elbow-length gloves, black kid with jet buttons:

The restaurant was beginning to fill up. Couples and small groups hurried across the courtyard from the street, eager to escape the icy winter air as they pushed open the painted double doors. The room was warm and welcoming, despite the high ceiling and a minstrels' gallery that overlooked it on the far side. She was wearing a black dress, her red hair swept up at the back by a couple of tortoiseshell combs, and she touched it now and then with a gloved hand. The fine black leather showed no marks, stretching over her fingers like a second skin, and tiny buttons marched in a row over the inside of her wrists. He had ordered as soon as they arrived, and she was sipping from a small glass of Saint-Véran while he drank from a bottle of Burgundy. A middle-aged couple sat down at the next table, exchanging discreet *Bonsoirs* with them before beginning a conversation punctuated by frequent hand gestures.

A waiter came to their tables balancing two huge white plates, barely hesitating before placing a carpaccio in front of her. Without hurrying, she undid the buttons on each glove and slipped her fingers out, pushing the black kid back to her wrists. He watched, observing as she picked up a fork that her nails showed the same red glints as her hair. She rolled a sliver of meat onto the tines, along with a few roquette leaves, and slipped it into her mouth. Her teeth were small and sharp and she chewed delicately for a few seconds, savouring the texture of raw beef on her tongue.

He swallowed. 'The Romans . . . the Romans believed it was an aphrodisiac.'

She looked at him.

'Roquette,' he said, gesturing towards her plate.

She said nothing, but permitted herself a tiny smile. He attacked his fish, eating too quickly. Even so, she finished first and pushed her place away.

He looked at her empty glass. 'More wine?'

'No thanks.'

She drank some water, sitting in silence while he dislodged the white flesh from the bones. When he finally put down his knife and fork, she signalled to the waiter.

'Deux cafés, s'il vous plaît.'

She held her hands in front of her, splaying her fingers and slipping them back into her gloves. Reaching across the table, she allowed him to fasten the buttons along her wrists. He was about to speak when she shook her head, her eyes flicking up in the direction of the minstrels' gallery. She waited a moment to make sure he had understood.

'One minute.'

She got up and crossed the room to the stairs, drawing admiring glances from men on other tables. An arrow pointed upwards, above the word 'Toilettes', and she began to climb, quickly disappearing from view. He glanced at his watch, rapped the table lightly with his fingers, then checked his watch again. Their waiter was nearby and he told him nervously, 'Je vais retourner dans un instant.'

He went up the stairs, pausing when he reached the top. A second arrow pointed to the right, down a short corridor with several doors, but a movement in the shadows to his left caught his eye. She beckoned, a gloved finger on her lips, and he shot an apprehensive glance towards the balustrade separating the minstrels' gallery from the floor below. He edged round a stack of gilt chairs, with a guitar case piled precariously on top, as she signalled him to hurry up. She drew him into the shadows, undoing his fly and taking out his penis.

'Mmm,' she said, cradling it in one hand and running a black fingertip along its length. It stiffened at the touch of leather, deceptively rough on his sensitive skin. He groaned as she stroked it, transfixed by the sight of his penis in her black-gloved hands, and glanced towards the balustrade again, sure that someone in the restaurant must have heard him. She shook her head, amused by his apprehension, and her movements got faster. Suddenly, without warning, she dropped to her knees, cupped his balls in one hand and used the other to guide his penis halfway in to her mouth. He froze, desperate not to cry out, and stared at her head, bobbing up and down above her black hands. She teased the glans with her tongue for a few seconds, sensed he could not hold back much longer, and took him fully into her mouth. He felt the touch of her sharp little teeth and seized her red hair in his hands, trying to keep himself upright as he came. She allowed him a moment to recover, then removed his hands and pulled away. She got up, wiping her mouth, and smoothed down her dress. Her gloves were rumpled at the elbows and she pulled them straight with a sharp tug.

When she was sure she looked as she had before, she gave him a half-smile and walked away. She reached the top of the stairs, shot him a warning glance over her shoulder and spoke loudly to someone. '*Ah oui, monseiur, vous avez raison,*' he heard her say, and he flattened himself against the wall.

He heard a man's voice, exchanging pleasantries with her in French, and scrabbled to dress himself as a grey head came into view. The man turned right without hesitation, following the arrow, and disappeared into the men's lavatory.

He gave himself a few more seconds to get his breath back, and returned to their table. She was drinking her coffee, and the bill protruded from a red leather wallet in the middle of the table. He reached for it as he sat down but she pushed his hand away. On closer inspection, he saw a wad of twenty-euro notes under the bill.

He leaned back in his chair, exhausted.

'Coffee's good,' she said, and he stared at her in surprise.

He lifted his cup and drank it in one gulp, even though it was colder than he liked. The cup rattled in the saucer as he put it down.

'Shit,' he said.

She raised her eyebrows.

His face reddened. 'Sorry, need a pee.'

He got up and crossed the floor, pausing to let an elderly woman climb the stairs in front of him. At the table, she rolled her eyes and signalled to their waiter.

'*Mon manteau – et un bout de papier.*'

'*Bien sur, madame.*'

The waiter picked up the cash and returned a moment later with a piece of restaurant stationery. He helped her into her coat, and she stooped to scribble a few words. Then she folded the paper and held it out.

'Could you give this to my husband?'

'Of course.'

She pulled the edges of her coat together, tied the belt and went to the door. Another waiter hurried to hold it open for her, and a blast of cold air entered the room. Thrusting her hands into her pockets, she gazed up at the clear night sky for a few seconds. Then she left the restaurant without a backward glance.

Girls' Own Guide to Gang Banging

DIXIE ATHEL

Me and Sonya Lingus are what the glossy magazines call new ladettes. We shag before the first date, we drink more beer than the blokes and we yell intelligent stuff like 'how's about it?' at cute boys from Sonya's hotted-up Torana. Thanks to a nifty new Dutch device called the P-Mate we've even tried pissing standing up, though I had second thoughts about this particular manifestation of feminine anarchy after missing the dunny and filling up an ugg boot.

Were our feminist foremothers thinking of urine-soaked lambskin when they fought for equal rights? Probably not. But me and Sonya like getting trashed, telling filthy jokes and treating guys like those disposable paper undies you get at the bikini waxers. Or at least we like saying we like stuff like that . . . Sometimes it's hard to know where one thing ends and the next thing begins.

I guess the point I'm trying to make is that if any two chicks were up for a wild night with two high-class hookers in the poshest brothel in town, it'd be us.

As things turned out, however, what should have been our boldest adventure ever ended in bleeding nipples, bitter recriminations and a nasty scuffle with a security guard the size of a kombi. It certainly wasn't anything like the girl-on-girl action in *Tonk* magazine, where four chicks only have to be in the same room for a matter of seconds before everyone's popping out their boosie wah-wahs for pillow fighting and multiple orgasms.

The trouble started when I turned up at work after another thrilling night of watching a bunch of strippers sit on each other's faces in tubs of lukewarm hydroponic plant jelly. Despite my new ladette pride, I didn't mean to become the jelly-wrestling correspondent for a dodgy men's magazine. Remember everyone saying they wanted to be a doctor or a zookeeper or an astronaut when they grew up? Well, back then, I wanted to be one of those things, too. It certainly wasn't my burning ambition that one day the editor of *Tonk* would send me out to write an investigative feature on the exact finger placement required for the jelly-wrestling six-pack hold. (For the record, you bend your index finger and thumb into a kind of C-shape before jamming them into your opponent's . . . oops, nearly forgot, the story's embargoed until next month so you'll just have to wait for the mag.)

My original plan was to become a journalist. But after four years of studying creative writing at uni, I emerged dazed and blinking into the real world to discover that the novel was dead and the only non-men's magazine writing jobs involved churning out endless advertorials for free community newspapers. Six-packing for *Tonk* seemed positively Lois Lane-ish in comparison. It also meant I got to meet Sonya Lingus.

The day I started work as *Tonk*'s token girl reporter, I was introduced to *Tonk*'s token girl art designer. She had a shock of spiky blonde hair, an *I Smoke So Fuck Off* T-shirt and a photo of a buxom blonde centrefold up on her computer screen. The centrefold's working name was Sapphire Diamond but she looked like more of a Rhinestone Bauble to me.

'Labia patrol,' Sonya Lingus said as she zoomed in on Sapphire's pink bits. 'We have to airbrush 'em out so we don't run foul of the government's censorship regulations. Girls' dangly bits break the DGD rule.'

'DGD?'

'Discreet genital detail. If *Tonk*'s labia are too outgoing, the mag'll have to be sold in a protective plastic sheath, and we all know that just doesn't feel the same.'

By the time Sonya had finished working her magic, Sapphire's undercarriage looked like it had been set to with a needle and thread.

'No wonder chicks are spending a fortune on designer vaginas,' Sonya snickered. 'We train our readers to expect Barbies then they freak out when they realise their birds have regular bacon sandwiches.'

I laughed, even though I felt a little sheepish about my

own asymmetric privates. A tactless high-school boyfriend had once said they looked like they'd been in a fight.

After relieving Miss Diamond of her labia, Sonya took me across the road to meet the rest of the *Tonk* editorial team in the skanky front bar of The Stiff Earl. It was 11 a.m.

'Beer-o-clock,' I said, shaking hands with everyone using my best crusher grip.

Sonya and I joined forces and before long our exploits were notorious throughout the office. If our workmates did twelve cocksucking cowboy shots at the pub, we did thirteen. If they made some gross comment about a lap dancer's bum, we made a gross comment about her bum *and* her boobs. Every so often I felt guilty about selling out the sisterhood, but it wasn't as if anyone was going to get anywhere at *Tonk* if they were all girly and menstrual and kept yakking on about their feelings and university degrees and stuff. Not unless they also looked good with a staple through their navel, anyway.

Not that you care about any of this. 'Bring on the brothel story,' you're yelling – maybe from a hotted-up Torana with a *Dukes of Hazard* horn of your own. 'Bring on the high-class hookers and the all-girl hoochie-coochie. And are you sure there wasn't just a little pillow fighting?'

Okay, well, what happened with the brothel was this. Just when me and Sonya thought we couldn't get any more amazed at the stuff guys get up to, we went to The Stiff Earl for lunch and discovered that *Tonk*'s team of executives had adopted a novel approach to corporate bonding. They'd just taken a clutch of Japanese investors to a new designer brothel called Voulez-Vous and had spent the afternoon drinking Moet and nailing hookers together.

'What, in the same room?' I asked Roger, *Tonk*'s executive editor and the only Voulez-Vous invitee at our table.

'Yeah,' he said, tiredly. 'I think it was called the Org-ecutive Suite.'

Roger used to be *Tonk*'s chief sub-editor and had written so many beaver headlines for so many beaver photos, he barely had any interest in real live three-dimensional women any more.

And he wasn't the only male staff member suffering beaver fatigue. Once we'd busted Dylan from photographic in the toilets jiggling over an imported copy of *The New York Times*. As he sprinted red-faced from the scene of the crime, we couldn't help noticing that the newspaper was open at a photograph of Condoleezza Rice.

'But back to Voulez-Vous,' I asked Roger, jabbing a blunt butter knife into one of The Stiff Earl's infamous five-dollar bar steaks. 'What happened, what did you do, what was it like?'

'I dunno,' Roger replied. 'It was pretty much like it always is, I guess.'

'*Like it always is?*' Poor old Rog dodged half-chewed steak flecks. 'How many of these company gang-bangs have you been to?'

A single squiggle of alfalfa twitched from the corner of the executive editor's mouth as he made some mental calculations. 'Oh, I don't know,' he said after a while. 'A dozen. Maybe more.'

My jaw hit the floor like a cartoon dog's.

'But isn't it uncomfortable having sex in front of each other like that? Doesn't it feel weird when you have to sit across from each other in the boardroom the next day?'

Roger shrugged and said he'd never given it much thought.

'Men are different to women,' one of the young guns from accounting chipped in. 'We have porn nights instead of sewing circles. It's just our way of bonding.'

That afternoon I could barely concentrate on work (and I had to write captions to go with X-ray photos of guys with champagne bottles stuck up their bums so I really needed my wits about me). The whole 'girls are different to boys' line drove me nuts. After all, weren't she-men like me and Sonya Lingus proof that gender differences were just a social construct?

What I have learned today is that – despite everything we have achieved in the workplace and in the pub – men still see us as little more than knitters, I emailed Sonya bitterly.

So what? Sonya replied. *What I have learned today is that brothel creeping with one's associates is an essential networking activity in modern business. In the interests of keeping up with the Joneses, therefore, I reckon we should give it a bash.*

I stared at my *Baywatch* screensaver – a close-up of Pamela Anderson giving another drowned scuba diver boob-to-mouth resuscitation – and pondered the magnitude of

Sonya's suggestion. Like every other twenty-something woman in the twenty-first century I was bi-curious, but was I Sonya-curious? The thought of the two of us watching each other have sex weirded me out, but, as always, the new ladette won out.

Fuck the Joneses, I emailed back. *I just want to keep up with the Rogerses. Let's do this thing.*

Rockin', wrote Sonya. *Tell Mike you wanna do a pervy story then* Tonk*'ll pick up the tab.*

Mike was the new features editor. He was so new he still hung round the photo studios hoping to catch a glimpse of the centrechicks' tits. Roger gave Mike three months before he Condoleezza Riced.

'Brilliant, love, brilliant,' he said when I dropped into his office and casually mentioned the Voulez-Vous idea. 'Two working girls meet two working girls. This is very *Tonk*, love. Very *Tonk*.'

Mike swung his Cuban heels onto his desk and adjusted his tight, mid-life crisis jeans. He asked how much the Voulez-Vous expedition was likely to cost and I suggested he look up the tax invoice from the afternoon before. Mike looked confused and I realised *Tonk*'s newest employee was still a few corporate rungs below the male version of the glass ceiling.

'I'll make some inquiries,' I said, returning to my desk to look up Voulez-Vous' website.

The place was swish, there was no doubt about it. Paparazzi shots from the A-list opening night showed celebrity hairdressers with streaming nostrils and soap-opera stars with fluorescent teeth. The world's oldest profession was suddenly very *now*. I clicked the link marked 'Our Ladies' and was swamped by a veritable tsunami of Destinys, Candys, Angels, Ravens and Cherrys. Voulez-Vous might be 'redefining the concept of pay-for-pleasure' but the fake names used by its working girls were as naff as those at any other two-bit bawdy house.

The online inquiry form invited me to nominate my preferred hair colour, figure and personality type. (Options for the latter included sultry, bubbly, naughty, loveable and, oddly enough, secretary.) After browsing through the profiles, I zeroed in on Mercedes, a 'busty brunette bombshell' from South America, who specialised in party bookings, massage and light domination. The accompanying photo was of a faceless woman standing over a naked man in the shower. She had huge slippery breasts and a mess of wet dark hair that clung to her shoulders. Mercedes' hips were way too Marilyn Monroe to ever make it into the pages of *Tonk* but that was fine by me. Like Roger, the albino stick insects we ran month after month left me absolutely cold. I stared at the photo of Mercedes and her jewel-encrusted riding crop for ages before dialling the number.

'Good afternoon, this is Voulez-Vous, how may I help you?'

'Mercedes,' I blurted out before hanging up.

I couldn't believe I'd choked.

While mustering the courage to try again, I emailed Sonya the website details and suggested she pick a bitch.

Mimi, she emailed back seconds later.

You're kidding, right? The only thing she's written under 'personality' is 'excellent service provider'...

And what are you hoping for? A conversationalist?

I had to admit she had a point.

I braced myself and rang Voulez-Vous again. The posh woman who answered said her name was Cordelia and asked how she could help me. I battled to quell the quiver as I asked how much it would cost for two people to hire Mercedes and Mimi for an hour in the Org-Executive suite.

'Has your boyfriend brought you here before?' Cordelia asked.

'My boyfriend?'

'Oh, I'm sorry. I mean, your husband.'

'Actually,' I said, summoning my best crusher voice. 'I'll be coming with a business associate. A female business associate.'

Voulez-Vous' unflappable madam almost flapped.

'So you're both women?'

'That's right.'

'And you're after a full service?'

'Exactly.' (I had no idea what a full service involved but I couldn't imagine the *Tonk* execs turning up and asking for just a half or a quarter.)

Cordelia paused again before clicking into professional mode. You could almost hear the whir of her hard drive.

'All right. Rates start at $150 for thirty minutes but there's a $100 surcharge per service provider for lesbianism. Our imported Belgium spas – all of which are cleaned with ozone jets between clients – cost an extra $30. Uniforms, fetish and toys also involve additional fees.'

I tried to splutter something outraged about the sexism of the lesbian surcharge but sound had ceased to come out of my mouth.

'Safe sex at Voulez-Vous is mandatory,' Cordelia continued. 'Fisting, role-play and kissing are up to the discretion of individual service providers and must be negotiated with the receptionist beforehand. We accept all major credit cards and there is a complimentary ATM on the premises. Would you like to proceed with a booking?'

I managed to squeak out a 'yes' followed by an equally high-pitched 'tonight, if that's okay'. Cordelia asked if I'd hold.

During the wait, I was treated to love-song dedications on a cheesy FM radio station. A mechanic called Warren wanted to know if a hairdresser called Shazza would do him the honour of becoming his wife. For some reason, he thought playing her 'Even the Nights are Better' by Air Supply would seal the deal.

'I'm sorry,' Cordelia said on her return. 'Tonight we only have one worker who does girl-on-girl. If you want two, you'll need to wait until tomorrow. Does 7.30 p.m. suit you and your . . . associate?'

I said that was fine and Cordelia – clicking back into computer mode – said Voulez-Vous' stunning service providers looked forward to fulfilling our every fantasy in an environment that was both classy and sensual. She also suggested

I bring the $830 in cash if I wanted to avoid a hefty credit-card surcharge.

Voulez-Vous was halfway along a deserted lane in the inner city. Its façade was dark and windowless and its front door was blank. Sonya and I barely had time to finish sculling our car beers before a woman with a short, furious bob appeared and ushered us inside. Clearly we'd been spotted on the brothel security system.

'Welcome to Voulez-Vous,' the bob's owner said. 'My name is Cordelia. I believe we spoke on the phone.'

Sonya mimicked the madam behind her back as she led us through a dimly lit hall to an even more dimly lit bar.

'Make yourselves at home,' Cordelia said, still in computer mode. 'You won't be interrupted. We have a total of twelve pre-service bars and lounges in order to offer our valued clients the absolute discretion and superlative quality of service that has made Voulez-Vous famous among short-stay hotels today. Would you care for a drink while you're waiting? Bunny and Crystal are just freshening up.'

Sonya sniggered. 'So Mercedes and Mimi are washing their hair tonight?'

Cordelia shot her an icy look.

'As I mentioned to your associate on the phone, this is a rather unusual request. We've never taken a booking from two women before. It took some time to find service providers who were prepared to meet your special requirements. Now, about the payment . . .'

After forking over the cash, Sonya and I fortified ourselves with Dutch courage followed by champagne courage, beer courage, then just a few shots of straight tequila courage.

'Bunny and Crystal must be really fucking fresh by now,' Sonya slurred after an hour-and-a-half of downing overpriced drinks and listening to Sade on the brothel stereo. 'Do you reckon we could request some Acca Dacca just for a change of pace?'

And that's when two of the blondest, thinnest women I'd ever seen pulled aside the bar's ruby curtain. Both had strappy evening gowns, towering glass stilettos and tiny ankle tattoos of roses.

'Hello,' squeaked one. 'I'm Crystal.'

'And I'm Bunny,' the other drawled in a broad Australian accent. 'How youse doin' tonight? Managed to tear yaselves away from the Bulldogs game, didja? Go the Doggies!'

The situation was so surreal that not even Sonya could think of a smartarse response. She did, however, belch loudly.

Bunny and Crystal led us through a maze of dark halls, closed doors and X-rated paintings, chatting relentlessly. Everything else about the place was deadly quiet. It was like a funeral parlour with porn.

'Check this out,' Bunny said as we reached the door marked Org-Executive Suite. 'The "o" in Org is a peephole so ya can check to see whether the guy inside's ya priest or whatever. Don't laugh. It happened to Tiffany last week. She coulda spewed.'

I made a note of this excellent insider info, but couldn't help thinking that Bunny was being a little too chummy – that she saw us as a couple of girly mates rather than as demanding clients whose every urge must be gratified.

'Well, here we are,' she said, leading us into a room painted in gun-metal grey. Hard-core porn beamed from giant plasma screens on the walls. There were two king-sized beds, a whole bunch of matching couches and a desk with an old-style phone.

'That's for when they want us to do Dirty Secretary,' Bunny explained. 'We keep our bobby pins and Nanna glasses in the top drawer.'

Our service providers asked us to take showers and wait for them in the spa, then disappeared.

Sonya and I looked at each other.

'Fuck,' I said.

'Double fuck,' said Sonya.

'This is so fucking weird.'

'This is *so* fucking weird.'

And then we did something we'd never done before. We giggled. Like a couple of schoolgirls. And it didn't stop. Giggling as we hauled off our jeans. Giggling as we showered. Giggling as we raced dripping from the ensuite to the spa.

'Saw ya boobies,' tittered Sonya.

'Saw ya front bum,' I teeheed back.

And that's what Sonya and I were doing when Bunny and Crystal arrived sans their sparkly evening gowns. Squealing and splashing water at each other like a couple of six-year-olds. We were having so much fun I was kind of disappointed that our service providers had returned.

'Mind if we join youse ladies?' Bunny said, waving a vodka bottle in one hand and a lurid pink vibrator in the other. 'We picked up some supplies.'

She and Crystal slipped out of their robes and slipped into the bubbles.

'Oh, well,' I thought with a gulp. 'Here we go . . .'

I couldn't have been more wrong. For a full half-hour, all Bunny and Crystal did was talk. About the awesomeness of their Russian eyebrow waxer, about the shittiness of their work hours, about the dodginess of Crystal's boyfriend who'd started selling weed out the back of his tanning salon. It was like they were going out of their way to avoid mentioning anything remotely sexy. Crystal had even sunk beneath the bubbles so we couldn't see anything.

As Sonya drank more and more of the vodka, I was struck by a hideous realisation. Bunny and Crystal expected us to make the first move.

Now, normally this wouldn't be a problem. We new ladettes are first-move maniacs. We think nothing of wall leaning and arse groping and space shuttling straight to fourth or fifth base. But sometimes it gets tiring always calling the shots. Just once it'd be a relief to offer the steering wheel to someone else.

Unfortunately Bunny and Crystal weren't those someones.

'Just out of interest,' Sonya finally blurted out. 'If we were men would you be fucking us by now?'

Crystal blushed and sank even further into the Belgium bubbles. 'Um, probably,' she said. 'But usually guys tell us straight out what they're after – you know, at the start of the session. So, um, what was it that youse were after?'

'We want to be like the groups of guys who come here,' I said lamely. 'You know, the businessmen.'

'Oh, right!' exclaimed Bunny. 'So youse are after a full service, then. Geeze, why didn't ya say something earlier? We're really gonna have to get cracking.' As we leapt out of the spa and started towelling off, Sonya asked our escorts if they were bi. Bunny said 'yes' and Crystal said 'no'.

You're not bi?' was the last I heard from Sonya as Bunny grabbed my hand and led me to the king-sized bed nearest the door. She plonked me down in front of a tiny light attached to a bendy antennae.

'Sorry, darl,' she said. 'You're gonna have to spread 'em for the VD check.' She flicked a switch and a vicious fluorescent beam speared between my legs like a Star Wars lightsaber.

'That red mark's just an ingrown hair,' I said defensively.

'No worries, darl,' Bunny replied, snapping off her pink latex gloves. 'You're clean as a whistle.'

Then, before I knew what was happening, she flipped me onto the bed and started wriggling up and down my body like an over-caffeinated goanna. Thanks to six months of *Tonk*, I recognised this as a body slide – the standard opening move of sex workers across the world.

Bunny had a bony body and breasts the size of marbles.

What she lacked in vital statistics, however, she made up for in chafe-eriffic enthusiasm.

'You're a rool treat,' she whispered, sliding up and down until our spa-dried skins crackled with static. 'Normally all I get to fuck are hairy old perves but you're a rool treat.'

Bunny squeezed my boobs and stuck her tongue down my throat. I'd always thought kissing was an absolute no-no for sex workers but she seemed really into it.

I tried to be into it, too, I really did, but it just wasn't working. Weirdly enough, the STD inspection had got me going a bit (I guess they don't make all those naughty-nurse porno videos for nothing) but after that I just felt, I don't know, removed or something. Everything was moving so fast.

After another quick pash, Bunny dived between my legs, shooting up a hand so she could keep pumping away at my boobs while she slurped. I glanced up at the ceiling mirror and noticed that Sonya and Crystal were in a similar position. Sonya's eyes were closed and her right hand was still wrapped round the bottle of vodka. Every so often she took a slug without looking. Crystal's head hovered between her client's thighs. Occasionally she slipped a hand round her back to massage a point just above her bum, but apart from that there was no movement at all.

Wow, I thought. Real-life sex is so much more monotonous and so much more *still* than it is in the movies.

Speaking of monotonous, I suddenly realised that despite (or perhaps because of) Bunny's cunnilingus callisthenics, I wasn't even close to having an orgasm. For a moment

I actually considered faking it. Despite her inane jacuzzi chitchat and her annoying football obsession, Bunny seemed like a nice person and I really didn't want to upset her. Then I thought about what that sewing-circle prick from accounting would say if he found out I'd faked an orgasm so I wouldn't hurt a hooker's feelings.

No, if this was going to happen it had to happen for real.

I closed my eyes and went through all my favourite masturbation fantasies hoping one would do the trick. But all I could think of was the ridiculousness of the situation. Here I was, experiencing the ultimate sexual fantasy in real life, and I was having to close my eyes and imagine I was jerking off.

I was about to tap Bunny on the shoulder and raise the white flag when the door to the Org-ecutive Suite slammed open and a woman appeared. A wild, dark-skinned woman with huge, shiny breasts and a mess of coal-coloured hair snaking down her shoulders. Mercedes wore black thigh-high boots and leather shorts that glistened and strained around her mighty thighs. A corset pushed her breasts into tight globes and sliced the flesh on her back into diamonds.

The dominatrix banished Bunny to a corner then strapped my wrists behind my back and forced my thighs apart with ankle cuffs and a steel rod.

'Adore me,' she said, standing over the bed so her legs towered above my face like skyscrapers. 'Adore me.' Her eyes glittered and the leather tip of her whip tasted sour. I gazed up at the swollen folds of her cunt, at the pierced, dangling lips, as hot piss rained onto my face and gushed between my breasts.

I came – a vicious, shuddering orgasm – just as the loud-speaker crackled and Cordelia informed us that our time was up.

'Good on ya, darl,' Bunny purred, emerging shiny faced from between my thighs. 'Just in the nick of time.'

I ran for the shower and scrubbed myself down with Voulez-Vous' grainy green soap. When I emerged, Sonya was lecturing a crestfallen Crystal about the exact function of the clitoris.

'I wasn't even close to getting off,' she said to me, shaking her head and slugging back the vodka. 'Not even close.' Sonya had a mean look in her eye. She gets like that when she's been drinking.

'Oh, God, I knew I should have practised beforehand,' Crystal moaned, looking genuinely distraught. 'Come back in three weeks and I promise I'll be better. Bunny'll help me – right, Bun?'

'Sure thing, darl,' Bunny said vaguely. She was back in her sparkly evening gown and sending a text message on her mobile phone. 'Just gotta remind Robbo to pick up some tampons on his way home.'

'Come on,' I said, helping Sonya find the armholes of her *Do I Look Like A Fucking People Person?* T-shirt. 'Let's leave them to it.'

Down at reception, Cordelia didn't look up from her computer as she asked if the Voulez-Vous experience had met our high expectations.

'Sure,' I said, trying to guide Sonya towards the door.

'Actually,' Sonya said, pulling free and splashing vodka over the posh brothel carpet. 'The Voulez-Vous experience did not meet our fucking expectations.'

'Excuse me?' We certainly had Cordelia's full attention now.

'No, I won't excuse you,' said Sonya, swaying. 'The goods were flawed. The merchandise failed to live up to its advertised promises. Your whores were dud roots.'

And that's when Cordelia said if we used that sort of language we'd have to leave and Sonya called her a stuck-up cunt and Cordelia said she was calling security and Sonya lunged and bit her on the boob and then, before we knew it, an enormous biker security guard appeared from a door marked 'fuses' and grabbed us by the elbows.

'This way, ladies,' he said, dragging us towards the discreet rear exit and propelling us into the street.

'Suck my cock,' screeched Sonya, scrabbling at the bitumen.

The security guard turned to stare at us.

'Chicks like you make me sick,' he said quietly. 'You talk so big and nasty but the truth is you're just little and nasty. And that girl you were badmouthing back there? Little Crystal? She's a single mum with two little boys and one of the nicest people you could ever hope to meet. You two don't deserve to lick her fucking boots.'

And he slammed the brothel door behind him and that was that.

After we got up and dusted ourselves off, Sonya suggested heading back to The Stiff Earl for a nightcap or twelve. I looked at my business associate with her scratched face and her dirty T-shirt and her drunken swagger and said I might just jump in a cab and head home. Sonya called me a total fucking girl but for once I didn't care.

The story I eventually wrote on Voulez-Vous was published under the headline 'Girls' Own Guide To Gang Banging'. It had everything a *Tonk* reader could want. Slow-motion pillow fighting. A zillion hot lesbo positions. Loads of mix and matching. Only Sonya knew what really happened and she's never mentioned it. For some reason we don't hang out as much as we used to.

I'm not sure how much longer I'll be at *Tonk*, either. Last week I saw an ad for a cadetship at *The Daily Globe* and sent in an application. Who knows what they'll think of my profile of Miss Nude Asia Pacific (her hobbies include – and I quote – Pilates, swallowing and pigeon racing) but I thought it was worth a shot.

As for Mercedes, well, not long after our visit I went back to the Voulez-Vous home page to see what she was up to. Her photo was gone. After a bit of hunting around, however, I did notice a new profile up on the website for Salon Correctional – a bondage parlour a few streets up from Tonk's head office.

Mistress M was described as a raven-haired Amazon who specialised in oriental rope bondage, medical play and slave training. *Perhaps you may be permitted to caress her stiletto heels and latex corset with your tongue*, the site read. *Then Mistress will decide whether you should be granted the privilege of worshipping her magnificent seamed stockings.* Next to this was the same shower photo I'd seen before. My asymmetric privates hummed.

Were our feminist foremothers thinking of urine-soaked dungeon fantasies when they fought for equal rights? Probably not, but I don't blame them. There's been so many revolutions within revolutions and backlashes to backlashes that no one knows which way's up in the gender war any more. In the meantime, I reckon the time has come to talk to Mike about one last story idea.

Acknowledgements

From the bottom of our lingerie drawer, we thank:

CURTIS BROWN
Muffy Kendall (Pippa Masson)
Buffy the Rock (Fiona Inglis)
Bilbo Waldemar (Jonathan Lloyd)

LITTLE BROWN
Bunny Hutchins (Jo Dickinson)
Sue-Sue Dorchester (Louise Davies)
Honey-Biscuit Lincoln (Kerry Chapple)
Fudge Rectory (Helen Gibbs)
Judy Pearson (Alison Lindsay)
Dante Reach (Alex Richardson)
Goldie Well Lane (Emma Grey)
Marilyn Lascelles (Caroline Hogg)
Domino Chestnut (Emma Stonex)

PENGUIN AUSTRALIA
Kim Roslyn (Ingrid Ohlsson)
Harry Shepherd's Hill (Julie Gibbs)
Patricia Brunker (Allison Colpoys)
Amos Rowallen (Belinda Byrne)

WILLIAM MORRIS
Sooty Bowlhead (Eugenie Furniss)
Guinea Manor (Alice Ellerby)
Shadow Pendene (Rowan Lawton)

The Editors

Contributors

Jessica Adams is the astrologer for worldwide editions of *Vogue* and *Cosmopolitan* and the author of six novels. She is a team editor on the bestselling *Girls' Night In* series.

Maggie Alderson was born in London, brought up in Staffordshire and educated at the University of St Andrews. She is the author of four bestselling novels: *Pants on Fire, Mad About the Boy, Handbags and Gladrags* and *Cents and Sensibility*, which have been translated into many languages. She has also co-edited two anthologies in aid of the charity War Child. Before becoming a full-time novelist, she was editor of *Elle* and *ES* magazines, and also worked for the *Evening Standard* and the *Sydney Morning Herald*. She is married with one daughter and lives in Hastings.

Emma Darwin studied drama and worked in publishing before becoming a writer. Her first novel, *The Mathematics of Love*, was published in 2006.

Louise Doughty is the author of five novels, five plays for radio and one work of non-fiction. She lives in London.

Stella Duffy has written ten novels, over thirty short stories, seven plays, and many feature articles and reviews. Her most recent novel, *The Room of Lost Things*, is published by Virago. In 2002 she won the CWA Short Story Dagger for her story 'Martha Grace', from *Tart Noir*, the anthology she co-edited with Lauren Henderson. She is adapting her novel *State of Happiness* as a feature film with Fiesta Productions and Zentropa. *Calendar Girl* was voted fifth equal in the international poll The Big Gay Read. As a performer she works with comedy company Spontaneous Combustion and Improbable, in *Keith Johnson's Lifegame*, and has acted in many plays and sitcoms for BBC Radio 4.

Imogen Edwards-Jones has written over a dozen books including the international bestselling *Babylon* series. She is married with one high-maintenance daughter and lives in London.

Esther Freud worked as an actress before writing her first novel, *Hideous Kinky*, in 1992. She has since published five further novels, the most recent of which was *Love Falls*. She lives in London with her husband and three children.

Joanne Harris lives in West Yorkshire. She gave up teaching to become a full-time writer and has written ten novels, including *Chocolat*, a book of short stories and two cookbooks.

Linda Jaivin is an internationally published author, playwright, essayist and translator. She has written five novels, including the comic-erotic best-seller *Eat Me*, as well as *Rock n Roll Babes from Outer Space*; *Miles Walker, You're Dead*; *Dead Sexy* and *The Infernal Optimist*. Her sixth will come out with Fourth Estate (HarperCollins Australia) in 2009. Her work has appeared on nerve.com and in Susie Bright's *Best American Erotica* series. She is also the author of the China memoir, *The Monkey and the Dragon*, and the collection of essays and journalism, *Confessions of an S&M Virgin*. She lives in Sydney.

Rachel Johnson writes for the *Sunday Times*, *Spectator* and *Easy Living*. She has written a novel, *Notting Hell*, and her next book will be published in the US and Britain in 2008.

Tobsha Learner was born and raised in England and has lived in both Australia and the USA. She is an international best-selling author and is also known as a playwright. Her novels include *Soul*, *Madonna Mars* and *The Witch of Cologne*, her collection of short stories – *Quiver*, and *Tremble – sensual fables of the mystical and sinister*. She is also a regular contributor to *The Times*. Her latest novel, *Sphinx*, is to be published in May 2009.

Even though **Kathy Lette** left school at sixteen (she says that the only examination she's ever passed is her cervical smear test) she has written ten bestselling novels which have been translated into seventeen foreign languages and are now published in more than a hundred countries.

Emily Maguire is the author of *Princesses and Pornstars: Sex + Power + Identity*, and the novels *The Gospel According to Luke* and *Taming the Beast*, an international bestseller and finalist for the Dylan Thomas Prize and the Kathleen Mitchell Award. Emily's articles and essays on sex, religion, culture and literature have been published widely including in the *Sydney Morning Herald*, the *Griffith Review*, the *Financial Review*, *The Observer* and *The Age*.

Chris Manby is the author of twelve bestselling romantic comedy novels, including *The Matchbreaker* and *Lizzie Jordan's Secret Life*.

Santa Montefiore has written nine novels that have been translated into over twenty-five languages and sell all over the world. Her latest, *The French Gardener*, is published by Hodder & Stoughton. She lives in London with her husband, historian and novelist Simon Sebag-Montefiore, and their two children.

Jane Moore is a national newspaper columnist with five bestselling novels to her name. She has written and presented several documentaries and is a mum of two.

Since 2000 when the *Evening Standard* identified **Adele Parks** as one of London's 'Twenty Faces to Watch', Adele has written seven bestsellers, including *Playing Away* (debut bestseller of the millennium), *Other Women's Shoes* and *Husbands*. She's sold over a million copies of her work in the UK but also sells throughout the world. Two of her novels have been optioned as movies. She has written articles and short stories for a number of magazines and newspapers. She lectures for the University of Surrey. Adele lives with her husband and son in Guildford, Surrey. They are, in her opinion, the most enchanting beings on the planet. She is an Aquarian, northern and she wanted to be a writer since she was a little girl.

Justine Picardie is the author of several books, including *If the Spirit Moves You*. Her most recent novel, *Daphne*, is published by Bloomsbury.

Bella Pollen is a writer and journalist who contributes to a wide variety of newspapers and magazines including *The Times*, *Sunday Telegraph*, *American Vogue* and *Spectator*. She is the author of four novels: *All About Men*; *B Movies, Blue Love*; *Hunting Unicorns* and *Midnight Cactus*. Bella divides her time between London and Colorado.

Helen Razer is a Melbourne writer. Her first novel is scheduled for publication in 2009.

Ali Smith was born in Inverness in 1962 and lives in Cambridge. She is the author of *Free Love*, *Like*, *Hotel World*, *Other Stories and Other Stories*, *The Whole Story and Other Stories*, *The Accidental* and *Girl Meets Boy*. Her story collection *The First Person and Other Stories* will be published in 2008.

Joan Smith is a novelist, columnist and human rights activist. Her latest novel, *What Will Survive*, is published by Arcadia.

Emma Tom is a Sydney writer and columnist who is slowly inching her way through a PhD.

Daisy Waugh's most recent novel is *Bordeaux Housewives*, published by HarperCollins. It's a work of solid genius, plus it's got lots of sex.

Fay Weldon is one of Britain's most influential, widely read and versatile writers. As well as having over twenty novels to her name, translated into many languages, she writes for stage, screen, television and radio. *Life and Loves of a She Devil* made history: her latest non fiction work, *What Makes Women Happy*, has created great public interest. She has a reputation, albeit a controversial one, as one of the formative influences in Britain's feminist revolution. She is familiar as a face on British TV, and a voice on radio.